The Tale of Jiraiya the Gallant

Volume I

Magical Toads—Monstrous Serpents

Lacuna
Lit
Press

The Tale of Jiraiya the Gallant: Volume 1 | April, 2025, 1st ed.

Edited by Joshua Smyser
Book Design by A.B. Hale
Cover Design by Joshua Smyser
Additional Graphic Design by Marshall Taylor, Rowan Media

Published by
Lacuna Lit Press (an imprint of Blue Feathered Quill LLC)
Evans, Colorado, USA

ISBN-13:
eBook: 978-1-965492-04-8
Trade Paperback: 978-1-965492-05-5
Hard Cover: 978-1-965492-06-2

Introduction

When I first came across *The Tale of Jiraiya the Gallant* some fifteen years ago, I was but a fledgling student of Japanese studies, reading manga and watching anime to improve my Japanese. One day, an episode of the popular anime series *Naruto Shippūden* titled *The Tale of Jiraiya the Gallant* led me to discover that the main character of the episode, Jiraiya, was based on a fictional character from the Edo period with the same name. This 'original' Jiraiya was the main character of a series titled *The Tale of Jiraiya the Gallant*, spanning 43 books published over 29 years. The internet told me that it revolved around Jiraiya's adventures as he used his toad magic to battle the forces of evil. The story even contained his nemesis from the anime, Orochimaru, a wielder of snake magic, and his friend Tsunade, who used slug magic. Just like in the anime. I could not wait to read it.

Much to my dismay, however, the series was written in premodern Japanese and had never been translated. That day, I decided that, should I ever possess the necessary skills to translate *The Tale of Jiraiya the Gallant*, I would. Even if only so I could read it myself. Roughly a decade and two degrees in Japanese language later, I started working on that translation, which you now hold in your hands.

Translating the original text took hundreds of hours, and restoring the images took hundreds more. I spent countless days, pouring over old maps to find locations now forgotten, and searching through classical Japanese and ancient Chinese novels and poems to understand obscure references that no one understands anymore. Transforming *The Tale of Jiraiya the Gallant* from its original premodern Japanese to English has been a mystery adventure on its own.

After 15 years, the journey has gone from curiosity to this finished book, which will hopefully be the first of three. For the first time ever, English readers can now take part in the adventures of Jiraiya, Tsunade, and Orochimaru, as they were first written in the time of the samurai.

—Andreas Kronborg Danielsen

Historical notes

This translation is meant as entertainment. For this reason, the amount of historical commentary is kept to a minimum and the text has been written to include as few notes as possible. However, in the following pages is some basic historical information both about the books and the authors, as well as information that the authors assumed readers would know. This includes things such as telling the time of day, money, locations, and measurements.

About the Books and the Authors

There are two major sources for the creation of the character Jiraiya. One is the plays about the real-life adventurer Tenjiku Tokubei (1612–c. 1692) written in the 1700s. In these plays, Tenjiku wields toad magic that he acquired in India, which he uses for vengeance against the *bakufu*—shōgunate. The other source is a tale from the Six Dynasties period in China (220–589) about the robber *Garaiya*.[1] In the story, the robber wrote 我来也, read "Garaiya" and meaning "I came" on the wall next to the door of every house he robbed. That name later became 自来也, *Jiraiya*, in Japan, still meaning "I came". The Japanese story of Jiraiya begins in 1806, with the book *Jiraiya Monogatari—The Tale of Jiraiya* (also known as *Katakiuchi Kidan Jiraiya Monogatari—The romantic story of Jiraiya's revenge*).[2] It borrows the name from the Chinese story of *Garaiya*, and is a story mainly focused on revenge and karmic causality. In it, Jiraiya ultimately dies as a result of his karmically dubious deeds, after having helped carry out a vendetta.

Later, in 1839, *The Tale of Jiraiya the Gallant* used the basic setting of *Jiraiya Monogatari*, but other than the idea of Jiraiya using magic taught by a toad hermit to get vengeance (borrowed from Tenjiku Tokubei), as well as a few names, it is its own work. It also changed the kanji characters in Jiraiya's name from 自来也 to the much more bombastic 児雷也, meaning "the young thunder". It can be said that it was not until *The Tale of Jiraiya the Gallant* that the story got fully developed and the character took on its now familiar shape. It was also the first long story about Jiraiya, stretching over 43 books of twenty-page long books, published over 29 years between 1839 and 1868. This long publishing period meant that it went through several authors and ukiyo-e artists, usually due to retirement or death. It is generally accepted that books 1–5 were written by Mizugaki Egao (1789–1846), books 6–11 by Eisen Keisai (1790–1848) under the penname Ippitsuan, books 12–39 by Ryūkatei Tanekazu (1807–1858), and books 40–43 by Ryōsuitei Tanekiyo (1823–1907). Based on forewords written by the varying authors, we know they worked with outlines left by whoever was the previous writer. In 1868, however, *The Tale of Jiraiya the Gallant* suddenly stopped being published after book 43, seemingly mid-story.

---

1. 今村, 与志雄. 唐宋伝奇集 下: 杜子春 他三十九篇. 岩波書店, 1988.

2. A summary of the story is available in Zhang, Jin. "The Didacticism of Katakiuchi Kidan Jiraiya Monogatari." Arizona State University, 2012, 2–46.

Legacy and Influence

The Tale of Jiraiya the Gallant gave birth to a slew of plays and retellings of the story. From Kawatake Mokuami's *kabuki* play with the same name in 1852, based on the first ten books of *The Tale of the Gallant Jiraiya*, to Sugiura Shigeru's manga *The Young Jiraiya* (*Shōnen Jiraiya*) in 1958. The story even made it to the west, with William Elliot Griffis' abridged English version of Jiraiya's story in 1880 in *Japanese Fairy World: Stories from the Wonder-lore of Japan.*[3]

Just between 1806 and 1914, Jiraiya appeared in no less than twenty different works, including eight kabuki plays. In the period 1912 to 1967, he starred in a staggering twenty-six movies. Interestingly, despite now being known as a ninja, it was not until 1918 that Jiraiya was referred to as a ninja for the first time, with the silent film *The Founder of Ninjutsu: Jiraiya* (*Ninja Ganso Jiraiya*).[4] This happened during an unprecedented boom in the popularity of ninja stories. The character itself did not change, however, as Jiraiya had always basically been what is now associated with being a ninja, if not by title, then by his actions. In 1958, the aforementioned *The Young Jiraiya* was published, and in 1988, Jiraiya was featured in *World Ninja War Jiraiya* (*Sekai Ninjasen Jiraiya*), a *Power Rangers* style TV-show with little else from the original except the name Jiraiya. In 1994, Hashimoto Masae published the three-book manga series *Jiraiya*, which was loosely based on the original story. Manga pioneer Nagai Gō even published a 200-page manga about Jiraiya in 1997, titled *Tales of Bravery: Jiraiya* (*Gōdan Jiraiya*), as part of a series of samurai themed manga.

Despite all this success of the character, Jiraiya disappeared almost entirely from popular media in the late 1960's. It can be argued this probably happened as Jiraiya had been squarely cemented as a ninja, and the 1960's was when the ninja craze ended. Apart from sporadic appearances, the character had practically disappeared from the media landscape in Japan until 2001, when Kishimoto Masashi brought Jiraiya back in the *Naruto* manga.

The Prints and How to Read Them

As mentioned previously, *The Tale of Jiraiya the Gallant* is a series of so-called *gōkan*—long versions of *kuzasōshi* illustrated books. The predecessor of the gōkan, *kibyōshi* (lit. "yellow cover") were only around ten pages long and stories lasted no more than three books. These were mainly aimed at children. Around 1806, the gōkan started hitting the market, most of them being between 20 and 50 pages thick and with stories that sometimes stretched several books. This allowed for more complex narratives, and mixing the text in with the images

3. Griffis, William Elliot. *Japanese Fairy World: Stories From the Wonder-lore of Japan*. Daily Union Steam Printing House, 1880, 126–140.

4. Nishimura, Yasuhiro. "Vanishing Hero JIRAIYA." *Artworld: Bulletin of Faculty of Arts, Tokyo Institute of Polytechnics*, no. 14 (2008): 1–6.

made the reading experience more exciting. Since the text was also more complicated, it also targeted a slightly older audience than the kibyōshi.

In the case of *The Tale of Jiraiya the Gallant*, each book was divided into two parts, which were sold separately. These divisions have been marked in the text of this volume. Although many of them occur during a natural narrative break in the text, others interrupt the narrative.

Gōkan are, in a sense, comparable to modern graphic novels, although a lot more text driven than image driven. Reading a gōkan without looking at the images takes away not only from the experience, but also important contextual clues not given in the text. For instance, the text might refer to a character as a mysterious stranger, but the observant reader might recognize the character based on their clothes.

To this effect, the text is interwoven with the image, appearing in various places around the page. It is, however, never structured like speech bubbles or the like, as one can find in lighter works of the same sort. That being said, there are a few instances where information is written in the image. These can be clues as to where the scene is taking place, or the sound of background conversations.

Therefore, it is inconsequential where the text is on the page, and thus not important to know for readers of this book. Nevertheless, it is noted where the corresponding pages start and end, so that the reader can follow the image that is meant to be enjoyed together with the text. It does, however, happen, that the image skips ahead of the text or lags. In all instances where there is text on the page that is separate from the narration, this has been translated below the image of the original page.

If one wishes to try following the text in the images, it always flows from the top right to the bottom left corner. Where the text jumps to somewhere else on the centerfold page, there is always some sort of glyph that indicates where to go. This can be anything like a triangle, a circle, a squiggly line, or a small box that says something like "to the right". The destination text will then always begin with a corresponding glyph or a box, saying something like "from the left". All named characters in the images are usually marked with a kanji or a few hiragana in a little blank circle somewhere on the character.

Figure 1 shows an example of how the text might flow on the page.

Figure 1

Time Period

Based on the information given in the books translated in this volume, the story takes place sometime during the Ashikaga shōgunate (1336–1573). However, in later books it is revealed that the *Kanrei* (the deputy Shōgun in charge of the Kanto area, who ruled from Kamakura) is Ashikaga Mochiuji (1398–1439), who was in office from 1409 to 1439. Furthermore, due to the mentions of Ashikaga Mitsutaka (1389–1417) and Uesugi Zenshū (died 1417) and references to what can only be the Uesugi Zenshu Rebellion of 1416, an educated guess would place the story circa 1409–1416.

Written towards the end of the Edo period, the setting was most likely a fictional mixture of the Kamakura and Muromachi periods, with a healthy dose of Edo period culture and realities thrown into the mix. These periods were a popular setting for literature in the Edo period, as they allowed writers to bypass certain censorship rules, such as the ban on writing about the Tokugawa shōgunate or any acts of rebellion against the system.

This setting, however, gave birth to many anachronisms. The story has references to positions in the hierarchy of the shōgunate, which were only relevant before the Edo period, while also having positions that only existed during the Edo period. For example, the *Kanrei* was an extremely powerful position during the Kamakura shōgunate up until the Edo period, and functioned like the deputy Shōgun. During the Edo period however, this position did not exist, but people still knew about it because of its historical significance. Furthermore, as mentioned above, Ashikaga Mochiuji was never actually the Kanrei of the Kantō region, but rather the *Kubō* of Kamakura. The title of Kanrei was with Uesugi Zenshū, who held the position from 1411 to 1415. The Kubō worked as a regional Shōgun, ruling the Kantō area from Kamakura. The Kubō, however, was subject to the actual Shōgun, who ruled from Kyoto. The Kanrei worked as a supreme commander in the Kantō region, whose main goal was to ensure that the Kubō followed the decrees of the Shōgun. In *The Tale of Jiraiya the Gallant*, this distribution of power seems to be missing, which leads to Ashikaga Mochiuji suddenly holding an office he never held. Nonetheless, because of the other historical figures and the references to the Uesugi Zenshū Rebellion, it still gives us a solid clue as to setting of the story.

As a final note on the use of titles, and as a segue to the anachronisms of the story, some titles such as *Hangan* (a high judge in a province) or *Gunryō* (an official in charge of military affairs in a province) only existed in the Edo period. However, had previous period titles been used, the reader might not have been able to grasp the exact position of the character. This is an interesting case of how anachronisms were used to make the story understandable to the reader, and perhaps even subvert censorship.

Another anachronism and hint towards one of these attempts to skirt the censorship rules, is the use of the pleasure district in Ōiso, where large parts of the story take place. During the Edo period, it was generally not allowed to write about the main pleasure district, the Yoshiwara. However, there are hints the author meant for the reader to imagine the Yoshiwara pleasure district when the scene is set in Ōiso. For instance, in book six, the character Chōbei, living in Ōiso, is supposed to safekeep a deposit for the Sanja Matsuri festival, gathered by people living in the area. However, the Sanja Matsuri festival took place at Sensōji Temple in Edo, some sixty kilometers away. If this scene is read as Ōiso being Yoshiwara, located in the area right next to Sensōji Temple, it makes more sense for the locals to be gathering money to pay for the festival. There are also several locations mentioned in the text as being right outside the Ōiso pleasure district, which were actually in Edo in the vicinity of the Yoshiwara district.

One final anachronism which is worth mentioning, is the presence of arquebuses called *tanegashima* in the text. These did not exist in Japan before the mid-1500s, over one hundred years after the period, established with the mentioning of the Kanrei. It's possible that the author was unaware of this information, but a more compelling explanation, I believe, is that the author deliberately crafted an anachronistic fantasy adventure. By setting the story in a distant past while incorporating the culture and innovations of his contemporary Japan, the author may have aimed to circumvent censorship and deliver a thrilling tale.

Names

All names are given in the Japanese order, with the family name first. However, in some scenes certain characters are referred to with several different names and sometimes even with a mixture of their different aliases. As a result, in the original text there are scenes where a character might be referred to with up to five or six different names by other characters or even by the narrator, who might use two different names for the same character, in the same sentence. In cases like these, the text has been streamlined so it is less confusing to read, choosing a single name per character to use, unless the dramatic structure of the story demands otherwise.

Concerning Jiraiya's name, it is worth mentioning that, when *The Tale of Jiraiya the Gallant* debuted in 1839, the character Jiraiya, and his true name Ogata Shūma Hiroyuki, were commonly known. As readers of the text will notice, Jiraiya's name changes from his boyhood name Tarō to Raitarō in book one. The story explains this change in detail, but the name Jiraiya appears between book one and two and is only briefly touched upon in the foreword of book two. When his true name is revealed in the text, this is also done very nonchalantly, signifying that the reader is supposed to already have some knowledge of the character and the name.

Distances

Below is a conversion chart for the measures of distance which appear in *The Tale of Jiraiya the Gallant*, converted from the traditional *shakkanhō* system to metric.

UNIT	METRIC VALUE
SUN	3.03 centimeters
SHAKU	30.3 centimeters
KEN	1.181 meters
JŌ/TAKÉ	3.03 meters
CHŌ	109 meters
RI	3.927 kilometers

Time

Time during the Edo period was announced via bell strikes, always starting with three strikes to declare that the time would now be announced. For that reason, the number of strikes announcing the time never went below four strikes. Sunrise and sunset were always when the bell struck six times, which makes translating the time directly into modern universal time impossible, unless we know the exact time of the year. As the seasons change, so does the length of the day and the night, meaning that an hour in pre-modern Japan changed many times during the year, with day and night hours almost never being of equal length. However, this system also means that when the text says the bell struck six times, we know it was either at sunrise or sunset, and we can imagine the scene based on this. Time was also divided into smaller units, with additional bell strikes indicating half-hour periods.

Below is a simplification of how timekeeping would have worked on the equinox, when the day and night are of equal length. It does not take into account the change from how time was kept when there was a change in timekeeping systems in 1844 from the *teikihō* to the *tenpōhō* system. It is based on this simplification that the times in *The Tale of Jiraiya the Gallant* are translated.

BELL STRIKES	TIME FRAME	ZODIAC ANIMAL
6	05:00 – 07:00	HARE
5	07:00 – 09:00	DRAGON
4	09:00 – 11:00	SNAKE
9	11:00 – 13:00	HORSE
8	13:00 – 15:00	GOAT
7	15:00 – 17:00	MONKEY
6	17:00 – 19:00	ROOSTER
5	19:00 – 21:00	DOG
4	21:00 – 23:00	BOAR
9	23:00 – 01:00	RAT
8	01:00 – 03:00	OX
7	03:00 – 05:00	TIGER

Money

Explaining the currency of the Edo period in a concise manner is near impossible and would require a small dissertation. One of the reasons for this is that changes were constantly made, and new coins were introduced while old coins were kept in circulation. What makes matters worse is the constant fluctuations in the value of gold which formed the basis of the value of coins, as well as the changing cost of living. Even if we assume an often-cited value of one *koban* (equaling one *ryō* measure of gold) coin being equal in value to one *koku* of rice (roughly 180 liters), the value of rice also changed based on harvests and rice stocks. In modern money, the value of one koban could vary from being worth 10,000–20,000 Yen, to being worth 200,000–400,000 Yen, which underlines how wildly its value fluctuated throughout the Edo period. Nonetheless, it is a good rule of thumb to imagine one koban coin to be able to pay for one year's worth of rice. Below is given the simplified relationship between the money that appears in *The Tale of Jiraiya the Gallant*, to give the reader an idea of their value.

15.6 grams of gold=1 RYŌ=1 KOBAN=4 KAN=400 SEN=4000 MON

Locations

Figure 2 is a map showing the main locations in the story, as well as outlining the relevant provinces as they were during the Edo period. Footnotes in the text indicate the approximate modern name or location. As some place names have changed or even been moved since the Edo period, this could otherwise cause confusion for anyone wanting to place the locations on a map. For instance, Shinano is currently a town in Nagano prefecture, but in the Edo period, it was the name of the entire prefecture. Another example is Jiraiya's hometown Nezumi-no-shuku, which has ceased to exist entirely and took quite a bit of detective work to locate.

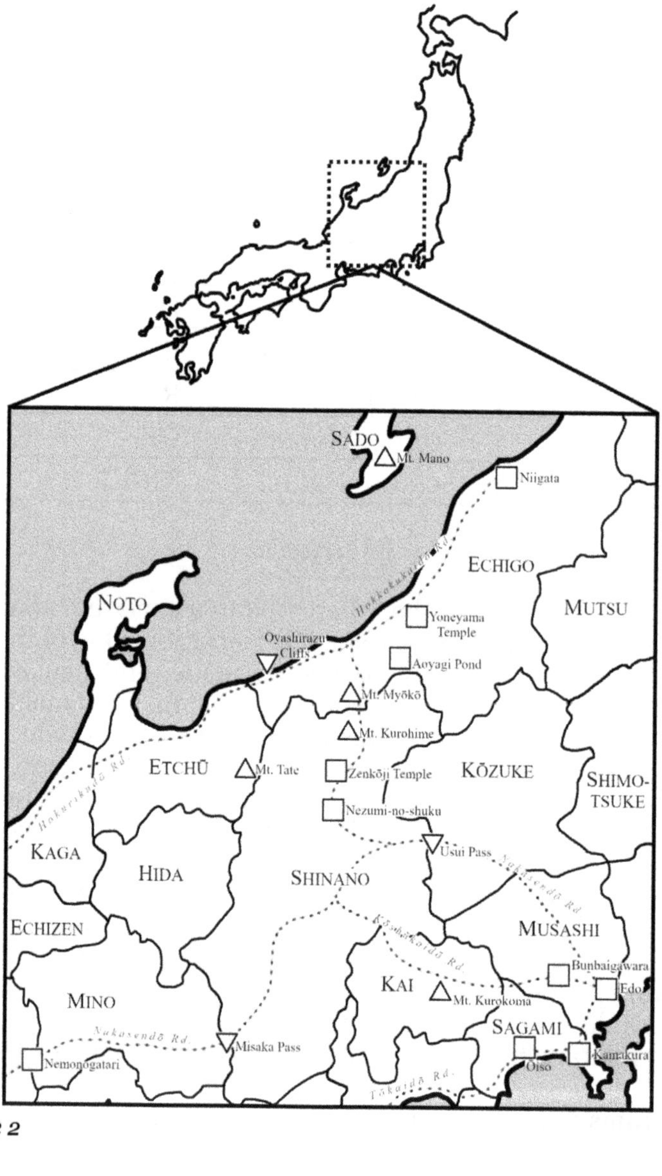

Figure 2

An Author's Mistakes

Book 20 starts with the following foreword by Ryūkatei Tanekazu:

> *Returning to previous books, the original story was written by Mister Mizugaki, and along the way, Ippitsuan took over as the author. Perhaps because it was a story he inherited, under Eisen many mistakes appeared in the text. A medicine box, which had returned to Jiraiya, is once again in Yuminosuke's possession. Kozue, who had been killed, is spoken of as being alive. In book two, Ogata Hirozumi was a lord somewhere in the Tsukushi area, but later the lord of Echigo. I have taken from Mister Egao's example, and specifically made Hirozumi from Higo province in Tsukushi. Furthermore, I have returned to the story about the Fubuki Katatsuki tea container from the first book, and the hag Okowa who disappeared in the night in book five. However, one thing has proven difficult to mend. Ekichi, who is really Jiraiya's adoptive sister Miyuki, has been treated as a completely different person. That being said, the medicine box and the dead person being suddenly alive could be a splendid plot device. If we see it as her being brought back from the death with medicine, it could make for quite the miraculous tale. If so, Ippitsuan's brush should be lauded as unrivaled, and the story viewed as an epic tale.*

This foreword addresses inconsistencies that, unfortunately, became rather prevalent when Ippitsuan took the reins as the writer of the series. Inconsistencies and plot holes in literature are by no means unique to *The Tale of Jiraiya the Gallant*, but as mentioned in the foreword translated above, the author Ippitsuan made quite a few mistakes, so it warrants mentioning.

Ippitsuan, which was the penname of ukiyo-e artist Keisai Eisen, is suspected to have written from around book 7 to 11. It is not entirely clear who wrote which books exactly, but it is generally accepted that Ippitsuan supplied the majority of the writing in those books.[5]

The inconsistencies are generally small and relate to character names being mistaken. Tagane and Ayame, who feature heavily in book 3, have their names switched throughout book 11. Kozue, mentioned above as maybe being alive, is called Azusa in book 11. Ogata Hirozumi is called Hirokado four times. Sumatarō is called Sumanosuke three times. There is a general confusion about whether Mount Kurohime is in Shinano or Echigo, which Ryūkatei shortly addresses in the foreword of book 14. Jiraiya's ancestral lands get confused as well, as mentioned in the foreword translated above.

Two character names I also wish to bring some attention to are the leader of the Sarashina clan, and one of Jiraiya's underlings. The first time he is mentioned, the head of the Sarashina is called Sarashina Saemon. Later, this name becomes Sarashina Hangan Mitsuaki, a

5. 大関, 綾. "『児雷也豪傑譚』における各編の作者と「嗣作」." 京都大学國文學論叢 44 (April 1, 2021): 1–13. 京都大学大学院文学研究科国語学国文学研究室

choice which I would argue might have been made in order to give the character more gravitas. The other character I wish to point out, is first mentioned in book 8 as Nobusuma Tenroku. Later in the same book, and again in book 9, his name is Nobusuma Tenbachi. This could be an intentional wordplay, as the only thing that changes is the final -roku and -bachi, meaning 'six' and 'eight' respectively. In book 11, however, he goes by the name Musasabi Tenbachi. This time, it is his family name which has changed from Nobusuma to Musasabi. This change, however, might be due to Nobusuma and Musasabi being almost synonymous. Nobusuma is the name of a *yōkai* in the shape of a flying squirrel, and Musasabi is the common word for flying squirrel.

These problems are easily dealt with and corrected in this translation, but Ippitsuan made three mistakes that cannot be fixed without rewriting large sections of text, which I would like to address here. First, as mentioned in the above foreword, Kozue, a character that dies in book 6, is talked about as being alive in a later book. This is never followed up on and can be considered a mistake. The next mistake, also mentioned above, is Ippitsuan writing Ekichi and Miyuki as two different people. The final mistake which demands notice, is the character Tatsumaki Arakurō/Onikado Yashagorō/Muyami Gundazaemon. In book 2, the story of how Tatsumaki Arakurō switches names to Onikado Yashagorō is told to Jiraiya, yet in book 10, when the two finally meet again, Jiraiya seems to have forgotten that Arakurō and Yashagorō are the same person and treats him like a stranger. This will strike most readers as odd, seeing as Arakurō, when he went by the name Yashagorō, killed the hermit who taught Jiraiya his *yōjutsu* and made himself Jiraiya's enemy. In fact, it seems that, following book 2, Arakurō's short stint as Yashagorō is entirely forgotten by everyone, including himself. In book 10, where Arakurō/Yashagorō/Gundazaemon finally meets his end, this unfortunately leads to a rather anticlimactic conclusion for readers who remember what happened eight books prior.

Characters

Here is a list of the characters in the following pages, as well as explanations of some of the puns and hidden meanings that the names carry. Because, even though *The Tale of Jiraiya the Gallant* is somewhat serious, many of the names are puns that describe the character.

Aogaki Shibuemon—A shrewd businessman. Possible meaning: "Bitter green persimmon".

Asuwa Hibanda—One of Takasago Yuminosuke's retainers. Possible meaning: "I'm off duty tomorrow".

Ayame—The number one pleasure girl of Kumadeya house. Possible meaning: "Iris flower".

Bitei—The Taoist immortal of Mount Tate. Possible meaning: "Slug trail".

Chōbei the dreamer—A leader of gaudy delinquents and self-styled humanitarians in the entertainment district of Ōiso. The name evokes the image of a dreaming butterfly.

Ekichi—a young man on a pilgrimage.

Fukai Chinonai—one of Takasago Yuminosuke's retainers. Possible meaning: "Has no deep knowledge".

Fukumaki no Takarako—A diviner and healer in Niigata. Possible meaning: "Someone who sows good fortune and brings treasure".

Fukutoji—the wife of Mochimaru Fukiemon. Possible meaning: "Many maids" meaning that she is so rich that she has a lot of maids.

Ganpachi—Miyuki's kidnapper and the murderer of Hatasaku.

Harisaki Togekurō—One of Tsuyaginu's clients and the real name of Suribaritarō. Possible meaning: "The sharp needle point".

Hatasaku—The adoptive father of Jiraiya and the father or Miyuki.

Himematsu Edanoshin—Most trusted retainer of the lord of Sarashina, and the father of Sumatarō.

Himematsu Sumatarō—The son of Himematsu Edanoshin and husband of Misao.

Inesaku—The right-hand-man of Mochimaru Fukiemon. Possible meaning: "Rice maker".

Iwane no Gakeroku—A mountain man carrying a great axe. The alias of Takasago Yuminosuke. Possible meaning: "Rocky cliff".

Jimoguri Kuroyasha—One of Orochimaru's henchmen. Possible meaning: "Dark demon who digs in the ground".

Jiraiya—The alias of Ogata Shūma Hiroyuki. "Young thunder."

Jitsumu—A pious monk and a miracle worker. Possible meaning: "A dream that has come to be".

Kamahira—The servant of Kurohime Yashagorō Onikado.

Koshiji—A lone woman living on Mount Myōkō. Real identity is Senso Dōjin.

Kozue—The widow of Himematsu Edanoshin and mother of Sumatarō.

Kurohime Yashagorō Onikado—The bandit lord of Mount Kurohime, formerly Tatsumaki Arakurō. Possible meaning: "Mount Kurohime's Yaksha of the Demon's Gate".

Matsuhei—The squire of Sumatarō.

Misao—The widow of Himematsu Sumatarō.

Miyuki—Daughter of Hatasaku.

Mochimaru Fukiemon—The richest man in Nezumi-no-Shuku and the father of Fukitarō and Osachi. Possible meaning: "Lucky and wealthy".

Mochimaru Fukitarō—Son of Mochimaru Fukiemon. Possible meaning: "Lucky and wealthy".

Nobusuma/Musasabi Tenroku/Tenbachi—One of Jiraiya's higher ranking bandits. The name is a play on the word for flying squirrel.

Ogata Saemon Hirozumi—The father of Ogata Shūma Hiroyuki.

Ogata Shūma Hiroyuki—The son of Ogata Saemon Hirozumi, and the real name of Jiraiya.

Osachi—The daughter of Mochimaru Fukiemon.

Osaga—Wife of Kamahira.

Raitarō—Jiraiya's name as a youth. Meaning: "Thunder boy".

Sarashina Hangan Mitsuaki (sometimes Sarashina Saemon)—The lord of Shinano.

Senso Dōjin—An ancient hermit who lives on Mount Myōkō and taught Jiraiya yōjutsu.

Shirotae—The concubine of Sarashina Saemon.

Suribaritarō—A bandit and the brother of Tatsumaki Arakurō. Originally the name of a legendary bandit said to have worked under the equally legendary bandit Kumasaka Chōhan in the late Heian period.

Tagane—The rightful heir of the Kumadeya house. Possible meaning: "Lots of money".

Takasago Yuminosuke—The brother of Misao and retainer of Sarashina Hangan Mitsuaki.

Tarō—A common name for young boys before they receive a more proper, adult name. Could be translated as just "boy".

Tatsumaki Arakurō—A retainer from the Himematsu household, brother of Harisaki Togekurō, murderer of Sumatarō and the former name of Kurohime Yashagorō Onikado. Possible meaning: "Tornado of violent hardships".

Tsumorinosuke—The son of Sarashina Hangan Mitsuaki, also known as "the purple millionaire".

Tsuruhashiya Kinosuke—Owner of the inn Tsuruhashiya and ally of Jiraiya.

Tsuyaginu—A high-ranking courtesan of the Ōiso pleasure district and Jiraiya's sister. Possible meaning: "Glittering fabric" referring to the beautiful kimonos she wears.

Yakama Shikarokurō—The sheriff of the Nagao clan, also known as Shikaroku. Possible meaning: a pun on *yakamashi* meaning "annoying".

Yokushirō—The proprietor of Kumadeya house in Niigata. The name denotes desire and greed.

Yokutsura Rinhei—A shrewd businessman. Possible meaning: "Greedy faced miser".

Yumeno Chōkichi—a young street brawler in Ōiso. The name is meant to mirror Chōbei the dreamer.

Book 1

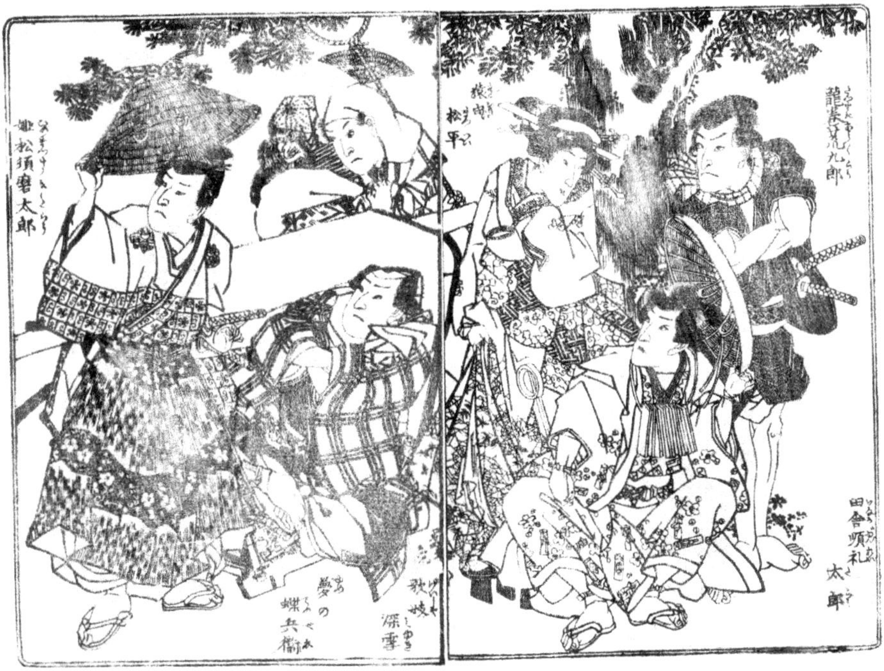

1.1

Tarō as a country pilgrim.
Tatsumaki Arakurō.
Matsuhei as a monkey tamer.
Miyuki as a geisha.
Chōbei the dreamer.
Himematsu Sumatarō.

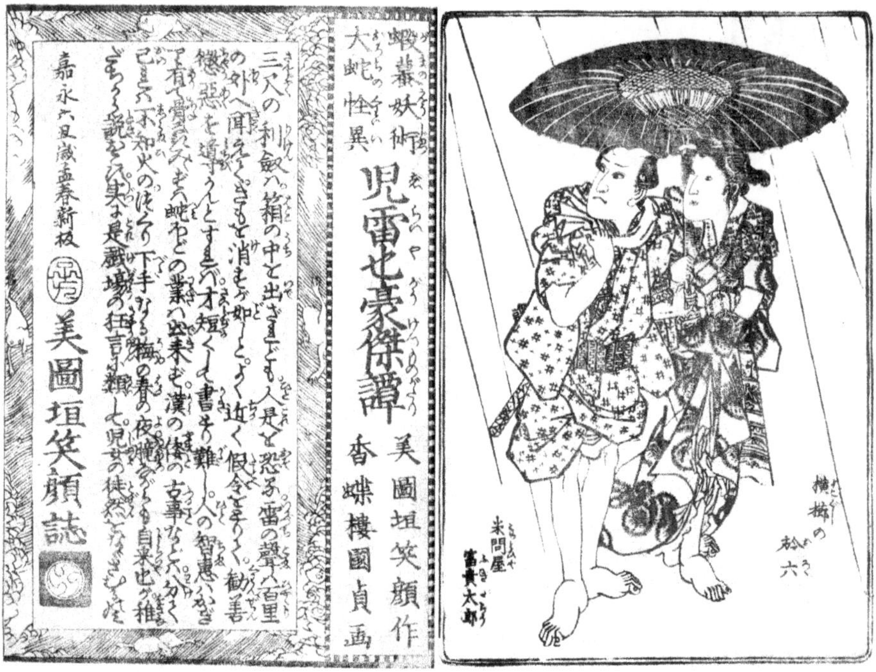

1.2

Left side:
Magical Toads and Monstrous Serpents
The Tale of Jiraiya the Gallant
Story by Mizugaki Egao
Art by Kōchōrō Kunisada

Right side:
Oroku with her comb aslant.
Fukitarō as a wholesale rice merchant.

A sharp, three *shaku* long sword is feared, even when left in its box. It is like lightning—heard from a hundred *ri* away, it still causes anxiety. With little talent, it is difficult to attempt writing tales of great poetic justice. My limited knowledge makes me like a worm—without a bone in its body, and incapable of doing the same feats as a snake. The old tales of China and Yamato are like the mystical ephemerally dancing *Shiranui* firelights over the seas of Kyushu—I would write their story as poorly as one would paint a picture of a plum blossom experienced in the dead of night in spring. Although shrouded in these mists of ignorance, our tale begins when Jiraiya was still young. It is like a comedic *kyogen* play on the stage—only for sating the boredom of boys and girls.

Tenpō 10—Year of the Boar—Spring (1839)
Mizugaki Egao

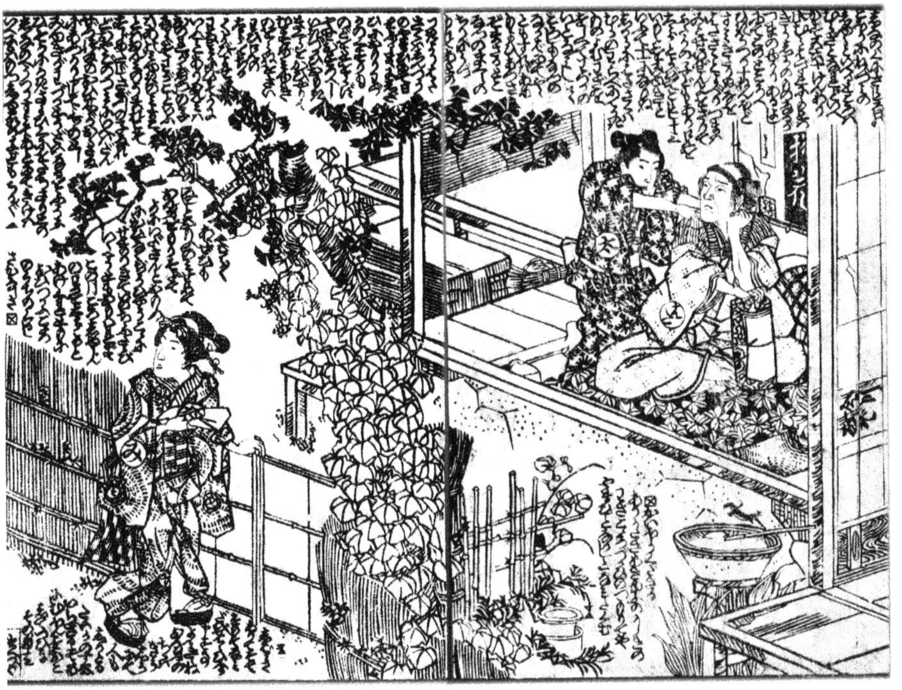

1.3

Part I

(1.3)
In the region of Shinano, in the Sarashina area, there was a place called Nezumi-no-shuku post station. Although it was a village with a post office, it only had fifty or sixty houses. Outside the village lived a man called Hatasaku. Although originally from Kyūshū, he moved to Nezumi-no-shuku some ten years ago, due to circumstances relating to his wife. She had died three years prior, leaving him with two children. The oldest was a boy of thirteen named Tarō, and the youngest a girl of eleven named Miyuki. Life wasn't easy, but he made a meager living by teaching the children of the village how to read and write.

It was mid-summer, when the heat was strong and rain was on its way, and Hatasaku had been struck with a painful heart disease a month prior. As the days passed, his condition grew worse. He hardly took any medicine and was wasting away. One day, when his daughter Miyuki was out, he propped himself up on his pillow and called Tarō to his side and spoke with tears in his eyes.

"I have a secret that I must tell you. You are not my real son. Only Miyuki is really my own child. The truth is, you were born to a grand warrior family, but due to sins committed by your parents, your house was eradicated.

"My wife Ohiki was asked by the lady of your family to take you in and flee the land in secret. You were three years old, and Miyuki had just been born. We moved here to Shinano, where we heard your estate had been confiscated and the children were scattered to the wind. It was regrettable, but nothing could be done. All I wanted to do was raise and protect you so you could make it in the world, but due to this illness I don't think I have long to live.

"Tarō, even though you are supposed to be my young lord, over these last few months I have worked you to the bone day and night. You have cooked my meals, nursed me, and showed me sympathy. Had I not already been sick, the sadness and agony in my heart, and the gratefulness for how you have treated me, would be enough to make me fall ill."

He paused to wipe a tear from his face with his sleeve, and then told Tarō, "Listen closely to what I am about to tell you. Your father is the descendant of a well-known and distinguished family in Kyūshū, but he followed some ill-gotten advice and committed treason, which led to his demise."

(1.4)

While telling Tarō about his father, Hatasaku quietly took out something wrapped in many layers of oiled paper from the Buddhist altar.

"Here, take this," he told Tarō. As he gave him the bundle Tarō immediately unwrapped the numerous papers, revealing a scroll with a beautifully embroidered fabric cover. "Inside this scroll is the record of the bloodline of your house. Read it, but do so secretly."

Tarō loosened the string and opened the scroll. As he read in silence, he saw for the first time the name of his father's house and learned his heritage. He then rolled the scroll back up, raised his head heavily, and spoke gently to Hatasaku.

"I thought I was your son, just an ordinary boy, but this scroll has told me who my true father is. The affection you have shown me is greater than that of a real parent, and my debt to you is immeasurable. I am thankful for the days spent reading and taking lessons from you, and I learned a good deal about the ways of the world. I think of Miyuki as my real sister, and you can rest assured I will pour my heart into raising her."

After Tarō spoke, Hatasaku told him to wrap up the scroll again and put it back into its hiding place before Miyuki came home. Tarō swiftly rewrapped the scroll and put it back in its original spot.

Hatasaku said, "Heed my words now. As you grow older, you will probably change your mind about these things. How happy it would make me, if only you would enter the priesthood instead and do memorial services for your parents and their retainers."

Tarō's heart ached at this, but he knew Hatasaku's words were spoken in kindness, so he chose not to argue. Grateful for the lesson he was given, he lamented the truth of his situation.

The door opened, and Miyuki rushed inside. She was a country girl of just eleven years, clad in dirty patchwork clothes. Somehow, despite this, she had an air of refinement, intelligence, and beauty about her. It was early evening, and she was clutching a package with medicine as she sat next to her father.

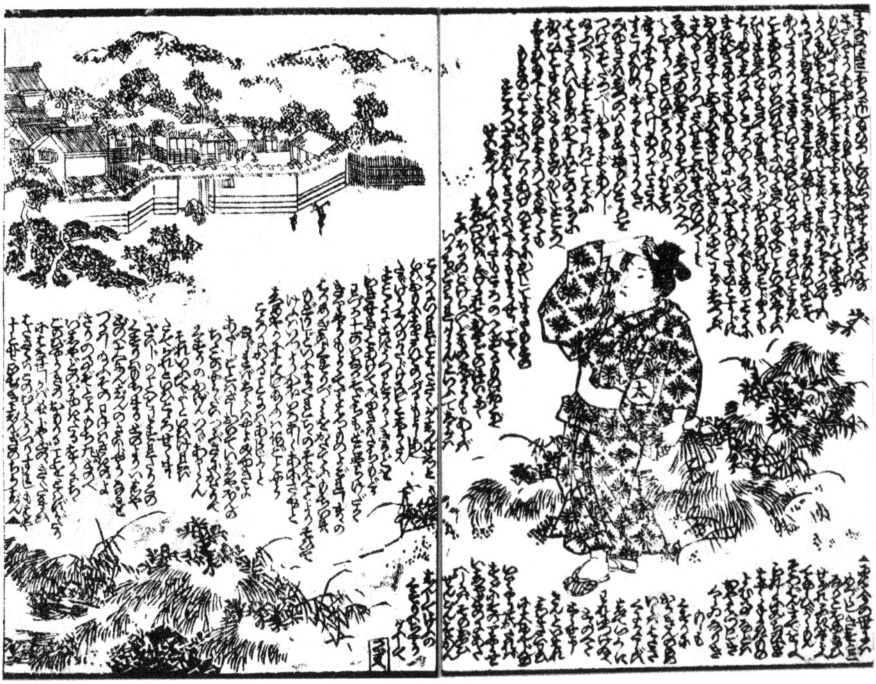

1.4

“Your complexion looks worse than usual today, father. Has something upset you? Have you been talking about something depressing with my brother again?” she asked accusingly in Tarō’s direction.

Tarō snapped back, “Miyuki, how about you quit the idle chit-chat and tell us how that quack of a doctor will adjust father’s medicine after you’ve told him all the details about father’s condition. That’s what we’re wondering about.”

“Oh yes! I completely forgot to tell you something important because it was getting dark, and I was in a hurry. This medicine is from a ginseng root of the highest quality, given to the doctor by Mochimaru-dono. Apparently, last evening, when the doctor went to see Mochimaru-dono, he told him about how serious father’s illness is.

“After hearing about it, Mochimaru-dono praised father, saying, ‘It has already been ten years since Hatasaku moved to our village. He is an honest and virtuous old man, which is a rare sight nowadays. He even taught my son Fukitarō literacy, the Chinese classics, and how to use an abacus. My son learned quickly, and his reading and writing skills have put even his parents to shame. If Hatasaku needs some expensive medicine, tell it to me but keep it a secret from Hatasaku. I will cover the expenses so you can stock up on it.’

“When Mochimaru-dono was told we needed ginseng root, he immediately gave the doctor the money for it. The doctor prepared today’s medicine and said he was astonished by Mochimaru-dono’s saintly charity.”

1.5

(1.5)

Hatasaku wept tears of joy, got on his knees, and bowed in the direction of the Mochimaru household.

"Don't you two ever forget this debt of gratitude!" he said to his children.

"Because of your honesty, father, we have been bestowed this blessing from the heavenly gods. I shall never forget this debt!" said Tarō with great reverence as he and Miyuki wept joyfully.

After quite some time had passed, when the day had long since ended, the lanterns had been lit, and they had cleaned up after dinner, Hatasaku called Tarō over to the stove and whispered to him, "I know the road might be difficult to navigate in the night, but could you please run over to Mochimaru-dono and thank him for the medicine? Leaving gratitude unsaid after receiving kindness from someone is exactly how you end up being resented."

Tarō got up promptly and quietly, retrieved his straw sandals, and said, "Sister, take care of our father," as he departed.

In his haste, Tarō carelessly stumbled over a rock at the side of the road he had not noticed. The tips of his toes hit the rock, ripping his toenails. He tore a bit of fabric from a handkerchief he had in his sleeve and tied it around the toes to stop the blood. Limping, he continued running towards Mochimaru's house. When he got there, he went through the kitchen entrance, looking for someone he could say his thanks to. There, by the hearth, sat the main man who worked in the house, Inesaku.

Giving Tarō a look, he asked, "What business do you have here?"

"I have come to show gratitude for the medicine we received today," Tarō said and gave his most heartfelt thanks.

"The Master has gone to the neighboring village on some business. I will convey your words to the lady of the house in a nice manner, so worry not. But be everything as it may, Hatasaku might still lose his life to this sickness. Make sure to nurse him back to health! If there is an emergency, send for me. And, should old man Hatasaku pass away unexpectedly, do not fret about the arrangements. I, Inesaku, shall help you take care of it!"

Inesaku's truthful and kind words made Tarō's eyes well up with tears. He knew he would have to take a rest in the grass at the side of the road on the way home. Promising to come again, he bid farewell and went home.

Back at the house, Hatasaku dozed off after having Miyuki rub his back. A rogue pushed his way through a hole in the fence outside. The rogue had concealed his face with a cloth, the hem of his kimono was tied to his belt to free his legs, and on his hip, he wore a sword. He checked the vicinity of the house when he set his eyes on Miyuki, and, without a word, he grabbed hold of her.

"Help, a bandit!" cried Miyuki, but the rogue gagged her tightly. He picked her up and held her under his arm, but as he tried to make his escape, the awoken Hatasaku stumbled at him and grabbed his waist, struggling take Miyuki back.

(1.6)

Annoyed, the rogue kicked Hatasaku to the ground, but Hatasaku clung to his leg to try and stop him from leaving. Then the rogue drew the sword from his hip and hacked it into Hatasaku's shoulder. He pulled out his sword from the writhing Hatasaku to mercilessly strike him again but heard people out in front of the house. The rogue was so startled and anxious, without realizing he had dropped a tobacco pouch from inside his sleeve, he fled out the back of the house, sword in hand and holding on to Miyuki.

Later, not knowing what had happened, Tarō stepped into the house and was surprised to find it totally dark. He called out to Hatasaku and Miyuki two or three times. There was no answer.

Puzzled, Tarō fumbled about in the dark, and remembered there was a fire striker under the stove in the kitchen. He hurried to find the fire striker, righted a knocked over lantern, lit it, and was shocked when he caught sight of Hatasaku. Tarō clung to Hatasaku and called out to him at the top of his lungs like a mad man in an attempt to bring him back to life. The injured Hatasaku opened his eyes slightly.

"You're late," wept Hatasaku. "Miyuki was kidnapped by a rogue just now. As he tried to make his escape, I fought him to hold him back, but he cut me down. Oh, curse this wretched body of mine, weakened by disease and with no strength in my legs or back! But as I drew my final breath, you called me back to life. What a strange and wondrous thing to happen."

Tarō's eyes were wide and filled with rage. With a trembling voice, he asked, "And who was this rogue?"

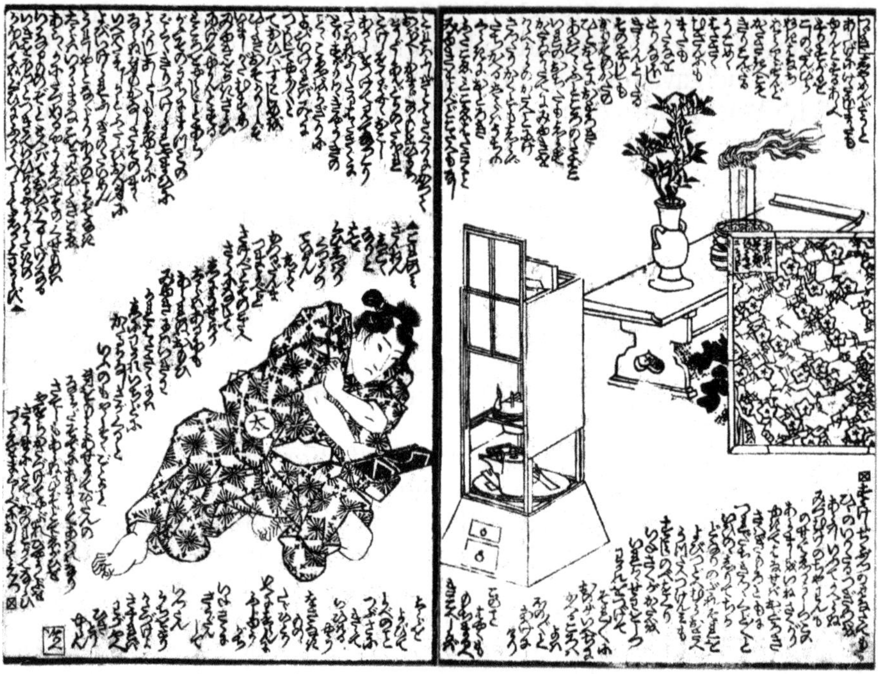

1.6

Hatasaku drew a pained, moaning breath and said, “The face of my bane was wrapped in cloth. I could not discern who it was. This is my biggest regret.” He gritted his teeth and writhed in agony. Hatasaku paled, and in his final moments, no matter how much Tarō called to him or yelled, he did not answer—he had passed away.

Tarō was distraught. It is said “Misery comes with company”; just so, Tarō lost his sister in life, and his father to death. Beset with grief, he wailed with such baleful tears that even his sleeve could not hide his sorrow.

Knowing he could not leave things the way they were, Tarō performed the rites one must follow when preparing the deceased for their final journey. He opened Hatasaku’s kimono and closed it again in reverse, right on top of left, and laid him to rest on the floor. Then he took a broken *byōbu* folding screen, turned it upside down, and placed it by Hatasaku’s right shoulder to ward off evil spirits. He took the table at which he had learned to read and write and placed it to the left of Hatasaku’s pillow. He put the soot covered flower vase from the Buddhist altar on the table, along with a cracked bowl, meant for offering water to the deceased.

After telling Inesaku what happened, there was a great uproar, and everyone went with Tarō to mourn. People from the neighborhood were called, and the village head was informed. After a formal inspection was conducted, they helped carry Hatasaku’s casket to the cremation site. When all had said their farewells and were heading home, night turned into early morning twilight.

1.7

As soon as Mochimaru heard what happened, he sent for Tarō and had him describe every detail of what transpired the night before.

Offering his help and support, Mochimaru said, "It is not reasonable to expect a child to take care of a house all by himself. Have Inesaku help you put your house in order. After that, we will take you in and you can live in our home. Concerning your lost sister, Miyuki, wait for five or six years and then go look for her somewhere lively with a lot of people. I am sure you will run into her."

(1.7)

"For you to help an orphan like me to such an extent, I will do as you command and get my house in order, and I will work to pay back this debt," said Tarō, his face swimming with tears of gratitude.

Here, an introduction to Mochimaru is in order. His full name was Mochimaru Fukiemon, and he was the richest man in the district. His wife was named Fukutoji, and they had two children. The oldest, and heir to the household, was Fukitarō. He was eighteen years old. Although his hair was in a topknot, he was still considered a boy, so his scalp was unshaven. Osachi was his younger sister, aged sixteen, whose uncommonly beautiful features could stop a man in his tracks. Mochimaru practiced compassion and charity as much as he could, and if he heard someone was in need, he would spare no expense to help them. Because of this, it goes without saying people would

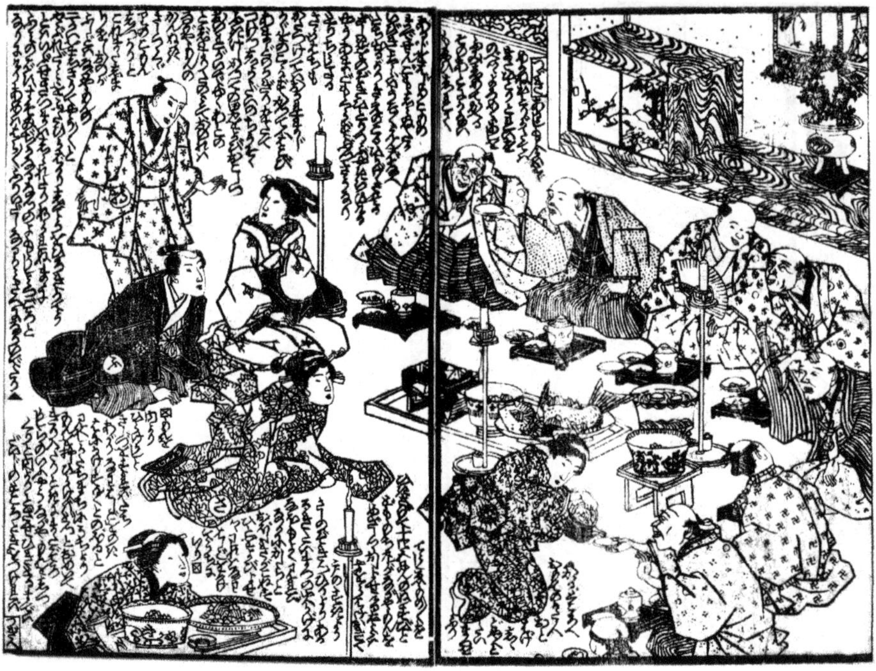

1.8

sing his praises, affectionately calling him the benevolent post station master.

The twenty-fifth day of the sixth month that year was Fukitarō's coming-of-age day, and many things had been prepared. Already from before daybreak, the house was in complete pandemonium with family members, relatives, and people from the village all having been invited for the event. From morning until evening, all manner of dishes were served on lacquered trays and tableware, which were rarely seen in the countryside. No expense had been spared for this feast.

Happy and intoxicated, one of the guests of honor suggested it was time to leave because they had stayed for too long. The lord and lady of the house were happy, and Fukitarō urged the guests, "It is not even midnight yet and there is another meal coming."

His younger sister, Osachi, also urged them, but they had all been at the feast since before noon, so they insistently took out their fans from their belt, as one needs to in order to bow, placed their hands on the floor, bowed, and said, "Let's call it a night."

(1.8)

When they started getting up, the lord of the manor agreed the event came to an end, and one by one, the guests said their thanks and stumbled home. After they left, everyone in the house, from the lord to the servants, collapsed from drunkenness and snored loudly.

Feeling uneasy, Tarō stepped out onto the *engawa* porch, from where he peeked into the parlor room. Shadows flickered across the room from a candle left burning, and Tarō muttered to himself, "Leaving the rain shutters open like this is unsafe, and all the plates and bowls can't be left strewn about as they are."

So, he gathered up the tableware and carried it to the kitchen, closed all the rain shutters, and blew out the candle in the candleholder. Then, he went and roused the men in the kitchen, ordering one to lock the door where the guests had left from, one to latch the gate in front of the longhouse, and one to tightly secure the small door next to the main door. Then he said he would go to his bedchamber on the second floor in the gated longhouse. His room consisted of two *tatami* mats, which had long since been worn out, and a paper mosquito net. He was in a foul mood.

That night was the type of short summer night where one would wear a gown short enough that the shins extended beyond the hem. Tarō could not sleep, and the night slipped into the hour of the ox,[1] when the veil between the worlds of the living and the dead grew thin. Rain trickled down and thunder rumbled in the sky.

Out front there was the sound of stomping feet. Lit by their torches, fourteen or fifteen bandits bearing arms pressed forward, aiming for Mochimaru's gated longhouse. Tarō sprang silently to his feet and peeked through the crack in the door. Because the dancing flames of the torches were as bright as day, Tarō could easily see them. Among them was one who looked like the leader. The leader called over one of the less important bandits and instructed him, "I will hang a rope ladder, go inside, and open the door from within."

The leader attached his rope ladder to the eaves of the building, and Tarō watched him scramble up. After a bit, the gate was pushed open from the inside, allowing the bandits to pour in.

"Make sure to shut the gate tightly from the inside. We don't want any disturbances until we retreat," said the leader, and everyone heeded his words.

(1.9)

They kicked down the rain shutters of the main house before storming inside. Startled, the people within tried to escape in great panic, but everyone was caught and tied to the house pillars. Their wrists were secured together behind their backs and ropes were tied from their necks down to their wrists. The bandits went deeper into the house where they tied up the Mochimaru couple, Fukitarō and Osachi, and dragged them before the leader.

"Hello there, Mochimaru," said the leader. "There is no one who does not know you have more treasure than you know what to do with. Well, tonight your luck has run out, because we intend to steal as much of your treasure as we possibly can. If you hand it over quietly, we won't hurt any of your staff, and we might not even do anything obscene to the women or your daughter." He turned to one of his underlings and ordered, "You lot go and open the door to the storehouse and take out all the treasure. Don't leave anything behind!"

---

1. 01:00-03:00

1.9

The bandits took out an enormous amount of treasure and piled it up. The Mochimaru family trembled with fear. There was no way they could object, and sat there with chattering teeth and faces pale as sheets.

(1.10)

The heavens became covered with clouds and a great surge of rain came down. As if cursing the very ground, lightning flashed, and thunder rumbled. The bandits were frozen in fear, as it looked like lightning might strike any moment.

Unfazed by the situation, the leader, who was called Suribaritarō, said to his men, "This downpour and lightning suits us fine. We will use it to cover our retreat!"

Thus, the bandits filled their hands with treasure and started for the front of the estate. However, as Suribaritarō leisurely made his way out, lightning tore across the skies and thunder roared. When it looked as if the sky might come crashing down, lightning struck with a tremendous boom and killed ten of the bandits, leaving their smoldering bodies scattered on the ground. The remaining four were knocked unconscious, along with Suribaritarō and all the people inside the main house.

At the same time, Tarō, who had observed what happened from the second-floor room, descended. When he looked closer, from within the lightning a mysterious beast sprang out and ran wild. It moved to try and climb one of the pine trees in the garden, but Tarō seized a spiked iron club from one of the bandits and struck it with all his might.

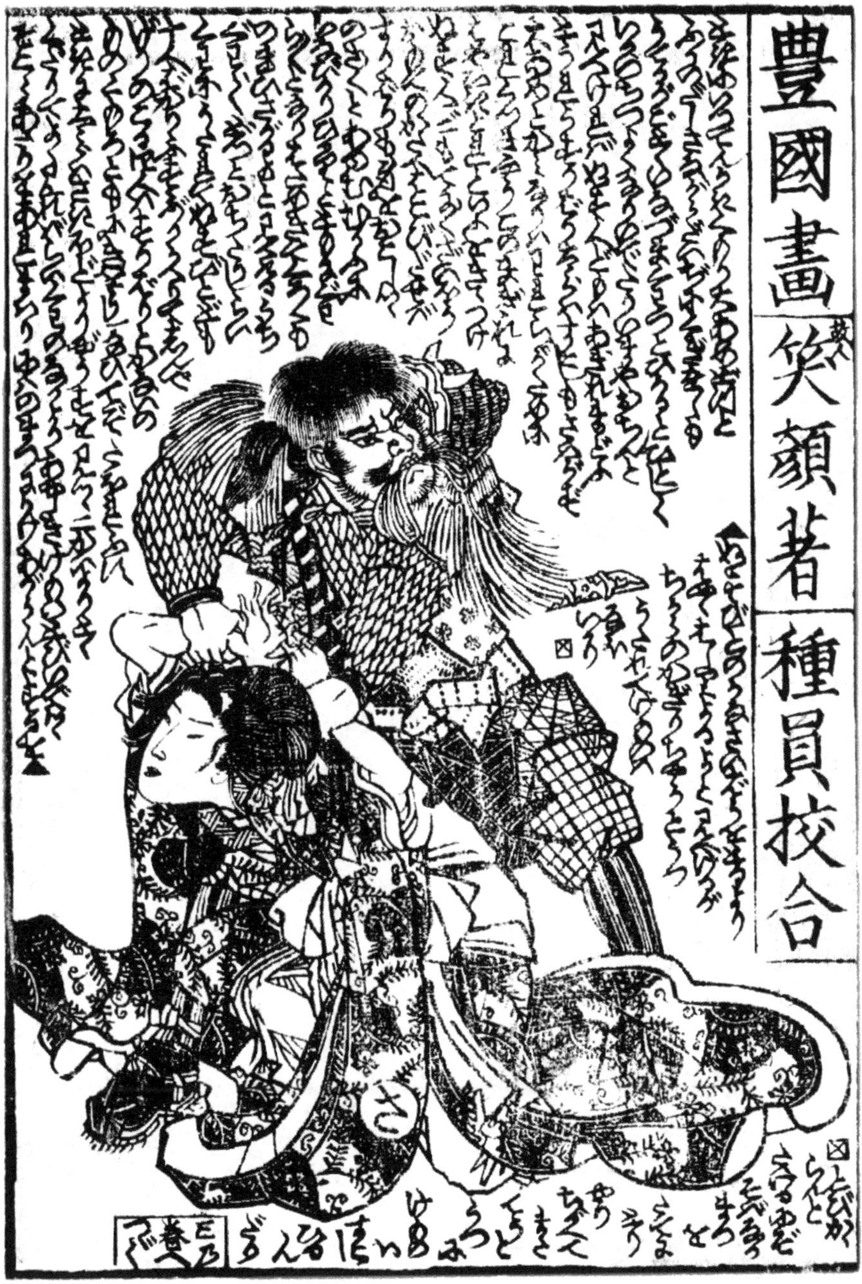

1.10

The beast, enraged by the hit, jumped violently towards the young man, but Tarō dodged behind the tree, which blocked its attack. Then he struck the beast again, causing it to recoil.

1.11

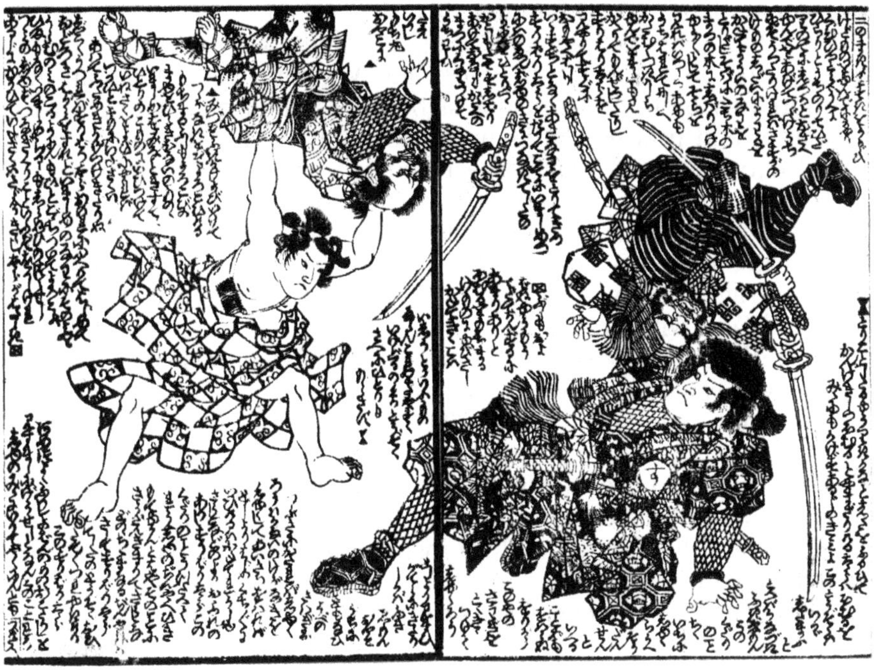

1.12

Part II

(1.12)

Tarō spotted an opening, and with his left hand, he grabbed the beast by the scruff of the neck and nimbly leapt onto its back. He struck it again and again while holding it down firmly. After a while, the thunder beast weakened. Tarō took out a rope he had prepared and tied the beast to the pine tree next to him. He then calmly looked to the sky and saw the rain was clearing and the moon setting towards the west.

He looked over his left shoulder, saw Suribaritarō unconscious from pain, and immediately ran to the main house and grabbed many hemp ropes. Suribaritarō's hands were bound behind his back, and another rope was tied from his neck to his hands, and then he was secured to a pagoda tree in the garden. The four underlings were tied up one by one without waking them, and fastened to a pine tree close to the other. He finished the task while letting out a laugh.

Tarō went and threw some water on the Mochimaru family to rouse them. Their faces lit up with relief, and he was happy to see they were unharmed. All the other people in the house were soon released. A boy was sent to fetch Inesaku, who came running back with the boy in a great panic.

After some time passed, Suribaritarō came back to his senses. At first, he was shocked, then grit his teeth while cursing the ropes that bound him. The remaining four bandits also woke up, but they had no time to rejoice. They were completely tied up and their sins were as numerous as the pearls on a string of prayer beads. Watching them bemoan their situation was quite an amusing sight. Inesaku turned to the lord of the manor and praised Tarō's work, deeply moved by his bravery and strength, to which not even the best trained warrior could compare.

Mochimaru then pointed to the beast and said, "Tell me again, is this the mystical beast you told us of? To think that Tarō managed not only to catch it alive so easily but also took every single bandit prisoner. What courage!" He was so impressed that his voice quivered as he showered Tarō with praise.

Tarō did not respond to the praise, but instead asked, "My liege, what do you wish done with these bandits?"

Fukiemon nodded and said, "Tell the village elder every detail of what has happened here and ask for his advice."

No sooner had the words left his mouth than did the village elder arrive. He had heard the commotion at the house and came to inquire. Fukiemon and his family led him inside and told him everything that occurred during the night.

After the elder finished greeting everyone in the house and thanked the heavens no one was hurt, he said, "The lord of Sarashina has already issued a warrant for this Suribaritarō. We will press charges for what has happened here and drag him to the lord's administrative office."

So, the decision was made, and the elder told them the directions to the lord of Sarashina's administrative office in Chikuma. Suribaritarō and his underlings were put on their feet and pushed along.

However, on a night with heavy rains, Suribaritarō kept a close eye for his captors to drop their guard, and when he saw his opening, he escaped.

(1.13)

When this reached the ears of the lord, he revoked the status of those involved, had the bandit cohorts decapitated, and ordered a thorough search for Suribaritarō's whereabouts.

Meanwhile, back at Mochimaru's estate, Tarō went to the lord of the manor and Inesaku and was put to tidy up the treasure which lay scattered in the garden. Afterwards, he went to them again and said, "Because this thunder beast, this *raijū*, came down, none of the gold and silver was stolen and the bandits were captured. When all's said and done, I practically did nothing, and the merit lies with the raijū. It would be heartless to keep such a brave beast tied to the pine tree just to let it suffer. Wouldn't it be better if we let it go?"

Fukiemon said, "You are quite right," and then immediately told Tarō to get to it. Tarō rejoiced and went straight over to the thunder beast's side, took its bonds and led it out the front gate. He took it to the middle of a field that was about twenty *ken*,[2] where he untied the ropes

2. Around 36 meters.

1.13

and cast them aside. When it was freed, the thunder beast looked back at Tarō and then went between the trees of the forest close to the field and disappeared from sight. The town was abuzz with the story of Tarō, who had captured thunder itself, and people called to him "Raitarō, Raitarō"—the young thunder. Even he himself started answering to this new name.

Armed with his new moniker, Raitarō returned to the main house where Fukiemon praised him, beaming with joy. "You did absolutely splendidly." Then his son Fukitarō, his wife Fukutoji, and his daughter Osachi all clamored, suggesting Raitarō deserved a reward.

Fukiemon said to Raitarō, "If there is something you wish for, please say it and I shall grant it."

Upon hearing this, Raitarō made a heartfelt request.

"Although it is a waste to give me a reward for doing such a small thing, there is one thing I would ask. As you know, I lost my father, and my sister has gone missing. I wish to report these dire things to Hatasaku's brother in Niigata in the land of Echigo. I also have not seen my uncle for several years, and I wish to use this opportunity to meet him. If you would allow me to go, there would be no greater reward than this."

Fukiemon sat in silent contemplation, but after a while he spoke, "Echigo is not very far away, but you are only thirteen, with your forehead still unshaven. It won't be too late even if you wait two or three years before you go. I will write your uncle a letter on your behalf, telling him all the details of what has happened. I am sure he will understand."

Hearing Fukiemon wanted to stop him, Raitarō responded, "I could never hope to express the debt I owe to you for everything concerning my father Hatasaku. Even in death, I shall not forget it. Please listen to what I have to say, even if you would wish to lecture me for suddenly bringing up this subject!" Raitarō gave no indication that anything could stop him.

The master of the house finally replied, "Since you have already set your mind to it, I suppose I ought to let you do as you please," and acquiesced to the wish, which brought great joy to Raitarō, who was moved by Fukiemon's sympathy.

The Mochimarus then went into the house and Raitarō went back to his room. Later, Inesaku came to Raitarō's room and asked him when he was planning to leave, to which the young man answered he would leave on the next day.

(1.14)

"Oh my, that is indeed sudden," muttered Inesaku.

To which Raitarō replied, "I've heard the day one makes up one's mind to do something is more auspicious for doing it. Would you please inform the master?" There was no way Inesaku could make any objections to this request, so he left and went back to the main house.

All alone in his room, Raitarō held his own council.

"I have heard the rumors of a man named Ganpachi, whom they say came to this area recently from Niigata in Echigo. They say he makes his living by gambling and other foul means, and everyone hates him. The tobacco pouch that was dropped in our home looks a lot like the one he supposedly carries. I should catch him to bring in for questioning, but such a scoundrel probably wouldn't stay in this area for long. I will set out on a journey to his hometown in Echigo and try asking around there."

Raitarō took the scroll with his ancestry and hid it together with his only clue, the tobacco pouch. Thinking he'd better retire early, he started preparing for bed, but someone from the main house called out, asking him to come quickly, and so he did.

When he arrived at the main house together with one of the servants, everyone waited there, even the master of the household.

Fukiemon faced Raitarō and said, "I heard everything from Inesaku about you asking permission to set out for Echigo tomorrow. This is not a bad idea, so I present to you this parting gift." On a piece of paper, he put five golden *koban* coins—enough to feed a single person with rice for almost fifteen years. On a cotton lined winter kimono, he put a *wakizashi* short sword for traveling, a scarf three shaku long,[3] a straw hat, and gaiters. All of these he produced and gave to Raitarō.

Fukiemon's wife, Fukutoji, took out a little purse and gave it to Raitarō, saying, "This is my husband's, but it is still brand new. It also has medicine inside."

"My rain mantle might be a little worn, but as a farewell gift I'm sure it should not trouble you," said the son, Fukitarō.

---

3. 1 meter.

1.14

When she heard this, Osachi fetched the rain mantle, and as she gave it to Raitarō, said, "When the next two or three days of summer have passed, autumn will be close, so please take care of yourself and don't catch a cold. And always keep an eye on where you are going. Beware you don't die young." Her intelligence showed itself through her words.

Weeping tears of joy and gratitude, Raitarō put his hands to the ground and said, "I have not properly expressed my gratitude towards you of late, and yet you have not gotten angry with me for my selfish ways. You have even given me these parting gifts. It is much more than I deserve. Words cannot express how thankful I am."

Tears streamed down Raitarō's cheeks as Fukiemon got up from his seat, saying, "We will see you again tomorrow. Then we will say our final goodbyes," after which everyone got up and left.

Raitarō awoke to the caws of crows, signaling daybreak. He gathered his farewell gifts and wrapped them in a small cloth bag. He took the money and put it inside the breast of his kimono, under the belt so it was against the skin. Then he went to the kitchen in the main house and thanked the servants for their everyday work. The Mochimaru family and Inesaku showed up as well and spent a lot of time saying farewell. Looking like they would never stop, Raitarō finished the sendoff and said his thanks. He put the main house behind him, and while looking back over his shoulder, set out on his way. He made a stop at the burial site where Hatasaku's remains were kept, gave the temple a small donation, and asked them to take care of making offerings for Hatasaku.

1.15

With his mind set to go to Niigata in Echigo to seek out Hatasaku's younger brother and this Ganpachi character who had kidnapped his sister, alone and lionhearted, he put the land of Shinano behind him, and set out on his journey to Echigo.

(1.15)
Seven years later...

In the town of Ōiso in the Sagami province, there was a quick-witted man named Kinosuke, who was known in all the tea houses of the pleasure district as Tsuruhashiya. Night was setting, so he hurried to cross the Hanamizu Bridge to go home. From behind him came a common foot soldier with his head wrapped in a scarf. Without a word, he thrust his hand into the breast of Kinosuke's kimono and snatched a letter. But Kinosuke was not going to let him get away, and grabbed the soldier by the belt to pull him back.

People turned to see the unsightly spectacle of the two men fighting on the bridge. The foot soldier then threw himself forward, tossed the letter into the river, broke away from Kinosuke's grip on his belt, and tried to get away. Kinosuke wrestled with him and pushed him in the back, toppling him, but the foot soldier kept going and disappeared into the crowd of onlookers.

(1.16)

Kinosuke gritted his teeth in frustration towards the crowd, who showed no sympathy for his unfortunate situation. In fact, they burst

1.16

into laughter at the scene, angering Kinosuke. But there was nothing he could do. Thus, with a frustrated look on his face, he hurried home.

At that time, a roofed entertainment boat came paddling down by the shore of the Hanamizu Bridge. The letter landed on the prow of the boat, making an audible sound. A samurai stepped out onto the forward deck and nabbed the letter. He tried to read the address, but the darkness of dusk had fallen, and he thought it would be a shame to open it because of the rain. Just then, a geisha stepped out and opened an umbrella next to him. Startled, he spun to face her. The geisha stuck her hand out from under the umbrella to feel if the rain cleared, and then closed it and went back inside the boat. As the samurai stuck the letter inside the breast of his kimono, a narrow river boat silently paddled up from behind.

A townsman could be seen on the other boat, and as he carelessly glanced at the samurai, they became acutely aware of one another. "Wait, isn't that...?" said the townsman and pulled out a lantern, which the samurai blew out. Without a word, they were both about to stand up in their boats, but both captains abruptly changed their courses, and the boats went separate ways.

(1.17)

Lord Yoriuji Anson of Kamakura, who was the constable to the Shōgun, was a great lover of tea ceremony paraphernalia. This being the case, he

1.17
Aside conversation on bottom left:
"Monji-san, when you go to Edo could you pick up some Senjōkō powder makeup for me? It's all the rage in Edo, so it must be wonderful."
"I'll go get it in a couple of days, so it will be a bit before you have it."

had borrowed a treasured tea container, named Fubuki Katatsuki, from the Sarashina family, who were the lords of Shinano. After Lord Yoriuji enjoyed it, it was time for it to return to its owner. It was entrusted to Sumatarō, the only son of Himematsu Edanoshin, Lord Sarashina's most important retainer. Alongside Sumatarō was Tatsumaki Arakurō, who served in the same household. They were strictly ordered to keep the container secret and safe, because it was a very dear and great treasure to the lord. With this in mind, they had brought it with them to the inn they were staying at in Kamakura.

(1.18)

Himematsu Sumatarō and Tatsumaki Arakurō had grown bored with the tedium of the inn and frequented Ōiso's pleasure district. Sumatarō had quickly fallen for a high-ranking courtesan, the *tayū* named Tsuyaginu, and the two were becoming very intimate with each other. Arakurō had other plans, and he spent all his time making sure the saké kept flowing and surrounded himself with *geiko* and jesters to make the evening more fun. To get away from the commotion of the party on the second floor, and to clear his head from drunkenness, Sumatarō and Tsuyaginu visited a room by the garden. There, Sumatarō had Tsuyaginu make some tea. When they were completely enthralled with each other, Sumatarō's squire, a man named Matsuhei came

1.18

running in a frenzy. No sooner had he set eyes on Sumatarō than he handed him a letter case, saying, "An urgent message from your homeland."

Sumatarō undid the case's string, broke the seal on the scroll, and opened it. What he read shocked him, and he burst into tears. After a moment, he turned to Tsuyaginu and said, "The message says my father has been killed in some sort of uprising in my homeland. I promise that I will be back tomorrow," and got up to leave at once.

Tsuyaginu was also shocked to hear this. She wiped a single tear from her cheek with her sleeve and said, "You say you will be back tomorrow, but because of your position, I don't think now is the time to play around. It would probably be best if we said our farewells. This is, after all, your honorable father you are talking about."

Sumatarō sternly told Matsuhei to hurry and go back to the inn, saying, "I will go later by palanquin. You go on ahead and pack up my clothes and belongings. I need to go tell Tatsumaki-san what has happened, and then we should hurry and go home." Sumatarō went and told Arakurō about the message and his father's death, which shocked Arakurō.

"There is not a moment to waste! You must hurry home!" urged Arakurō.

Sumatarō said his parting words, got in the palanquin in a hurry, and headed for the inn.

(1.19)

Arakurō got up and left with no sense of urgency. What could he have been thinking? Sumatarō set out on the way back, and Arakurō left the pleasure district and nervously went to the top of

1.19

one of the surrounding embankments. There he picked up a small pebble and threw it, and three men came rushing from below the embankment.

"We hid here earlier and have been awaiting your signal," said the men in unison.

Arakurō gave them a nod and said, "The man you just saw is the target. If he is too much for you to handle, I will help. Now go hide!"

They all gave one another a nod and concealed themselves. When the rushing palanquin came by, the men drew their swords and surrounded it. Shocked, the bearers fled without looking back. From within, Sumatarō kicked the palanquin open and cut down one of the attackers. He grabbed another and restrained him on the ground, then dodged one who charged at him and cleaved his torso from the collarbone across to the lower abdomen, ending him without pain. Sumatarō readied his blade to stab the man prostrated below him, when he was struck from behind. The sneak attack cut him from his shoulder down to below the nipple. Sumatarō screamed from terror at the river of blood and his final moments were excruciating. With his face concealed, Arakurō carefully checked his surroundings and then put an end to Sumatarō. Without hesitation, he also killed his own last surviving ally. Now no one could mess up his carefully laid plans, and grinning to himself, he crept away like a rat.

On that very same evening, Arakurō snuck into Sumatarō's room in the inn, stole the Fubuki Katatsuki tea container, and quietly bolted from Kamakura, leaving no clues as to his whereabouts.

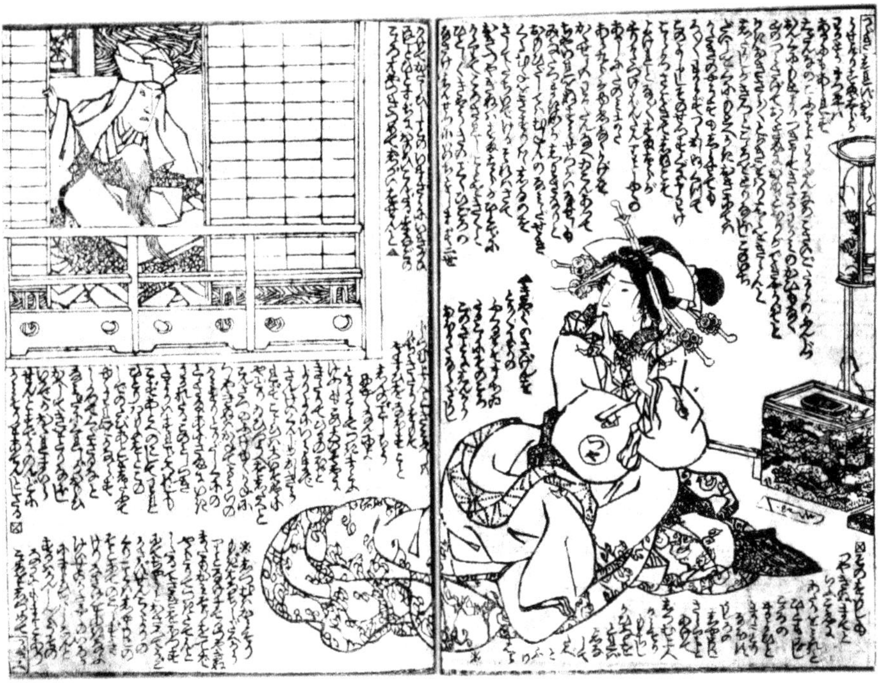

1.20

(1.20)

Sumatarō's squire Matsuhei was at a total loss. How would he face Sumatarō's mother and tell her what had happened to her son, despite him having come all the way together with Sumatarō? How would he tell the lord the unexpected news, that the young master had met his end, and that his treasure had been lost? He wrote a suicide note, intending to cut open his belly when he finished, but he had a change of heart.

"Telling what has happened in a suicide note won't be enough for them to figure out who the murderer was. It would be best if I go back home, make my amends and apologize, and only then save my honor by slicing open my stomach and dying."

With great sorrow, he asked the owner of the inn to take care of Sumatarō's body. As he set out for Shinano, with tears of regret and a heart filled with hatred, he thought about how Arakurō's unexplained disappearance must have been because he had some sort of grudge against his young master, and how both the stealing of the tea container and the murder must have been that damned Arakurō's doing.

Elsewhere, upon hearing how Sumatarō had been slain, Tsuyaginu was beset with maddening grief. The love they shared, and the sweet words of their undying affections, only made her maiden heart lose all reason to live. As she entertained guests, she waited for the night to come, while considering ending her life.

Around that time, in this town where devout believers were few and far between, there was a man called Jitsumu the Saint. It was said that, like the Buddha, he healed the sick through prayer, that he had many followers, and that old and young, men, and women alike paid him respect. On this very day, he came to Ōiso and stayed the night because he had been unable to break through the crowd of worshippers since noon and all the way until evening.

As the town was on its head from all the commotion, the evening grew late and a weeping Tsuyaginu took out a razorblade she had prepared.

"In all these years and months since I was separated from my father and brother in my homeland, I have sent them letters but never received any replies. I have been abandoned, and now the only man who cared for me has died. Please don't be angry with me for following you now in death," she said, and as the blade was on her throat, something happened.

"Tsuyaginu, wait!" a voice called out in an attempt to delay her hand and make her come to her senses. The voice made her look around, but no one was there. Before Tsuyaginu got lost in despair again, the *shōji* screen behind her opened, and Jitsumu the Saint appeared and grabbed the arm holding the razor.

"Just let me die!" cried Tsuyaginu, trying to break free. Jitsumu pulled the razor from her hand and threw it down on the floor with a clatter. Tsuyaginu thrust her hands out to grab the razor, but Jitsumu restrained her and would not let her move.

(1.21)

"I was outside the shōji for the past hour and heard all your lamentations. Being a courtesan who sells her love to customers, it is no wonder you would be taken in by their charm and now feel like dying. Even in lies, there is truth, and you have my deepest sympathy. But please, still your heart and listen to me. If you kill yourself, it will cause your father and brother tremendous grief, and it would be a great loss to the owner of this house. You would be committing grave sins of faithlessness and breaking filial piety, which are inexcusable sins. So listen to my words—there are things a hundred times sadder than your wishes to die right now. Please, for now, just stop."

Gradually, Tsuyaginu raised her face and said, "I needed to hear the sermon you gave me just now, you truly are like the living Buddha people revere you as. The words you speak are..." she trailed off as she stared deeply at Jitsumu's face. "Seven years ago, I was separated from my older brother. I could swear you look just—"

"Namu Amida Butsu! Namu Amida Butsu!" interrupted Jitsumu, reciting the *nembutsu* prayer.

"The Buddha teaches us to save all, whether or not they are related by faith or blood. Not straying from the path is the shortest road to enlightenment. But, all of that being as it may, for now let us adjourn to another room," he said, and so he went with Tsuyaginu.

1.21

Who exactly could this monk be? Maybe the mystery will be solved as we commence the second book.

To be continued...

2.1

Book 2

In olden texts, characters sometimes have nicknames. In *The Tale of the Heike*, the lord governor Suenaka of the Dazaifu government is called *Kokusotsu*—the black governor, because of his dark countenance. In *Fukurozōshi*, minister Takayoshi is called *Aoemon*—the pale minister, because he was said to be so pallid, etcetera. Kokusotsu, Aoemon, the list goes on and on. Just like *Kaoshō*, the flowery monk, and *Kyūmonryū*, the nine-tattoo dragon, from *Outlaws of the Marsh*, who took aliases that would spread far and wide, so did Jiraiya. Already in the first volume, he captured the raijū and proved his knowledge, benevolence, and courage.

The spirit of the boy of three turns to the spirit of the man of a hundred. Even if I only spun the tale up to ten, like a frog sitting on a platter, I place my hands on the ground, and as always, I pray for good reviews.

Tenpō 12 (1841)
Mizugaki Egao

2.2

Left side:
Kurohime Yashagorō Onikado the bandit leader.
Harisaki Togekurō the rōnin.

Right side:
The concubine of Sarashina, Shirotae, who is actually Jiraiya.

2.3

The loyal and fierce retainer of the Sarashina clan, Takasago Yuminosuke.

Ogata Shūma the rōnin.

Koshiji the mysterious woman.

2.4

Part I

(2.4)
And so, the story continues.

After holding back Tsuyaginu from killing herself, Jitsumu said, "There is something I have a moral obligation to tell you." Jitsumu took Tsuyaginu to a quiet room, where he turned to her and in a hushed voice said, "The two of us alone in a lively brothel where people are coming and going like this almost looks like I am trying my best to cause a scandal. But there is a reason why I must talk to you in secret. So, if you would, please still your heart and listen."

With the fabric of his sleeve, he wiped the tears about to overflow from his eyes, and then he told Tsuyaginu his tale.

"Around seven years ago, a time so distant now it feels almost like a dream, a man named Ganpachi attacked Hatasaku with a sword and kidnapped you, separating you from your family and disappearing without a trace. Hatasaku sadly perished, leaving not only you, but also me, orphans. Because, you see, I was also brought up by Hatasaku. The Mochimaru family took me in and even though they showed me infinite kindness, I left, telling them I wanted to go visit our uncle. I wandered around from place to place and came to Niigata in Echigo. I asked around for Ganpachi, but no one knew of him.

"My heart was wrought with worry for you, but to no avail. Obsessed with finding out where you were, I spent years as I went around working as a servant. Three years in one place and then two years somewhere else. Last year, however, I was heading towards Kamakura, and there was a revered monk who came from the capital. I asked to become his disciple and started in his service, but his ties with this earthly plane were thin, and he soon moved on to the next. And now, the other remaining disciples have nominated me to be a teacher of the dharma, so we will soon be going to the capital so I may get ordained.

"We are believers in the dharma and the merits of chanting the nembutsu prayer. Through it, we have saved an untold number of people who suffered from plague and other grave illnesses. Because there has so far not been anyone who has not made a full recovery, our reputation has spread, and we have gathered many loyal followers. I've spent several days here at the pleasure district of Ōiso because I was invited here, but to my surprise, the pleasure girl named Tsuyaginu, desired by all, is actually my little sister Miyuki."

While telling his story, his fingertips were running through his prayer beads, but even his denouncing of the 108 poisons of the mind came to a halt, as his eyes welled up with tears of happiness upon this long-awaited reunion.

(2.5)

After listening to the monk's long story, Tsuyaginu could no longer hold back. As she gazed at Jitsumu's face, tears poured from her eyes, and she told him her own tale.

"Every day and night of this wretched life of prostitution, I have wondered how my brother was doing. My brother, who was separated from me when we were so young. And tonight, the Buddhas have seen pity on my sincere heart and have guided you to this unexpected reunion. Dressed like the Miroku Bodhisattva, destined to appear and guide the world back to the dharma, you have come to be my guide to the ways of Buddhism.

"The life of harlotry is especially sinful for women, and I was plunged into it by that scoundrel Ganpachi's doing! On that evening when you were out, he came with his face wrapped in a cloth and cut down our sick father with a sword. He kidnapped me and ran off, and your story now is the first I have heard of what happened after.

"While my kidnapper and I wandered, I was worried sick about father. I sent letters from far away, asking about his well-being, but never got any responses. I guess he was already dead at that time. Next, that loathsome fiend sold me on the way, and I was passed between whorehouses in places like Niigata in Echigo and Mikuni in Echizen. I have no words to describe to you the pain of being a pleasure girl or the horrors of harlotry.

"Later, I was sent to this pleasure district, and again I wept into my pillow alone every night with every changing guest. But as I worked here, I fell deeply in love with Himematsu Sumatarō, a vassal of the Sarashina family in Shinano. Alas, a man named Tatsumaki Arakurō, who worked with him, had a lover's grudge against him and attacked him in the darkness. When I had heard what happened, I was so miserable

2.5

that I could think of nothing else, not even myself or anything in this world. Just as I resolved myself to end my life, I was stopped by a monk who turned out to be none other than my brother. Even in tragedy, I guess, there can be joy."

As she told her story, she broke down crying. Jitsumu did not tell her they were not truly siblings by blood, nor did he tell her of his true intentions. Those he kept locked away deep in his heart.

During their conversation, someone spied from a crack in the shōji screens behind them. Jitsumu noticed this but pretended to be unaware.

From a sleeve he took out a single sheet of folded paper and gave it to Tsuyaginu. "This is a vow I wrote when I was not busy with my work. Open it in private and learn its lesson. It is the written teaching of the Buddhas, showing the road to paradise between the plane of the present and the plane of the future. Until we meet again, consider it and let it bring you peace."

Then he got up to leave. Tsuyaginu was reluctant to part with him, and Jitsumu could not look back at her. When he went down the ladder from the second floor, one of his companions called for a palanquin, and Jitsumu got in and headed home.

From the main gate of Ōiso's famed entertainment district, people fled, yelling about the fight that had broken out, crying like crows in the morning. Steel flashed as a *rōnin*, enraged by a grudge, and a man, who

2.6

was the well-known leader of delinquents and knights-errant in the entertainment district, squared off. The latter saw the floating world as nothing but a dream and went by the name Yume no Chōbei—the dreaming butterfly. They were quite evenly matched, and when Jitsumu came upon the fight, he had his followers put down the palanquin at a good distance from it. Then he shoved the door open, and without fear of the shining blades, he rushed in between the two men trying to cut each other down. He wrapped Chōbei's blade up in his clothes and stopped the rōnin's *katana* with his fly whisk.

(2.6)

Then, quietly to the two men, he spoke, "Here in the pleasure district, the custom is to bring forth peacefulness through desire and to shun violence. What immature behavior, brandishing your swords in a place like this. If you have a grudge with each other, you should let go of it."

At these dignified words of mediation, Chōbei's face let up. "We have indeed gotten into a fight over something trivial, causing problems for passers-by and amassing sin by making hardship for an honorable pilgrim. If you also wish to retract your blade and sheath it, then let this grudge be water under the bridge."

The rōnin nodded in approval. "To draw my katana over a fight about a pleasure girl. I am embarrassed for what the priest is thinking of us. Let's put our blades away."

They both sheathed their swords and agreed the matter was settled.

With a pleased look on his face, Jitsumu said, "Even though my monkhood does not require me to get involved, if you had hurt each other you would have regretted it. And I am like an old grandmother, so I always worry about the problems of others. How splendid I could convince you to stop." Then he took his leave from the two, got in his palanquin, and departed with his companions. Afterwards, the two men looked each other in the face, gave a forced smile, and went their separate ways.

After seeing the rōnin off, Chōbei thought to himself, "That man was definitely the one who picked up the letter that fell on the roofed boat I passed at Hanamizu Bridge the other day. I've heard a rumor that he became Tsuyaginu's client. His name is something like Harisaki Togekurō. The fight he instigated with me started this morning in the Tsuruhashi tea house, and it ended in a right mess with heated words. They say this monk Jitsumu is like a living Buddha, and thanks to his mediation, our fight ended in a draw and we both saved face." His mind now broadened by his meeting with the monk, he walked leisurely down the main street towards home. This Chōbei was, by the way, also known as one of Tsuyaginu's clients.

While the fight outside the gate was happening, Tsuyaginu opened the piece of writing given to her by Jitsumu, and was surprised by what she read. She kept it a secret, and the very next morning she sent for Tsuruhashiya Kinosuke. She whispered something to him for a long time, making sure no one overheard. Later that day, Kinosuke gave a lot of money to the owner of Tsuyaginu's contract, telling him that Chōbei, the dreamer from Umezawa in Ōiso, was taking her as his wife. Chōbei buying Tsuyaginu's contract made the owner very happy. All of this, Tsuyaginu whispered to Kinosuke to keep secret from Harisaki Togekurō, and after Kinosuke did as Tsuyaginu asked, he went home.

Tsuyaginu waited for Togekurō, and when evening fell, he came accompanied by Kinosuke. He brought a jester, and they sang and danced, causing quite the ruckus. Togekurō was completely absorbed with Tsuyaginu and got so drunk he didn't notice his entourage went home. He went with Tsuyaginu to her room to lie down, where he soon overcame his intoxication. When he looked at the woman, he saw her depressed and worried expression. This was very rare for her, so he asked her what was wrong. He asked her gently with a kind expression, and Tsuyaginu slowly raised her head.

"You are so sweet to me, so I am embarrassed to have to answer your question, but as you know, I have many clients. The confident ones are rude, and the gentle ones are weaklings. There are very few whom I can truly give myself to. It has been decided Chōbei the dreamer, whom you already know from before, is to buy my contract and take me as his wife. I must show love for him, otherwise he will spread rumors about me, and I won't be able to get any clients afterwards. But when I am with you, even if you are a client, in my heart I don't see you as some stranger. Tomorrow, I have a way to not have to go to Chōbei, but the only one whose strength I can rely on to help me is you. I cannot show I

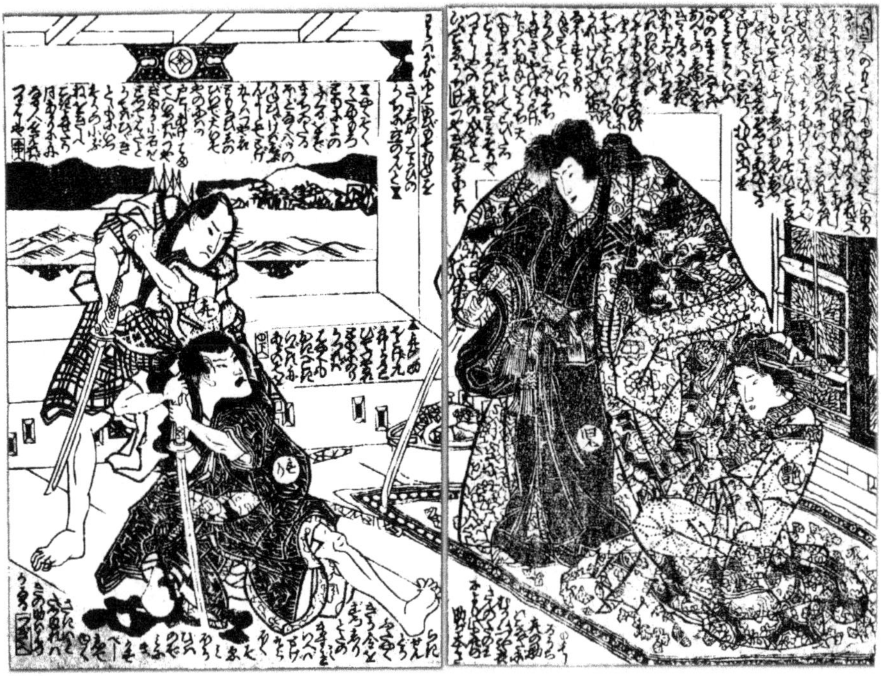

2.7

have another love, but if I am asked, I will have to tell everything about my unrelenting feelings for you."

(2.7)

As she said this, she snuggled up close to Togekurō and sank into quiet wistfulness. Overwhelmed by the heartrending winds of love after having been told this truth, Togekurō swallowed into his palpitating chest and said, "If what you tell me is true, tell me what this way you have is. If I can live up to the task, I will take you away from this place. We will hide somewhere far away from here and we can be husband and wife. How does that sound?"

Hearing this, Tsuyaginu was pleased and drew even closer to him. "Here is my plan," she said, and put her lips up to his ear and whispered her plans. Togekurō clapped his hands together. His face lit up with joy. He was so elated he could jump through the ceiling.

"Then Tsuruhashiya Kinosuke is going to—" he started, but Tsuyaginu cut him off and pointed a finger at her chest.

"Let us keep the rest in our hearts and leave this place tonight," she said, sealing their promise to each other. Then they waited for nightfall.

Before long, the eighth bell was struck, signaling the hour of the ox.[1] Judging it to be the right time, Togekurō snuck out with Tsuyaginu. He opened the door in the garden of the pleasure house, and they went to the beach. There, Tsuyaginu picked up two pebbles and struck them together. At the sharp clack, a single small boat rowed up to the shore.

1. 01:00

2.8

The light of the moon revealed the man on the boat to be Tsuruhashiya Kinosuke. Togekurō rejoiced, boarded the boat with Tsuyaginu, and frantically rowed out into the waves away from the reefy, windswept coast.

Kinosuke said to the two, "By Tsuyaginu-san's request, I, Kinosuke, have worked hard and hired two boatmen for which I humbly ask payment."

"Leave the payment to me," said Togekurō. "By the way, where are we headed?"

(2.8)

"If you tell one of the boatmen on that ship where you want to go, he will take you there," Kinosuke said and pointed to a large vessel far out in the water. He sped up his rowing. Before long, they reached the stern of the ship.

On the ship, five or six boatmen appeared and helped the three climb on board. One of the boatmen grabbed Tsuyaginu's hand and forcefully pulled her along, saying "The master has been waiting for hours, we must make haste!"

Shocked, Togekurō ran at them while drawing his sword, shouting, "What are you doing to that woman?"

Without Togekurō seeing it, Kinosuke drew the sword and slashed at him from behind. The cut was deep, but Togekurō still turned around to strike back. Kinosuke ducked down below the attack and cut Togekurō's left leg with a swish. Kinosuke held his enemy at bay on the floor and turned to the main cabin of the ship.

"I believe this is the man you requested," Kinosuke called, "Please enter and confirm his identity!"

Tsuyaginu came out from the cabin, surrounded by many boatmen, and a young man was with her. His complexion was white and fair, and his eyebrows thick. His eyes were vivid and overpowering, and his features were gentle and honest. He was clad in a purple *kosode* short-sleeved kimono, a pale turquoise belt of ruffled crepe fabric, and on top he wore a large, black overcoat with a dragon embroidered in golden thread. Behind his back was a great wakizashi short sword, and brandished before him was a magnificent longsword. The man sat on a storage chest facing Togekurō.

"Isn't this a rare sight to see you here, Suribaritarō! Not only once, but twice now you have fallen and been brought shame by my hand. Do you understand the limited scope of your own abilities now?"

Stupefied, Togekurō, also known as Suribaritarō, eyed the man and slowly said, "You are the one from seven years ago, when we went to rob Mochimaru. The one who captured the raijū and defeated and hogtied my men. That wild and fearless boy, Tarō. How you have changed since then. The other day I picked up a letter that fell on a boat at the Hanamizu Bridge. All that was written in the address was 'Rai' and the seal said 'Ki'. Now that I think of it, it must have been yours. And last night I secretly listened as you claimed yourself to be Tsuyaginu's sibling. And now you are a pirate?"

Kinosuke drew to Togekurō's side. "You are the one who picked up our secret letter? And to make matters worse, I know you came to my inn where the Fubuki Katatsuki tea container was being held, and that you saw where it was. You reported it to your leader and made a mess of everything. Tell me where the tea container is, immediately!" His accusation was harsh, so Jitsumu stepped in and stopped him.

(2.9)

Jitsumu then turned to Togekurō and spoke in a pleasant tone, "It is as you say. I have assumed the name Jitsumu, and the common folk respect me. This is, of course, all part of my current plan as a pirate. You know, when people are about to die, they tend to always get very good with words and speak their mind. So, if you have something you want to say, I will listen. And while you're at it, you should also tell us where the tea container is."

Having been spoken to with such decency, Togekurō answered Jitsumu in a wavering voice. "As punishment for the evil I have done, when I die, I will surely go straight to hell, where I will be cut to pieces on the mountain of blades. So, I will tell you the truth and hopefully gain some manner of redemption. I have an older brother who served as a retainer in Sarashina in the land of Shinano. His name is Tatsumaki Arakurō. We were born by a handmaiden and left the manor where she worked when we were infants. After our mother's death, I became a bandit. As the years passed, Arakurō, who called himself my brother, was viewed as a friend of misfortune. My brother then killed one of his comrades over a lover's grudge and stole the tea container, and he too

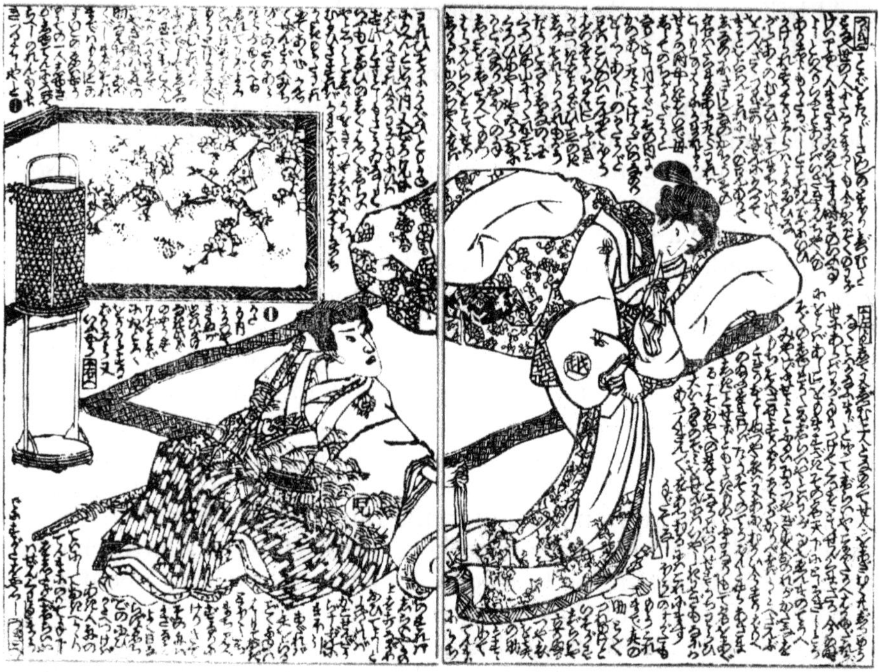

2.9

became a bandit. He hides on the Kurohime mountain in Shinano and now goes by the name Kurohime Yashagorō Onikado—Kurohime's Yaksha of the Demon's Gate. He commands many followers and lives a selfish life of pleasure. But be that as it may, I was planning to steal the tea container and trade it for money, but my older brother beat me to it, so I don't have it. This is all I can tell you for certain."

As he spoke, his wounds caused him great pain, and Jitsumu listened carefully from start to finish. Jitsumu said to his sister, "If what he says is true, then he also shares a part of Sumatarō's grudge. I am glad his evil heart has been led to good and we now know the whereabouts of Arakurō. Very soon, my long-held ambition shall come to fruition. Now then, we will ship out and set sail for Shinano. Until we return, I shall leave Tsuyaginu with you, Kinosuke. Your Tsuruhashiya inn is both prosperous and the equal of the inn of Zhu Gui, one of the heroes from the Chinese classic *Outlaws of the Marsh* who set it up as a lookout to gather information."

Togekurō was shocked by this unexpected situation. "And will you again assume the guise of Jitsumu the monk and deceive people? If you do not even dare to use your real name, I doubt your plans will ever come to fruition!"

Jitsumu raised his voice and proclaimed, "If the legendary bandit lord Hakamadare were still in this world, he would answer to me and do my bidding! If the ancient outlaw Kumasaka were here now, I would have him give me foot rubs! For I am Jiraiya—the young thunder, the leader of bandits and the one whose name reverberates beneath the heavens! Take that with you as a souvenir, when you go to see Lord Enma in hell!"

With sword in hand, Jiraiya strode past the trembling Tsuyaginu, lobbed off Suribaritarō's head and threw it into the sea.

Tsuyaginu said to her older brother, "Suribaritarō already told us who the ringleader was. To make a name of yourself as a proper warrior is how you show loyalty to your family. There was no reason for all this wretchedness."

Jiraiya interrupted her halfway through her sentence with a laugh and said, "Vile acts mean nothing if you are trying to accomplish a great ambition. And there is no better way to do this than by amassing wealth. Even donning the guise of a monk has helped me tremendously thus far. Now, Kinosuke, make haste and take her with you."

Hurried along, Kinosuke picked up Tsuyaginu who was struggling to stand, and put her in the tender boat. Jiraiya peered across the waves and called out, "We have a good tailwind!" and the boatmen unfurled the mainsail. The ship darted away like an arrow fired from a bow, and soon disappeared among the waves.

Met with favorable winds and currents, it wasn't long before they arrived in Niigata in Echigo. There, they disguised the ship as a merchant vessel and dropped anchor. Jiraiya then left on a tender boat with some of his underlings and took on the appearance of a pilgrim on his way to the Zenkōji Temple in Shinano.

(2.10)

Later, as they were passing by the foothills of Mount Myōkō in Echigo, the sky darkened with a thick layer of early winter clouds. A fearsome gust came with rain. Jiraiya and his men were worried about the steep mountain slopes, and the clouds made the road impossible to see.

Soon, Jiraiya lost sight of his men and walked aimlessly. After a while, he found himself on a mountain road when the rain finally stopped. The clouds lifted, revealing mountain pines with treetops colored by the evening sun and a gently sloping mountain path, covered with green grass. He turned around and saw a single straw-thatched house. It had a wicket gate, and the breeze blew through its eaves. The gate swung open, and out came a young gardening girl of about eleven or twelve years of age.

Jiraiya asked her, "Is the master of the house inside?"

She pointed her sickle towards the house and, while leaving, said over her shoulder, "Go in and ask for yourself."

Jiraiya entered the straw-thatched house while looking over his shoulder, and there he saw the master of the household. A woman—no more than twenty years old. She was a beauty, with lovely features entirely unsuited for the countryside. Jiraiya told her how he had gotten lost and separated from his comrades, and modestly asked if he could spend the night in the stranger's hidden house.

With a smile exuding an overwhelming charm, the woman answered him, "The deluge also struck here, and the winds shook the roof and

2.10

made the walls creak. Surely you must have been worried for your safety. You have my permission to stay, but the service and sleeping facilities that mountain houses can offer are poor. If this does not pain you..."

Upon hearing this, Jiraiya rejoiced. "How could I ever say no to that? Please let me stay." Then he sat on the bamboo stoop of the house. The woman brought warm water to wash his feet, but Jiraiya stopped her and did it himself. Then they went to the *zashiki* parlor, and the woman brought tea and the trays for the evening meal. Jiraiya enjoyed the hospitality, and after finishing dinner, they talked about various topics while the woman prepared the futon.

"Now you should go to sleep," said the woman while looking over her shoulder as she left the room, but Jiraiya stopped her.

"At first glance it looks like you are someone who lives alone in the mountains, but your words and your mannerisms are like someone from the capital. If it is not too much to ask, I wish to hear your true identity."

The woman cast down her face which was red as an autumn leaf from shame.

"My name is Koshiji, and I have left my parents to live on my own. I manage to pass the time, but I sit lonely at my spinning wheel, repeating the same things day in and out. I talk to myself, for there is almost no one to talk with, and I make friends with the plants on the mountain. For months and years, I have wasted away like this. Please have pity on me."

She cried a single tear, and as if drunk, Jiraiya thought she was more beautiful than a sakura flower with drops of rain on it. His heart, previously occupied with misfortune and living a short life, fell deeply in love with her.

He drew close to her side and lied: "I am a retainer from a house in Sarashina in Shinano, and I have come to these lands on some business from which I am now returning. It must be the work of karma that I have come here, bothering you to let me stay the night to escape the rain. Your story has moved me to tears, and if you give yourself to me, I will take you with me to my homeland immediately and take you as my wife. How does that sound? Please, my love, agree to my proposal," he said with passion.

Koshiji didn't give him any answer, but kept her eyes down. Finally raising her gaze, she said, "Even though you say this temporary stay is where you have found a destiny that only happens once in a hundred years, the hearts of men are like autumn clouds—floating, and not something I can trust. Please excuse me!" She got up and left for the next room, closing the sliding door behind her.

Jiraiya's heart was filled with rage. "Then I will intimidate her into being mine!" he thought and drew his sword. He went and opened the sliding door to the other room and peeked inside, where he saw Koshiji facing a lantern, reading some piece of women's literature. Koshiji did not acknowledge him as he entered the room with sword in hand, but instead kept reading. Angry, Jiraiya raised his blade in an intimidating display and drew near to her. In that moment, Koshiji reached under her sleeve and pulled out a pistol of Tanegashima make, and with a calm demeanor aimed it at Jiraiya, telling him the safety cap was off, and she would fire if he stepped any closer. Jiraiya knew getting near her would be difficult and lost his nerve. Not even if he sprang at her like a bird in flight could he make it. Then Koshiji snatched his sword from him and snapped it into several pieces with her bare hands.

"For a woman to be so daring is uncanny, I will show you!" said Jiraiya and tried to pull his short sword, but he could not draw it from its sheath. Despite his frustration, his limbs would not move, and they were as if frozen. Bewildered, all he could do was grind his teeth.

(2.11)

Koshiji sneered at Jiraiya and mocked him. "No matter how fierce your fighting spirit is, against me, it is useless. And what's more, you say you will take care of me? For your heart to be moved so easily by a woman. Your spirit is weak! But, if you abandon your evil intentions towards me and show me some respect and faith, I will forgive you right here and now."

Her voice echoed like thunder in Jiraiya's ears and head. Stricken with fear, he thought this was not any normal person. With a respectful tone, he politely said, "Please, forgive my actions for the foolish pranks they were. I did not know you were such an extraordinary person, but now I see."

As soon as he said these words, his limbs returned to normal. Koshiji's face softened and she said, "I have been waiting for you for a long time. There are things I must explain to you about our unexpected meeting today and me testing your courage." Koshiji's words surprised Jiraiya, and his respect for her grew.

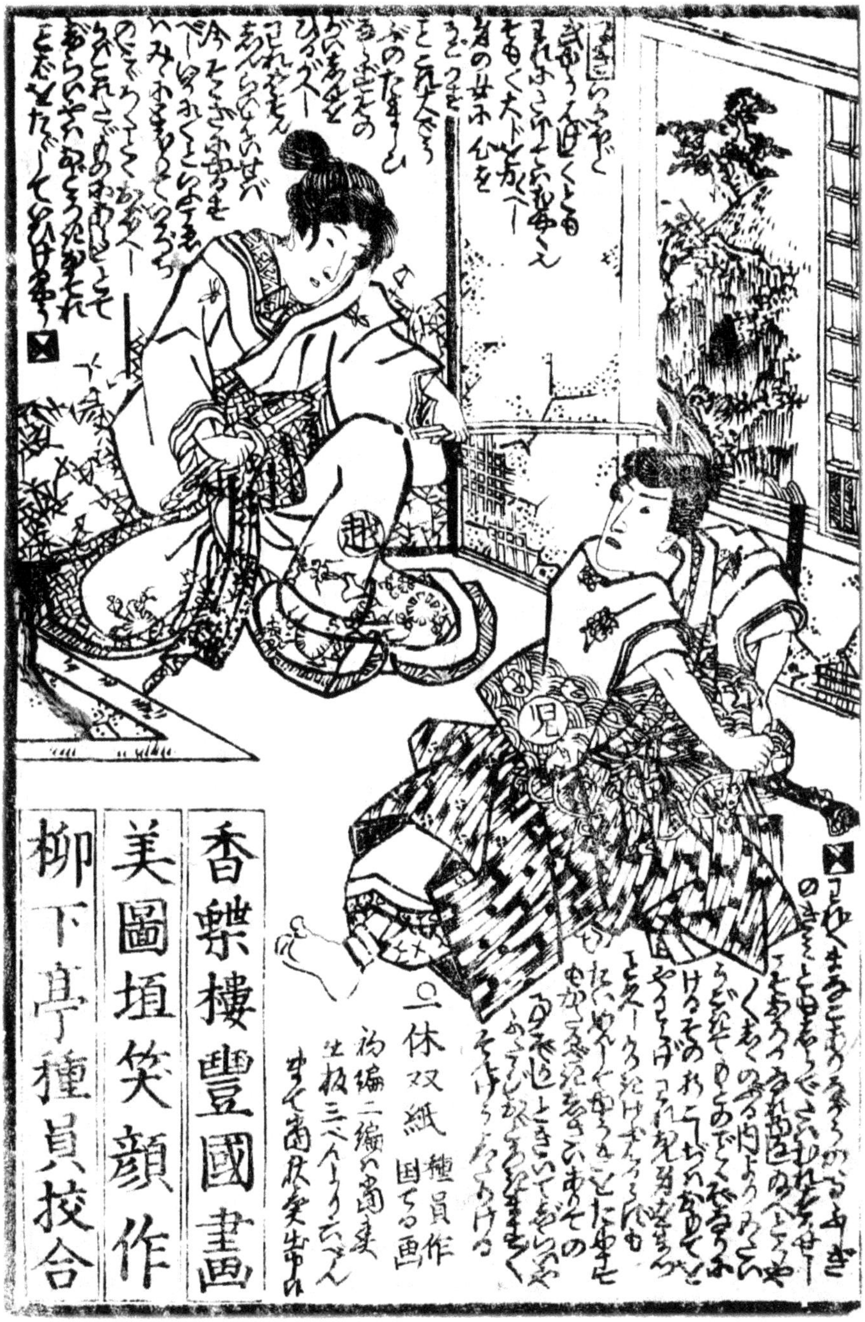

2.11

2.12

Part II

(2.12)
Then, the most mysterious thing happened. Before Jiraiya's very eyes, the woman became a white-haired hermit, skinny and feeble looking, but with well-defined muscles and bones, and eyes shining with a sharp light that swept all before them. The hermit was like an auspicious omen sitting in a place of great honor, and without thinking, Jiraiya prostrated himself before him.

With a smile, the hermit spoke: "I have lived on this mountain for hundreds of years, having long imbibed the mist and practiced Chinese alchemy and gained everlasting life. I can conjure fog and call upon the winds and the rain. I can ride clouds and travel the universe at will, and with my mystic powers I can turn flat lands into raging seas. I am called Senso Dōjin—the immortal hermit. It is with my powers that I have brought you here today, Shūma Hiroyuki, so listen well. You have gone the way of the bandit to amass wealth for military use, but you will not achieve your heartfelt desire like this. Nevertheless, I admire your sturdy and chivalrous heart, never wanting to needlessly kill people, and I have decided to teach you my magics. However, once you have learned to use these techniques, if a snake, big or small, drinks of your blood, you will be instantly defeated. They will be your most powerful enemy. Now, still your heart and learn!"

The hermit beckoned Jiraiya to come to his side, and for a long time instructed him on how to weave *mudra* signs with his hands and chant secret spells. Jiraiya repeated the teachings with great care and put it to memory, and was soon well-versed in all that the hermit had to teach.

Impressed by Jiraiya's talent and intelligence, the hermit decided to tell him something. "You lost your father when you were very young. I doubt you are even acquainted with his face. Through my powers, I will now let you meet him."

He then weaved signs within his sleeve and chanted a spell, and the rugged mountain became shrouded in mist, obscuring everything. After a little while, a great wind came and swept away the fog, and from across the mountain and echoing through the valleys came the roar of war gongs and *taiko* drums, the sound of flags fluttering in the wind, and the sound of war cries. As Jiraiya kept his eyes firmly on the lookout to see where the army making the sound was, a castle appeared, and it was in the middle of a battle.

(2.13)
As he watched, a great host poured through the wooden castle gates in droves, and as the people fought without being able to tell friend from foe, the castle burst into flame. Then a man, whom Jiraiya thought to be the commander, appeared. Like someone who had seen much battle, his armor was torn to pieces and so filled with arrows that it looked like he wore a straw raincoat. With no fear of death, the man ferociously charged, his work on the battlefield like that of a rampaging demon, and the attacking army fled before him. But then, an arrow was let loose

2.13

from its bow. It whistled directly for the warrior and struck with a loud thwack. Hurt, the warrior staggered towards the spacious veranda of the castle, stood himself up, grabbed his sword, and ran it through the left side of his belly, cutting all the way across to the right side.

Senso Dōjin turned to Jiraiya and said, "The warrior who was just shot and ended his own life was Ogata Saemon Hirozumi, famed in Tsukushi. He was your father, and these were his final moments."

Without even hearing the hermit through to the end, Jiraiya's eyes became bloodshot, and he saw red. He gritted his teeth in frustration as he looked down and saw the roaring inferno spreading, burning down every part of the castle until it was lost to ash.

Jiraiya's anger grew and he turned to the hermit with a look of resentment. "Seeing my father's final moments as he left this wretched world is more than I can bear. Who was his attacker?" he asked the hermit, who laughed.

He explained to the angry Jiraiya, "What you saw was brought forth by my powers, and it has been twenty years since it happened. You should already have learned all about your father's rebellion from what Hatasaku told you. The one who took down your father was Sarashina Mitsuaki, the lord of Shinano, who was a guard of the capital at the time. He was only doing his duty, so to resent him for this would not be right."

(2.14)

Senso Dōjin continued, "It is time for you to leave this mountain. There are people you need to meet," and grabbed a scroll on a table next

2.14

to him. "I will give you this text, and you must read it many times and remember what I have taught you," he said kindly.

Jiraiya abased himself before the hermit and showed him the respect a student must show his master. "My teacher, some day, I will repay my debt to you for your lessons."

Then the hermit took the scroll and threw it towards the adjacent mountain, and in the most mysterious way, it unrolled and became like a walkway, forming a path. "Hurry up and go," said the hermit, urging Jiraiya, reluctant to leave.

Jiraiya finally set out, and as he stepped cautiously onto the footpath, the top of the mountain became distant. When he looked up, he saw Senso Dōjin's figure being wrapped in the thick mist and eventually disappearing from sight.

Before long, Jiraiya arrived back at the foothills of Mount Myōkō, where for a moment he contemplated the mystic powers of the hermit. Before he knew it, the footpath on which he had come rolled up and became a scroll again, which landed on a large jutting rock beside him. He became even more astounded than before.

"Now, I wonder where my underlings are," thought Jiraiya, worried about the whereabouts of his men. "This is a great place to test one of the techniques I received." He chanted a spell and weaved some signs he had learned, which was supposed to summon his men. And strangely enough, from afar his bandits appeared, saying, "Your orders sir!" and bowed before him.

Jiraiya laughed and said, "So, you are all in good health?"

2.15

(2.15)

The bandits answered in unison, “Yesterday, when we lost sight of you, Master, we spent a lot of time searching the mountain. But just now, as if in a dream, someone told us where you were, so we all rejoiced and came here.”

When they said this, it was clear to Jiraiya what they had seen was an illusion. He instantly became impressed with his own conjuring. Together with his band of thieves, they set out on the way to Shinano, but at the side of the road was a collapsed mountain brigand, an untouchable *hinin.* He was sick and suffering, rolling on the ground from pain, moments away from death. The bandits mocked him, and went to kick him. Jiraiya scolded them, “This man is a human being! *We* are human beings! He is not trying to rob anyone, so he is at the very least purer than we are. Who are you to look down on him?”

Jiraiya went to the untouchable’s side, said, “Even if you are a hinin, your illness must be troubling you greatly. Get yourself some medicine,” and gave him a bit of money.

The untouchable slowly raised his head and said under pained breaths, “I am very grateful for this gift, but I am so weakened from my sickness that I cannot even stand, so even if I have money, I cannot buy medicine. What good is money when I lack even the strength to use it to save my own life? If you have any medicine, would you extend your mercy even further and give me some? I appreciate the gesture, but you can put away your money.”

2.16

Jiraiya took the medicine box from his belt and gave it to the untouchable.

"In that case, please accept this and take care of yourself. Now, I must be off!" Jiraiya said, and left with his men.

The untouchable bowed and prayed with both his hands towards Jiraiya, who did not look back but returned to the road, his figure shrinking in the distance.

The untouchable then stood up on his toes, stretching to see the disappearing figures off, and proceeded to closely inspect the medicine box. As he smiled, the loud resounding crack of gunfire filled his ears, and he threw himself to the ground.

(2.16)

Lifting his straw hat, he saw a bullet had gone clean through it. Shocked by the endangerment, he got up like someone in perfect health, with not a trace of what had so far been a dire sickness. He glared at his surroundings, sweeping all directions in a way no ordinary person would. The way he stood there, it was obvious he was a great warrior who had disguised himself and hid from the world. Who this untouchable was, will be revealed in book three.

Now the story takes us to a different place, at a different time. The provincial governor of Shinano, Sarashina Saemon-dono, was having his lover brought from the capital. Her beauty was without equal, and keeping her trip a secret was impossible, so the rumor of her was on everyone's lips. She was now in the countryside, having left the capital and crossed the Misaka pass in the Kiso mountains. One day, she reached the Seba post town where she stayed the night, so the inn was busy beyond words. Early the next morning, the lady and her retinue set out from the inn. The Sarashina manor was not far from the road to Zenkōji Temple, so they went at a leisurely pace.

From a small hiding place among the trees ahead, a large force of mountain bandits appeared, brandishing swords. The lady's entourage was unprepared for an ambush. They lost their composure and panicked. Not one of them stopped for even a moment, and they abandoned the lady, whose name was Shirotae-dono, in her palanquin. Those who were supposed to protect her fled without looking back. The bandits chased off Shirotae's incompetent people and stole not just her immense luggage, but also the palanquin she traveled in. Happy with a job well done, the bandits hurried on the road in high spirits at great speed. As if flying, they climbed mountains and crossed valleys, going to some faraway, unknown place. Shirotae, inside the palanquin, thought she would surely die and bemoaned her situation alone. To make matters worse, the ruffians violently shook her flowery palanquin up and down, making her even more worried and anxious, and so she kept lying down in the palanquin. At around the seventh bell of the afternoon,[2] they finally reached a house and put down the palanquin in some strange room.

Scared, Shirotae surveyed the surroundings. The walls of the house were carved into a rock and the pillars were wild trees. She did not need to ask to know this was a bandit dwelling.

The bandit commander here had come to the area not long ago. He stood almost eight shaku tall[3] and was immensely strong. On his pale face were thick, bushy eyebrows and bulging eyes. A truly unparalleled fiend and outlaw. The mountain was called Mount Kurohime, and the bandit had taken this name as his own, calling himself Kurohime Yashagorō Onikado. Yashagorō killed the previous commander and made himself the ruler of the mountain. He stole riches, kidnapped beautiful women from the nearby lands, and was consumed with drinking and making good-looking girls sit on his lap and fornicate with him. A cruel and villainous monster was he! Because he heard the concubine of a lord was coming from the capital, he ordered his bandits to bring her to his bedroom. Thus, they kidnapped her as she traveled.

The day waned, so Yashagorō put up many candles, making the parlor as bright as noon. In the middle of the room, he sat on two or three stacked futons, and his many underlings were cramped close together. In front of him was a spread of food and snacks, and on his left and right were beautiful women, pouring him saké.

(2.17)

While drinking from an oversized saké cup, he said to his men in a great booming voice, "Bring that coquettish woman you captured earlier today, Shirotae or whatever her name is, and put her before me!"

2. 16:00.

3. 2.5 meters.

2.17

"Aye!" answered one of the underlings and went to the adjacent room. Shirotae trembled with fear as he forcefully pulled her to Yashagorō's side and pushed her down. "There you go."

Yashagorō softened his expression. "The rumor said you are a noblewoman from the capital, but you are much more beautiful than I heard. There is nothing for you to be afraid of. If only you follow my whims, you will lead a life of pleasure a hundred times better than you would with the lord of Shinano. Now come over here!" He laughed loudly, grabbed Shirotae's hand, and pulled her towards him.

Shirotae's teeth clattered. "Is this Enma, the ruler of hell, or is it the demons inhabiting Mount Ōeyama from the stories of old, here to bring me suffering?" With tears flowing from her eyes, she prostrated herself on the floor. "Please let me go!"

Her words amused Yashagorō, to whom her voice was like the first cries of a bush warbler in spring entering the ears of a mountain eagle. He grabbed her hands and pulled her into the next room. The underlings gathered and poured drinks for one another, drinking themselves into a drunken stupor, passing out among the scattered cups and plates.

While they drank, Yashagorō went into his bedroom with Shirotae. He spoke words of seduction, lust written all over his face. When he drunkenly came at Shirotae to ravage her, Shirotae grabbed his dominant hand, twisted it, and immobilized him. This surprised Yashagorō, and after a while he pulled his hand free.

"You attack me unprovoked, and although you are a bit strong and fearless, this is not a problem for me. Now, I will show you my might

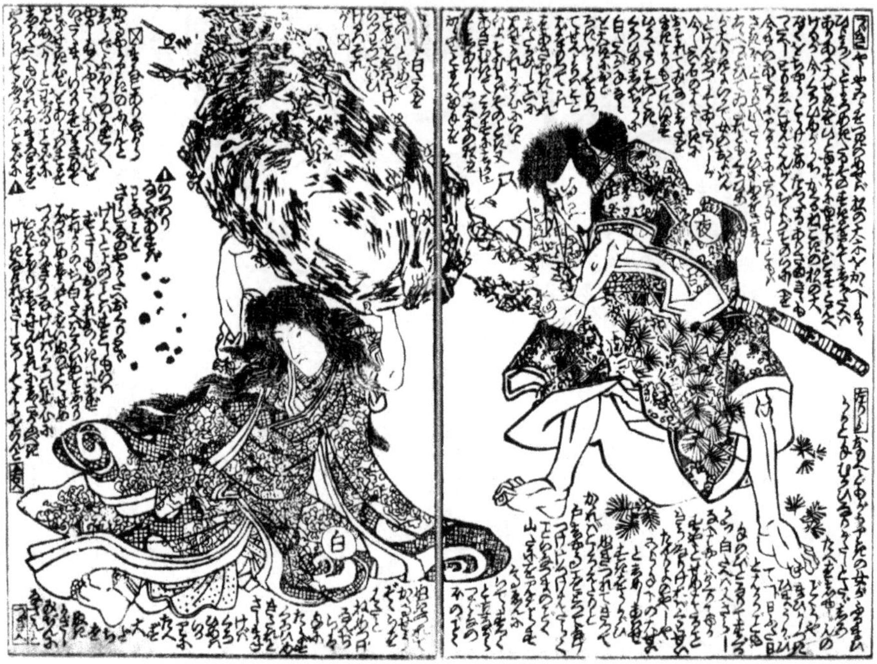

2.18

and crush your spirit!" cursed Yashagorō as he jumped to the garden where he uprooted a pine tree and swung it about in display.

Shirotae also jumped down into the garden and laughed out, "If you call something like this *might,* you must be joking!"

(2.18)

Furious, Yashagorō flourished the pine tree. Shirotae dodged it several times and pushed Yashagorō so he stumbled and tottered. Seeing her opening, Shirotae grabbed on to a massive boulder that happened to be there, gave it a shake, and hoisted it up. Yashagorō swatted at her with the tree, but Shirotae managed to block it with the boulder. The sight was like Tomoe Gozen or Lady Hangaku, the two legendary female warriors of the olden times, standing before one's very eyes.

The underlings were awakened by the fighting and gathered in the garden. When they saw Yashagorō's great strength matched by the woman, they were dumbstruck and refrained from getting any closer.

Yashagorō, surprised by Shirotae's skill, thought, "Instead of using strength, I will use words to deceive her and pretend to go along with her. Then, when her guard is down, it will be the perfect time to strike and kill her."

He threw away the tree and raised both hands to Shirotae to stop her. With friendly words, he lied to her, "We did not know you are such a mighty lady, but now we see. Please forgive us for our transgressions. We will not give in to evil thoughts again. Quell your anger and see my sincerity."

His apology made Shirotae's rageful eyes soften. "If there are indeed no lies in your words, you will take me to the Shinano manor tomorrow!" Without a trace of fear, she spoke no more on the matter.

After this, Shirotae scolded Yashagorō, disgraced him, and berated the bandits without end. Yashagorō thought, "She is the one who should be doing *my* bidding. I should just stab her and kill her. That will quench my anger."

Yashagorō's resentment grew, but knew it would be difficult if he carelessly attacked Shirotae, as she was his equal in strength. For the moment, he would treat her with respect as if she were his master and await his chance for a day or two. But before his plan could come to fruition, Shirotae demanded, "Take me to Sarashina already, and be quick about it!"

The fiery and short-tempered Yashagorō ordered his many underlings to gather. Thinking this was their chance, they all drew their swords.

"Ready yourselves!" they cried, and tore through the shōji sliding doors. They poured out with lightning speed, and in the garden overlooking the valley and mountains, they were numerous like the ears on kunai grass.

"All of you together will not be enough to take me on. Yashagorō, come fight me!" Shirotae called, fiercely glaring at the bandits and their blades.

(2.19)

Yashagorō, overcome with fury, drew his great sword and held it over his head, wanting to cut Shirotae to mince. He rushed at her, but Shirotae was not troubled in the least. She chanted a spell and weaved signs with her hands. An enormous wave sprang forth, taller than the trees in the garden, and the sound of the torrential rise of the water was deafening. In the blink of an eye, the mountains and valleys changed into a raging sea, and Yashagorō and his underlings struggled in the water. Great waves carried them up and down, floating and sinking them, making them suffer. Yashagorō managed to grab to a branch of a tree and tried to climb higher, but the branch broke, dropping him back to the water with a splash. He tried to swim, but his arms and legs were numb, and his body was unable to move. Then came the raging wind and rainfall.

"I guess this is as far as my life goes," thought Yashagorō, but someone grabbed his hand and saved him. He had no words to express his gratitude, and was only halfway conscious. He vomited a huge amount of water, and with one foot in the grave asked, "Who saved me?"

Yashagorō strained his eyes and saw it was none other than Shirotae. He then tried to get up, but Shirotae stepped over him and pressed him down with her knee, immobilizing him. With an ice-cold demeanor, she took a sword and thrust it to his chest, raised her voice, and called to all the bandits lying exhausted and squirming in the garden.

"All of you worms who got a taste of the water from my conjuring, see what I have done to Yashagorō! My whim dictates whether he lives

2.19

or dies. If you make me your leader and respect me, I might forgive you. But if you show me any hostility, I will make you regret it!"

(2.20)

Her sharp voice cut through the shaking bandits. "From today, we will respect you as our leader," they said, prostrating themselves in the garden.

Shirotae spoke to Yashagorō again. "I was planning to kill you, but I've had an idea, so I won't finish you off but rather leave you alive a while longer. For now, I will forgive you for what you have done. Change your ways and work for me! When you hear my real name, I bet you will be surprised."

Shirotae firmly grabbed Yashagorō's collar and threw him aside. Yashagorō was frustrated, but feared Shirotae's mystical conjuring. Although brave and daring before, he thought attacking her would be a foolish idea. So, vile and cunning as he was, Yashagorō chose to pretend to do the same as his underlings, submitting for now so he could hear that true name.

Shirotae took the seat of honor in the parlor and said, "I am the one who will not needlessly take a person's life and does not covet the money of women, the young or the old. The great man who only steals riches obtained through foul means and who practices great virtues, and yet knows dirty tricks and commands bandits to reach his ambitions. The one who saves the weak and crushes the strong. The bandit leader whose name is known by all and puts crying babies to sleep. My real name is Ogata Shūma Hiroyuki, but I am better known as Jiraiya!"

Yashagorō had heard those gallant and beautiful names before, and finally, for the first time in his life, he felt what it meant to respect another.

2.20

From then on, Jiraiya made that place his mountain fortress and gathered his men there to live safely behind its walls. Yashagorō moved away to Mount Togakushi in the same area, where he made his own stronghold, and occasionally would return to attend drinking parties.

The frost set in as the year reached the end of the eleventh month, and Jiraiya secluded himself to his room, where he read classic literature. Contrary to his intentions, he had gotten extremely sleepy and now lay collapsed on his table.

Someone roused him from that state. When Jiraiya opened his eyes, he saw Senso Dōjin, his teacher whom he had parted with on Mount Myōkō. Jiraiya hopped up and bowed. The hermit, drenched in a cold sweat, spoke to Jiraiya with a pained expression.

"I made a vow with you in the past to be master and student, and now I have come to you because something grievous has befallen me."

Without beating around the bush, Jiraiya said, "My debt to you as my master weighs more heavily on me than a great mountain. No matter what, I will not turn my back on you! Tell me what has happened."

Senso Dōjin let out a lamenting sigh before saying, "Many years ago I came to my mountain and have lived there without a care ever since.

But recently a great serpent has come from Mount Kurohime and has made me suffer relentlessly. I have been fighting against it with my conjuring for days now, but the great serpent is powerful. Within the

2.21

next three days, my strength will run out, and the serpent will devour me. Please, come quickly. Eliminate the snake and free me from my suffering. I am counting on you!"

(2.21)

Jiraiya was shocked at Senso Dōjin's haggard complexion and sad breathing. He accepted the request. "I will do as you command! Rest assured I shall go at once." After hearing these words, Senso Dōjin's figure faded and disappeared.

Worried about Senso Dōjin's safety, Jiraiya hastily got up, grabbed his two great war swords, and an arquebus as well as plenty of gunpowder and match cord. Using his mystical *yōjutsu* magic, he was on Mount Myōkō in the blink of an eye. There, the rocks and towering boulders pierced through the clouds, and the growth of pines and daimyo oaks was so thick one could not even see the sky. The waterfalls at the mountain top were hidden in the clouds, but the sound of the water reverberated into the valleys. Valleys a thousand fathoms deep, much too deep for an echo to bounce back. If one gazed into them, one could see the lines of the running rivers, winding around the base of the mountain like sheep entrails. Truly, it was like staring over an immense precipice, peering through from heaven and all the way down into the depths of hell. Mount Myōkō was a mountain that would make anyone lose their courage, but without a second thought, Jiraiya traversed the mountain, searching high and low, holding his two swords and carrying his arquebus. He then took shelter by an old cedar tree and scanned his surroundings.

2.22

As this book ends, we find Jiraiya on the mountain, but will he be able to take down the serpent? This will be answered in detail in book three, but for now, I must store my brush.

3.1

Book 3

Previously, Kanwatei Onitake has written myths and tales about Jiraiya. Over the years, mister Tōri's *Onna Jiraiya*—woman Jiraiya, has been published here with Kansendō publishing house. In books one and two, which were cheap paperbacks, the amusing devices like the ideas of Mount Myōkō and the fight between toads and serpents were published. Amateurish work spat out by Mizugaki pretending to be an author, it was like water off a frog's back.

Like sitting on a stone for three years to warm it up, this third volume continues again this year.

Like the hands of children clapping, beat the taiko and blow the mountain winds! Hear the Amaguruma, its sound tremendous and like the pouring rain! The Ōdorodoro drumming lures buyers to an eerie mountain backdrop. Thus, I have written this foreword, so the newest print may jump out like a frog, as we lift the curtain on this book.

Tenpō 12 (1841)
Mizugaki Egao

Also on page:
Kamahei's wife Osaga.
Himematsu's retainer Matsuhei.

3.2

Himematsu Sumatarō's wife, Misao.
Ekichi the pilgrim of the 24 temples with his ladle.
Yokushirō of Kumadeya's daughter, Tagane.
The son of the Sarashina clan, Tsumorinosuke Yukitaka. Also known as *the purple millionaire.*
The pleasure girl of Kumadeya, Ayame.

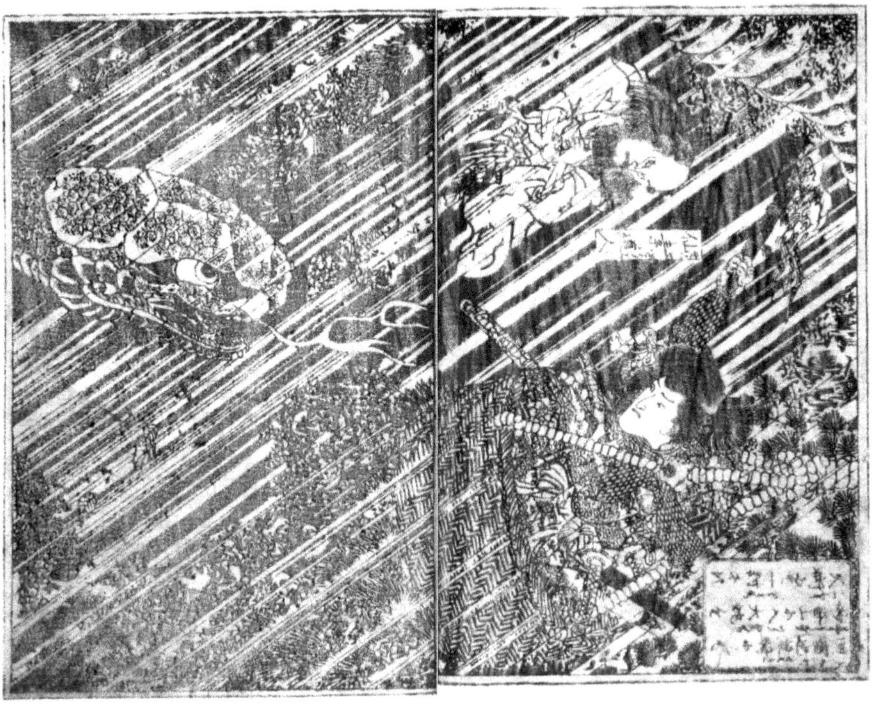

3.3

Jiraiya, having traveled alone to Mount Myōkō, shoots at the great serpent.

Senso Dōjin.

3.4

Part I

(3.4)
And so, the story continues.

Jiraiya made his way through Mount Myōkō with great difficulty, and when he stopped at a cluster of cedar trees to scout around, the mist cleared slightly. Tired from the troubles of walking the roads, he propped up his arquebus on a nearby rock and rested. He glimpsed over yonder and saw a flickering like firelight.

"What is this now? I think I see a fire," thought Jiraiya, and steeled his eyes, drawing closer to see.

And there he saw it. The great serpent. Its head was like that of a hornless bull. Although its entire body was hidden behind a thicket, it was like an old fallen pine tree, and what had looked like lights were its two eyes. From its mouth darted a tongue like fire—lighting up the area around it in a horrifying glow. Then the great serpent moved, aiming for a faraway ridge. The sound of the trees being moved by the snake was immense, like tremors of an earthquake.

Jiraiya, excited to have found the great serpent, thought, "This must be it. The great serpent my master told me about." He loaded his arquebus with gunpowder and readied the match cord. As he was about to remove the pan cover and take aim, he glanced at the mountain again and saw something that looked like a small hill, moving about. Upon closer

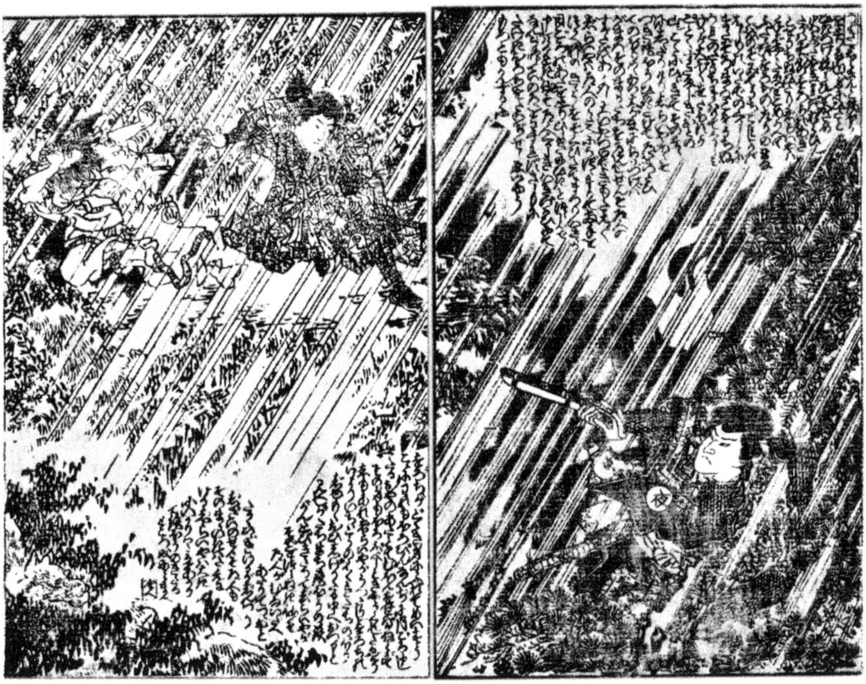

3.5

inspection, he saw it was an enormous toad, lying and glowering at the great serpent. "It must be my master Senso Dōjin in his true form after having had his magics broken!" he thought, and swallowed, sweating profusely like a mountain spring.

(3.5)

Jiraiya scowled at the serpent. He said, "This will teach you a lesson!" and readied his arquebus. He held it tight to his body, steadied his hand, and removed the pan cover. He fired. True to his aim, he shot clean through the serpent's jaw. Jiraiya loaded another bullet and took aim again, now at the snake's left eye, and fired again. The snake writhed and twisted in pain from its first wound and from having its eye pierced. With a tremendous sound echoing through the mountain and valley, like a mighty tree falling, it succumbed.

With a content smile, Jiraiya lowered his arquebus and followed the mountain path up to the giant toad. When he approached, it changed shape and appeared as Senso Dōjin, who took a deep breath and was about to faint. Jiraiya knelt by Senso Dōjin's side with both hands on the ground, and with great reverence said, "Master, I have saved you from danger and brought down the enemy that has been hounding you."

Under pained breath, Senso Dōjin said, "You truly have not forgotten the way of master and student, and you have so heroically defeated the ferocious serpent. I am deeply impressed, but the serpent's poisonous breath has touched my body. I will probably perish here. Please,

3.6

"Here I made the picture like a nigao *portrait, so you can show it to kids."*

remember you must not try to avenge your parents against the ones I told you about all those months ago. It will cause a rebellion and you will surely fall."

At the moment he finished this sermon, a single string of vapor rose from the mouth of the great serpent, which had fallen in an overgrown thicket after being shot. A steel bullet from an arquebus flew straight through Jiraiya's sleeve and hit Senso Dōjin in the chest. It was followed by the loud ringing of gunfire, and Senso Dōjin, who had thus far seemed almost omnipotent, drew his final breath.

(3.6)

Furious, Jiraiya glared towards the direction of the shot, and when he was about to run down to the thicket, the sky became enveloped in clouds, the mountain rumbled, and rain fell. Trees creaked in the wind. As Jiraiya watched, Senso Dōjin's body disappeared in the mist. At this time, cut off by a mountain ridge, a lone wolf kept a lookout with sharp eyes, and when it saw Jiraiya lower his arquebus and go down into the valley, it hid in a thicket of bamboo grass.

Incidentally, Yashagorō had been visiting Jiraiya's mountain stronghold from Mount Togakushi. When he heard Jiraiya went to Mount Myōkō with the first morning light, he wondered what for. So, he grabbed an arquebus and also went to Mount Myōkō. There, as one might expect, he found Jiraiya on a faraway ridge, speaking together with a hermit. Next to them, spitting up blood and dying, was the great serpent. Thinking Jiraiya must have shot it when the mountain shook earlier, Yashagorō was awestruck at how skillful Jiraiya was with the arquebus. Just then, the snake expelled a white steam which touched Yashagorō, instantly sending tremors throughout his body. Almost immediately, he remembered his feelings of the day Jiraiya defeated him, and his malicious heart awoke.

"I have feared Jiraiya's courage since that day, and he defeated me with mystical swordsmanship, but in physical might I am his equal, so there is no reason for me to fear him now. If only he cannot summon his magic. This hermit must be the sage who taught him his illusions. First, I will shoot the hermit dead with my arquebus, and then I will take down Jiraiya." The serpent's grudge completely took hold of Yashagorō's body. He steadied his aim at Senso Dōjin and fired.

Killing Senso Dōjin brought Yashagorō great joy. He decided to wait for Jiraiya to come down the mountain to put him down as well, and so went into a thicket of bamboo grass to hide.

Agreeing with himself that the gunshot must have come from that direction, Jiraiya loaded a bullet and fired his arquebus into the thicket to check. Yashagorō, caught by surprise and startled by the sound of the fired arquebus, appeared from the shadows of the bamboo grass. He slipped past Jiraiya, and from behind, without even calling out, he attempted a foul sneak attack. Jiraiya noticed the flash of the blade and dodged. Yashagorō attacked again. Jiraiya barely stopped the blade with his arquebus. The morning fog finally cleared, and they stood face to face.

Jiraiya gave him a death stare, and with a voice trembling from fury said, "Yashagorō, I thought I already beat the hostility out of you, but you just don't learn. Stand down!"

With a cackling laughter, Yashagorō said, "Now that I have taken away the source of your illusions, your *magics* are insignificant. Fighting me with words will get you nowhere. Now, have at you!" and came at Jiraiya.

Yashagorō was different from usual, dexterous and fearless, but to Jiraiya it still meant nothing. He blocked the man's attacks using only his arquebus, and at first, he did not touch his sword. But Jiraiya knew from Yashagorō's words that he was the one who killed Senso Dōjin. There was no way Jiraiya could let Yashagorō be. When he saw his chance, he threw away his arquebus and drew his blade. And then, with a loud clash of swords, they fought.

As they battled, the bamboo grass rustled, and a large wolf appeared. Without fear of their blades, the wolf stood on its hind legs, grabbed Yashagorō's back, and pulled him away.

(3.7)

Both shocked, the two separated and stared at the wolf. When the wolf threw back its head, they saw it was actually a man wearing a wolfskin. On his back were hunting arrows, and in one of his hands a bow. By the light of a concealed torch, he stared at their faces. From his

3.7

expression, they could tell he was no ordinary person. In the blink of an eye, Yashagorō fled upon seeing the hunter. The hunter ignored Jiraiya and chased after Yashagorō. Needing to avenge his teacher, Jiraiya followed.

At roughly the middle of Mount Myōkō, there was a famous bridge made of the vines of a wisteria plant, which connected to the peak of a neighboring mountain. The valley river below had a swift current with torrents more vicious than waterfalls. It was so fearsome that simply looking down on it was enough to send one's eyes spinning, even if the bridge had been made from stone. Breathing heavily, Yashagorō fled to this place, but looking down, he became unsure on the halfway point of the wisteria bridge. Behind him came the mountain man from before and following him came Jiraiya. Upon seeing his foe, Jiraiya lunged at him with his sword and the mountain man used his bow to stop Yashagorō. The three were now in a perilous situation. The wisteria bridge swayed with their footsteps.

"Do not get in my way!" yelled the mountain man as he pulled Jiraiya back as the bridge rocked.

Yashagorō attacked, and the mountain man deflected his blade with the nock of his bow. The blade fell with a clatter on the bridge, and seeing his chance, Jiraiya stepped in and grappled Yashagorō. The two men wrestled, and Yashagorō summoned his superhuman strength to try and push Jiraiya into the valley. Even though he was pressured, the fiercely courageous Jiraiya did not let Yashagorō have his way.

Impressed by Jiraiya's valor, the mountain man decided to let him capture Yashagorō. Afterwards, he would take the man into custody himself. Thus, letting Jiraiya have the fight, he overlooked the duel while leaning on his bow as if it were a cane.

Jiraiya and Yashagorō were entangled for a while, but their might was evenly matched and neither seemed to be losing. But in the end, for a brief, almost unseen moment, Jiraiya overpowered him. Pinned down, Yashagorō frantically tried to push Jiraiya off and get on top. In an attempt to free his hands being held down from above, Yashagorō mustered his strength and pushed up. They scrambled to their knees and accidentally stepped over the edge of the wisteria bridge. Locked together, the two fell towards the valley river a thousand fathoms below, disappearing in the white, cloudlike mist whipped up by the water.

The mountain man looked down from up on the bridge, clicked his tongue, and muttered to himself, "I finally managed to locate Yashagorō, and then he falls off the bridge with some stranger. His body must surely have been smashed to pieces on the rocks. I missed my chance and now all that investigating is wasted!" He looked around, put away his bow, and with the creaking of the wisteria bridge under his feet, he left.

(3.8)

On one of the valley rivers surrounding Mount Myōkō, where the shallow water had tumultuous currents, there were people who cut down trees and stacked up the branches on their boats and sailed them down river to sell. Quite a few people made their living this way. On this day, a man named Kamahira from the foot of the mountain was going down the river with his boat, heavily loaded with firewood. As it was being swept along, faster than an arrow, something fell on the boat with a thud. The staggered Kamahira saw two young and muscular men, locked in a mutual death grip. Even though they were not breathing, neither let up his hold on the other. He wanted to separate them, but Kamahira could do nothing because he had to steer the boat, so it sailed five or six *chō*[1] before it finally came to the rocky outcropping where he usually moored it. He extended a pole and tied a rope to a pine tree on the rocky shore. Then he poured water on the two and made them drink it to nurse them. Yashagorō started breathing again and woke up. After inspecting his surroundings, he thanked Kamahira for bringing him back to life. Jiraiya had already awoken earlier, but chose to play possum and kept lying where he was.

Yashagorō pointed to Jiraiya with his chin, and told Kamahira, "That person who fell on your boat together with me is the outlaw Jiraiya. It is fortunate he hasn't regained consciousness. I will tie him up and give him to you. That way you can take him to the Sarashina estate and hand him over for a handsome reward. You should consider yourself lucky."

Kamahira said, "My liege, do you not recognize me? It is I, your servant Kamahira."

---

1 545–654 meters.

3.8

Yashagorō was greatly surprised to hear this and gave him a closer look. “Well, this is unexpected. If it isn’t my old servant Kamahira!”

“By your orders I secretly killed Himematsu Edanoshin, fled Shinano, and with my reward I married a prostitute I liked. Now I live in a cheap lodging house down river. I make a living by sailing up and down this river, and I have promised myself to live in poverty, not soiling my hands with dirty money anymore.”

Yashagorō did not listen to more than half of what Kamahira had to say before interrupting, “Men should not whine! I too have committed murder. I killed Himematsu Sumatarō over a grudge and stolc thc Fubuki Katatsuki tea container” He then shared his story from beginning to end.

Kamahira heard Yashagorō’s tale and cheered, “I shall also become a bandit and be your underling!”

(3.9)

“This Jiraiya I just told you about, he is a mysterious fellow who can use yōjutsu. He is not someone who can be held with mere ropes. Thinking I could leave him to you was a foolish mistake.”

He stood, picked up Jiraiya, and threw him into the raging river. Jiraiya bobbed pitifully up and down in the water as he floated along. Feeling good about himself, Yashagorō laughed with Kamahira. Leaving the boat moored, Kamahira shouldered his pole and led Yashagorō towards his home.

3.9

After they had gone, a pillar of water one *jō*[2] high erupted up from the river, and on top of the water stood a dim figure like a shadow. It was Jiraiya, untouched by the water, with a dazzling new set of clothes. He had a mild look on his face, eyes that gleamed like the moon, lips as red as a flower, and beautiful eyebrows. An elegant and refined man who would outdo even Prince Hikaru Genji.[3] Two female travelers and their servant, who happened to be passing by, stared fixedly and wide-eyed at the mysterious yōjutsu spectacle. As the three of them stared up at it from the side of the river, the water and the figure disappeared in a gust of wind.

The two female travelers were in fact Kozue, the widow of Himematsu Edanoshin, the most valued retainer of the lord of Sarashina in the Shinano area, and Misao, the widow of Sumatarō. Kozue was in her fifties. Misao had just turned nineteen, and was a beauty to behold. With them was the loyal Matsuhei, carrying all their heavy travel luggage on his shoulders. The three of them traveled as masters and servant. As they walked, they talked about the strange and mysterious thing they had seen. The rocky mountain road ahead wound up and down, and Misao had weak legs. To make matters worse, she also carried an infant at her bosom.

Misao muttered to her mother-in-law Kozue, "We have walked on this mountain road since morning. I am starving. Mother, surely you must be tired by now."

2 3.03 meters.

3 Hikaru Genji is the protagonist of the classic story *The Tale of Genji*.

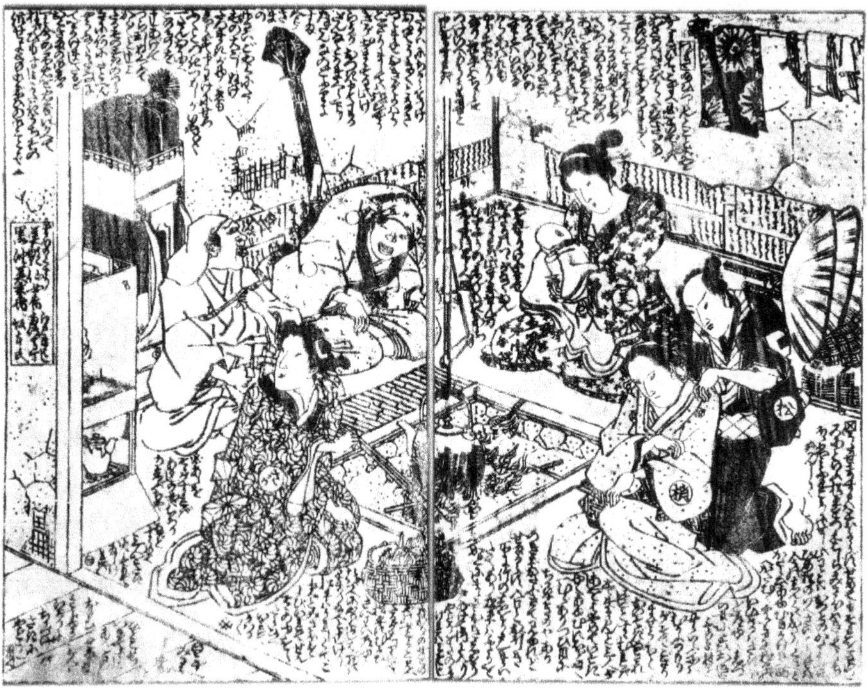

3.10

(3.10)

Kozue said, "Last month we left our homeland, just the three of us. We have been traveling constantly and without a goal ever since. And what's more, you are young and bright, yet you must bear the grudge of your husband and your father-in-law, all while carrying an infant on this depressing journey with no roof over our heads. That is what is truly heartbreaking." She said this while crying as old people often do. This, however, was purely from the wretchedness of it all.

In an effort to cheer them up, Matsuhei said, "Milady, even if you say we are but stuck in this floating world, let us at least cheer each other up and be buoyant in spirit! If you let yourself be overtaken by faintheartedness you are apt to get sick. This humble servant was with the young master going back from Kamakura, when the old master unexpectedly passed away and the young master met his end.

"As the useless and spineless mongrel that I am, I didn't know where Arakurō went, and wanted to commit seppuku in atonement. But I had to go back to our homeland and report on what had happened. When I told everything that transpired and wiped my face of my tears, lacking words to describe the sadness I felt, I reached for my blade to end myself. But you, Milady, scolded me, saying, 'Take your broken loyalty and mend it by carrying out my wish for vengeance,' with pity and compassion. Since then I have accompanied you two and made sure you were safe. Now finally, after untold trials and tribulations, we are so close to capturing Arakurō and getting our revenge. Try to look forward to that at least."

Misao smiled after hearing Matsuhei, whom they had come to trust and rely on. "The child I carry at my bosom is the spitting image of my husband. When he reaches adulthood, he will restore our house, and all our suffering will be nothing but a story we tell," said Misao, and she looked to the sky where the sun was descending to the west.

"I heard from some peasant girl that there is a place called Fumoto Village up ahead. It is probably just beyond this forest. Let us make haste," said Matsuhei, and urged them on.

"Indeed, let's hurry and get going," said the three, and hustled onwards.

After a long span of walking, they came upon a village, where they saw a straw-thatched house. The eaves looked crooked, but the house was not too small. At what looked like the entrance, there was a single latticed bamboo door. Matsuhei made the other two wait outside the gate, opened the lattice door, and went inside to ask if they could spend the night. A woman in her thirties, who looked like the wife of the household, came running out.

"If travelers on the road of prosperity ask for lodging, I shall give it to them," said the woman to Matsuhei, who rejoiced and called Kozue and Misao inside. The lady of the house then poured warm water in the tub for foot washing, and in turn they all washed their feet. She offered them all a strong green tea from a kettle and welcomed them to her fire. Kozue and Misao could finally relax and feel a little safe. The three of them sat by the fireplace where they met travelers who had arrived before them.

(3.11)

One was a Buddhist pilgrim, carrying sixty-six copies of the lotus sutra to leave across Japan, and the other was a *gōze*—a blind shamisen player. Because there were no other lodgers, Misao relaxed, and took her child out from her bosom and nursed him. Matsuhei proceeded to give Kozue a shoulder rub. The lady of the house made rice porridge and offered it to them for dinner, also offering some for the pilgrim and the gōze. Then she gave the travelers as many futons as they wanted, albeit the futons were rather thin. The travelers rested as they pleased.

The lady went to the main house, and after a while someone came home. A voice came calling from the front door, "Osaga! Osaga!"

The lady of the house ran out and saw her husband—Kamahira. They went inside together and greeted all the travelers one by one. After seeing the trio of travelers, he snuck back to the main house, and in a great panic ran out the gate. There in the shadow of a pine tree was someone wearing a straw rain mantle, whom Kamahira whispered something to. Then the two went around the house and went in through the back door.

3.11

3.12

Part II

(3.12)

That evening, when the bell had rung five times,[4] Kozue, Misao, and Matsuhei lay sound asleep on their thin bedding, tired from the trip. But at some point, even this night dawned, and from the kitchen the voice of a woman could be heard, and there were sounds of rice being cooked. The lodgers woke up and were offered breakfast like they had been offered dinner the night before. Each ate their meal and made preparations to leave. The pilgrim and the gōze gave some money for their stay and left the house and went on their way. The trio also readied, making sure the strings on their gaiters were tight, revealing they were very used to making this preparation. It was rare to see a party with women being this accustomed to traveling. Then, Osaga went to pick up Misao's son. It looked like she was going to cradle him, but she snatched him and ran for the main house. As soon as Matsuhei saw this, he pursued Osaga. The shōji doors on the house flew open, and a man came out, holding the young boy with one hand and a sword with the other. Following him came Kamahira and Osaga, both holding bladed weapons, and they surrounded Kozue and Misao.

The man holding the child raised his voice, "Kozue, wife of Edanoshin, and Misao, how long it has been since I saw you two last."

They scrutinized his face, staring with eyes that could kill.

"You! Tatsumaki Arakurō!" said Kozue. "Suffered, we have, searching for you. You killed my husband Edanoshin and fled. And the treasure of our house, the Fubuki Katatsuki tea container—"

Misao interrupted, "And you killed my husband Sumatarō too, you atrocious beast!"

The two drew closer to Yashagorō. To protect them, Matsuhei drew his sword and attacked Osaga to take her down.

Yashagorō laughed and cursed at them, "You noisy bitches! The one who killed both Edanoshin and Sumatarō was indeed I, Tatsumaki Arakurō! If you come at me to take your revenge, oh warrior's wife, then I will simply stab this brat. I have been in love with you since I worked in the mansion, so if you do as I say and become mine, I will let your mother have a pleasant retirement." His last words had a shadow of affection in them.

(3.13)

Yashagorō held the child hostage, and as Misao and Kozue inched closer, the three of them exchanged looks. Kozue and Misao clenched their fists and gritted their teeth while shedding tears of anger.

Misao finally raised her head and said with seductiveness in her voice, "I will do as you ask if you give back the child. But please, it is embarrassing to do it in front of my mother and my baby," and gazed at Yashagorō's face.

His expression softened a bit. "So you say, but if I hand over your son, will you truly do as my heart desires?"

---

4 19:00.

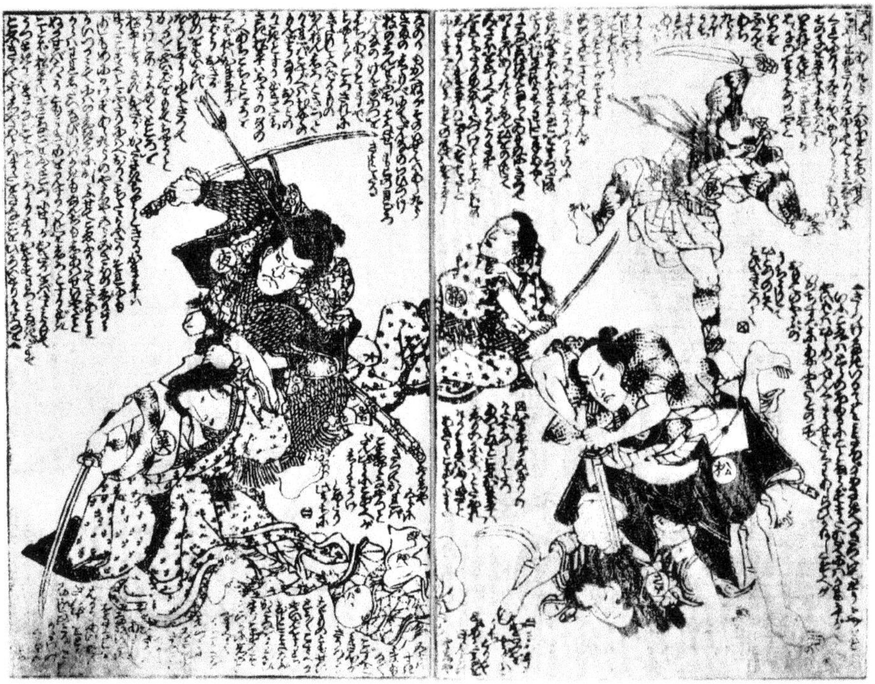

3.13

As he said this, Misao snatched the child and handed it to Matsuhei. She drew her sword and slashed at Yashagorō, who stretched out his long arms and pinned her down.

"Take care of those two!" Yashagorō said, and they followed his command.

Kamahira scowled at Kozue and said, "My name is, as it has always been, Kamahira. I used to be Yashagorō's servant, and by my master's orders, I am the one who took down Edanoshin. I learned swordsmanship from my master and now I will use it to strike you down. What a fool you are, to have come all this way to be killed. Now resign yourself to your fate!" He lunged at her with his sword.

"What pointless talk. This one is for my husband!" yelled Kozue, and pointed the tip of her sword at him.

Matsuhei, worried for both Kozue and Misao, was torn about what to do. Without a word, Osaga attacked him with a knife. He parried with his blade, sending her into a stumble, and cut into the top of her shoulder.

Kamahira and Kozue had stepped into the garden—locked in combat. Not paying any attention to this, Yashagorō grabbed Misao by the scruff of her neck and pushed her down on one of the stepping stones in the garden.

With a trembling voice, he spoke, "What happens now is up to me. Submit, and I will make you and your brat happy. Resist and you will be sorry. What is your answer?"

3.14

Matsuhei had been holding the child, but when he took down Osaga, the child had fallen from his embrace. Hearing the cries of the child, Yashagorō picked him up and put his blade to him while holding him up in front of Misao.

With a voice like a tiger's roar, he bellowed at Misao, "So, what will it be?"

Kozue's life was already in danger, and Matsuhei could not deal with both situations. In that moment of most dire need, an arrow like lightning came flying from the thicket in front of the house, impaling Kamahira's right shoulder. In a cry of pain, he fell on his rear with a thud. Surprised, Kozue attacked Yashagorō, who blocked her blade with his sword, and said, "You impudent little—"

While this happened, Matsuhei finally went to finish Osaga off. Without any delay, and unfazed by Kozue and Misao's attacks, Yashagorō threw Kozue's blade to the ground and stole Misao's sword. He trampled Kozue, held her down, and grabbed Misao by the hair bun. With his left leg, he kicked away the crying infant. Then he readjusted the grip on his broadsword and prepared to take care of them one at a time.

(3.14)

As he was about to cut off Misao's head, yet another arrow launched from the thicket. This one lodged itself in the shoulder of Yashagorō's sword arm. The pain sent the man backwards while still holding his blade. Relieved, Kozue and Misao looked over towards where the arrow came from.

3.15

Matsuhei finished off Osaga, picked up the crying child from the garden, and gave him to Misao. When he did this, five or six sparrows came flying from the tall thicket, fluttering their wings, and a man crashed through the bamboo gate, holding a bow and arrow. He walked calmly towards them and took a seat above Kozue and Misao on the porch.

"This cannot be! Takasago Yuminosuke-dono, I did not know you were in these parts," exclaimed Kozue.

"My dear brother, you left your post last year because you said you could not fulfill your ambitions," said Misao. "Since then, my husband was slaughtered, my father-in-law died, and the Takasago house ceased to exist. It has been nothing but hardship and sadness. But to know you are safe and sound makes me happy."

Matsuhei bowed his head. "I went with the ladies to take revenge, and as a result we met Arakurō today in this place. We were happy to finally get a chance to fight him, but he was much too strong for us to handle."

Yuminosuke said to the three of them, "Just today I was going to do an investigation on this Kamahira, and when I came here to look for him, I heard the clash of swords. I snuck up to the bamboo fence to see what was going on, and when I saw Kozue-dono and my younger sister Misao in danger, I shot down Kamahira. And in order for you to get proper revenge against Arakurō, I was careful to not hit any of his vital points when I shot him afterwards. But it sure was a close call." He finished with a joyful expression.

(3.15)

This truly was the heroic Takasago Yuminosuke of Sarashina in Shinano, whom everyone knew of as an amazing and mighty young warrior.

Without warning, Yashagorō sprang up, tore out the arrow stuck in his shoulder, and fled into the main house. Yuminosuke, gritting his teeth, went in pursuit, but then a pillar of white steam appeared, obscuring everything so he couldn't tell up from down.

Yuminosuke was at a loss, and when the steam cleared, he said, "I did not know Arakurō could summon a pillar of white smoke like this. I might have let him slip this once, but when the time comes for his divine punishment, I shall capture him with my own two hands. Lady Kozue, my dear sister Misao, this Kamahira is the servant who killed Edanoshin-dono. As part of your vendetta, go finish him off and pay him his final respect."

The two ran over to Kamahira and gave him the death blow, having enjoyed watching him squirm and suffer so far. Matsuhei threw Kamahira and Osaga's corpses into an old well nearby.

Yuminosuke went and sat back down in his previous seat. "Last year, the reason I left our homeland was because I was secretly ordered to do so by Lord Sarashina Saemon-dono. I purposefully spread the word among the retainers that it was because of a lack of filial piety.

"The lord already informed me all about the assassination of the trusted retainer Himematsu Edanoshin, the theft of the precious tea container and the butchering of Sumatarō, as well as the fact that it was Tatsumaki Arakurō who orchestrated all of it. The lord sent a secret letter to my hideout, so I already know all the details. But I never expected the disaster which has befallen the Himematsu household. And my sister who married into that house now carries her child with her on a quest for revenge. Thinking about you and Kozue, strong-willed yet so unused to traveling, searching aimlessly, is too much to bear. Bless the lord's heart, for he had the idea to send me to help your female-led vendetta. I was already out searching for the last forgotten remnant of Ogata Saemon who fell to ruin in Kyūshū. It is unknown where he might be, so last year, I was sent out under strict orders to find him, which is why I left Shinano. The first frost of the year fell, so I moved to Echigo in search of some greener pastures, and I moved into a village in a river valley at the foot of Mount Myōkō. I became a tree cutter and a hunter, carrying with me my hunting bow as I went every day from mountain to mountain, and made a life of hunting animals. When I came to Fumoto Village I came on a raft and heard of a man on a firewood boat, who went by the name Kamahira. I heard a rumor that he apparently came recently from Shinano, and I concluded this might be the fiend Arakurō. So, I secretly came to check, and when I saw his face, I knew it was actually Arakurō's servant Kamahira. I came here to capture and question him, and that is what led to today's events."

Hearing this, the three travelers felt safe. Leaning on his bow, Yuminosuke added, "It has been so long since I have seen you and have

3.16

missed you so. Please, will you not come with me to my hideout? There we can talk leisurely about how to carry out our revenge." Then he guided them to his hideout.

And now, the story takes us elsewhere, at around the same time, to Niigata in the land of Echigo. Niigata was a flourishing place, making wealth through all its brothels. They were built roof to roof and, like normal houses, wherever and however people saw fit. It did not discriminate high from low among its guests.

(3.16)

Geishas sang and played the shamisen seductively, and the jesters chanted and drummed to excite and entertain. Here, one could not distinguish nighttime from daytime. In one of these prosperous and lively houses, the Kumadeya house, known throughout all of Niigata, was a man named Yokushirō. His eyes were sharp like a hunting hawk or a hungry bear, and he was so stingy that he would burn fingernail trimmings in his lanterns instead of wicks. He would strongly reprimand the working girls, and would scold and punish the young geisha apprentices until they were bruised and bloody. Seven years prior, he married into the house bringing with him a dower, and day by day he increased his wealth, and was now a rich man. However, he had a twisted personality, never helping anyone in the family when they were in need, always lending at a high interest rate, and not taking care of others who struggled. He had married into the family, but he grew increasingly selfish and thought poorly of Tagane, the daughter who was to inherit the house. He cursed at her and worked her hard, but after her mother had passed, Tagane respected Yokushirō as her real father. Since he had increased the fortune of the house, she served him with a gentle attitude, never going against his will.

Roughly seven or eight days earlier, Tsumorinosuke-dono, the son of Lord Sarashina, who was the provincial lord of Shinano, had announced a tour of Echigo. However, in secret, he had gone to Kumadeya to be with the girl Ayame, who was in the prime of her career. In the inner rooms of the second floor, the young samurai brought by the lord threw around money, having boisterous fun and merriment.

On this day it snowed, and the world turned to silver. On the backside of the second floor, the young Tagane lounged with a young apprentice and a geisha, appreciating the snow-covered scenery. Absent-mindedly, they looked down to the outside of the outer wall and saw a young boy, roughly aged sixteen or seventeen. The hair on his forehead was white from the snow and pulled back over his shaved scalp, and his features were not too shabby looking. He was what one would call a *wakashū*—a tender boy, not quite yet a man, awaking lustful thoughts in men and women alike. He was dressed in the robes of a pilgrim visiting the twenty-four temples of the disciples of the monk Shinran, and on his back he had a straw bundle for carrying food.

(3.17)

His worn-out bamboo hat flapped about in the wind and broke in half. He walked in snow so deep that only the head of the ladle he carried on his hip was visible. His hands had been in the snow and were so cold they seemed frozen. He cried out in agony, and it was unbearable to look at.

Tagane's eyes filled with tears at the sight and turned to the two other girls. "We three sit here, enjoying the nice view and the snow, while there is a young man down there outside our wall, suffering and freezing in it. I want to save him, but due to father's temperament, there is no way to do so."

The apprentice answered her words. "They say saving someone in pain is rewarded with being saved yourself, so of course you would want to save him. Tagane-sama, let's do this...." and whispered something to Tagane.

Tagane smiled, and after finishing their talk, the apprentice went down from the second floor and snuck out a paper umbrella. She put it up, raised the hem of her kimono, and went out into the snow. After walking across the yard to the wall, she cautiously put her hands on the servant door and tried to open it, but it was frozen shut and would not budge. Applying more force, she finally managed to open the door.

She stuck out her head and the umbrella and called out, "Young Mister pilgrim. If you stay out there in this heavy snow forever, you will freeze and die. The young lady Tagane-sama has kindly told me to bring you inside without anyone seeing. So, hurry up and come inside the yard."

3.17

The pilgrim raised his head, and said with a trembling voice, "I want to get going before you get caught and scolded, but my legs were frozen by the cold and I cannot stand, and the snowfall is only getting stronger. I was sad because I thought I would freeze and die in the snow here today, but since you speak such kind words to me..." His legs were deeply buried in the snow, and as he tried standing, he fell over.

He was half covered in snow and his clothes were so frozen that icicles hung from them. A truly lowly and unbearable sight. But the apprentice reached out to him and together, teeth clattering from the cold, they went inside the wall. Tagane snuck the pilgrim into the shed where they kept firewood and gave him rice balls and warm water. The pilgrim finally found relief and returned to his normal senses.

The sun had set on that day, but because of the snow it was still so bright, when one thought it was early evening, it had long since become night. It was the fourth quarter of the hour of the rat[5] and the pleasure house had been bustling since early in the evening. The hallway became chaotic with the owner, Yokushirō, cursing at the top of his lungs. He grabbed his daughter Tagane by the hair bun and the pilgrim by the scruff of his neck, dragging them out into the hallway.

He yelled, "This blasted girl, bringing in some beggar from who knows where, keeping him in the woodshed, entertaining him, giving him food and saké, rubbing her bosoms all over him! And you, you cursed young thief, pushing your luck saying you're a pilgrim on the

5 00:30-01:00.

3.18

Shinran trail, a shame on your parents' face! Now, tell me who you are! Speak your name! But don't you think you can use any of your thieving tricks on me, or I will hang you from a tree, young man!"

(3.18)

With a quivering voice, he replied, "I really am a pilgrim. Your honored daughter showed me pity."

Without care, Yokushirō said, "Stop spouting pointless things and shut up."

"I will make this youngster confess, so you just stand there and watch!" he said to Tagane with a crazed look in his eyes, and then kicked and stomped on the young man.

Yokushirō had the prostitutes take Tagane to the kitchen and ordered the men to tie up the youngster. The young son of Lord Sarashina, Tsumorinosuke, led by Ayame, his companion for the night, saw the commotion and approached. When he called out to Yokushirō and came near, Yokushirō leapt backwards and planted his head on the tatami mat, bowing with great respect.

Tsumorinosuke-dono said to him, "I have been listening since the beginning, and I heard everything. Tagane's true intentions will only bring harm to the pilgrim, and the troubles he would face would be truly pitiful." He turned and clapped, calling over his samurai attendant.

"My liege?" said the approaching samurai. Tsumorinosuke cupped his hands and whispered something into the samurai's ear. Then the samurai retrieved a gift-envelope wrapped with a beautiful string. Judging by the size of it, it had a significant amount of money in it. He placed the envelope in front of Yokushirō and withdrew to the next room.

Tsumorinosuke said, "This pilgrim caused a ruckus in this house tonight, and although he is detestable, this whole situation is obstructing my merriment. For tonight let him stay in the woodshed or something and chase him out in the morning. It would be wretched if he went into the snow now and froze to death. Laugh, laugh and be happy! Like this, tonight not only can we handle the pilgrim and the young lady offering hospitality without permission, but you also make money."

With a smile, Yokushirō said, "Such inspired words, my lord, and such a generous tip. I shall see to it that it is done as you say. And you, pilgrim. Your life seems to have divine protection. If it wasn't for the lord, you would have faced dire consequences. Consider yourself lucky." That smile twisted into a frown at the pilgrim. To Tsumorinosuke again, he said, "And you even extended your kindness to my daughter. Ayame, make sure to take good care of the lord. Please show him our gratitude for what he did today. When it gets dark, spend the night in his room and have fun. And you, young man. Hurry off to sleep with the firewood!"

Frightened, the young man tiptoed back to where he came from. Yokushirō took the money and counted his riches on his fingers with a smile on his face, bid farewell and took his leave. Then Ayame took a lantern and walked in front of Tsumorinosuke, leading him into her private parlor.

Now, this Tsumorinosuke was very concerned with what the world thought of him. Everything he wore, from his overcoat to his short sleeve kimono, the wrapping cord on the hilt of his swords, and even his belt, stood out with purple felt and velvet. Because of this, there were none who did not know him as "the purple millionaire".

(3.19)

As the night wore on, Tsumorinosuke abruptly woke from his sleep and searched for Ayame, who was not there. He called out, "Someone, come here!" Answering to his call, someone opened the shōji screen and entered. With scrutiny, he saw it was not Ayame, but the daughter of the house, Tagane.

Tsumorinosuke lowered his voice to speak in an apologetic voice, "Rather than the Ayame I called for, an even better view has appeared. The young branch on a plum tree, sprouting its first flower. Your long sleeves are so vivid with blossoms. I must make you mine!"

Tagane lowered her head and hid her face with her sleeve. It would be embarrassing not to say anything at all, so after a moment of silence, she finally spoke up.

"I am nervous speaking by your side, but I thought I should pay my respects for your blessings earlier today. Not only did you save me and the pilgrim from trouble, but you also gave my father money. But since Ayame was not here to bring you my message, I could not give it to you. Being the idiot that I am, happiness overcame me when you called out

3.19

and I went to you. Just you talking to me is making me happy, but you are only teasing me, a country bumpkin, and making wanton sport and embarrassing me."

Tsumorinosuke silenced her. "Finding a beautiful courtesan in this world of river reeds is truly rare, and they can make for a good pastime. But unlike them, your honest and kind intentions, which you showed when you saved the pilgrim from freezing in the snow, have made me infatuated with you. Now, I am overcome with passion. Tagane, let us melt the snow with our love tonight!"

He brushed the sleeve away, and Tagane's face was as red as an autumn leaf.

"Please excuse me!" said Tagane, attempting to flee.

But Tsumorinosuke drew even closer and kept a firm grip on Tagane's sleeve, saying, "Love is love! But I also have something else I want to ask you about. So, for starters, come here.

"Here is my question. You are not the real child of the proprietor Yokushirō. I already heard from Ayame that your father recently married into this house and is merely your stepfather. I need to know exactly who this man is, and I am certain you know all about it. Nothing would make me happier than if you were to tell me this."

Without thinking any further, Tagane spoke in a hushed voice, "Now that I think about it, it has been almost eight years since my father came to this house. Fighting brewed here in Niigata, and he was supposed to go

3.20

help quell it, but apparently mistook the place and ended up here. Back then his name was Sune'emon. He came into our care and married into the household. Long ago though, he lived in Shinano where he was a gambler and only associated with bad people. I think his name back then was something along the lines of Ganpachi."

(3.20)

Tsumorinosuke said, "I don't need to hear the rest to know what happened then. He is a cunning man, and he raised the fortunes of the house, taking good care of it all. He has been making it a pleasant place for himself to live, while you have been waiting for a good husband to come. I can be that husband, so give yourself to me and your business shall soar!" Tsumorinosuke grasped her hand. Tagane trembled and shirked away.

From beyond the byōbu folding screen next to them, the courtesan Ayame had been listening for a while. Tsumorinosuke spoke in a hushed voice, and although she could not hear them very clearly, every now and again she heard some words and could tell the man's tone was amorous. She had spent her days with him, not wanting to pillow with anyone else. She had climbed the mountain of love, and now as she looked down on this scene, the flames of animosity burned within her.

"Even if she is the owner's daughter, she has crossed my path of love and I will get back at her! If she sleeps with him, I will not let her off easy," she thought, and her eyebrows stood on end. She bit down on her sleeve and tore at it.

Her feet on the tatami mats gave off a sound as she was about to enter, and realizing who it was, Tsumorinosuke hurried Tagane out of the room. Although she didn't understand what was going on, Tagane slipped away into the hallway.

Yokushirō snuck up on Ayame and grabbed her hand. He pulled her sleeve to signal for her to come with him for a bit. She didn't even turn to him but tried to run to the other side of the byōbu screen and made a fuss. But Yokushirō put his mouth to her ear and whispered something while forcefully dragging her with him into the hallway. Tsumorinosuke could guess what was happening, but he pretended to sleep, not making a sound. Yokushirō finally managed to lead Ayame to an empty parlor, where he spoke to her quietly.

"As a courtesan, feeling a raging jealousy and cursing Tsumorinosuke after seeing him together with Tagane is only to be expected. But there is a reason why I forcefully brought you here, which I must tell you. Tagane might be my stepchild, but she is a nuisance no matter what I put her to do. Let's say you were to take this *tantō* of mine. Sneak into Tagane and Tsumorinosuke's room while they sleep and stab them to death to your heart's delight. It would clear up your lover's grudge immediately. Not only that, but there is something else which you must know. Do not be surprised by what I am about to tell you. It is the honest truth.

"That man might have come here under the pretense of being the young Lord Tsumorinosuke of the Sarashina house, but this 'purple millionaire' is in fact from the same land as I. He is the son of a country samurai from the town Nezumi-no-shuku. His name is Tarō, but now he is known as the great bandit Jiraiya. I have a grudge against him, so I am going to kill him tonight. I have informed the local authorities, and on my signal, they will come if he proves too much to handle. That way, we can outnumber him and tie him up. You can kill Tagane and clear your grudge then.

(3.21)

"When I opened the envelope with money that he gave me earlier, there was a tobacco pouch in it. One I have a memory of. When I thought hard about it, there was no doubt it was a tobacco pouch I dropped when I killed his father Hatasaku many years ago. After realizing this, I captured and tortured one of Jiraiya's underlings, who was pretending to be Tsumorinosuke's page. He confessed Jiraiya already knew my identity, and that he gave me the money so he could hand me the tobacco pouch to test me. So, prepare yourself, because tonight will not pass without incident."

Ayame did not respond, but simply let out a deep resounding sigh.

In that moment, outside the shōji screen, it became as bright as day. Shocked, Yokushirō opened the shōji and saw a huge toad in the garden. It was made from snow and spewed a great flame which rose high into the sky. Yokushirō was baffled by this, and from behind him came *shinobi*, dressed in white clothes, hoods, and masks. They came from his left and right, restrained his arms, tied him up with rope, and

3.21

gagged him. Stunned, Ayame was similarly caught, hogtied, and gagged. When they were restrained, more shinobi came from the garden, and with roaring footsteps they filled up the porch and the garden and bowed down.

(3.22)

From the second floor, Jiraiya silently undid the mudra he had formed with his hands, opened the shōji and looked down on the garden. He smiled to himself, went down from the second floor, and addressed his men.

"You did a great job waiting for my signal. Now, take those two and put them in palanquins. Bring them to the place we have prepared. Also, the bastard Yokushirō captured one of my underlings and interrogated him in the storehouse. Release him, and also take Tagane, the daughter of the house. Put her in a palanquin and bring her along behind me."

"Aye!" answered the men in unison. Jiraiya stepped into the garden, got in his own palanquin, and left through the door in the garden wall. His great host followed, but one went back, grabbed some snow, aimed for the firewood shed, and threw. At the sound of the shed getting hit, the door opened from the inside and the pilgrim, whose name was Ekichi, came out. He picked up his straw bundle and followed Jiraiya towards an unknown location.

3.22

What follows in the start of book four is vengeance, and you will be able to read everything about Ekichi the pilgrim. But for now, this book has come to its end.

4.1

Left Side:
Leader of the Nezumi-no-shuku town in Shinano, Mochimaru Fukitarō.

Right Side:
The Tale of Jiraiya the Gallant: Book Four
Story by Mizugaki Egao
Art by Kōchōrō Kunisada

Book 4

Tales of frog battles start in texts of old. In the *Shoku Nihongi*[1] during the time of empress Shōtoku in the seventh month of the second year of the Jingo-keiun era,[2] a great battle formation of frogs was spotted in Yatsushiro in Hi province.[3] The formation was seven jō[4] across and left in a southern direction. By sundown it had disappeared to who knows where. In *Chomonjū*[5] it says that during summer in the third year of the *Kangi* era[6] under emperor Go Horikawa, in the ditch on the southern side of the Kōyōin Temple, thousands of frogs assembled. There, they formed two armies and took up positions opposite each other. Then they fought, biting each other to death, and for several days, the citizens of the capital watched as the frogs fought, even when they were halfway dead. In texts written in later times, such stories are abundant. Here you can see snakes fighting frogs, and a frog using a slug to kill a snake. This is also in Konzan's essays.[7] I put it here in the foreword to show the connection between toads and serpents.

Tenpō 13—Year of the Water Tiger—New Year (1842)
Mizugaki Egao

---

1 *Chronicles of Japan—The Sequel.*

2 768 CE.

3 Province in Kyushu.

4 About 21 meters.

5 *Kokon Chomonjū—A Collection of Notable Tales Old and New.*

6 1231 CE.

7 Gotō Konzan—famous doctor in Edo who wrote important books and essays.

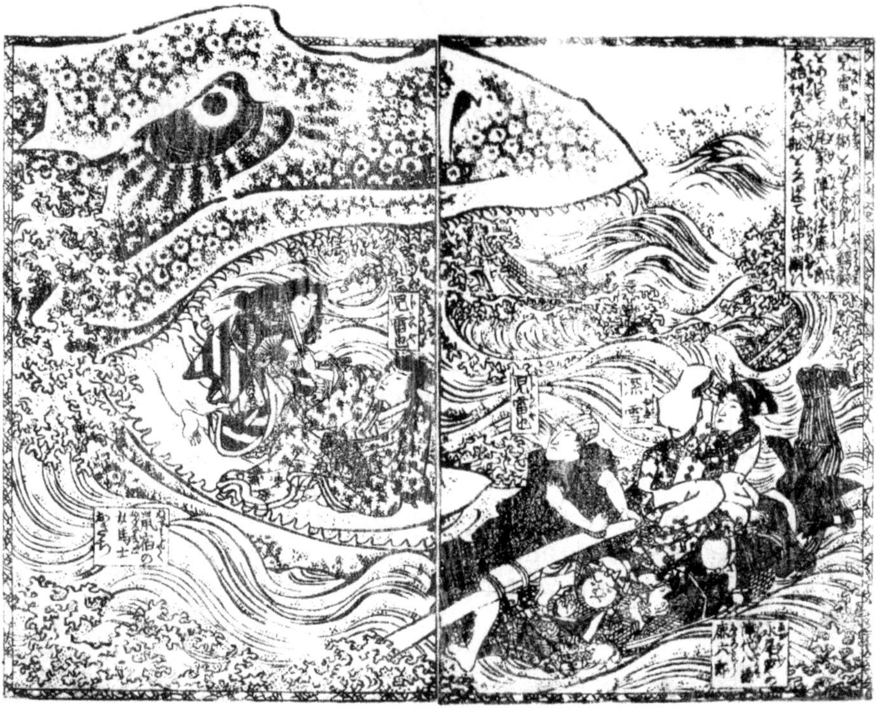

4.2

Jiraiya uses his yōjutsu to copy himself and summon a great shark. With it, he capsizes the pursuing warships with Yakama Shikaroku, the sheriff of the Nagao clan, and sinks them into the sea.

Yakama Shikaroku, the sheriff of the Nagao clan.

Miyuki.

Jiraiya. [1]

Jiraiya. [2]

Osachi, the lady of Nezumi-no-shuku.

4.3

Oroku, geisha of Ōiso, with her comb aslant.

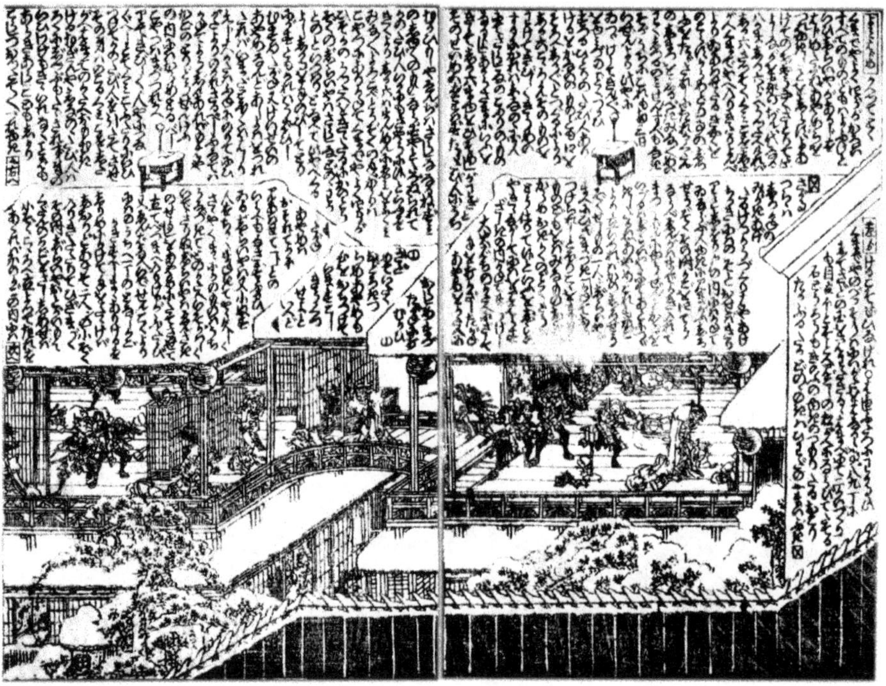

4.4

Part I

(4.4)
And so, the story continues.

In the late hours of the night, unbeknownst to all the people in the Kumadeya house, Jiraiya had kidnapped the proprietor Yokushirō along with Tagane and Ayame. As the day dawned, so did the realization of what happened, and the people called for the sheriff of the Nagao clan—Yakama Shikarokurō. Shikaroku, as people called him, went with his constables and apprehended every guest who had stayed at the house since the previous evening. To figure out the facts of what had happened, they questioned everyone, because someone was bound to know. But all they did was cause problems for the guests. When they thought there was nothing left to do, Shikaroku found out from the staff there was a traveler who had stayed at the house for the past three days, pouring away money like hot water. They put him under severe interrogation and found out he was from the Sarashina area in the land of Shinano. He was very candid about this. Shikaroku knitted his brow and intentionally skipped asking what his name was, simply asking the traveler, "You wouldn't by any chance happen to be from the Nezumi-no-shuku post station in Sarashina?"

"Indeed I am," answered the traveler.

A smile spread across Shikaroku's face, and he called out, "Everyone, rejoice! This person has a clue to finding the bandits. According to an investigation by Kumadeya's Yokushirō, the bandit Jiraiya came here disguised as the son of the Lord Sarashina. Even though he has evaded capture for now, he took with him the young Tagane and the courtesan Ayame. Their legs are weak, so they cannot have made it very far. They will most likely try to make their escape from Niigata by ship. If we ready sailors in advance, Jiraiya will be like a bird in a cage, and we will have him in custody before the day is over. For now, take this person back with you and lock him in the hold."

Shikaroku ordered two of his constables to take the traveler away and left for the coast with the rest of his men. The traveler was in a truly pitiful situation. No one would listen to him when he tried to explain the truth, and as they berated him, the men took him to meet his inevitable fate.

Here the story takes us elsewhere. Roughly eight or nine chō[8] outside of Niigata, there was a villa owned by the Kumadeya house. It was an impressive two-story building on the shore looking across the water to the land of Sado. Under the branches of the pine trees overlooking the house were stone lanterns, covered in snow from the day before. Icicles stretched down from the eaves of the thatched cypress bark roof of the stately mansion, sparkling like polished silver. It was early morning, and inside the garden, past the creaky wicket gate, were people dressed in clothes so white they were easy to lose in the snow. Just then, four palanquins were carried in and placed right next to the engawa porch. The first person to exit was Jiraiya, who stepped out with a casual composure. Next came Tagane, followed by Ayame. After they disembarked, one of the white-clad men took a knee before Jiraiya.

"As per your instructions, we have locked the caretakers of the house in the shed. We have finished clearing the property."

Jiraiya paid him no attention and entered the parlor overlooking the garden. He sat next to the large brazier set up in the room and put his hands over it. Tagane and Ayame came next to him.

He said, "Tagane, you must be very shocked right now. And Ayame, calm down and try to maintain your composure."

Despite his words, Tagane and Ayame glanced at each other, shaking with fear, and they didn't reply with as much as a word. Jiraiya called one of his bandits close and whispered something to him for a while. The bandit nodded and withdrew to the garden in a hurry. Jiraiya then had Ayame put up the shōji screen towards the veranda and led her inside the room. He stepped back out on the veranda, giving a sideways glance to the remaining doorless palanquin which was left sitting in the garden. He clapped his hands, bringing forth two of his men through the gate to kneel before him. Jiraiya pointed to the palanquin with his chin and the bandits opened its side. Inside, gagged and hogtied, was Yokushirō, scowling at Jiraiya.

8 872–981 meters.

4.5

(4.5)

With a great smile, Jiraiya looked around and called out, “Miyuki. Miyuki.”

Although he could not speak, Yokushirō was shocked to see the one Jiraiya summoned was the pilgrim from the night before. Jiraiya ordered his men to take out Yokushirō and stand him up but leave him bound.

Jiraiya removed the gag from the man’s mouth. “Hello there, Yokushirō, formerly known as Ganpachi! I came to Niigata a while ago and, while I stayed at your brothel, you unexpectedly managed to figure out from the confession of one of my subordinates that I am the bandit Jiraiya. Because I hold a fierce grudge against you, my plan was to have Miyuki disguise herself as a pilgrim and sneak in to take our revenge on you, but you informed the Nagao clan’s sheriff. You left us no other choice but to bring you here. Look at you, like an animal with no legs you are. It would not feel right if we were to take our vengeance with your arms tied up like this. Those arms of yours that murdered Hatasaku. Grab your blade and have a fair duel with Miyuki.”

Yokushirō was a strong-willed man, but completely taken in by Jiraiya’s overwhelming presence. Although his words were soft-spoken, they felt like booming thunder, and Yokushirō could not even raise his head out of fear. After a moment, he managed to let out a sigh.

Yokushirō mumbled, “And as payback for me killing Hatasaku, you will gang up on me, two against one.”

4.6

Jiraiya laughed. "For an animal like you there is no reason for me to do anything. A woman will be more than enough. Now, get on with it!"

Jiraiya's words emboldened Miyuki, who grasped her sword, eager to proceed. Two of the subordinates understood what they had to do and untied Yokushirō. They let him prepare, and then gave him a sword and pushed him to an open space in the garden. Miyuki followed closely after him. In order to give them some space, Jiraiya oversaw the duel from the veranda. With a snappy and fluid motion, Miyuki drew her sword and called out to Yokushirō.

"You killed my father Hatasaku. You sold me to be a prostitute. For years I suffered, and now, on this day, I finally get my revenge. Prepare to die!"

Yokushirō smiled wryly. "You are nothing but a whore who puts up a bold front now that you have a crowd to back you up!"

(4.6)

No more words were said, as Miyuki boldly, and with all her force, came down on Yokushirō with her sword, trying to cleave him in two. She was completely absorbed in her attack as Yokushirō parried her unrelenting assault. The fighting was even fiercer than Jiraiya anticipated. He swallowed and watched without taking his eyes off them.

However, Miyuki was a woman, and although she was in high spirits, her swordplay grew dull. Due to her excitement, she ran out of breath. When Yokushirō realized this and stepped in to strike her, Jiraiya made a toad out of snow on a tray next to him and threw it at

4.7

Yokushirō. True to Jiraiya's aim, it struck right between the eyes and shattered. The flurry of snow then turned into a mass of frogs, and they clung to Yokushirō's sword arm, immobilizing it. Miyuki did not see this, but did see Yokushirō shocked and losing composure, which she took advantage of. She flanked him and pierced his torso. As he writhed in agony, blood gushed from him, staining the snow crimson red.

"Well done! Bravo!" cheered Jiraiya. "And now for the finishing blow."

Miyuki pushed Yokushirō down, stepped over him, and with great spirit, stabbed him through the neck. Jiraiya put on *geta* sandals for going into thc garden, stepped off the veranda, and sliced off Yokushirō's head. He sheathed his katana and took the head with him back to the veranda.

Jiraiya reopened the shōji screen to the veranda. Miyuki took her place beside him. Tagane and Ayame also came out.

(4.7)

Miyuki turned to Jiraiya. "After all these years, our father's bane Yokushirō ha—" said Miyuki, but Jiraiya interrupted her with a cough.

"Fix your disheveled hair. You are all flustered and agitated," he told her, and Miyuki borrowed a hairpin from Tagane, who was sitting next to her, and tied up her hair. "And after today you should no longer use the name Miyuki. Better that you stay disguised as the wakashū Ekichi."

Halfway through Jiraiya's sentence, one of his subordinates returned, anxious and in a hurry. He took a deep breath before saying, "As you ordered, I prepared the boats, but there is something else I must inform you of immediately. For some strange reason there are seventeen or eighteen roofed boats in the water at the entrance to Niigata. We should be careful."

"They are probably trying to surround and capture us," said Jiraiya. He arose and called his underlings close to him. "Take the women to the main ship as fast as you can. Even if they have placed tens of thousands of boats to close us in, I'll make it so you can leave without worrying."

Then the three palanquins from earlier were brought over, and Tagane, Ekichi, and Ayame got in. Jiraiya's men took them towards the ship with great urgency. Jiraiya tossed Yokushirō's head and corpse into a well. He also released the caretakers of the house who were tied up in the woodshed, telling them to take care and watch the fire. With one of his bandits, he left at a leisurely pace.

Sheriff Yakama Shikaroku closed off the mouth of Niigata, boarded a fast rowboat, and inspected the boats in the water. Among them was a single, large vessel. By his command, seven or eight small boats paddled close to it.

"Please wait while I inspect your ship," he called out to stop the ship.

(4.8)

But pretending not to hear him, the ship rowed at top speed to get away. Something was suspicious about this, so he ordered at the top of his lungs, "That one is Jiraiya's pirate ship! Stop it and seize them!"

At his command, like an arrow in flight, the constables rowed the boat and drew near the ship. At that moment, the straw siding of the ship was raised, revealing a line of arquebus barrels. They gave off a volley with a loud report, shooting down several of the pursuers. Even so, they were many, and as more and more boats came rowing, their courage grew along with their number of allies. They clamored over one another, not wanting to let the ship escape. But when it looked like the mass of pursuing boats was about to capture Jiraiya's ship, something mysterious happened. A fog rose up, making it difficult to see even a short distance. It was followed by a wind across the water, making waves like crashing mountains roaring with a tremendous sound. The many boats drifted, like leaves dancing in the wind, as they swayed up and down in the waves. The pursuers lost their bravado, and as they swallowed the spray, they screamed and lamented at the top of their lungs. Sheriff Shikaroku was dumbstruck and panicked, and he rushed the boatmen to retreat to shore. As he scrambled to flee, Shikaroku looked back and saw an enormous shark, wrapped in the spray of the sea as it floated on top of the water. It went against the waves, large enough to reach the skies, and the sharp light emanating from its eyes was beyond words. As he watched, his allies' ships sank in the sea. The

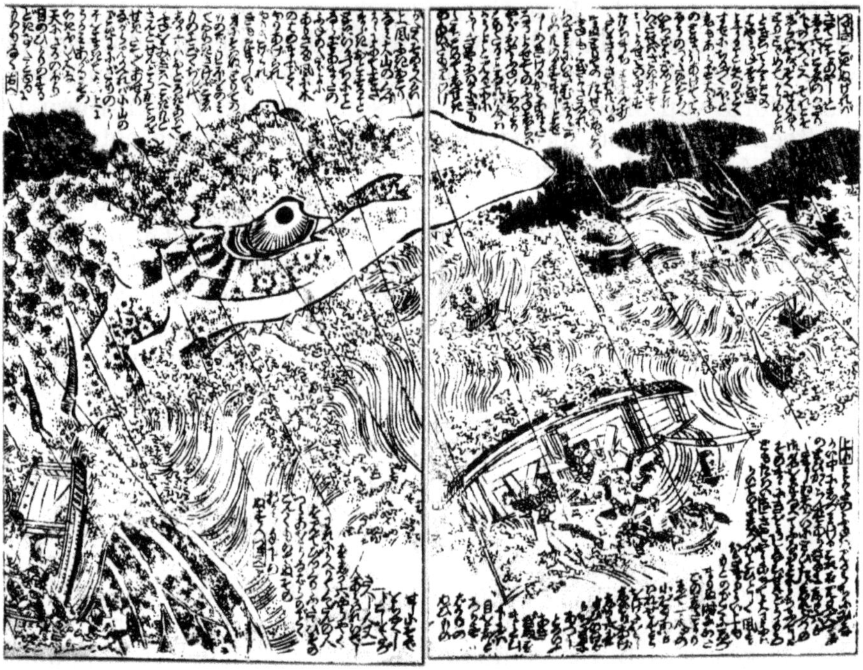

4.8

great shark looked like it was going to charge, sending Shikaroku's valor flying to the heavens. All he could do was chant the names of the gods as he threw himself to the bottom of the boat where he lost consciousness along with all the boatmen.

Finally, the shark sank to the bottom of the sea, the winds died, and the waves returned to normal. Then, out from under the floorboards of Shikaroku's boat came a bandit. He kicked over the boatmen and tied them up, and as he tried to bring Shikaroku back to consciousness, another person appeared. He wore a thick hemp *atsushi* kimono, like that of the northern lands of Ezo.[9] Underneath he wore a short-sleeved kimono with dazzling embroidery, and on his hip, he carried a sword. Shikaroku finally came to his senses, and when he saw the man, his face turned as blue as the sea. Before he could say anything, the bandit said to him in a strict and threatening voice, "You are before my master. Get down on your belly!"

(4.9)

Shikaroku thought if he refused, he would surely be killed. Thus, he bore with it and lay on the floorboards of the boat, trembling. The man, who was Jiraiya, then sat neatly over Shikaroku and spoke to him.

"The reason I came here was not to steal gold or silver. The man you know as Yokushirō was the bane of the parent of someone whom I have a relation with. I only came here to help carry out the revenge. People might know me as a bandit and hate me, but I would never take

9 Ainu clothing. Often used in Kabuki to make someone look exotic and foreign.

4.9

someone's life without reason. We got our vengeance, so now I have no reason to stay in this land anymore. Nevertheless, just because you have a little bit of power, you wanted to take down me and my subordinates and came at us with a horde of men. How laughable! You made an enemy out of me, but I won't take the life of the likes of you. Consider yourself to have divine protection, both from the great shark and my yōjutsu!"

Jiraiya then pointed to a ship sailing far out to sea.

"Yonder is our main ship. It will already be twenty ri[10] away from Niigata before you can even blink. It would do you well to tell the local lord what happened. How I spared your life today, and that I am a man of virtue."

As he talked, a fast rowboat which was farther out to sea spotted them and approached. Jiraiya and the bandit boarded the other boat, and Shikaroku finally felt like he could breathe easy again.

He said to Jiraiya, "You truly are a great man unlike any other. Be it your virtue or your bravery, you are as gallant as the rumor says. I am both shocked and ashamed at myself for being so overwhelmed. You have my gratitude for sparing my life."

The boatmen all rejoiced. Jiraiya signaled the bandit with his eyes. The bandit understood the message and rowed the boat out to sea. After seeing them off, Shikaroku turned his boat towards Niigata and headed home. Jiraiya's boat made it to the main ship, which smoothly rowed

10 79 kilometers.

4.10

out to sea where it caught a favorable wind. With the three women, Jiraiya got on the tender boat and returned to his hideout in the Kurohime mountain.

The year had ended, welcoming springtime, and the Kurohime mountain was clad in the mist and colors of the season. The plum trees in full bloom, scattered among the pines on the cliffs of the familiar mountain, were a rare sight to see. The bush warblers of the valleys sang their first songs amongst the eaves, and inside, behind the shōji screens, Jiraiya enjoyed the sound. Together with him were Ayame and Tagane, and between them was an oriha game board, and the fight between the white and black pieces raged. Ekichi was sitting next to Jiraiya, reading 'The Cicada Shell' from the Tale of Genji, and the heated talking and noise from Ayame and Tagane's game was distracting.

(4.10)

Ekichi said, "Their game of oriha is like the 'The Cicada Shell' story, when Hikaru Genji had to do a ceremonial stop at the inn by Nakagawa River and saw the two ladies playing *igo.* One too pretty to even be able to play properly."

Jiraiya laughed and replied, "The younger one—Iyonosuke's pretty daughter—was too immodest, but the older one—her stepmother Utsusemi—was so gentle, it made prince Genji fall for her all over again."

When Tagane heard this, she put down the bamboo cup for the oriha dice. "I could swear I see Prince Genji right here and now," she said, and slid herself close to Jiraiya.

Ayame gave her a sharp look and snapped at her, "Your sweet and spoiled words do not hide your intentions. And you, oh strange Genji, giving two women such unseemly knowing looks!"

She grabbed the oriha board and flipped it, scattering the black and white pieces, erasing any sign of who was winning. Ekichi and Tagane knelt next to Ayame and quarreled.

Jiraiya stared at them and said, "For three young women in the spring of their lives to fight over something like this is shameful. Tagane, to the inner room. Chop-chop, Ekichi," and gave her a signal. She understood and took Tagane away. Ayame also left for her room, looking over her shoulder at Jiraiya and stomping on the tatami mats as she went.

In solitude, Jiraiya picked up the *Tale of Genji*. When he reached the 'Leaves of Wild Ginger' story, he sighed to himself.

"Ayame's jealousy is like the concubine Rokujō, whose vengeful *ikiryō* spirit possessed and tormented Lady Aoi no Ue. I only brought them here out of a sense of justice, but it seems I have given the women pointless concerns. Nothing could shame my father more than this," he said, while nodding away as dusk fell.

(4.11)

Ayame, who had gone to her room, locked herself in and wallowed in melancholy alone. The flames of her anger burned hot as she sat by the brazier in the light of the lantern and talked quietly to herself.

"I remember when Jiraiya came disguised as the young lord of the Sarashina family and I met him for the first time. I loved him so much that even after I learned he was the bandit Jiraiya, and even if he were to kidnap or kill me, I wouldn't hold a grudge against him. Do I not please you, Jiraiya? Morning and evening, Tagane never leaves your side. A woman will naturally get frustrated when treated like she isn't even there. She was the owner's daughter and should show some restraint. Making comparisons to Genji together with Ekichi, saying all those things right out in the open. I dare not think of what kind of things she says when she sleeps with the master. That little bitch, I won't let her get away with this."

Ayame puffed on her pipe and blew, and from within the wafting smoke, slithered a single, eerie snake. The snake was the incarnation of Ayame's jealousy, but she did not notice it. She exclaimed, "Oh how sleepy I am," and fell asleep right there on the spot.

The horror story of Ayame will continue in the next book. Open it and see what happens.

4.11

4.12

Part II

(4.12)
Jiraiya had something he needed to discuss with Tsuruhashiya Kinosuke and mulled over plans for setting out on a trip to visit him in the pleasure district in Ōiso in the Sagami province. He had gone to bed but was yet again having a sleepless night when Tagane entered the room.

"I know this is a stupid complaint to come with now," she started, "but even though my father was a stranger, I owed him for bringing me up. After you defeated him, I left my hometown to come here with you, and although I am happy that I did, my house has ceased to exist, and I cannot carry out mourning rites for my real parents. This has been weighing very heavily on my heart. The months I have spent with you have been truly wonderful, but lately, I have had a lot of troubles with Ayame. She wears her envy on her sleeve, and when there is no one else around, she says all kinds of unreasonable things. She gets angry over the slightest words and says such hateful things I wish I'd never heard." Tagane mumbled this last bit as tears welled up in her young maiden's eyes, and Jiraiya gave a sigh at her downhearted appearance.

He said, "Yokushirō, or Ganpachi as was his name, was the bane of Ekichi's father and I had an obligation to help her get her revenge. Concerning who will be the successor for Kumadeya, I have a plan, so you should not worry about it. About Ayame's recent bouts of envy, I know it is hard. I will think of some ideas to help give you peace of mind. For now, bear with it for a bit longer."

Without any wind in the room, the strings from the scented *kusudama* ball hanging on one of the pillars squirmed and took the shape of thin snakes. They raised their heads and laid their eyes on Tagane, getting ready to strike. Tagane threw herself into Jiraiya's lap with a scream, where she lay shaking. Jiraiya did not falter for a moment and drew his short sword to cut the snakes, but when he looked closer, the snakes had vanished and the kusudama was back to normal. This made Jiraiya suspicious, so he wanted to send Tagane to her room, but she was in such a state of shock that her face was pale, and her legs shook. When he saw Tagane could not stand, Jiraiya called Ekichi and told her what happened. Jiraiya told her to take care of Tagane, and Ekichi knew what to do. She took Tagane to her room while consoling her. Jiraiya then returned to his bedchamber.

(4.13)
After this night, Tagane became gravely ill, and every day her suffering worsened. She was delirious, crying out, "Snakes! Snakes are crawling at my pillow! Chase them away, please!"

Ekichi, who stayed by the young woman's side taking care of her, told Jiraiya what Tagane cried, but he could not find any snakes. All he could do was worry, for there was nothing that could be done.

Ayame did not care at all for visiting Tagane on her sickbed, but she assumed Jiraiya and Ekichi would think badly of her if she didn't. So,

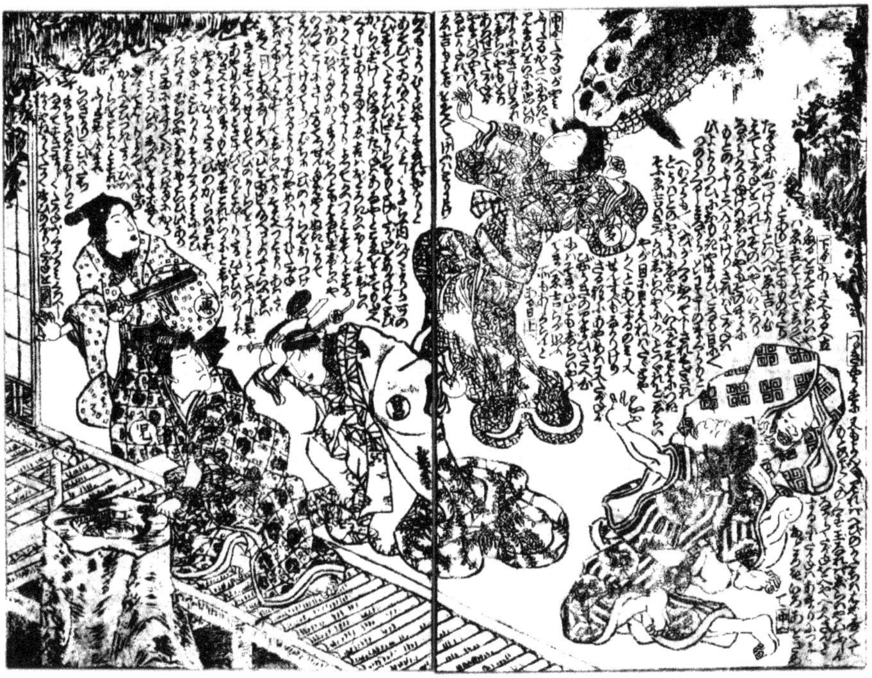

4.13

one day, she said she wanted to visit Tagane. Because it was so unexpectedly kind of her, Jiraiya joined her.

As they discussed Tagane's illness, Ekichi also joined the conversation. "She looks like she is in a much better state today than usual, so you can see each other for a bit."

As the three talked, out from nowhere slithered a snake. It raised its head and targeted Tagane, who shrieked and writhed in pain. Shocked, Ekichi went to help her. Jiraiya ran over and caught the snake. He tried to throw it away, but it wrapped itself around his arm and would not let go. Furious, Jiraiya took out the steel fan from his belt and went to the washbasin in the garden where he pinned down the snake's head.

"It's dangerous! Let the snake escape, don't do this!" cried Ayame in a panic next to Jiraiya, not looking back at the suffering Tagane.

But Jiraiya did not hear her, and struck the snake on the head with his steel fan. When he did this, for some mysterious reason, Ayame cried out. Blood came from her forehead, and she fainted while trying to staunch it. Confounded, Jiraiya struck the snake again with his fan, severing its head. The head flew at Tagane and bit down on her black hair. Jiraiya was stunned. First Ayame and now this. Jiraiya cast off the body of the snake still wrapped around his arm and ran to Tagane to pull off the snake head latched on to her hair. But when he tried this, the head, which had so far been small, inexplicably grew to the size of a terrible, enormous python. While biting down on her hair, it danced around in the air, floating up under the rafters, hoisting up Tagane. The

4.14

sight frightened Ekichi so much that she threw herself to the ground and did not dare to look. Standing tall, Jiraiya drew his sword and held it up, glaring at the great serpent's head. Intimidated by his courage, the head dropped Tagane on the tatami mats and vanished.

(4.14)

At this point, several underlings came in and aided Tagane and Ekichi. When the two women came back to their senses, Jiraiya ordered his men to wake Ayame and give her some medicine. When she regained some of her consciousness, Ekichi took care of her and brought her to her room. Jiraiya, rattled by all the strange occurrences, first consoled Tagane, and then brought her to her chamber where he put her to bed. As the day grew into evening, Jiraiya retired to his room and read a book on military tactics by the light of a lantern, with the late hour going unnoticed.

Apropos, the reason why Ayame's forehead bled when Jiraiya struck the snake on the head, and the reason why the tiny snake's head became that of a great serpent, lay in Jiraiya's past. It was the hateful grudge of the great serpent Jiraiya had shot with his arquebus. The serpent had previously possessed Yashagorō and now entered Ayame's jealous heart, showing Jiraiya all these unnerving sights.

Around this time, Ayame suffered from the cut on her forehead and developed a terrible fever. She ran around the house like a madwoman, cursing at anyone she saw. When she met Ekichi, she insulted her, and then went to torment Tagane, bedridden with her illness. Ayame clawed

4.15

at Tagane and pulled her up. Tagane panicked and tried to shake Ayame off to no avail. Tagane called out, and many underlings came running to pull Ayame from her. But she thrashed and kicked fiercely, not letting any of them get near her.

(4.15)

"I have always thought you were infuriating, Tagane. And now I will torture you to my heart's content and make you suffer!" Ayame cursed, as her eyebrows stood on end and her hair whipped around. Her eyes were terrifying, and her mouth split open at the corners, making her spew blood. She looked so furious that even a man as wild as an *oni* would not dare to come near her.

Unconsciously, Tagane howled, like a bush warbler panicking when faced with a snake. Jiraiya, who was alone in a parlor room deeper in the house, was surprised by the commotion and ran to see what was happening. Seeing Ayame's form, his head filled with anger, and he drew his sword with ten times the courage as he normally did. When he got near, Ayame scowled at him over her shoulder.

"Now see what you get for being so cold and not wanting to lie with me!" she bellowed, and sank her teeth into Tagane's throat. She then pointed at the suffering Tagane and opened her blood-soaked mouth in cackling laughter. The sight was so terrible to behold that most would look away, but Jiraiya was not in the least bit afraid. He lunged at Ayame, grabbed hold of the hair on top of her head, and drove his sword through her torso.

Ayame gave a startled yelp at the excruciating pain, but did not let go of Tagane's body even while falling over. Jiraiya adjusted his grip on the sword and decapitated Ayame. When he lowered his sword, the mountain rumbled, and the earth shook. A great torrent of wind and rain came like poles of *shino* bamboo and flying pebbles. Then, the hair on Ayame's head bundled up and stretched like a long rope, and the head flew into the sky in a spiraling pattern. The black hair was like a large snake, and in the center was Ayame's head with its mouth open and the tongue sticking out. Jiraiya did not blink. Like a wheel, the head spun and flew around in the clouds. Jiraiya, not in the least disconcerted by the horror of Ayame's dying will, kicked her body into the valley below and again stared fixedly at the skies.

(4.16)

At the same time, on the hillside opposite from Jiraiya's fortress, a shinobi sat perched on one of the upper branches of a big pine tree. Clad in black and using a grappling hook, he had climbed the tree before the events in Jiraiya's fortress occurred. Using a bandit's lantern, he observed everything. After the skirmish concluded, the shinobi hid himself deep between the branches of the pine tree. The mountain wind cleared the clouds and the rain, and Ayame's ghostly head disappeared. Jiraiya stood tall. Without changing his expression, he lowered his blade and sheathed it.

In silence he found Tagane's dead body and said, "Oh this poor girl. I killed her father for his wickedness, and because of me she lost her home. Today she met an unnatural and untimely death. Was this her fate in life? Woe to have such a pitiful destiny!"

Jiraiya chanted the name of the Buddha as tears filled his eyes, and he wallowed in sorrow despite himself. Then he called his underlings, told them to take care of Tagane's body, and gave other various orders. Finally, he withdrew to his private parlor.

When the ridges of the mountains to the east turned white, Jiraiya woke and ate a breakfast he had prepared the night before. He was at the washbasin rinsing his mouth when Ekichi came and said, "I have made my preparations and the men have all scattered, so you can rest easy."

"You should also get going already," said Jiraiya with a smile.

Ekichi answered with a short "Yes," and departed.

From out of nowhere, and without a sound, the shinobi from earlier snuck up on Jiraiya and grappled him. He struggled with the shinobi and dragged him along, taking one step after another towards his katana holder. Jiraiya grabbed a katana, but the shinobi saw an opening and used the tip of the scabbard on his wakizashi short sword to hit the hand attempting to draw the katana. Jiraiya slipped and staggered, but took a step and extended his arm, using the momentum to hit the shinobi on the ribs. With the wind knocked out of him, the shinobi toppled, landing on the floor with a thud.

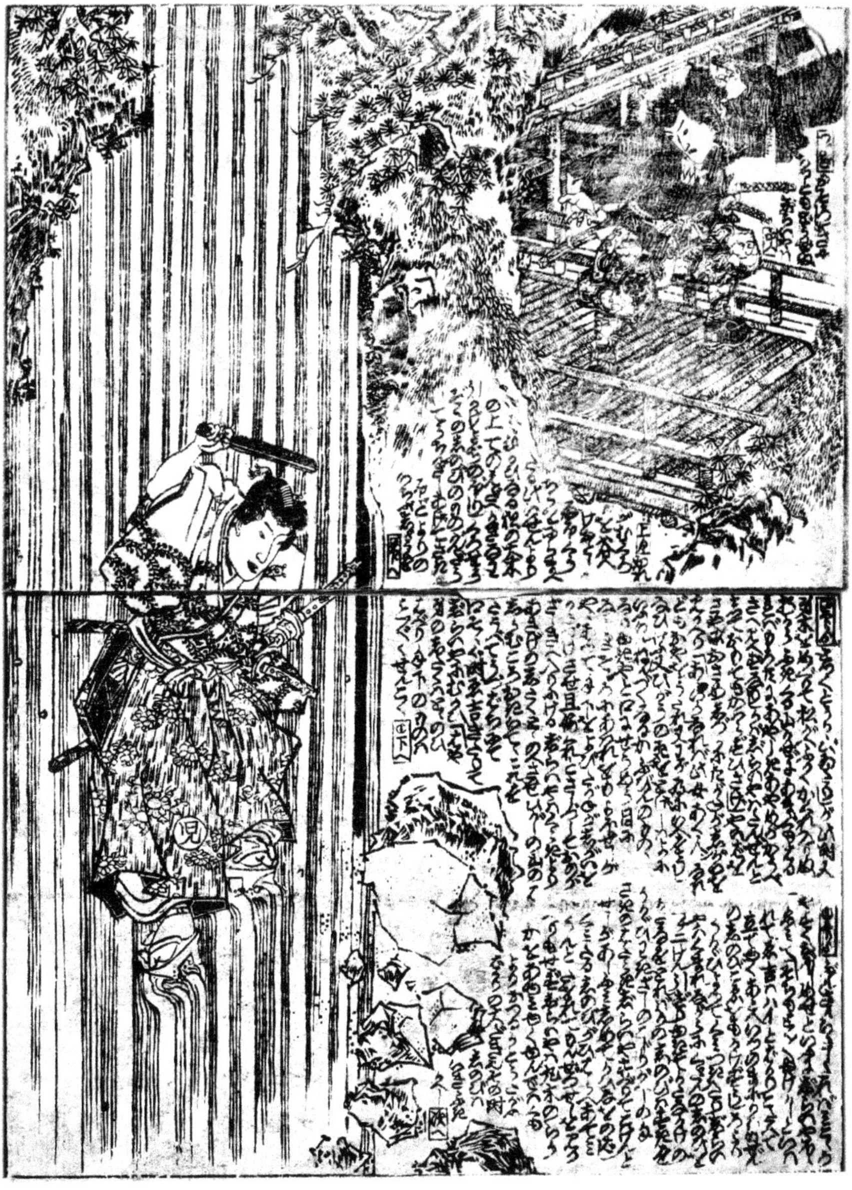

4.16

Without looking back, Jiraiya went down the log walkway, to the left of which was a great waterfall so big it looked like it might have been falling from the clouds. The shinobi caught his breath again and chased after Jiraiya, who calmly leapt sideways off the walkway and into the waterfall. The shinobi grabbed the stone washbasin next to him and hoisted it up above his head, took aim, and hurled it at Jiraiya.

4.17

(4.17)

What happened next was most uncanny. Jiraiya stopped his descent, standing mid-air in the waterfall. He looked up, pulled out his steel fan, and hit the washbasin falling towards his head with a loud crack, smashing it to tiny pieces which went flying in all directions. The waterfall crashed against the rocks and sent its roar throughout the mountains, and Jiraiya then rode it down, disappearing without a trace into the faraway valley tens of *také* below.[11] This was a display of Jiraiya's mystical yōjutsu.

The shinobi will appear again in book five, where we will learn more about his identity.

When Jiraiya reached the bottom of the waterfall, Ekichi was already waiting for him. At some point she had clad herself in the travel yukata of Tsuyaginu, and carried a bamboo cane and a small, woven straw hat. Jiraiya also changed out of his conspicuous clothes, covered his head with a scarf, and strapped his travel straw hat on his shoulders. He put his short wakizashi on his hip, and in high spirits, wrapped the strings of his straw sandals around his deep blue gaiters. Under the carefree spring sky, the two looked at each other and set out, leaving the road to the Koshi region[12] behind them, setting their hearts on the road crossing the misty mountains to Shinano.

11 1 také = 3.03 meters.

12 West coast. During Edo consisted of Echizen, Etchū, Echigo, Noto and Kaga.

4.18

Now the story takes us back to Niigata. Previously, following the turmoil at the Kumadeya house, the sheriff of Lord Nagao, Yakama Shikarokurō, had come to capture the bandit Jiraiya. To do this, he had sent many small boats with pursuers. With his ship encircled, Jiraiya used his yōjutsu to conjure an enormous shark, which capsized the boats of Shikaroku's comrades. But when Shikaroku himself was in danger of being sunk to the bottom of the sea like his men, Jiraiya had inexplicably saved him.

(4.18)

Confused, Shikaroku returned to his mansion, but because he thought it would not benefit himself if his master, Lord Nagao, knew about it, he kept it a strict secret, making even his subordinates keep quiet.

However, because Yokushirō had secretly reported that a traveler staying at the Kumadeya house was from Nezumi-no-shuku in Sarashina in Shinano, the same village and land as the bandit Jiraiya, Shikaroku captured the traveler under suspicion of being in cahoots with Jiraiya. He had been locked up securely in a cage, but one day Shikaroku pulled him out for questioning.

"There is no doubt you are together with the bandit leader Jiraiya. Stop resisting and confess. Otherwise I will torture you and make you suffer," said Shikaroku, eyes wide with anger.

"As I already said the other day, that bandit coming here has brought me nothing but misery. All because I happen to be from the same village as him and was visiting the Kumadeya house. It does not matter how many times you ask; I do not know this *Jiraiya* person," replied the traveler.

Shikaroku did not listen to his words and only said in a demeaning tone, "There are plenty of people in the villages I govern who I do not even know the names of, and it is not as if you are the head of Nezumi-no-shuku in Sarashina in Shinano. But I have people to find out what your name and background is, so there is no need to ask you about this anymore. For now, maybe I should give you all the water you could ever possibly drink."

Not showing any fear of Shikaroku's threats, the traveler, who was in fact Fukitarō, answered, "Even in small villages there are many people. Many, due to their employment, go to other towns and lands and go to Kyōto and Kamakura for trade. Among them are bound to be plenty who use the name Jiraiya and commit banditry. Please, you must take this into consideration."

Despite Fukitarō's words being proper and compelling, Shikaroku did not lend him any ear. "We'll see how it all is once I make you confess. Now get going!" he commanded his underlings, who stripped Fukitarō naked. They mercilessly tied him to a ladder and placed it on the ground so he faced the sky. They put water-filled pails next to him, and as Shikaroku watched, two underlings fetched frayed bamboo sticks and positioned themselves at Fukitarō's sides. In turns, they beat Fukitarō and poured water from the pails down his mouth.

(4.19)

After a while, whenever Fukitarō would thrash from pain, they poured water all over his eyes, nose, and mouth, making it impossible for him to breathe. He suffered so much it was unbearable to watch. When his stomach was swollen like a taiko drum, he finally stopped breathing. At that point, Shikaroku stopped his men, wanting to torture Fukitarō again the next day. They untied Fukitarō from the ladder, forced him to throw up all the water, and gave him some medicine. When he started breathing again, they stood him up and took him back to the cage. They tortured him repeatedly in this fashion, but Fukitarō had committed no crime, thus had nothing to confess.

Now the story takes us back to Nezumi-no-shuku in Sarashina in Shinano, where six years prior, the rich village headman, Mochimaru Fukiemon, had passed away with his wife following shortly after. Fukitarō had become the head of the house, but due to a youthful mistake, he had gone towards Echigo on business and met with the misfortune of being locked in Sheriff Shikaroku's prison. Such, at least, was the report from the people who were with him. Following Fukiemon's passing, Fukitarō's younger sister Osachi married Inesaku, her father's faithful right-hand man over many years, and they moved into their own house. But when Inesaku heard what had befallen Fukitarō, he headed for Echigo to try and save him. However,

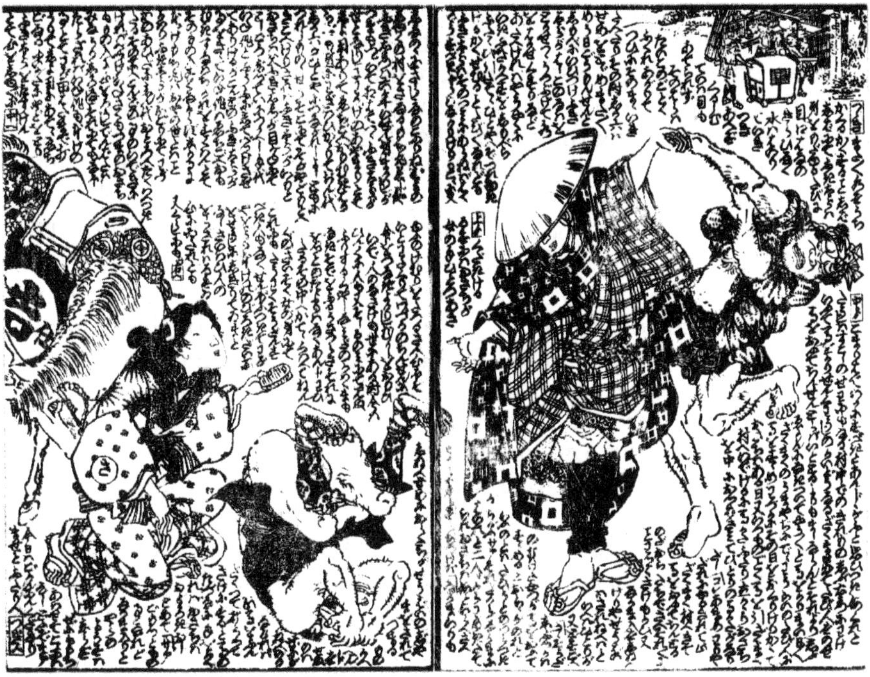

4.19

the expenses from this were not insignificant. Unlike his parents, Fukitarō led an extravagant lifestyle. And in a short time, the family fortune diminished, running out entirely when he was captured by Shikaroku. Inesaku and his wife Osachi were worried sick, so they sold all their fields to raise money, but it still did not suffice. Inesaku then sold the fields of the head household as well to pay for various expenses and to get lodging in Niigata in Echigo to save Fukitarō. It broke his heart in many ways to do this.

Osachi was left alone and disheartened, and took care of the house. In the morning and evening, when smoke rose from the kitchens, she spun cotton strings to make a bit of money to live by. She reminisced about a time when all was still good. Back when people had sympathy. Now, people slandered her for being impoverished and pretended not to see her. The bitter tears she cried into her sleeve were all but dried up, and on top of it all, she had no husband to rely on. To add to her miserable and worried state, she also had to pay land taxes, and being a woman, she was perplexed and had no one to ask for advice. In the end, she had to sell her house and move back into the house of the main family. There, she had put up shōji screens in the spacious kitchen, making a living space where she could be when no one was around. But when she faced problems with her living situation again, she worried about what to do and soon thought of a plan.

"There is a shrewd businessman in town, Shibuemon, whom I can probably rely on a little. I will explain the situation and borrow a horse from him, and use it to carry travelers on the road from Zakumaku[13] to the Zenkōji Temple. It will certainly be better than spinning thread."

Then she wept to Shibuemon, who eventually let her borrow a horse. Every day afterwards, she went on the post station road, picking up travelers and taking them along. And so, her days went by.

On a day like all others, as Osachi set out for Zakumaku Village while pulling the horse, two packhorse drivers were blocking the middle of the road. They boxed her in and one of the drivers said, "Hey, woman! Who said you could take your horse here to Zakumaku Village and charge people money? If you don't buy us saké and drink with us and become a part of our crew, we won't let you do no business here!"

Then the other one added, "Yeah, that's right! And if we have a pretty and clever little thing like you inviting people to ride, people will have a different look on their faces when we tell them to get on our horses. So, you should join up with us already."

Osachi knew not what to do or say and fidgeted in place.

The first one said, "Is the reason you don't want to join our crew because you want to get in the way of our business, woman? Or aren't you answering because you don't have any cash? If that be the case, then I'll take your horse and sell it for saké!" He grabbed the reins of the horse, startling Osachi, who pushed him.

"You are absolutely right, but I don't know anything about joining crews and I do not bring money with me. So please, just today, let me go," she said while rubbing her hands together apologetically.

(4.20)

The horse driver took advantage of the situation. "Do you think asking us to excuse you will settle this? Now, you little thief, come with us! We'll take you to where the rest of our crew is, and then beat you!"

As the two grabbed her arms to pull her with them, there was a traveler concealed by a big straw hat, who had parked his palanquin at a tea house a bit away from the scene, where he was resting. He dashed to the incident and flung the two horse drivers to the ground. They brushed off the pain and encircled the traveler from both sides.

"I don't know who you are, traveler, but you'll regret having this thieving woman's back!" one yelled before charging. They moved faster than the traveler could manage to pull out the stick he carried for self-defense. Instead, he pivoted, grabbed the dominant arm of one of the men, twisting it upwards, and kicked over the other, stepping on him and holding him down. The traveler then rummaged inside his breast pocket to retrieve two golden koban coins.

"Here is your membership fee," he said, and scattered the money on the road.

Osachi, astounded by the traveler, clasped her hands together and said, "You have not only saved me from my predicament, but you have also given all this money. I don't even know what you look like and yet you have suffered this loss on my behalf. The gods will surely frown upon me for this. I am certain the matter would have been settled if these

13 Present day Jakumaku.

4.20

two dragged me away with them and had their way with me. Take your money and put it away. And then hurry and get away from here. If you stay, more trouble is sure to come your way."

Without as much as glancing at Osachi, the traveler grimaced at the two horse drivers. "Take your money and get going!" he demanded, and pushed away the arm he was twisting and kicked the man he had been stepping on. Disgruntled, the two men picked up the two koban.

"Consider this as letting you off easy!" one yelled over his shoulder as the two fled as fast as they could.

After seeing them off, the traveler returned to the tea house. "We have spent too much time here. Get the palanquin ready!" he said, and fixed his clothes and climbed into his palanquin. Osachi thanked him while pulling on the hem of her kimono to straighten it, and the departing traveler waved.

Osachi fell to her knees and prayed in his direction. "There are all kinds of people in the world, and there are many travelers, but only few who would give out money and save a perfect stranger from trouble, and then not even listen to their words of gratitude. I wonder what land he hails from. He arrived in the nick of time, and I don't even know his name. If only I had at least seen his face, I might have been able to find him later. Curse me and my lack of wits!"

Osachi's hair was in total disarray because her wooden comb had come out and fallen to the ground during the commotion. She picked it back up and gathered her hair so it looked like a blooming flower, making

4.21

her look like she was not someone who should be making a living by driving a horse. Osachi then pulled herself together and continued taking travelers on the horse. She didn't make much money, so she chose to call it a day and went home early.

(4.21)

The next day, Osachi was preparing to take the horse to the road like usual, when Aogaki Shibuemon, the wealthy man who only recently moved to town, came by. Without reservation, he walked right into the house, sat down as he pleased, and spoke at Osachi.

"Today I don't want to hear any more of your excuses, so I have no intention of letting you open your mouth. All this time you have been loitering around, saying 'village headman this' and 'village headman that,' but there is not even a scent of money on you! You have a pot and a teakettle, don't you? Sell them and your tooth-blackener too while you're at it!

"Your older brother is a self-conceited, sniveling child who only became the owner of the head family's house because the master died. He let you into the house because he felt sorry for you, and I exchanged what little fields you had for money. But all that is left now is a dilapidated house about to fall over and the land it stands on.

"Out of pity I lent you some money, since no one else in this entire village would help you. But now, Osachi, I will have you leave this place! Your bills are long overdue, so I won't listen to any complaining. Get going as fast as you can. I want you out before noon!"

He then heaped verbal abuse at her so terrible no one should wish to hear it. He was absolutely detestable, and nothing would be enough to stop his tirade. There was nothing Osachi could do, so she swallowed her tears, bowed with her hands on the floor, and replied politely.

"Indeed it is as you say, but this house serves the important function of being the home of the village headman, and even if I were to hand it over to you, I would have no explanation for my brother or my husband. Inesaku will most likely return sometime this month. Please, give me a little more time."

Shibuemon heard half of her words and looked at her with gaping eyes, and then shouted, "Why would I wait for this Inesaku, or whatever, to come back? It is already long past the due date. It says right here at the top of our contract that if you go past the due date, I can do whatever I want! And not only that, but you also borrowed a horse with which you used to make money every day. I have half a mind to demand that money as well now!"

Osachi bawled. Shibuemon grabbed her hand and dragged her up. Annoyed, he said, "You stubborn wench! If you won't do as I say and leave this house on your own, I'll throw you out myself if I have to!"

A pair of samurai clad in travel clothes appeared from the front door. One put a white wooden tray table, filled with a pile of silken fabrics, on the collapsing entry step leading up from the kitchen. Then he stepped out of the way and the other samurai took his place, holding another white tray with rolls of gold-brocaded satin damask, stacked like Mount Fuji. The ends of the rolled-up *obi* fabric revealed a deep crimson fabric inside. He put the tray down next to the other one and stepped outside the house. Shibuemon was flabbergasted and let go of Osachi's hand, gawking at the two trays.

Osachi, equally surprised, muttered towards the front door, "This gift surely cannot be for me. I cannot accept this."

(4.22)

Then one of the samurai ran inside and said, "This is without a doubt Mochimaru Fukiemon's house. Our master will now make his entrance."

Not a moment passed before a magnificent and imposing samurai appeared. He wore a *haori* coat for traveling, and carried a set of swords with golden inlay.

"Pardon me," he said, as he stepped in leisurely and went to the parlor room. Osachi and Shibuemon jumped after him, falling over each other with worried faces as they tried to see who he was.

4.22

To be continued...

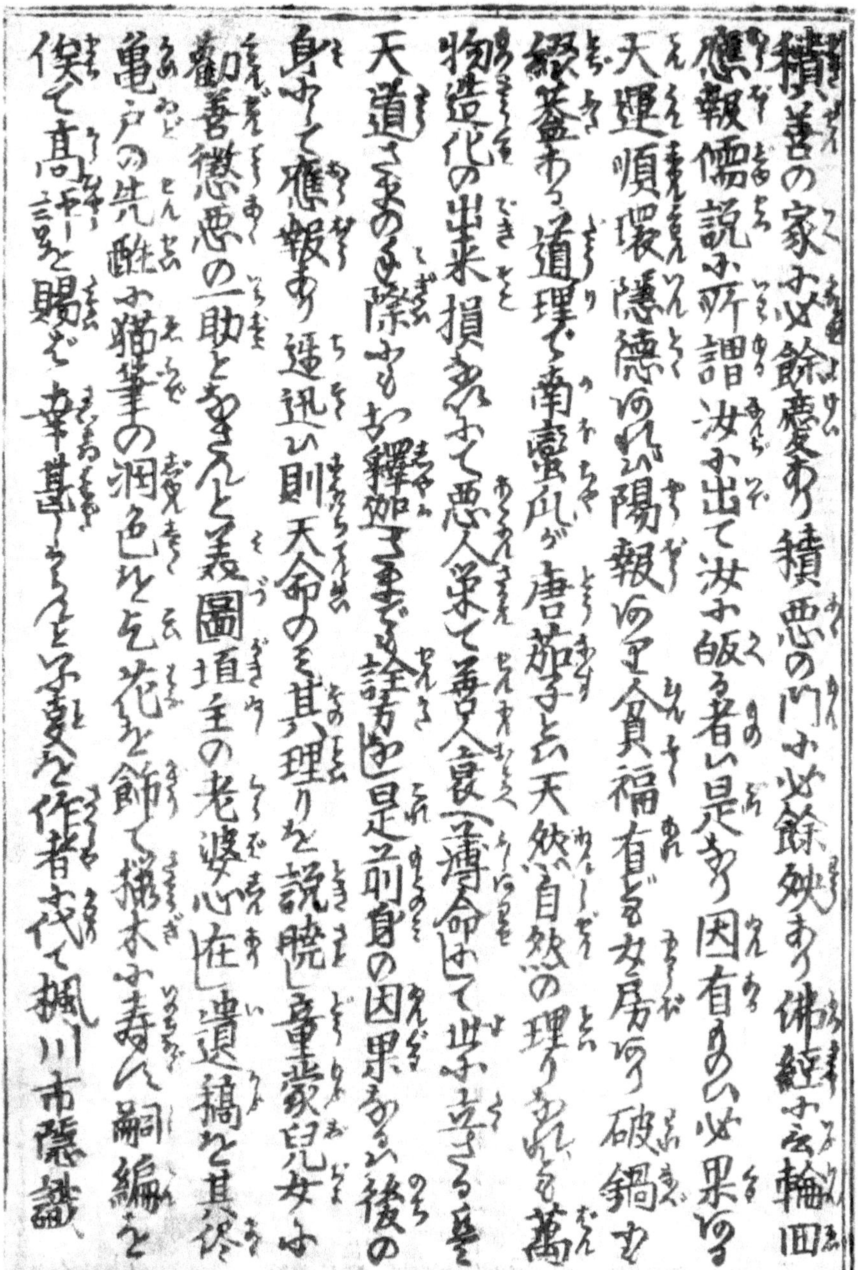
積善の家に必餘慶あり 積悪の門に必餘殃あり 佛經に云輪回應報儒說に所謂汝に出て汝に皈る者は是なり 因有ものは必果あり 天運循環 隱德あれば陽報あり 貧福有ども女房あり 破鍋にも綴蓋あるの道理 南齋氏が唐茄子と云 天然自然の理りなれば萬物造化の出来損なふて悪人栄て善人衰 薄命にして世に立ざる是天道さまのお際にもお釋迦さまでも詮方なし 是前身の因果なれば後の身にて應報あり 遲速は則天命のみ 其理りを說曉し童蒙兒女に勸善懲悪の一助となさんと 義圖直主の老婆心 在遺稿を其終亀戸の先醒に猶筆の潤色を乞 花を飾て梓木に壽んし 嗣編を俟て高評を賜ぞ 幸甚ならんと 不文を作者に代て 楓川市隱識

5.1

Book 5

Mister Kanwatei has told us the story of how, long ago, there was a bandit named Jiraiya. This book has taken that name and written it 児雷也, but it is a very different story. Since it was first published, the series has been popular beyond what was hoped for. So, year after year it has been published, and now we have reached the fifth book. Probably the most important reason why it has had such success, is because professor Mizugaki has kept coming up with new and bizarre ideas. Thus, in this fifth book, a story of the way of karma shall be told to all the ignorant boys and girls, to teach them that good is rewarded and evil is punished. It is this publishing house's most sincere prayer that it lives up to expectations and previous volumes.

Respectfully,
Kansendō publishing house

Kōka 3 (1845)
Story by Mizugaki Egao
Art by Utagawa Toyokuni III

5.2

The mountain dweller, Iwane no Gakeroku.
The fortuneteller Takarako, sprinkling riches.
Okowa the demon hag.

5·3

Part I

(5·3)
And so, our story continues!

Osachi, the sister of Mochimaru Fukitarō of Nezumi-no-shuku in Shinano, had borrowed money from Shibuemon after her husband, Inesaku, had gone to Echigo. When Shibuemon came to demand his money back, samurai came to the house to announce an arrival, and they placed gift after gift on the kitchen step. Shibuemon and especially Osachi were astounded by the presents. The samurai opened the outside door, and an unusually outstanding warrior entered. Without further thought, Shibuemon and Osachi cleared the parlor room and put their hands on the floor. The warrior smiled, and without delay grabbed Osachi's hand, leading her back to the parlor room. Osachi, still wary and flustered, tried to stand, but the warrior stopped her.

"Come now, Osachi-dono. There is no need to stand on formality. Have you forgotten me? It is I, Hatasaku's son, Tarō. The one whom the Mochimarus took such good care of. I found employment with a samurai family in Kamakura and have had more success than I could have ever imagined. I wanted to visit and see how you were doing earlier, but my work offers me no free time. I finally managed to get some time, which is why I have come here today to see you. How is Fukitarō? Is he in good health?"

5.4

After the initial surprise subsided, Osachi said, "After our parents died, Fukitarō inherited everything. But because of his poor conduct, as you can see, the fortune is gone, and the house is dilapidated. But your fortunes sure have change—"

Standing upright with a jolt, Shibuemon interrupted, "Hey mister samurai, and you too, Osachi. If you have something to discuss, do it outside. This house is mine now. I've brought laborers who are going to tear this place down."

Over his shoulder, Jiraiya called out, stopping Shibuemon in his tracks. "I have been listening outside for a while now, so I know what is going on," he said, reaching into his belly band and pulling out fifty-one *ryō* in gold coin. He tossed it to Shibuemon, saying, "Now get out of here!" and glowered at him.

(5.4)

Shibuemon, eyes bulging with fear, collected the money, stepped down to the garden, and hurried to leave. But with a swift hand, Jiraiya threw a shuriken that went clean through Shibuemon's throat, who fell to the ground with a yelp. On Jiraiya's orders, the two samurai handed the money back to Jiraiya. Then they threw the body into an old well there in the garden.

"What are you—" Osachi exclaimed in disbelief.

Jiraiya interrupted her, "He was a wicked rat. Taking care of him like this was more an act of charity than anything else. Now, about what happened to you. Looking at the state of your solitary life in this wretched abode, I suppose it would be hard for you to talk about. Where has Fukitarō gone? I wish to meet him."

Osachi considered what to say. Then she returned the gifts on the step to Jiraiya, and with a trembling voice she said, "You might not think people know this, but there is a bandit who I believe goes by the name of Jiraiya from Nezumi-no-shuku in Shinano. They are hunting for him with wanted posters. About my brother, he went to Niigata in Echigo on business three months ago. Due to youthful indiscretion, he went to the whorehouse called Kumadeya in Niigata for a single night. At the same time, that Jiraiya character came there dressed as the young lord of Shinano. Because of the drinking and merrymaking, they lowered their guard, and Jiraiya kidnapped two prostitutes known as the mother and daughter of Kumadeya and disappeared. Fukitarō-dono was staying there and by mistake came under suspicion for being involved. When they verified where he is from, and told Sheriff Yakama-dono that he is from the birthplace of Jiraiya, the sheriff arrested him and put him in jail for interrogation.

"When I heard of this from my husband Inesaku, I fell to the ground in tears. Inesaku could not bear to see me like that, so he sold our fields and used the money to set out for Echigo and save Fukitarō-dono. That was last year, and it has taken so long that all the money has dried up. But the letters asking for money keep coming. Being a woman, I worried for him, so I sold all my kimonos and tools and sent a bit of money, but everyday life has become difficult, so I became a horse driver.

"My hardships have been many, like pearls on a string, and it is all thanks to that bandit Jiraiya's doing! I hate his poster and your face is the spitting image of it. Returning a present in anger might be the shallow act of a woman, but for you, it does not seem like such an evil action. If you had known of filial piety in the depths of your heart from when you were a child..."

As she said this, she slipped out a hidden dagger and lunged at Jiraiya to stab him. He grabbed her arm and pushed her back, then dodged as she came at him again. Jiraiya grabbed his two swords and threw them on the ground.

"Please, wait a moment! I will not resist you, Osachi-dono. This is the first I hear of your brother, and although I did not do this myself, something went wrong and now he suffers in prison because of me. You are completely in your right to be furious with me, but there is a good reason why I became a bandit. Only the gods could have known Fuki-dono was staying at Kumadeya on the night I caused a commotion. And on the same floor as me even. Please, still your anger and listen. I have a plan to save Fukitarō-dono."

Osachi finally put away her dagger and sat. Jiraiya regained his composure and said, "I was on my way to take care of some business in Sagami, but I will leave that for now and head to Echigo. Rest assured, Osachi-dono, I have already come up with a device to save Fukitarō-dono. I will leave here tomorrow and within a few days there will be good news."

Upon hearing this, Osachi's face softened, and she said, "I will gladly await to hear how you can take this disaster, which you gave us in return for our kindness, and turn it into gratitude."

Jiraiya only listened with half an ear as he called over his page and told him, "Leave the palanquin here and go back out on the road. I will call you in a bit to come back." The page understood and left with the other people.

Then Jiraiya spoke to Osachi. "I came here to this village yesterday, and amid the hustle and bustle on Zakumaku Road, I saw a horse-driving woman being harassed by two other horse drivers. I stepped in and gave them money and took care of the situation, but to my surprise it was you, Osachi-dono. To see you in such a state brought tears to my eyes and I had to hide them in my sleeve as I said farewell."

Taken aback, Osachi replied, "It was you who saved me yesterday? I could not tell who you were because you were wearing a travel hat. What about your little sister Miyuki? Have you found out where she is, or haven't you met her yet? Please tell me how she is doing."

Going to Echigo weighed heavily on Jiraiya's mind, and being asked this question, he thought it would take too much of his time if he had to set up a meeting with Miyuki. Therefore, he kept it a secret and cleverly avoided the subject.

(5.5)

"Although I wish I could tell you, I have not found out where she is yet. I was heading for Ōiso in Sagami because I have a small lead there," he said and then changed the topic. "About your parents, it is regrettable that they have already passed and that I cannot meet them. Also, concerning what happened to Shibuemon here, please do not report it to the authorities."

As he said this, Jiraiya's men came around the front with the palanquin. Then Jiraiya stood and turned to Osachi. "My business in Echigo is urgent, so I must take my leave now and go. I know it is disheartening, but for now, wait for a bit."

After saying these words of comfort, Jiraiya hustled into the garden. Osachi followed him as far as the veranda, where she bowed in gratitude. Jiraiya then entered the palanquin and departed with his men.

Later that same day, Jiraiya wanted to see Mount Kyōdai which was in the same area, so he climbed it and met with Tsuyaginu at the summit. He told her how the Mochimarus had passed away, how Osachi had married Inesaku, and how they had made their own family. He also told her how Fukitarō had gone to Echigo, stayed at Kumadeya, and then been thrown in prison. When Tsuyaginu heard this, she wept at the downfall of the Mochimaru house and the wretched fate that had befallen Fukitarō and Osachi.

Jiraiya had Tsuyaginu assume the guise of a young pilgrim again and had four or five of his bandits disguise themselves. Some as pilgrims heading for the Konpira Shrine, some as traveling samurai or couriers. He ordered them to escort Tsuyaginu while staying out of sight, and then sent them on their way on the Nakasendō Road towards Ōiso in Sagami.

5·5

Reassured, Jiraiya commanded his remaining men to go to Niigata ahead of him and seek news about Fukitarō, promising he himself would come later. He donned a straw hat, hiding his face, and set out towards Niigata alone.

On the second day of his journey, Jiraiya entered Echigo Road as the sun set, but he was late in finding any lodging, so walked on, worried about what to do. That was when he saw an old *torii* gate next to the road. Delighted, he said, "There is bound to be a wayside shrine here where I can spend the night."

He passed through the torii gate and came upon a long stone staircase. After he climbed the many steps, he saw a singular abode for the shrine's kami. The cedar trees around the shrine were close together, leaving no gaps between them, and the sun would disappear any moment, making it dark like midnight. Jiraiya did not know what kami resided there and could not see inside the shrine, but he paid his respects and then relaxed on the old porch, where he was struck with a severe cramp. The pain felt like being impaled. Even for the gallant Jiraiya, there was nothing that could be done, so he agonized and gritted his teeth.

(5.6)

A large man who looked like a tree cutter came before the altar of the kami. He carried a great battle axe and wore a mountain scarf made from wisteria vines draped around his neck. He saw Jiraiya suffering from the cramp and came closer.

5.6

"My name is Iwane no Gakeroku, and I live at the foot of this mountain. It is so dark that I cannot see your face, but I can tell you are suffering from a sudden illness. I have strong medicine with me. Try some." He handed over a medicine box, which Jiraiya took and grabbed some medicine from.

"Nothing works better against the pain from a strong cramp than good medicine," Jiraiya said, and took the remedy. The mountain dweller rubbed Jiraiya's back. He eventually recovered from his cramp and returned to normal.

Jiraiya thanked the mountain dweller profusely, but the dweller laughed. "The worst thing to happen for a traveler is to have an accident in a place like this. And it is so dark now I can't even see who I'm talking to."

(5.7)

He arose and fumbled around for some dry sticks, and with flint and steel lit a fire. The fire lit up everything like it was the middle of day. This was when they first saw each other's faces, and both tilted their heads, feeling like they had met somewhere before. The mountain dweller remembered something, held up the medicine box, and looked at Jiraiya.

"I have a story that is very much like this situation we are in now. Some time ago, I fell to ruin and was a mountain outcast. Back then, just like you with your cramp, I was writhing in pain and was about to die, when a magnificent samurai passed by. I thought he might have

5.7

been a warrior from a noble family from the capital, but no, he was apparently a bandit leader. He disciplined his underlings for mocking me and gave me this medicine box. The medicine was extremely effective, and the following sound of gunpowder in my ear snapped me back to my senses."

Jiraiya slapped his thigh and said, "And you probably reacted in a way completely unfit for an untouchable hinin. And would you look at that, the medicine box has a *netsuke* toggle in the shape of a toad. And there's a dragon flying over Mount Fuji gilded into the lacquer work. The same way I would like it."

The mountain dweller said, "And here I have finally once again met that skilled marksman from Mount Myōkō. The one who fought the toad's shooter and fell off the wisteria bridge into the frothing waves—Jiraiya, what a rare event this is!" While he said this, he grabbed the handle of his axe and edged closer.

Jiraiya, not the least bit flustered, said, "Ah, so you are the trickster who disguised himself as a beast, and later in the spring infiltrated my mountain fortress using a rope hook to see what was going on inside!"

"Where I saw the brave young man, who did not falter at the malevolent visage of the head, consumed with jealousy. Because I heard the villain I was looking for had become a mountain bandit, I climbed Mount Kurokami and was disheartened when I didn't find him there. Nonetheless, I managed to catch him elsewhere, but he broke free from my grasp and jumped sideways into a waterfall."

"And with the ability to crush even stone," added Jiraiya.

"Because of his magical steel fan, he did not drown in the water," said Gakeroku.

Jiraiya boasted at the top of his lungs, "Nor does fire burn him, and he can go wherever he wants under heaven! For *you* to try to catch *me*, Jiraiya, is nothing short of ridiculous. Compared to me, you might as well be a mere toddler!"

This sent Gakeroku into a furious rage. "Then have a taste of my battle axe!" he bellowed, and attacked with ferocious energy. But Jiraiya sidestepped Gakeroku, swept his leg, and jumped into the air, nimble as a flying bird. He descended, picked up the medicine box from the ground, and threw the netsuke frog at the trees. In the most mysterious way, the frog attached itself to the base of a great cedar tree and spewed a strand of white smoke which rose and hung mid-air, like a faint rainbow.

(5.8)

Without looking at the strange sight, Gakeroku roared, "Jiraiya, prepare to die!" and swung his axe to cleave the man in two, but as if erased from existence, Jiraiya disappeared.

"Damn it, I lost him," the mountain dweller muttered to himself, and skulked down to the halfway point on the stone staircase. The rainbow in the dark of the night shone with a glittering light as it stretched across all the land. All the way to the sea in Echigo, to the white sails in the waves, it was as visible and all-reaching as if it were the middle of day. And on top of the rainbow, walking placidly with the medicine box in hand, was Jiraiya, strolling along as if on level ground.

He looked back at the mountain dweller and boomed, "I heard rumors of you, Takasago Yuminosuke, brave retainer of the Sarashina clan. I sympathize for the months and years you have toiled and brought yourself low to aid in taking your lord's revenge. If fate will have it, we shall meet again. Now, fare thee well!"

As the chilly northern winds of the autumn night blew, it swept away the rainbow along with Jiraiya, leaving Iwane no Gakeroku on the dark road, dumbstruck by Jiraiya's courage and extraordinary conjuring. Going down the stone stairs, the bell struck eight[1] and he headed back to the village where he lived.

Here, the story takes us elsewhere. To Misao, the wife of Himematsu Sumatarō, and Kozue, her mother-in-law. After parting with Yuminosuke, they had spent half a year in Echigo looking for the object of their vendetta, Arakurō, but found no leads, so they decided to head east. At the onset of autumn, they left the town of Koshiji and set out for Shinano again. They prayed towards Lord Sarashina-dono's mansion from a distance, and traveled to the temple where the family grave was, but did not visit the temple itself. Only the graves. Then they left the area and traveled the Zenkōji Road, crossing over the Usui pass between

1 01:00.

5.8

Shinano and Kōzuke.[2] The hardships of travel still weighed heavy on the little party of three, consisting of the two masters and the servant. The child, now named Sonematsu, had turned two this year and was more adorable by the day. So, Matsuhei worked hard and diligently to support his two mistresses.

One day, Kozue said to Misao, "People from all over go to the Yukaho *onsen* here in this land.[3] If we go there, we might be able to find a lead."

Misao nodded. "Indeed. My father-in-law in the underworld and my husband in his grave must be pleased with you, toiling on these travels despite your age. And with Matsuhei for taking such good care of us. The gods must surely be on our side as well, because my child, so prone to tantrums, grew strong without even taking any medicine."

When she said this to Kozue, Matsuhei added, "The power of the gods will surely lead us to our man. Nevertheless, we should make haste!"

Kozue's brow furrowed as she said, "I have gotten even more blisters on my feet today than usual, and it has been hurting for a while now." Then, smiling, she added, "Look at me, making mountains of molehills. Let's get going!" and bore the pain as she carried on, being considerate of Misao and Matsuhei.

In time, the party came upon a hunter carrying two monkeys, one big and one small, with all their limbs tied up. On his shoulder he carried an arquebus and when the trio approached him from behind, Kozue

2 Present day Gunma. Proper name Kamitsukeno.

3 Modern day Ikaho onsen.

5.9

saw the bigger of the two monkeys was dead, probably shot by the hunter. But the smaller one, although tied up, moved its arms and legs and squirmed deplorably while shrieking.

Kozue, who was deeply compassionate, approached the hunter. "What are you going to do with the little monkey? Are you going to keep it, or will you sell it?"

(5.9)

"When I gut the big one, I'll also kill the small one and sell it," the hunter said, contentedly.

To the others, Kozue cried, "To live a life of killing! I want to buy the small monkey and set it free in the mountains as a prayer to the gods."

"There can be no greater act of meritorious mercy than that. Let's do it," agreed Misao, and Matsuhei went to negotiate with the hunter.

Grinning, the hunter said, "I guess the happiness of this critter will cost you two silver *kan*."[4]

Kozue reached into her travel bag and pulled out first two, then three silver coins and handed them to Matsuhei, who said to the hunter, "Here is what you asked for, and then some!"

The hunter was delighted with the silver and untied the monkey. He handed the monkey over to Matsuhei who took it in his arms. The hunter said a word of gratitude and left them. With a look of happiness, the little monkey raised its behind as it bowed in thanks.

---

4 Silver coins worth 1000 mon copper coins a piece.

"Even an animal knows how to do this. I guess that bastard Tatsumaki has just been outclassed by a monkey!" said Misao, pointing.

Matsuhei interrupted her, "Milady, really, such blunt talk is best left at a drinking house. Now, little monkey, go wherever you want." She untied the rope around the monkey's neck.

The monkey did not acknowledge the mountains, instead he ran straight to Kozue. They did not know what to do with it, and no matter how they yelled at it or tried to push it away, it whimpered and refused to leave her side.

Matsuhei clicked his tongue and said, "Well, I guess we'll take him along with us. We can't suffer any more delays." And as they walked, the little monkey followed happily.

On that day, they passed through Sakamoto and Matsuida and were in such a hurry that when evening fell, they had completely forgotten to get lodging. The next inn was far ahead, and in her hurry, Kozue, whose feet were already hurting, kicked a rock on the road. She bloodied her toes and fell over in the grass with a yelp. Misao and Matsuhei ran to her side, sat her up and took care of her. With some paper they dressed her wounds. Kozue finally managed to stand up a little, but she could not walk. Misao and Matsuhei shouldered her and kept walking. Soon, however, the road split in two, and they could not tell which was the main road. As they stood there bewildered, from the right side of the road came an old but sturdy-looking retired woman holding a cane. She was clad in a soft haori overcoat and a kosode kimono of black, coarse silk. On her head, she wore a scarf. She was accompanied by a maid carrying a small bundle, and they approached in a graceful manner.

Seeing the three bewildered people in the middle of the road, the old lady called out to them, "Are you travelers? It looks like you are in trouble, worn out, and with a hurt foot." She down the road and continued, "And it is at least four or five ri[5] to the next lodging, a distance that would be difficult in your current state."

Then the maid added, "And the lodging behind you is equally far. Are you indeed in trouble?"

"As you guessed, I have hurt my foot and we are in trouble," answered Kozue.

The old lady smiled and said, "Today is the death day of a Buddha, who is very important around here. As a sign of my appreciation to the Buddha, I will let you stay at my retirement home. One of my children is a merchant, so a lot of people live in our house, and it is terribly busy all the time. Because of all that commotion and noise, I chose to retire and live together with my maid in a separate, yet unforgiving, house. If you stay tonight to recuperate, your pain should go away by morning."

Her kind words cheered up Misao, who said, "Your kindness has made me regain my courage."

Matsuhei, rubbing his hands together, asked in a pleading voice, "As you see my companions have weak legs, so please, let us stay in your house."

---

5 16–19 kilometers.

5.10

"Since you ask so nicely, follow me," said the old lady, and the three were overjoyed. After proceeding around four or five chō,[6] they came to an enclosure of cedar trees. The old lady and maid entered together, and when the trio looked through the trees, they saw a single detached house, much shabbier than what they had imagined.

(5.10)

The old lady turned to the three and said, "You can rest at your leisure. I will go for a bit to the main house." Then she called to the maid, "Make sure to give them dinner!" and left.

The three extended their gratitude while washing their feet, then went inside where the maid brought Kozue trays with boiled barley and rice. Misao sat next to Kozue and breastfed Sonematsu. Matsuhei waited on them while also feeding the monkey. All three were worried about how dirty the tableware was, so they only ate a little before giving the trays to Matsuhei to put away. Then the maid came into the room, said her pleasantries, and took the trays to the kitchen.

After a while, the lady of the house came back. The three knelt and thanked her deeply for the food. With an apologetic look, the old lady said, "There is no need for you to thank me. This backcountry dwelling is nothing like a proper lodging place. By the way, we can't forget about the medicine. A little way outside this village, you can get some very good ointment. It is such a miracle cure, people from all over come here

6 436–545 meters.

looking for it. It is troublesome, but if your escort would be so kind as to go and buy some..."

"I am most indebted to you. I will go and buy some now," said Matsuhei ecstatically.

The old lady pointed and said, "Go out from here and then go seven or eight chō to the right. There should be a street sign with a trademark for the medicine on it."

Matsuhei said to Kozue and Misao, "Please excuse me as I go and get this miracle ointment." Sonematsu, whom Misao was holding, threw a tantrum and chased after Matsuhei to be carried by him. Matsuhei picked Sonematsu up, saying, "Come here, you." He thrust a sword into his belt, put on his footwear, and was off.

Then the old lady called for the maid. "Now, do as I told you and get the *lodging fee* for tonight from this lot," she said while signaling with her eyes.

The maid nodded, pulled out a carving knife she had been hiding, and brandished it at Kozue and Misao.

"Now you two, it seems following us here was the end of your luck. If you give us all your travel money and take off your clothes, I will spare your lives. If you dawdle, I will cut you up. Now, what will it be?"

And the old lady, who had seemed dignified earlier, removed her scarf, revealing a few solitary hairs growing on her head like silver needles, unkept and hanging down by her neck like rat tails. She stared with eyes that sparkled like they were filled with stars, and her dreadful appearance was like that of a demon hag. Truly a terrifying robber.

"Time is running out. If you have any interest in your own safety, you will hand over the money," said the horrific hag as she drew closer, also brandishing a knife.

In unison, Kozue and Misao cried out, "Even if you are an inhuman, evil hag, we will not die by your hand!" And from their straw bundles, each pulled out a sword. They unsheathed the blades, and guarded themselves, making it clear anyone who drew near would be cut down.

"These two are tougher than we thought. Better take them apart before the other one comes back!" said the demon hag to the maid, and she lunged at Misao while the maid went to fight Kozue.

When the demon hag was about to be killed by Misao, the maid ignored her target and went to help. Kozue chased after the maid, but tripped over an ashtray at her feet and collapsed from the pain from her wound. Noticing this, the hag jumped at Kozue, sat herself on top of the woman, and raised the knife to stab. The little monkey, who had relied on Kozue earlier, pulled and scratched at the demon hag's legs, and Kozue struggled to push the hag off. Misao flew in a fit of rage and valor, and cut down the maid. The demon hag grabbed the bothersome monkey and threw it in an attempt to hurt it.

She raised her knife again and turned to Misao. "What now? If you make a move, I will stab this crone. Or maybe I will cut her? Are you upset now that I have a hostage?"

She cackled in ridicule, and her expression was so detestable no amount of hate towards her would ever be enough. Although Misao was flustered, there was nothing she could do in this situation. She reluctantly backed off while glaring at the hag and crying tears of regret.

As if guided by a sixth sense, Matsuhei had turned back on the road, and upon seeing what was going on in the house, he jumped to their defense. He grabbed the demon hag by the hair on the scruff of her neck and threw her with tremendous force. Saved from the jaws of the tiger, Kozue and Misao rejoiced. The demon hag arose, knocked over the lantern, and disappeared into the darkness with her knife in hand, escaping to who knows where.

Matsuhei gritted his teeth. He handed Sonematsu to Kozue and made ready to give chase, but Kozue stopped him, saying, "Rather than chasing after someone who has no more business with us on an unknown road in the middle of the night, we should leave this place as soon as possible."

(5.11)

Misao added, "You are right. There is no knowing what disaster will befall us if we thoughtlessly try to catch that evil crone. Don't give in to a long chase, Matsuhei!" While she spoke, she gave the death blow to the fiendish maid and put her sword back in its scabbard.

Misao tied up Kozue's messed up hair, and when she looked at Sonematsu, she saw he had already fallen asleep. Misao smiled at how innocent he was, and then tied up her own hair and took Sonematsu in her arms. Matsuhei returned to their side and got ready for departure. He put the two swords back in the straw bundles, took some bamboo from the enclosure around the house, and made torches, which he lit. Then he took the luggage on his back, and while taking care of Kozue, who was still with an injured foot from the mountain path, he and Misao kept a close watch as they left, followed by the little monkey. At some point, the temple bell struck, and Matsuhei counted five strikes,[7] and after a little less than one *koku*[8] they arrived at a village. They begged the head of the village for lodging and spent the night there. When night lifted, they set out again, but did not go towards Yukaho. Instead, they continued on the road to the east.

7 19:00–21:00.

8 Two hours.

5.11

5.12

Part II

(5.12)
Yet again, our tale takes us elsewhere. For lately, a woman had moved to the port of Niigata in Echigo from Kamigata.[9] She was a diviner and a spellcaster, who often healed the sick, and because she was adept at divination, it was as if she could see into people's hearts. The people praised her and called her a *miko*—a servant of the gods, and there was none who did not know of her. Her real name was Fukumaki no Takarako. She was about eighteen or nineteen years old, and a stunning beauty. She lived a quiet life alone on one of the backroads of Niigata Road, where no one came.

Every day, Takarako was requested to go somewhere, and today, as usual, she wore something akin to a glossy white, silken *kariginu* dress. This was only normal wear for a noble or a priest. She had a white *gohei* staff with white *shide* paper streamers and a black handle shoved into her belt behind her back. Her raven hair was tied up with a purple string, bangs hanging loose, and her topknot was swept forward, looking like a tea whisk. In her left hand she carried a black handled bell stick, and in her right, a wickerwork straw hat. She wore *bokuri*, a woman's high, wooden sandals, with a single metal tooth on each. She looked like a willow tree as she walked, exquisite and swaying in the wind. None who walked past her did so without diverting attention to her.

As she walked, someone who looked like a traveler took off his straw hat and called to her from behind, stopping her in her tracks.

She turned to him and said, "Is it me you call upon to stop? Do you have some business with me?"

With such kindness in her words, the traveler bowed. "Indeed I do. You look to me like you are the miko everyone is talking about around here. I know it is sudden, but please, could you tell me where you live? I have a small thing to ask of you, so I will wait for a day when you are home."

Takarako nodded, took out a card from a folding paper case inside the breast of her kimono, and gave it to him. On it was the information he sought. The traveler read it to himself and said, "Thank you for this. Now I know where you live and when you are free. I will come early tomorrow."

"I will be awaiting you," said Takarako with a smile, and with those few words she left. The traveler put his straw hat on and went back in the direction where he came from while looking over his shoulder.

While the two were talking, a splendid-looking samurai had stopped to watch. He wore a straw hat covering his whole face and had two swords. He whispered something to one of his servants, who swiftly followed after Takarako. The samurai then left, bringing with him the rest of his retinue.

The next morning, the lone traveler arrived at a small, quaint house on the backstreets of Niigata. Next to its lattice gate was a nameplate with "Takarako" written on it in a woman's hand. When he read the

9 Present Kyōto/Osaka area.

5.13

nameplate, the traveler nodded to himself and called out, "Excuse me?" as he opened the entrance door in the gate.

Takarako greeted him with a smile. "Come in, come in," in a hospitable voice, and led the traveler into the parlor room.

(5.13)

After they sat and exchanged seasonal greetings, the traveler spoke to Takarako with tears in his eyes. "The request I stopped you for on the street yesterday is this:

"One of my relatives has been arrested by Yakama-dono, the sheriff of this place, and thrown in prison for a long time for a sin he did not commit. I have been racking my brain to think of various ways to save him, but they say he is in league with a famous bandit and won't release him. Until they catch the bandit, he is an important prisoner to them, and they torture him every day.

"I managed to sneak a peek at how he fares, and he is so very weak that his life hangs in the balance. Even when he is unconscious, they torture him horrendously with water and fire, and he will inevitably end up confessing association with the bandit, if only to avoid the suffering. Once they hear his confession, he will truly be beyond saving. When my wife back home heard about this, she fell crying to the ground, completely distraught. Despite my attempts and my sympathy for him, I have not been able to come up with any plans, so please, would you tell a fortune or two? Will he finally die under these false accusations, or is there some way to rescue him?"

His misfortune made Takarako's eyes glisten over. "I guess it is true there are those who have no luck in this world. I understand the situation. Please wait here," she said and straightened up, turning to what looked like an altar, veiled behind a white cotton curtain. She chanted a prayer for a moment and clapped her hands. She picked up the gohei staff on the table and waved it at the traveler's head. After shaking her bells, she closed her eyes and fell silent for a while. Finally, she opened her eyes and put the bells on the table.

She said, "This is a severe tragedy. The person is the blood relative of your wife, and even if he is innocent, this is all due to a fate from a past life. He will most likely die in three days. There is not much that can be done with the power of a mere human. You should return to your homeland. If you stay here any longer, it will only lead to more disappointment. Leave it to the gods in the heavens for now, because even if there is still someone for you to turn to, in eight or nine out of ten scenarios, your relative will die a violent death. I pray the heavens grant him life." She paid her respect to the altar. Then she left the table and spoke no more, and when no words of appreciation were spoken, she cleared her throat.

The traveler sighed and said, "As the name miko—servant of the gods—would imply, I suppose what you say is true. The reason I am having all kinds of thoughts about it is because of the confusion of my heart. My heart, which only wants to save him. If his life will last no longer than three days, the least I can do is stay here for two or three days more and give him a small memorial service. Afterwards, I will go back home."

While saying this, he reached into the breast of his kimono, pulled out a small silver lump, put it on a piece of paper, and respectfully pushed it in front of Takarako.

"Please, accept this small token of my appreciation," he said kindly.

Takarako pushed it back, saying, "I have no desire for gifts. I cannot accept anything more than ten *sen* as an offering to the gods."[10]

Even though the traveler offered it repeatedly, Takarako would not take the silver, and reluctantly the traveler gave ten sen. With a sorry expression, he thanked her deeply and went on his way.

After the traveler left, one of the front doors slid open. A single manservant entered and said, "I am a messenger of Yakama-dono, the sheriff of this town. My lord has tasked me with inviting and escorting you to him. So, if you would please follow me, we shall be off at once."

Elated, Takarako answered, "Why, mister messenger, I will go right away. Just wait a little bit, if you don't mind." She made her preparations like she always would, and then left following the manservant towards the sheriff's mansion.

The reason Sheriff Yakama Shikaroku had invited Takarako was because he wished to solicit her fortune telling powers. Or at least that is what he said, for the truth was different. When he had seen her in town the day before, he fell in love with her, and since his wife had

10 1 sen = 1/100 of a kan.

passed away before him, no one could hold it against him. So, on this day, he had called for her to lavish her with gold and silver and take her as his concubine. Takarako did not know any of this, and when she arrived at Shikaroku's house with the manservant, the delighted sheriff invited her into the parlor.

Without even glancing at Shikaroku, Takarako scanned the room and went to the *tokonoma* alcove, where a scroll of Yōryū *Kannon*, the Willow Bodhisattva of healing, was hanging. Takarako spoke to it in a polite tone, as if it were a living person.

"Last night, you visited me in a dream unexpectedly, but I had no idea this would be where you actually were. Words fail to express how happy and fortunate I am to have been invited by the master of this house to come here today."

The Kannon in the picture then nodded and smiled. Neither the master Shikaroku nor the male and female servants who were peeking into the room had ever seen such a strange occurrence, and they whispered how mysterious it was. Takarako drew even closer to the scroll, tilted her head, and put her ear close as if listening for something.

She raised her face. "You say you want to bestow fortune on Shikaroku, the master of this house? In that case, would you hand me the pot you are carrying?" Takarako held out both her hands. The Kannon handed the small pot it held to Takarako, who took it and held it up with reverence.

Shikaroku was intoxicated with the wondrous sight before his eyes. Upon hearing Kannon's commands, he was so grateful for being bestowed such luck that his smile covered his whole face. He worshipped at the scroll of the Kannon, pouring in all his heart and soul. Takarako took a table and placed it in front of the alcove, where she prayed and shook her staff and bells.

(5.14)

"Let it be as the Buddha of ultimate truth commands," she prayed, and with the pot she was given in her hands, she ambled over to Shikaroku. His lustful and shamelessly blasphemous character was written all over his face. As he bowed and scraped, his eyes were riveted on the pot Takarako carried.

Then something miraculous happened. Money spouted from the pot like water from a mountain spring. Like a golden waterfall in the mountains, it overflowed onto the floor. Golden koban coins and silver nuggets rained down over Shikaroku's head faster than it could be picked up. Startled by this, he shoveled it up with both hands, his eyes sharp like a predator. When they saw this, the squires, the manservants, and the maids came running, trying to pick up the silver nuggets scattered farther away. Shikaroku scolded them with wild and glaring eyes, and they fled to the kitchen under disgruntled murmurs.

Takarako tipped the pot, turning the bottom up, and said to Shikaroku, "You were given this wonderous gold treasure because, every day without faltering, your devotion is unyielding. If I request it,

5.14

there might be an even larger divine reward for you. So it would be best if you bolstered your devotion even more."

Holding the pot in great reverence, she turned to the Kannon in the hanging scroll and presented the pot. The Kannon reached out, took it, and returned to its original position—smiling and sitting on a boulder. With this, Shikaroku's gratitude, respect, and devotion increased, and he prostrated himself countless times. When Takarako sat, Shikaroku stacked the money he had picked up in three piles on the alcove. He was jubilant, and from thereon he completely changed his impression of Takarako after seeing what she could do. His thoughts of her as a lover were changed to respect, like she was an honored Buddha or Bodhisattva.

(5.15)

Afterwards, they adjourned to a different parlor where food and drinks were served. After some time had passed, Takarako said her goodbyes and tried to go home, but Shikaroku would not allow it. To have Takarako stay the night, he had more and more food and drinks brought. She decided to humor him by having a drink and took the opportunity to speak with him.

"If I put in my best effort and work through the night, and then pray to this Kannon, through her great powers I can beckon all the money of the world to come here. But in order to do that, you must place all the money you have in the alcove and put up many votive lights. When you worship the money, money from other places will be drawn to its

5.15

essence. It will gather up and come flying here at godlike speed. This would not work for someone who is frugal with money and doubts this prayer, but I do not desire any of the money myself. Only to bestow the blessing upon one who is devoted and reverent every day."

"Takarako-dono, so straight to the point you are. I will put out my money as you have said, so please make sure to grant the blessing to me," said Shikaroku eagerly, and slid closer on his knees.

"Do not worry. I accept your request and shall do it tomorrow," answered Takarako.

Elated beyond words, he gave her money and a kimono, praised her as the *miko*, messenger of the gods, and respected her as if she were his master.

Shikaroku then said, "I have an unpleasant duty I must perform the day after tomorrow. I am not sure if I should be telling you this, but I have caught one of the underlings of Jiraiya, the bandit who is on everyone's lips right now. I have had him in my prison and tortured him for a long time, and I think he will die soon. If he dies in prison, no one will know of my good deeds. So, while he still draws breath, I will take him to the beach here in Niigata, and there I will behead him to weaken Jiraiya's spirits. Ah, there really is nothing in this world as tough as doing one's duty."

Takarako raised her eyebrows. "Such dreadful stories will only serve to dampen the mood of this feast."

Shikaroku laughed and said, "Just pretend I didn't say that then," but the mood had died.

5.16

With the evening growing late, Takarako asked to take her leave and went home. Shikaroku was exceedingly drunk, so he simply passed out.

And so, the night grew ever later. The prison inside the walls of Sheriff Yakama Shikaroku's estate was extremely strict. It had three stone walls and bars made from latticed logs, and next to the cell were the three tools made for capturing humans—a *tsukubō* push-pole, a *sasumata* spear-fork, and a *mojiri* sleeve-entangler. It rained, and a woman appeared with her face wrapped in a scarf. She snuck close to the lonely cell to have a look.

(5.16)

The two night-guards on duty spotted her, and one of them called out, "An intruder!" and raised his pole-lantern. The guards surrounded the woman and tried to bring her down. But the woman grabbed the guards by their collars without hesitation and threw them aside. After looking inside the cell, she vanished from sight. The guards got back up but could not find signs of anyone nearby. They looked at each other, shuttered, and then returned to the guardhouse.

The following evening, as she had promised, Takarako came to Shikaroku's house and Shikaroku welcomed her warmly. As Takarako had instructed, he took all the money he had unjustly made over the years, two thousand ryō in gold, plus the money from the night before, and put it on display in the alcove. Then he put a great number of votive lights and showed the setup to Takarako.

She said, "Tonight, at nine and a half bells[11] you must start praying and then stop at eight bells.[12] Kannon will then appear, and the lights will go out all at once. The money will emit its own light, and more money will come flying from all directions."

Shikaroku rejoiced. "And for you, Lady Takarako, I will give you whatever reward you wish for."

Then a feast was served, and as time passed the ninth bell finally struck. Takarako refrained from taking any more food or drink and she rinsed her mouth and washed her hands. She made sure her preparations were in order and readied to pray. As the time for the nine and a half bells grew near, she went before the alcove. There, as she always would, she grabbed her gohei staff and her bells and sat on a straw mat facing the table. She started praying, making a hundred prostrations to the hanging scroll and chanting something like invocations. This lasted a long time, and all the men and women in his house sat reverently, but they became terribly sleepy. Without noticing, they nodded off and fell asleep. Shikaroku alone did not sleep even for a moment. His eyes were like saucers, keeping a close watch of what was happening. The gonging sound of the eighth bell rang, and just like Takarako had said, as if by a gust of wind, the lanterns and candles all went out with a whoosh. From out of nowhere came a tremendous sound like thunder, and Shikaroku and the people in the house all threw themselves to the floor with a cry.

After a while, they got back up, lit a candle, and looked around. Takarako had disappeared, and all the money on display in the alcove was gone as well. Not only that, the Yōryū Kannon was also missing. Left behind on the hanging scroll where the Kannon had been, were only three letters.

児雷也—Jiraiya

"I have been duped by Jiraiya!" Shikaroku howled furiously. He gnashed his teeth and looked like he wanted to burn down everything around him.

(5.17)

He pulled down the hanging scroll and tore it to shreds. He smashed and stomped on the lanterns and other things in the alcove. After lambasting his servants, he went to his bedchamber, but could not sleep. Deep in thought, he realized Jiraiya must have disguised himself, entered his house, deceived him, and taken his two thousand ryō and his other treasures. If the daimyo ever heard about this, it would surely influence Shikaroku's position, so he gathered all the men and women in the house.

"You must not under any circumstance let the world know what transpired here tonight," he ordered. When he was alone again, he put his hands together in contemplation, but his frustration only intensified. Even if he lay down, he could not sleep, and he clenched his fists and stomped around, cursing, "Damn you, Jiraiya. When the night has lifted, I shall dry out the waters and part the grasses to root you out!"

11 Exactly 00:00. Midnight.

12 01:00.

5.17

He continued like this until the crows of the morning cawed and dawn broke. He had a hurried breakfast and called for his constables to assemble.

"I know for a fact the bandit Jiraiya, whom we are already searching for, has been prowling this area recently. Search him out in secret and then capture him. He has disguised himself as a woman, so be vigilant. Now, get going!" he ordered sternly, and the constables set out in great numbers.

Shikaroku then called for an additional five or six constables and said to them, "Today is the day we shall pass judgment on Fukitarō, the prisoner from Shinano whom I informed the daimyo about. We have no more use for him."

The constables confirmed. One said, "The arrangements have already been made. We await your arrival."

Shikaroku nodded and went inside the house to make his preparations. He and the constables headed for the Niigata beach which was to be the execution ground.

The place where the deed was to be done was surrounded with a fence made of young bamboo. A great number of constables had been waiting for a while when Sheriff Shikaroku arrived.

(5.18)

He sat on a folding chair and called to his constables, "Bring out the offender!"

5.18

At Shikaroku's order, they brought him out—the innocent prisoner from Nezumi-no-shuku in Shinano, Fukitarō. He was in a pitiful state. His hair had grown out, his skin was pale, and he was scrawny and withered. His chin was covered with a beard, his eyes were sunken, and his arms and legs were like a skeleton. Without mercy, he was forced down on a mat of rice straw.

Shikaroku frowned at him. "Greetings, Fukitarō the sinner. Based on the confession you gave me the other day, there is no doubt you are in league with the bandit Jiraiya. The judgment you will be given today is therefore divine punishment. Consider it your reward for your sins. Speak your final peacc. Get on with it."

Fukitarō could not hold back tears of regret. With a voice weaker than the sounds of a diminishing insect in autumn, he said, "Even if it is in view of the gods, dying an unnatural death for a crime I did not commit will only garner spiritual malice."

His miserable words were ignored. One of the men took a sword, went behind Fukitarō, and raised the blade in the air.

A wind like a gale blew in. The sky darkened with clouds, and raindrops the size of pebbles started falling. It was altogether terrible. They heard the sound of wings, and an enormous eagle swooped down from the sky. First, it knocked over the man with the sword, and then, eyes gleaming with fury, it flapped its wings. This sent sand flying and leaves dancing through the air. The eagle grabbed two guards and hurled one to the sand and dropped the other in the sea. It landed on a

5.19

boulder and everyone in attendance fled in terror. When Shikaroku panicked and tried to flee, the great eagle spread its wings and came at him with its talons. He drew his sword and flailed it around. The eagle ignored this. With a single beat of its wings, it sent the sheriff somersaulting, landing him on his back. The bird did not falter for a moment and settled on Shikaroku. It grasped one leg with its talons, and bit down on the other with its beak. With a bone-breaking sound, it tore Shikaroku asunder.

When the events had played out, Fukitarō passed out. The fierce eagle picked him up and flew away with him, high above the sea. The wind died down and the rain stopped. When it was finally quiet again, the constables, who had previously fled, nervously came back. They found Shikaroku torn to pieces, and many of the constables who had not managed to escape were either clawed to death or torn and only halfway alive.

The constables reported the incident to the daimyo, and after samurai had come to investigate, Shikaroku and the departed constables' bodies were handed over to their relatives. Since the disaster was the work of a wild eagle, nothing could be done, and hunters were given strict orders to take down the eagle if they ever saw it.

(5.19)
Inesaku had heard Fukitarō was to be decapitated on this day, so he had blended in with the crowd to see how Fukitarō was doing. Being so

5.20

distraught, the tears he cried in secret were like a waterfall. When Fukitarō had been forced down on the straw mat and the man with the sword had gone behind him, it had started raining and a great eagle appeared. It kicked over the man with the sword and tore apart the sheriff. In the confusion, all the people who had come to watch fled left and right, sweeping away Inesaku who then left the area. After a while, the rain died down and it got quiet again. When Inesaku heard the talk of the people walking around, it seemed there was a pile of corpses left and the criminal had been taken by the eagle.

Someone said, "Even if his life was worthless, by now he has probably been torn apart and eaten by the eagle. How terrifying."

Hearing this, Inesaku was saddened beyond words, and he lay down on the ground, crying over his own uselessness. Just then, two or three constables came looking. Without a word they grabbed Inesaku by his arms, immobilizing him. They hogtied him and threw him in a palanquin without a door. With great haste, they carried him away.

Now we turn back to the wild eagle from before. After it kidnapped Fukitarō, it flew high above the sea routes of Echigo in an instant. When it spotted Mount Myōkō, it beat its wings and flew even farther, to the border between Echigo and Shinano, where it rested in the shade of a mountain. It let Fukitarō down on a bed of brushwood and landed on a large branch of a great pine tree. Perched there, resting, it observed its

5.21

surroundings with hunting eyes and flapped its wings. This sent leaves flying and the bluster echoed across the mountain. As if shuddering with fear, the great pine shook and creaked. The various birds hid in the grass, not making a sound out of dread, and the monkeys fled down into the valleys without as much as a cry and concealed themselves.

(5.20)

Truly, it was such an immense eagle one would think it must have been living in the mountains for hundreds or thousands of years for it to get so big. It beat its wings many more times, standing on its claws while looking around. Then, for a moment, it was still, and the most inexplicable thing happened. The eagle shuttered, and it split open from chest to stomach. From inside the eagle stepped out a handsome and refined man. This was indeed none other than the bandit leader Jiraiya, famous in all the lands, whose real name was Ogata Shūma Hiroyuki.

Jiraiya straightened his clothes while standing firmly on the branch of the pine tree. The great eagle, perched high in the tree with its unparalleled wings, mysteriously faded away like morning mist before the sun, and after a while it was gone.

(5.21)

Jiraiya jumped from the top of the tree and floated gently down to the grass. There he sat up Fukitarō, still passed out since the morning. From the medicine box he wore on his hip, Jiraiya took out a restorative remedy. Using his folding fan, he parted Fukitarō's clenched teeth and put a bit of the medicine in his mouth. From a valley stream he took some water in his hands and poured it into Fukitarō's mouth. When Fukitarō swallowed the medicine, Jiraiya held him close and spoke into his ear.

"Fukitarō. Fukitarō. You can't possibly still be unconscious, can you, Fukitarō?"

After Jiraiya called to the unconscious man a couple of times, the medicine took effect. With a heaving gasp, Fukitarō breathed in deeply and regained consciousness. Slowly, he opened his eyes and surveyed his surroundings. When he saw Jiraiya, he stared in blank amazement and said nothing.

5.22

The story of what Jiraiya and Fukitarō did next, will follow in the beginning of book six. Now I put down my brush for this spring.

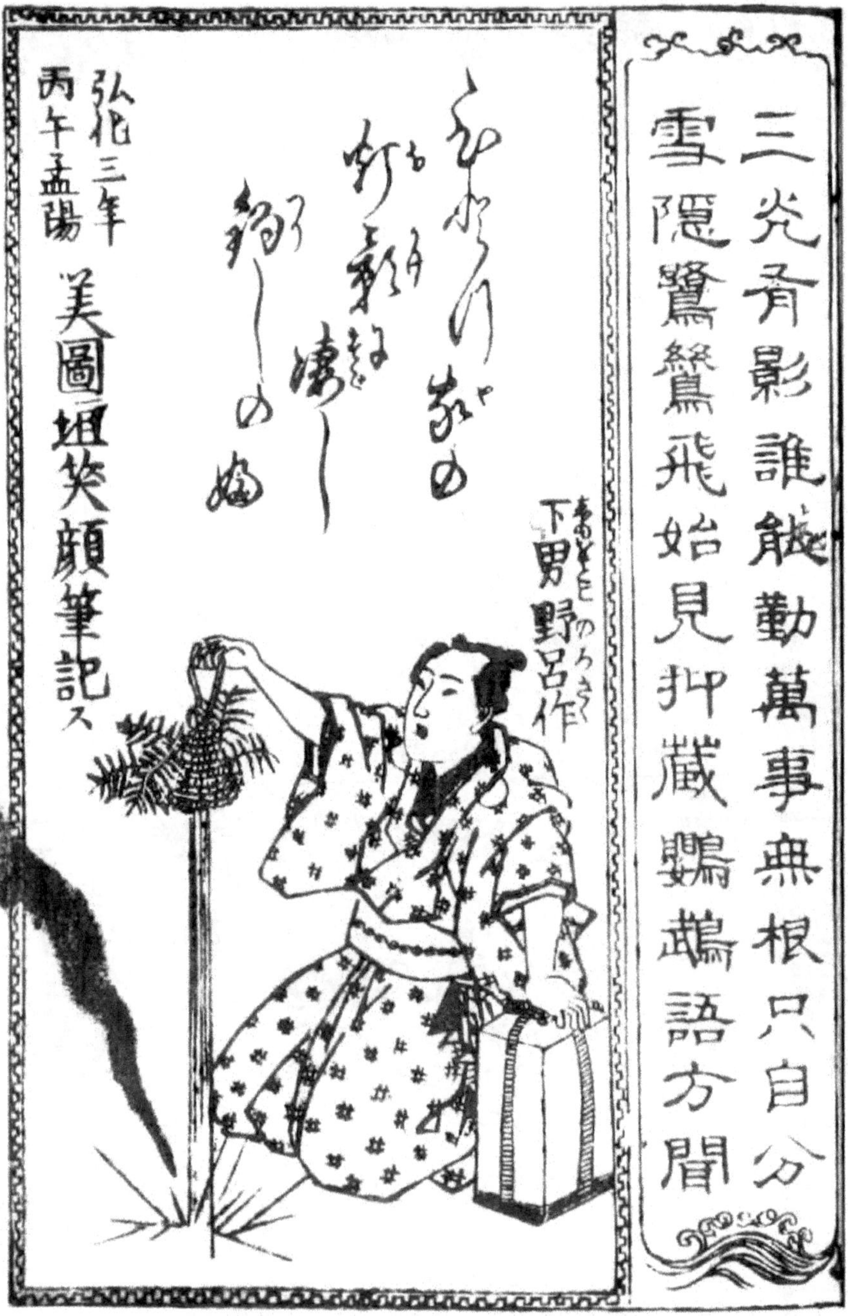

三光有影誰能動萬事無根只自分
雪隱鷺鷥飛始見柳藏鸚鵡語方聞
下男野呂作
弘化三年
丙午孟陽
美圖垣笑顔筆記ス

6.1

Book 6

"The three lights cast shadows, who can endure? All things have no roots, they only grow on their own. When snow conceals, herons and egrets take flight; when willows hide, parrots' chatter is heard."[1]

A lonesome fern ball hangs in the shifting firelight of a solitary house.

Kōka 3—Year of the Fire Horse—First month (1845)
Mizugaki Egao

Also on page:
Norosaku the servant.

1 This poem is from *Jin Ping Mei,* a novel written by the Ming Dynasty novelist Lanling Xiaoxiao Sheng.

6.2

Gōtekisai Muyami Gundazaemon, teacher of the Meppō sword style,[2] rides a golden dragon and flourishes his spear techniques.

Knight-errant Chōbei the dreamer

Jinza of Ōiso.[3]

Knight-errant Enma no Kiroku.

2 Fictional fighting style usually used by villains. Means "Destruction of the Dharma School".

3 Unknown character, possibly a reference.

6.3

Oyoshi the candy seller.
Matsuhei the monkey tamer.

6.4

Part I

(6.4)
We find ourselves back with Jiraiya tending to Fukitarō. As Fukitarō gradually regained his senses, he surveyed his surroundings and realized he was on an unfamiliar mountain. Initially stunned, his attention was soon captured by a figure—a man seated at ease on the root of a nearby pine tree. Before Fukitarō could utter a word, the man spoke.

"Tell me Fukitarō, have you completely forgotten who I am? It is me, Tarō, who once received such invaluable help from your family!"

Upon hearing this, Fukitarō exclaimed in great surprise and wonderment, "Now that you say it, I do have some recollection of your face from my childhood. How remarkable that such a fortuitous encounter has taken place here in the middle of the mountains. What a mysterious turn of events."

Jiraiya smiled and laughed. "It is no mystery why we have met here. It was all part of my grand plan. I sought to express my gratitude for the assistance I received all those years ago, so consider your rescue as a small token of my appreciation."

Jiraiya proceeded to recount the events that unfolded in Niigata to Fukitarō. He described his discovery of Ganpachi, the nemesis of Hatasaku, disguised as Yokushirō, and how Miyuki had ultimately defeated him. Jiraiya also provided intricate details about his encounters with Sheriff Shikaroku at sea.

After hearing the entire tale, Fukitarō said, "During my leisurely stay at the Kumadeya house in Niigata, I was unexpectedly captured by Shikaroku. He accused me of hailing from the same village as the bandit Jiraiya, subjecting me to torture and beatings."

In a hushed voice Jiraiya spoke again. "I did not know you were imprisoned until I had already left Kumadeya. I only heard about it and the details when I talked with your sister Osachi, and I immediately knew I had to do something. The suffering that had befallen you was a consequence of my actions. I abandoned my plan to travel to Kamakura and returned to Niigata. There, I assumed the guise of a miko and planned to fool Sheriff Yakama Shikaroku so I could rescue you. Coincidentally, Shikaroku invited me to his home, presenting the perfect opportunity to put my scheme into motion. Shikaroku was a reprobate, ruled by his carnal desires, and I knew he would demand me to become his concubine. How laughable. So, I told him about the benefits of the Willow Bodhisattva and had him take out all the money he had amassed through many years of wicked acts. With my yōjutsu I showed before his very eyes that I could make his gold increase tenfold. My plan set in motion, I left for the night, intending to seize every last coin Shikaroku had. However, my concern for your well-being consumed me, so in the dead of night I returned and went to the cell to see how you were doing. It relieved me to see you still in one piece. Although I considered breaking you out that very night, I feared it might bring even more misfortune on Inesaku and Osachi. Therefore, on the evening when I stole all of Shikaroku's money, I snuck back inside later to eavesdrop. It was then that I overheard them say the accomplice of the bandit Jiraiya was to be taken to the beach in the morning and beheaded. Certain of what was to happen, I hatched a plan. Utilizing my yōjutsu I transformed myself into a wild eagle. At the appointed hour I swooped down from the heavens and tore Shikaroku apart. The others I kicked and scattered, ensuring an unencumbered rescue. Rest assured, there will be no investigations into the actions of an eagle or your subsequent whereabouts. No one will suspect our involvement in this elaborate scheme."

(6.5)

Overwhelmed with joy, Fukitarō exclaimed, "I thought my life was forfeit, but it was miraculously saved, and I was given refuge. But be that as it may, your appearance bears an uncanny resemblance to the infamous bandit Jiraiya, known throughout Echigo and all the provinces. Even your age is—"

"There is no wonder in our resemblance, for I am Jiraiya. It is my alias, but my true name is Shūma Hiroyuki. I have a burning wish, and for that reason, I became a bandit leader to amass military funds."

Fukitarō was flabbergasted by what he just heard.

Jiraiya then called over his shoulder, "Bring that palanquin here!" and from behind came two men dressed as constables. "Aye!" they

6.5

exclaimed, and brought a traveling palanquin, tied shut with straw rope. They placed it before Jiraiya, who looked as they untied the ropes on his command. What came dropping and stumbling out of the palanquin was Osachi's husband Inesaku. The surprise and joy left Fukitarō momentarily speechless, lost in thought.

Kneeling on the grass by the roadside, Inesaku bowed in silence to Jiraiya. Then, after celebrating that Fukitarō was safe and sound, he said to Jiraiya, "I overheard the entire story from inside the palanquin. I am overwhelmed with gratitude for what you have done for us. I never could have imagined that Fukitarō could be rescued so easily. But be that as it may, what will we do after Fukitarō has settled down? This matter is of the utmost importance."

Jiraiya smiled at him and replied, "I have taken measures for that as well, so do not burden your heart with such worries. Shortly we will finish our business here and I will hasten to Kamakura. I will bring Fukitarō with me and we will go in disguise. Inesaku, you shall go back to our homeland as swiftly as possible. Tell Osachi-dono what has transpired here and make sure she is safe."

Jiraiya called over the men dressed as constables and said to them, "Prepare everything as I instructed. Snap to and see it done!" The two men immediately understood what they had to do, kicking the palanquin off a cliff and into the valley below before departing. From within his pocket, Jiraiya fished out a hundred ryō in coin and gave it to Inesaku. "It is but a trifle, but use some of it for the road," he said, handing over the money.

6.6

However, Inesaku politely refused, saying, “I appreciate the gesture, but I have my own travel funds. Please do not trouble yourself.”

Jiraiya extended the money once more. “Don’t be so stubborn, Inesaku. I understand your concerns. Not accepting this money because it comes from a tainted bandit is excessive moral righteousness. Take back your fields and the mansion and restore the Mochimaru family as the head of the village. Have them hold on to this money and take it as a funeral gift for when Jiraiya has passed away.”

Inesaku could not argue against his words and took the money. “In that case I shall do as you say,” he said, and tucked it away beneath his obi belt.

Fukitarō, weakened and relying on Jiraiya for his safety, entrusted his sister Osachi’s well-being to Inesaku.

(6.6)

Their paths would have to separate on the mountain road to Kamakura, but they were among men, so they stifled their parting tears with great pain.

A great host of Jiraiya’s men appeared carrying two palanquins and a yoke holding two boxes. The men were clad in resplendent attire and wielded spears inlaid with mother of pearl, resembling a samurai entourage preparing to travel. Jiraiya opened the lid on one of the boxes, and he pulled out clothes and a set of swords which he donned. His men did the same for Fukitarō, changing his clothes and presenting him with a set of swords to look like a sickly samurai. Jiraiya then promptly got into one of the palanquins and Fukitarō did the same. The men attached the poles and lifted them.

"And now, I bid you farewell!" declared Jiraiya.

"Please take care of Fukitarō!" Inesaku responded, bowing deeply.

They gave each other a nod, and as if to signal their parting, the crows let out their evening caws, startling Inesaku. As the road split like the flowing sleeves of a kimono, Inesaku stood on the mountaintop for a while, watching Jiraiya and his retinue descend the mountain road leading down from the pass. As Inesaku stood dead in his tracks up high on the mountain, Jiraiya and his followers shrunk into the distance until they looked like a flock of colorful birds in flight. Inesaku was lost in the sight of watching Jiraiya and his men go when two mountain dwellers appeared.

"You must be in league with that notorious Jiraiya we just witnessed. Prepare to be captured!" one exclaimed. They came at Inesaku from both sides to grab him. Taken aback, he jumped out of the way, causing the two men to fall over. Inesaku had always been frail, so he tried to run away, but the two men hopped back on their feet. They pulled out batons and one swung at Inesaku. As the baton came down on him, he did something unlike anything he had done before. He grabbed the arm holding the baton midair and twisted it upwards. Just then, the other man came at him, but as he drew close, he was flung several steps to the side. Inesaku was mystified, having no idea how the man had been thrown in such a manner without Inesaku touching him.

(6.7)

Inesaku put the man whose arm he was holding into an armlock and threw him where the other had landed. Completely baffled by his own sudden strength, Inesaku surveyed his surroundings and caught sight of the ethereal figure of Jiraiya suspended in mid-air.

"Well I'll be..." thought Inesaku just as the two men got up again. With a kick, Jiraiya sent one of the men into the valley below, and then picked up the other and tossed him in as well.

Inesaku gave his thanks and began to depart, but Jiraiya stopped him. "In a place like this, calamity is bound to strike if you let your guard down. Make haste and leave!" As Jiraiya spoke, he slowly faded away, disappearing without a trace. Inesaku understood the message and burst into a run on the road to his homeland, Shinano.

Since ancient times, Kamakura was lauded as a lively place, and nowadays, beyond description. Egara Tenjin Shrine was especially popular, with visitors lined up like teeth on a comb. People performed spectacles and acrobatics, and there were festival vendors abound. All were lined up in a narrow space, and among them was a single young woman. Her head was wrapped in a cloth, and she wore a sleeveless haori overcoat in a flashy pattern. In a bundle holding candy on her back, she carried a child of just two years, held in place with her obi. She had a mat made of small bamboo sticks, tied together to form a long

6.7

screen. By manipulating it with her hands, she could make it look like a ship or a fishing rod and many other things. While she did this, she told amusing stories and children came running and formed a crowd. Those who bought candy from her were given a little kite as a gift.

The sun had started its descent towards the west when visitors to the shrine dispersed. From a distance, a monkey tamer came carrying his monkey on his back. The monkey was nicknamed Konomi—fruit of the tree, because it loved to climb trees and pick fruit. The tamer had worked from morning till dusk, and he carried a heavy load of coins and white rice. Without thinking, he called out "Lady Misao!" as he approached, but immediately put his hand over his mouth. "I know you told me not to speak your name out loud, but I forgot," the tamer apologized. "It has gotten late, so perhaps it is time to call it a day? Just listen how happily the young master laughs inside his bundle."

Misao glanced around and said to the tamer, "Since we started living near this town last month, we have had to take care of mother due to her eye illness. Our one sliver of hope has been to rely on the winds of fortune as traveling merchants and look forward to one day meeting that man we so desperately seek. I pray to Egara Tenjin that this day will come soon!"

(6.8)

Tears welled up in the tamer's eyes. "The grudge that you and I carry is made of hardship upon hardship. To think that we still have

6.8

not found the man we seek, is such bitter frustration. It is as if the kami and the Buddhas themselves have abandoned us."

Misao listened attentively, but instead of wallowing in their resentment, she wiped the tear from the tamer's eye with her sleeve. "Waiting for our time to come in this floating world is something that cannot be done if we are impatient," she said. The child she carried cried, so she jingled a small bell to cheer him up. The child giggled. Misao then tightened the straps of her straw sandals, and the monkey tamer, who was none other than Matsuhei, followed closely behind her as they left for their lodging.

In the backstreets of the renowned Hasedera Temple in Kamakura stood a dilapidated house. There, Kozue, the widow of Himematsu, who was the chief retainer to the lord of Sarashina in Shinano, lay sick. Recently, Kozue had developed a sickness of the eyes, and she could not even lift herself from her pillow. Misao, her daughter-in-law, sold candy, while Matsuhei, their retainer, worked as a monkey tamer. They had picked up the monkey a long time ago when it was very small. They traveled for a while, and Matsuhei taught it all manner of tricks. The purpose of this was so it might play with the child, but it had learned so many tricks that Matsuhei one day thought, "I should make use of all these tricks I've taught the monkey. I can take it with me and go out as the smoke rises in the morning and come home when it rises in the evening. That way we can make some money and be helpful."

Knowing the day when one decides to take action was the most auspicious, he set out immediately with the monkey. He went to houses with large gatherings of people or to temples with bustling crowds. There, he laid out a straw mat, took a seat, and called out, "Come one, come all! Every coin in my box means rice on my table!"

Monkeys were said to be only three hairs away from being human, and as Matsuhei made the monkey dance, coins were generously tossed their way. When the first smoke rose in thin wisps, Matsuhei finally left. Misao felt she could not sit idly by, and so decided she would try a different approach by selling candy and captivating children with her tricks. Together they made money and used it to take care of Kozue as she suffered from her eye condition. They treated her with kindness and stayed up all night to take care of her. In this manner they carried on, but even with the two of them making money, their lives remained far from easy. To make matters worse, Kozue's illness grew more severe each passing day, leaving no room for negligence.

Then another problem reared itself. Matsuhei became ill and the doctor gravely diagnosed him with typhus. Misao did not know what to do on her own and was at a total loss with worry.

One day, the doctor told her, "I have a miracle cure for the eye disease, but acquiring one of the ingredients is incredibly difficult. I can give you what I have of it, but it will be hard to make use of it."

He let out a deep sigh as he said this, so Misao inquired about the treatment.

(6.9)

"There is a powdered medicine passed down in my family. It must be combined with the raw liver taken from a monkey and the liver taken from a living man, born in the year and the month of the tiger. With this medicine, there is no illness that cannot be cured in an instant. It is a most extraordinary elixir, but obtaining a human liver is no easy task, so it is not a light undertaking."

As she listened, Misao edged closer to the doctor. "Could I possibly receive what you have of this family medicine? Even just a little bit? Truly you cannot mean to say that you carry none with you." She paused for a bit and then slapped her thigh, exclaiming, "Please, I implore you!"

"In that case, I shall dispense it now," agreed the doctor without arguing and got his medicine kit. He made the compound and gave it to Misao, elated with joy. As she received the medicine, she expressed her sincere gratitude, after which the doctor promptly went home.

Misao did not know what to do with herself. She was lost in thought until the next day dawned. Just like every other day, she shouldered her wares and set out.

"If only I can gather the two required ingredients by tonight," she thought, each step driven by determination. So focused was she that she forgot about the road and her child, making the little one unhappy. With her sleeve, she gently wiped away the child's tears and pressed on, attending to her business.

6.9

Matsuhei, who had heard the doctor the previous day, made up his mind on his own. Fortunately, Misao had left the house, so he said to himself, "I won't survive this anyway, and I gave up on my life the moment we set out from our homeland. I have accepted my fate. We still have no clue to the whereabouts of the man we seek, so our trials and tribulations have been for naught! Amongst all this misery, the mistress has become ill in the eyes, and to add worry to lady Misao's hardships, I have also fallen sick. I doubt I will ever recover. I cannot help my ladies carry out their revenge, but by sacrificing my life to help make the elixir, at least I will be able to properly apologize to my two masters while in the underworld. I was born in the year and month of the tiger, so my liver, and the monkey's, will suffice."

Matsuhei tried to stand, but he stumbled and fell hard on his backside. The monkey was sleeping at the foot of the futon, but the crash startled it and woke it up. It climbed up on Matsuhei's lap and settled there. He gazed at the monkey through tear-filled eyes.

"Since the day we bought you, you have not left our side for a moment. You even learned all those tricks and did your best to help us make a living. You are such a splendid companion."

As he petted the monkey, it clung to him and buried its face in his bosom.

"How am I to take a blade to you? Even if it is for the sake of my master, over the past year we have become so close. I love you more than I would my own child. It's all so wretched! The cruel and heartrending task I must do now. I, an ignorant fool who knows less than an animal. How absurd it all is."

Matsuhei remained immersed in the depths of sorrow for a while. Then he wiped his tears and muttered aimlessly to himself until the time came. He lifted the monkey from his lap and put it on the tatami floor. It was as if the monkey knew what was in Matsuhei's heart and had comprehended his words, despite being just an animal. It closed its eyes and put its hands together, like a person in prayer who accepted their fate. Witnessing this robbed him of all his courage and willpower to carry out any action, let alone swing a sword. He was reduced to tears, his heart shattered.

"If you would but cry and scream because you want to live or run and hide to save yourself. I would have to exert myself to catch you, and I could kill you with a rash heart. But you are so much braver than any human could ever be, and I do not have the resolve to do it!"

Matsuhei turned away from the monkey in tears. Bright as it were, the monkey then tugged at his sleeve, seemingly urging him to hasten its own demise. Matsuhei wept bitterly and steeled his weak heart like that of an oni. He grabbed the sword lying by his pillow, and while clinging to a pillar, he pulled himself up on his legs while wavering from side to side. He walked behind the monkey and clenched his trembling fist. Finally, he drew the sword. There was to be no more suffering, so he closed his eyes and cried out, "Namu Amida Butsu!" and brought the sword down, severing the monkey's head.

(6.10)

He grieved for a while, weeping at the monkey's tragic end and clasping its lifeless body to his chest. When he regained his composure, he crawled on his knees and got a bowl. Then he cut the monkey open below the chest, pulled out the liver, placed it in the bowl, and breathed a sigh of relief. From in front of the house, Matsuhei heard the sound of people. In a hurry, he covered the monkey's corpse with his futon, closed the shōji screen to his room and lay down, feigning soundless sleep.

Unaware of what had just transpired, Misao returned home. She put down her candies and supplies, took out the sleeping child from her bosom and laid him down. He did not fuss, so Misao took off her sleeveless haori and went up to the second floor to see how her mother-in-law was doing. Finding her fast asleep, Misao quietly descended the stairs so as not to startle her. Then she peeked on Matsuhei, who was also in deep slumber. Relieved by seeing everyone in good condition, Misao took a sip of the lukewarm tea left in the earthen teapot and calmed her heart while looking at her child's face. Then, she cried in silence.

"You were born to such unfortunate circumstances. You never even knew your father's face, and you have endured constant hardships from our perpetual travels. Now mother and Matsuhei are gravely ill, and taking care of them means we can't live a proper life. I go to trade during the day and stay up all night caring for the sick. All the stress has

6.10

made my milk dry up, and you have grown so skinny. To make matters worse, the elixir the doctor told me about yesterday has proven to need someone to be murdered. My son, a woeful duty lies upon you. They say that sometimes one must kill a smaller insect to save a bigger insect. Choose the lesser of two evils. Truly it is unlucky for you that you are born in the year and month of the tiger, but it is a great display of filial piety to your grandmother. When I have done what I must do now, pitiful as it is, I must also take the life of the little monkey. Although man and beast are different, the thought of taking two lives with my own hands terrifies me. This is even lower than being a hunter who must live by killing."

She wailed and bit down on her sleeve, tearing it apart.

Gradually, Misao regained her composure and said, "If I am too weak and delay, I will regret it a million times over. Accept my devotion and help cure my mother-in-law!" She prayed to Egara Tenjin and the Jizō Bodhisattva, "Lead this child, protect him from cruel judgment, and deliver him to my husband."

She wiped the tears falling from her face and drew her sword. Just as she grabbed her child and was about to plunge the sword into his chest, he awoke in a cheerful mood, smiling and laughing. Misao's hands went numb, and she cast her sword aside, embracing him tightly. She wailed, but being mindful of her surroundings, she bit down on her sleeve and sank to the floor. Forcibly, she willed herself out of lamentation and once again placed the child on her lap. She was about to take the blade to her child once more, but the shōji screen behind her burst open. Matsuhei emerged, staggering. His abdomen was cut open and with a pained voice, he spoke.

"Lady Misao, please refrain from doing anything rash! I will give you the liver of a monkey and that of a man born in the year and month of the tiger!"

Misao turned around, horrified by the scene. Even Kozue fumbled her way down from the second floor to check what was happening. Matsuhei pounded his chest and took a pained breath.

He continued, "Remember how the young master Sumatarō met an unnatural and untimely death while traveling because of Arakurō. Shamefully, even though I was traveling with him, I did not seek immediate revenge. I wanted to slice open my belly and die for my lack of loyalty, but I realized someone had to report this murder in the homeland. With no one else to do it, I wiped away my tears and returned home. There, the master of the house also met an untimely death, leaving only his widow and you, Lady Misao. Together we embarked on our quest for vengeance, and the years spent have been heartbreaking. And now, this sickness eats away at me day and night, making my life ever shorter. Everything has since worsened, and I want to stomp my feet in frustration. But luck has bestowed upon me the opportunity to bring about the medicine the doctor spoke of. For I am fortunate enough to be born in the year and month of the tiger. It took a long time, but finally, I might be able to transform my disloyalty into loyalty. How splendid that my death was delayed, and my life can be of use. But now, you must act swiftly!"

Matsuhei gestured towards the room beyond the shōji screen with his chin. Discovering there were two bowls with livers in them, Misao retrieved them.

(6.11)

She said, "To be so devoted and loyal to bring us this medicine... Mother, come quickly and witness Matsuhei's virtuous deed. What a joyous thing!" She got out the powdered medicine from before, placed all the ingredients in a bowl, and mixed them together. After administering the medicine to Kozue, the most miraculous event unfolded. Kozue opened her eyes almost immediately. To Misao's astonishment and Kozue's amazement, her fresh eyes scanning the room were as bright as polished mirrors. Seeing Kozue look at every nook and cranny made Matsuhei happy, and he told the story of the monkey's bravery at the end. Then he smiled with joy, for he had proven his loyalty. Inside, however, he suffered greatly, his complexion growing pale. Blood spurted from his wound, and he collapsed, drawing one last breath.

Kozue and Misao wailed, but the young child did not understand. He crawled over to the lifeless body and moved it, making it rock a bit, which made him laugh. In a voice thick with tears, Kozue said, "The old are a burden and should depart first, but due to this unexpected eye disease, I have brought hardship on you and Matsuhei. May the kami and the Buddhas welcome these two for saving me, who has no reason to go on living. I am forever indebted to the skilled doctor's concoction and Matsuhei's loyalty."

Kozue prostrated herself. Together with Misao, they chanted the name of the Buddha, weeping even more than before. After regaining their composure, they recounted the story to the neighbors. The village elders spread the word of the life and death of the most loyal retainer. They hired people to take care of the corpses of Matsuhei and the little monkey, and as a token of their appreciation, they carried out Buddhist funeral rites every seven days for seven weeks thereafter.

And so, Misao was left disheartened with Matsuhei's passing, and needed to rely on her mother-in-law as well. Like always, she carried her child as she conducted her business. Without fail she went every day and provided a meager living for her mother and child.

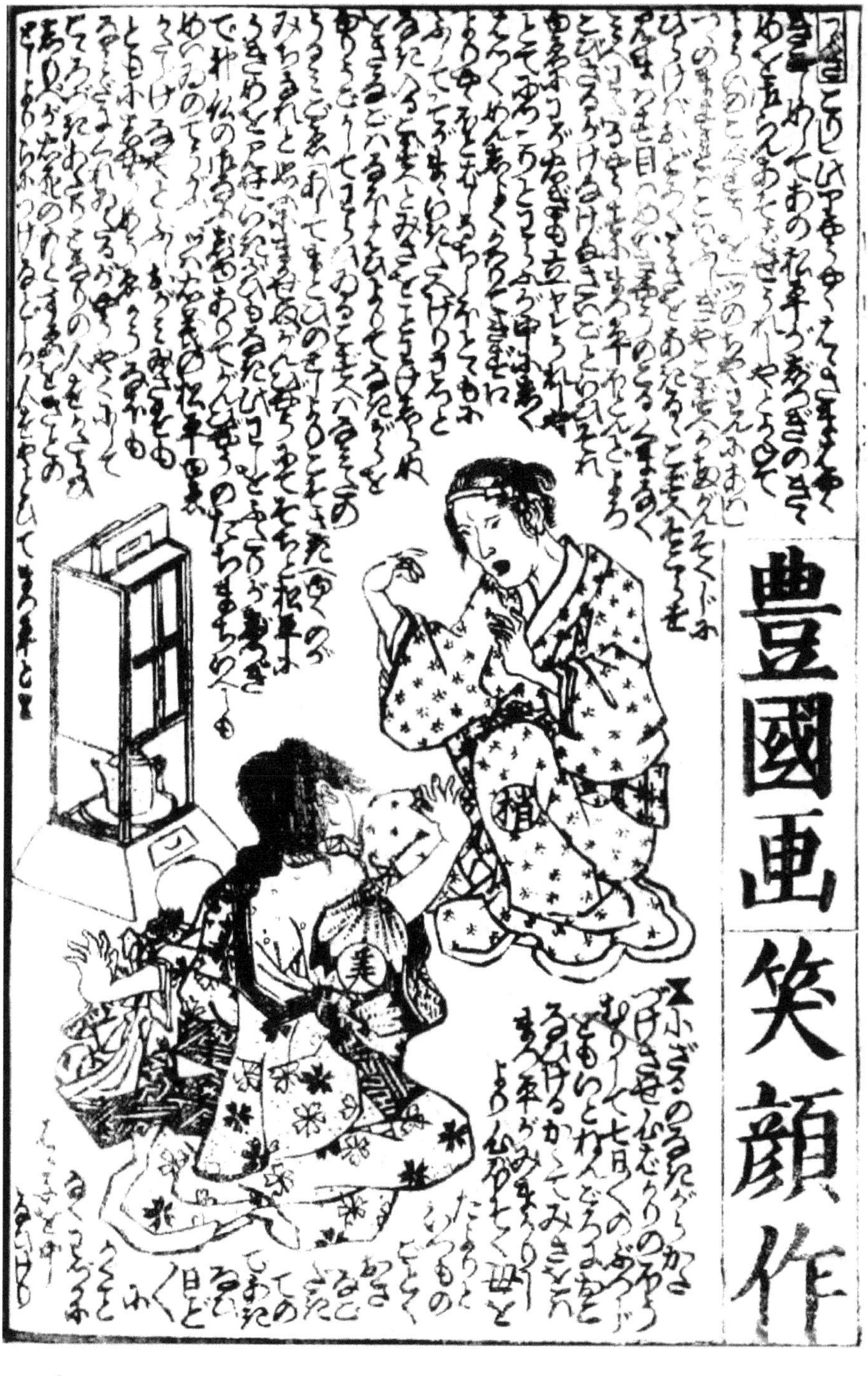

6.11

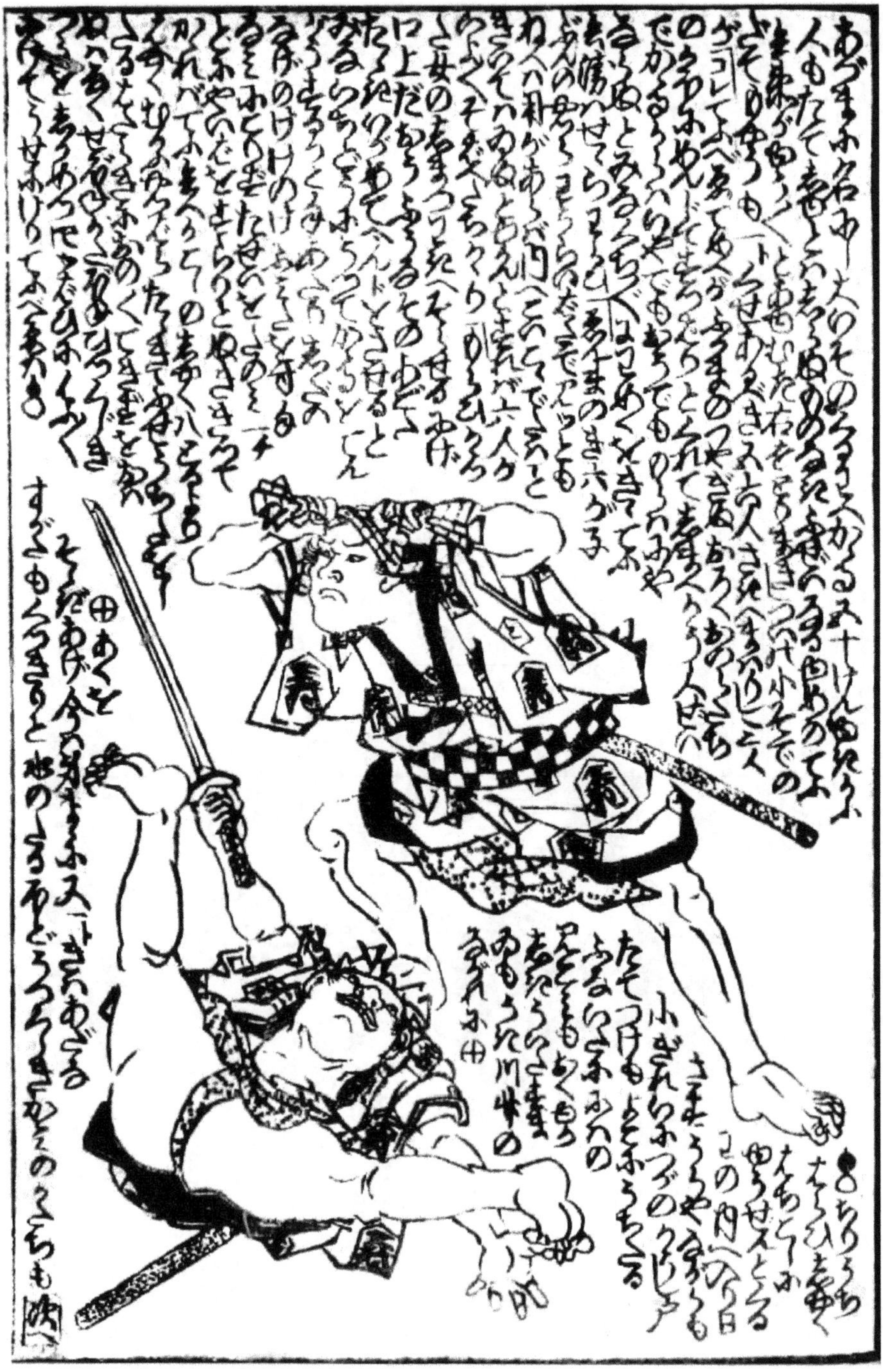

6.12

Part II

(6.12)
On the famed main street running through the Ōiso entertainment district in the east, Chōbei the dreamer strolled leisurely. Among the people frequenting the district, there was none who did not know of Chōbei—the dreaming butterfly and chivalrous delinquent. As he walked, a group of five or six men wearing matching kosode kimonos in a gaudy pattern came and surrounded him. Three circled in front of Chōbei, clamoring over one another, and announced, "Chōbei! You always keep Tsuyaginu Oroku to yourself, but we demand that you hand her over! If you want to keep doing business here in Ōiso, whether you agree or not, we must have her!"

"Enma no Kiroku's henchmen sure are a disgraceful bunch, causing such a scene at the side of the road! If you have business with me, come inside. I will not entertain your drivel out here," Chōbei retorted, and continued walking.

The six men closed in on him, saying, "You're just trying to distract us and avoid giving over the woman we've come for. We'll beat the answer out of that arrogant mouth of yours!"

They all rushed at him simultaneously, falling over one another in a haphazard advance. Lacking any finesse, they tried to rely on sheer numbers. It appeared as though they intended to pummel, kick, and trample Chōbei. However, at once they all drew swords and tried to cut him down. With a swift hand, Chōbei grasped the *shakuhachi* flute at his hip and beat his attackers to the ground. None of them escaped the beating without injury. With their backs and shoulders sprained, they crawled away on all fours, howling while covering their faces, and escaped. Chōbei brushed off the dust from his clothes and calmly returned the shakuhachi to its place. He proceeded into the entertainment district to a house in the back alleys.

The house was in the sun, neat, and had a latticework door of southern Japanese hemlock which was closed up tight. The walls were covered with overlapping boards resembling a ship's hull and the garden was deep and reserved. In this alluring house was a stunning woman—Tsuyaginu.

(6.13)
Free of her contract, and in a world where the beauty of courtesans rivaled that of bamboo swaying in the flowing rivers, she stood out for her unfiltered honesty, like a patch of scum floating on the river's surface. Her hair like flowing water was done up in the common *shimadawage* hairstyle. She emitted a subtle plum blossom fragrance, and her face radiated beauty like a polished gem, untouched by the powder commonly used to whiten complexions. Hence, she was aptly called Tsuyaginu, meaning "shining silk". Since the turn of the year, however, she had taken the name Oroku. Yet, no matter how time passed, her fame endured, evident from the incessant sound of geta sandals outside her abode.

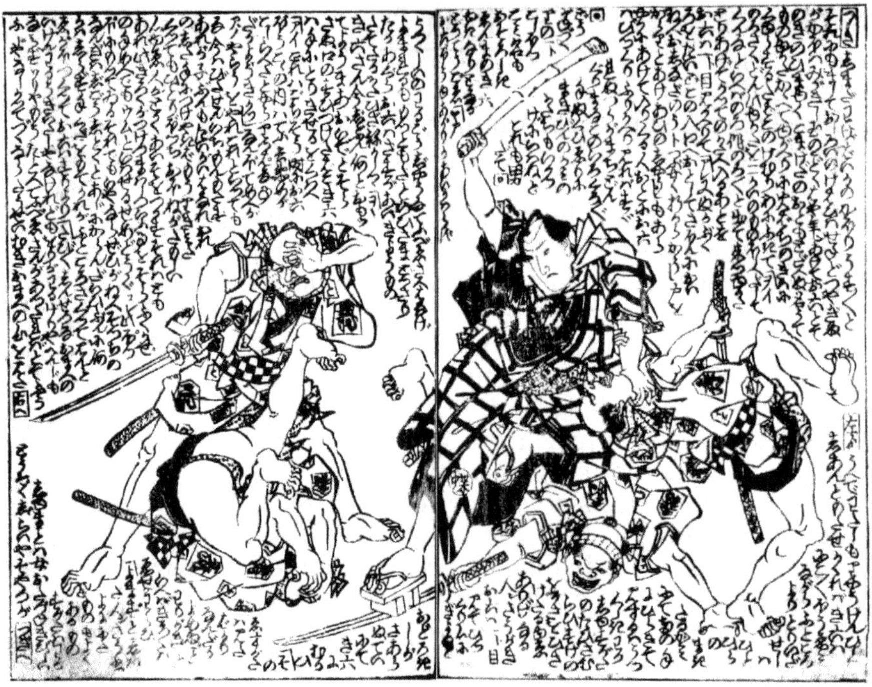

6.13

She had just come home from the public bath, carrying a yukata bathrobe in her arms. She sat down by the brazier, puffing on her pipe and blowing smoke rings.

"Hey, Norosaku, you sluggard!" she called out. "Take my yukata and put it upstairs and hang it to dry."

Norosaku appeared, slowly got the yukata, and sluggishly went through the kitchen door.

Oroku looked back at Norosaku and added, "And you dropped the rice bran bag at the entrance to the kitchen again. You're such a dunce."

As she mumbled these words, the lattice door rattled open and the shōji leading to the room was opened violently. Startled by this entrance, Oroku spun to see a man with a repugnant complexion and a wicked glint in his pitch-black, chestnut-round eyes. He wore a scarf around his neck and his hair was done up in a *makibin* hairstyle, giving him a rugged look. It went without saying that he was a ruffian who saw himself as virtuous. He carried a crude sword which was shoved unceremoniously into his obi, and his name was meant to inspire fear—Enma no Kiroku, Lord Enma's demon.

He bellowed, "Hey, Oroku! Did you just come home from the bath? You're looking lovely as always. You really are leading that stubborn and ill-tempered Chōbei around by the nose, aren't you?" As he spoke, he sat cross-legged without waiting for an invitation.

As expected from someone as captivating as Oroku, she raised one of her knees and leaned on it while saying in a straight fashion, "Kiroku-san, what is going through your head, coming here at this hour?"

Oroku gave the pipe she was smoking to Kiroku, who took it and bit down on it. "Thank you for the smoke. By the way, Oroku, this place that reprobate Chōbei has set you up with is all well and fine, but you need to listen carefully to what I have to say. That bastard talks a big game, but he doesn't have a coin to his name. He has dismissed most of his underlings, who have all come to work for me. Despite his swagger, he is all alone. Because he is base and vulgar at heart, people have long lost their fondness for him. But be that as it may, I have followed up on some things. Right here, in my breast pocket, I have something. A torture device, if you will, that can make someone as carefree as you agree to my advances. If you still refuse, I suppose there will be nothing for it, and you will suffer the consequences of your own actions."

Kiroku's words were convoluted and Oroku did not understand what he meant. "I've heard your kind opinions on numerous occasions, and although it doesn't sound bad, I haven't had the chance to respond. However, even though I have a relationship with Chōbei, it's not bound by marriage. I am free to act as I please. If you tell me what is on your mind, I might also have some ideas of my own." She said this slyly as she put on a smile and edged closer to Kiroku to detect what he had in his breast pocket.

With a grin, Kiroku revealed what he was hiding—a rolled-up piece of paper that he unraveled and held up with both hands. On it was a picture of a beautiful wakashū dressed like a traveling samurai, holding a small, bamboo hat. From the looks of it, it was a wanted poster. At the first glimpse of it, Oroku became stunned. Her heart skipped a beat, but she pretended nothing was amiss.

She said, "I have never seen this portrait before. I cannot read it, but it looks like some explanatory poster."

(6.14)

Kiroku replied, "Even if you can't read it, it is a very well-known wanted poster. There are indeed many people who look like this, and yet, although it looks exactly like a wakashū, it is actually a woman. A woman who is the sister of the notorious bandit Jiraiya and goes by the name Tsuyaginu. Wait, is it Tsuya—no, it is just you, *Oroku*. This picture sure does look like the spitting image of you. If only I can get a simple 'yes' from you, I promise to tear this wanted poster to shreds and burn it to ash in the brazier."

Oroku stared intently at the wanted poster, comparing her face to that of the poster in her mind. Then it dawned on her what Kiroku's scheme was.

"Even if it is someone else, I look exactly like this wakashū—"

"Indeed, you do."

"In that case—"

"Yes. The way I see it, I can tie you up, hand you in, and collect the reward money. I will leave it to you to figure out what choice is the right one. So, let's hear your answer." With a dominating attitude, Kiroku edged closer to Oroku as he said this.

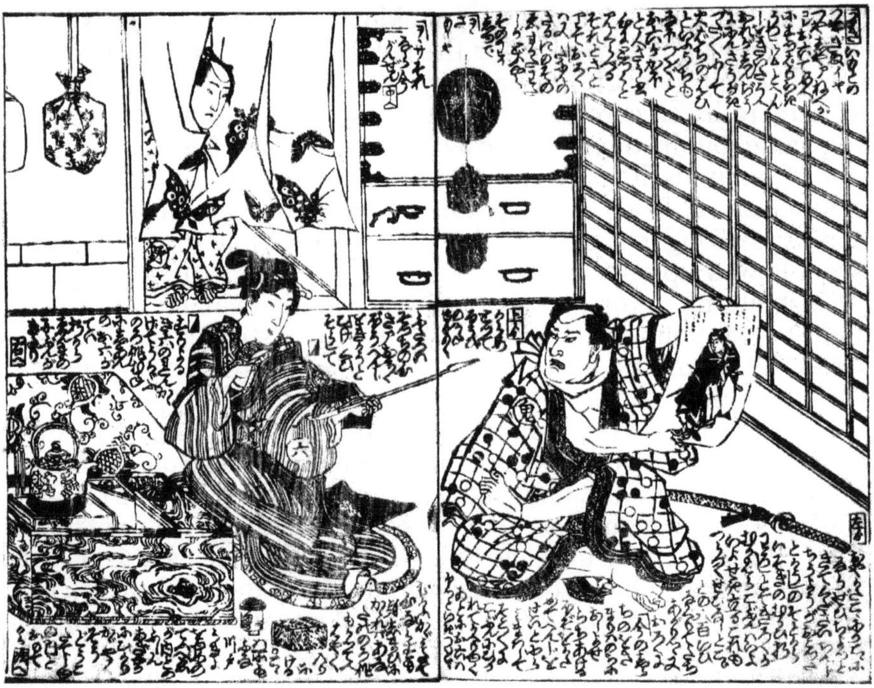

6.14

Norosaku was peeking through the *noren* curtain, observing Oroku, who appeared to have devised a plan. However, just then the voices of Kiroku's henchmen were heard outside the lattice door.

"Boss, are you in there? If you are, could you please come with us? Something terrible has happened!"

They were in a hurry to get their boss to come with them. Kiroku got angry, but his henchmen insisted. They showered him with arguments, saying it was a matter of saving face, and begged for immediate action.

Kiroku got up and said to Oroku, "I will return and resolve this matter once I've dealt with my business. So, make up your mind and give me an answer by then!" His menacing scowl swept the room, and then he left, pulled along by his henchmen.

After Kiroku departed, Oroku let out a sigh and turned to her mirror. Unwillingly, she started getting dressed up, and Norosaku disappeared into the servant's kitchen.

In Funakawado stood the house of Chōbei, for whom the world was like the floating dream of a butterfly.[4] From the outside it was radiant like a shrine, with copper plating all over which shone in the light. It was clear this was the house of a knight-errant.

(6.15)

At that time, there came the sound of many people gathering in front of the house. Within moments, Kiroku's henchmen came through

4 Funakawado is most likely based on Hanakawado, which was in Edo, close to the Yoshiwara pleasure district and right next to Asakusa.

6.15

the door. They bore wounds all over their bodies and heads, which were covered with ointment.

"Chōbei! Are you here?" they bellowed. They stepped into the house and sat cross-legged without waiting for an invitation.

The master of the house could be heard getting up in a room farther inside. Stepping into view, he said, "What's this now, coming into someone's house uninvited? Have you come to get payback because of yesterday?"

A voice rang out from the front of the house. "I have already settled that quarrel!" It was Kiroku, who entered the house and strutted leisurely to the main seat of the room.

"Chōbei, please pardon my subordinates. They were rude and stuck their noses in where they didn't belong," said Kiroku, leering at Chōbei.

"Yesterday, I was in a foul mood and ended up injuring your men, so I suppose you would be upset."

"After their petty fight, these good-for-nothings wouldn't stop pestering me until I went to speak to you. But let's put that aside for now. Chōbei, as we both know, next month is the Sanja Matsuri festival. The funds entrusted to you for the festival belong to everyone—a collective pool, you might say. This year, I have been appointed as the cashier, and I have come to get said money. I have already prepaid all manner of things for the festival."

This demand came like a bolt out of the blue and caught Chōbei off guard.

"Come now, Kiroku. The festival is still a month away. Surely you don't need the money today?"

Kiroku opened his eyes wide and retorted, "Next month might sound like it's far away, but today is the twenty-fifth! Chōbei, you can't possibly mean to say that you've spent the deposit money, can you?"

"Well that money—"

"Is for the festival, so if you have it, hand it over already! But it doesn't seem like you have any money now, does it? I bet you spent the entire deposit on that house for Oroku," Kiroku said, staring offensively at Chōbei.

Chōbei got upset, but upon reflection, he had indeed spent the money and had nothing on him to offer. Thus, he sat there without saying a word, looking like he had no idea what to do.

Kiroku chuckled to himself and taunted, "What's with the long face? Aren't you supposed to be a 'knight-errant' and an honorable man? Don't think you can charm your way out of having spent the money people broke their backs to earn. Just so you don't try to get by on your good looks, here's what I'll do." Kiroku raised his pipe and brought it down on Chōbei's forehead, causing a spurt of blood.

"Isn't this a bit too much?" Chōbei exclaimed, standing with a mortified look on his face.

This made Kiroku yell, "Too much? Don't be making a fuss! I will be going through your finances next!"

As Kiroku threw his weight around, a wallet came flying from the front door and landed on the floor with a thud. Kiroku was startled, and Chōbei picked up the wallet. He turned it in his hands and read out, "Dowry," which was written on the back. During this, Kinosuke came in, dressed as a samurai, accompanied by Oroku. Norosaku, who actually hailed from Shinano, also entered, carrying a ritual saké barrel.

Kinosuke said to Chōbei, "Questions later, right now just hurry up and take the money you need so we can settle this."

Chōbei nodded in agreement.

(6.16)

The money in the wallet made up one hundred ryō in koban gold coins, which Chōbei threw before Kiroku. "I hereby give you the money for the festival. Take it!"

Picking it up, Kiroku responded, "Of course, why wouldn't I? Don't suspect it's counterfeit copper imitations either. I will admit my defeat. You are indeed an honorable man, compensating the money pool with this dowry. However, I still have a score to settle with you regarding my men!"

Chōbei immediately grabbed his katana. "You have insulted my honor, and I demand satisfaction!" As he got up, Oroku got in front of him, while Kinosuke held up a saké flask and cup and stepped in between the two.

"Though I am not a matchmaker, today I shall play the role of one!" Kinosuke said, adopting a conciliatory tone. "It is a glorious day, for

6.16

Chōbei is taking a bride. But the celebration is just for close friends, if you understand."

Kiroku had a sour look on his face and said, "This will be your last toast as man and wife. I will make you weep with the wanted poster. You just wait and see!" His anger was evident, and his words filled with venom.

"I will not let you!" Chōbei retorted, rising again. But Kinosuke was quick-witted, so he stepped in and insisted Chōbei and Oroku exchange saké cups, as is tradition during a wedding.

Choosing to vent his anger on Norosaku, who was idling in the room, Kiroku kicked him. This outburst also turned over both the table and the saké barrel, spilling the liquid all over the tatami mats.

The commotion was Kiroku's way of getting revenge, so he departed with his men, stomping on the tatami as they left. The remaining three exchanged sorry looks. As Kinosuke and Oroku calmed Chōbei down, Norosaku tidied up the barrel and the table, taking them into the kitchen.

Kinosuke turned to Chōbei. "We seem to have defeated Kiroku by overwhelming him with money and with this sudden marriage and your bride moving in. The world is yet again at peace. You and Oroku are now a genuine married couple. Norosaku, since you're here, could you go cook some rice or something?"

Chōbei's complexion finally returned to normal, and he furrowed his eyebrow in disbelief. "I can hardly grasp what is going on, Kinosuke-san. But you took all the burden upon yourself by giving Kiroku that deposit. One hundred ryō is quite an enormous sum."

Kinosuke nodded. "That money was provided by none other than Oroku-san's older brother. There's no need to thank me."

With a perplexed look on his face, Chōbei blurted out, "I had no idea you had a brother, Oroku. What kind of man is he?"

"My brother is a warrior in the capital. He will come visit me this year, and you can meet him then," Oroku answered.

Hearing this, Chōbei tried to ask about Oroku's past. "You've never told me about this brother, but the rumor—"

But Kinosuke knew it would be a lengthy tale, so he interjected, "We can always have that conversation later. The sun is setting, and I still have to finish my duties as the matchmaker. So, Chō-san, Oroku-san..." and made ready to leave.

Together, Chōbei and Oroku said, "We cannot thank you enough for taking care of us today and bringing us this happiness."

After saying their parting words, Kinosuke set out for home.

In the bustling Ōiso district on the eastern roads, truly famous through all the provinces, the tea houses were lined up tightly with their open fronts. The food was lavish and the saké overflowed. One of the guests was said to be a close friend of the Ashikaga clan, who had ruled Kamakura for generations. He was a master of the Meppō martial arts school, well-versed in swordplay, military tactics, and heroics. His name was Gōtekisai Muyami Gundazaemon.

(6.17)

He was an elderly man with hair as white as snow but a young-looking face. He possessed a selfish disposition and an affinity for heavy drinking. On this particular day, he had brought along five or six of his pupils to revel in merriment. On the streets, the well-known Oyoshi played her small *surigane* gong and sang popular songs. Inside her candy container, her laughing child made up the cargo. The candy was selling more than Oyoshi expected, but Gundazaemon was watching with a disgruntled expression. Struck by a thought, he yelled out in a dismissive voice, "What a racket that surigane makes! My ears are ringing. Hurry up and go somewhere else!"

This caused Oyoshi to examine him closely, and she was surprised at what she saw. Although on the verge of rushing toward him, she remained, as if making up her mind about something. Eventually, she quickened the pace on the surigane, headed out the district's main gate, and hurried home.

That night, after the bell had rung eight times,[5] sending its echoing voice out into the lonely night, traffic on the embankment along the river ceased, and the seventh bell drew near. Misao had put her child to sleep on a folding chair inside a roadside tea house and had concealed herself behind a reed screen, keeping a watchful eye on a palanquin on the embankment. Diligently, Kozue had come with her, armed with her trusted sword.

5 01:00.

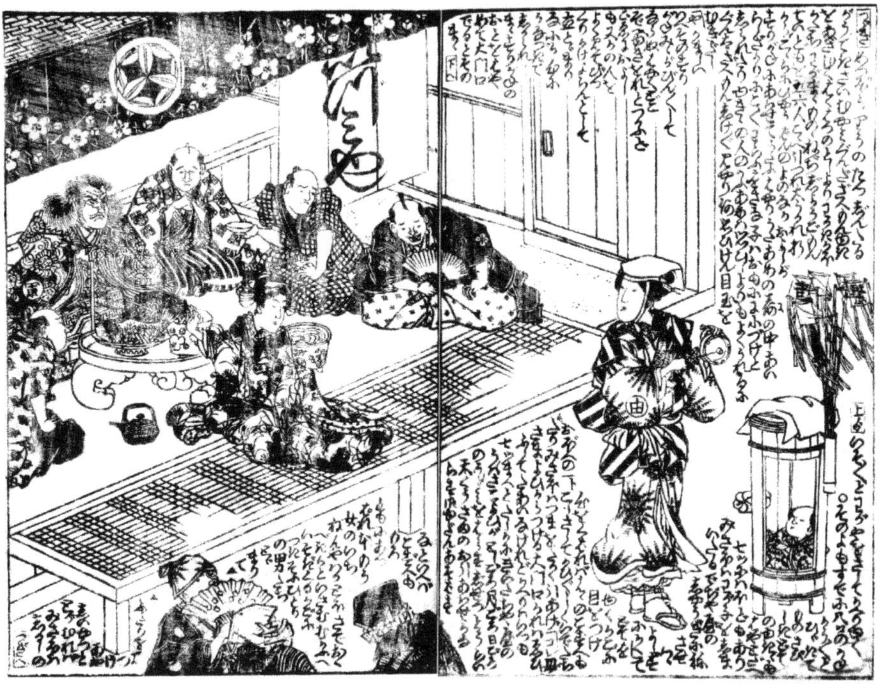

6.17

The palanquin swiftly came closer and one of the men accompanying it halted as he caught sight of the two women. "Who goes there?" he questioned.

(6.18)

Without hesitation, Misao knocked over the man carrying the lantern, and Kozue yelled out, "Get out of our way, man!" as she advanced with her sword. Alarmed, the man crossed swords with Kozue.

While they fought, Misao unleashed her wrath upon the palanquin. "Tatsumaki Arakurō! Reveal yourself at once! You may have dyed your hair white, but I will *never* mistake your face!"

Misao made ready to draw her blade, frightening the bearers who panicked and threw down the palanquin before fleeing. She stepped closer to the palanquin. Inside, Gundazaemon was snoring. He woke up, and without making any fuss, he said, "Such pretentious yelling about vengeance, you better prepare yourselves, you bitches!"

Gundazaemon stretched his legs, kicking open the door. Misao was staggered but did not waver. She slipped in close, planning to draw her blade and cut the man in one smooth motion. Gundazaemon, however, was nigh on invincible, and from inside the palanquin he grabbed his broad-bladed sword. There was a flash, bright and fast as lightning, and Misao was cut down.

Then he turned to his retainer and said, "Take care of that one as well. She annoys me."

6.18

Misao hitched up the hem of her kimono and said to Kozue, "Listen now, mother. What I heard in the tea shop is that he will always, no matter how intoxicated he gets, go home before the seventh bell from the main gate. Tonight, the time for us to fulfill our grudge that we have held for days and months and years has finally come. The gods have guided us to this point, so do not let your guard down!"

Kozue replied enthusiastically, "Finally, we shall have satisfaction! A determined woman never lets up!"

6.19

Encouraged by Gundazaemon's words, the retainer stepped forward and attacked. Although his opponent was not any ordinary old woman, witnessing Misao being overcome shattered her resolve. He took advantage of this and cut Kozue down. He then moved over Kozue and delivered the final blow. Severely injured, Misao gritted her teeth as she could only watch. From within the roadside tea house, the sound of a baby crying could be heard. Gundazaemon ordered his retainer to locate the infant. He did not put his swords to the child, but instead threw him off the embankment. The seventh bell tolled, and numerous palanquins started showing up as they were heading home. Gundazaemon, fearing questioning, lacked the time to finish off Misao. Therefore, he left his palanquin and fled undercover with his retainer.

Weakened by pain, Misao tried to crawl over to Kozue's lifeless body, but instead fell down the embankment. Rain trickled, and by the steps on the road at the foot of the embankment, a palanquin was settled. One of the bearers bowed and said, "Pardon me, sir, but this rain has caught us off guard, so I must run and get my rain mantle." Then he ran off, and the other bearer followed suit, claiming he also had something he had to attend to.

(6.19)

The grass rustled as the child, merely two years old, crawled around crying. The curtain of the palanquin opened at the piteous sound, revealing a man. His name was Samezaya Jiroza, a handsome and well-known rōnin who had recently moved to town. When the rain had slowed to a drizzle, Jiroza put on his low wooden *komageta* clogs and looked closer. Among the grass, he noticed a woman's corpse, stained crimson red. The cries of the child were deplorable, so Jiroza stepped closer and tried to console the infant.

"There's a good boy. Don't cry, don't cry."

The child stopped crying, and the woman rose, groaning, "Damn you, fiend! I won't let you escape!" She used her sword like a cane to stand but fell to the ground again in pain.

Jiroza spoke out to her. "I understand you may be delirious, but still your heart and look closely. I am not the fiend you seek. I only just arrived here, yet I can see you need my help. Start by telling me what has transpired."

The wounded woman stared at Jiroza and then prostrated herself before him. With pained breath, she said, "I do not know who you are, but I have one request of you." The child nestled up to his blood-soaked mother and took to her breast. The woman gazed single-mindedly at the child's face. "Together with my mother-in-law and my child, we set out on a vendetta. After many trials and tribulations, we finally managed to come across the target of our vengeance. We thought we would finally get satisfaction, but it did not go as we would have it. After all, we are but weak women as you can see, and the tables were turned against us. Thankfully, the life of this young one was spared, but I worry he will now grow up an orphan."

While listening intently to her tale of suffering, Jiroza leaned against his palanquin. Blinking his eyes rapidly, he spoke in an encouraging voice, "No, Milady, your wounds are not too deep. Rest assured, you will be fine. However, could you kindly tell me where you come from?"

The wounded woman took a long breath before saying, "I am ashamed of my story, but here it is. My home is with the lord of Sarashina in Shinano. I am Misao, the wife of Himematsu Sumatarō, and my mother-in-law is Kozue. My husband and my father-in-law were both killed by a man named Tatsumaki Arakurō, who served alongside my husband. Since then, our lives have been nothing but struggle. This boy is all that is left of my husband. I beseech you, consider the wretched and miserable future my child faces. I beg you to have some compassion. Deliver him to my older brother and make sure we are avenged."

Taking this to heart, Jiroza asked, "And who is your brother?"

"My brother serves in the same house as my husband did. His name is Takasago Yuminosuke, and he is an incredibly valiant warrior. He was going to help us get our revenge, but alas, he was called on different business by his lord and had to return home."

Jiroza wiped the tears welling up in his eyes. "Your misfortune truly has been cruel. Your story is too much for me to bear. But worry not for your child. I will make sure to deliver him to Takasago and tell him everything, even if it kills me!"

(6.20)

His kind words made Misao forget about her pain for a moment, and she spoke to her child. "From today you will be in the care of this kind

6.20

man. Do not throw any tantrums or cry excessively. Hurry and become a man, and avenge your grandfather, grandmother, father, and me."

Misao, weakened by her wound, finally felt at ease and relaxed. Then her eyes closed, her face went pale, and she collapsed.

"Children being separated from their parents. Such is the way of this material world. Come with me little one," Jiroza said, his eyes welling up with tears once again as he reached out his hand.

The boy clung to Jiroza's hand, and as Jiroza held him, the child smiled and laughed. He never looked back at his poor deceased mother. His innocent and young heart was quick to accept new people, not just his mother, who had always been by his side.

Just then, Kinosuke arrived in a hurry, panting. Disturbed by what he saw, he asked, "What is all this?"

Amidst Kinosuke's disarray, Jiroza replied, "First, tell me what happened with the thing I asked of you." Jiroza listened as Kinosuke whispered something close to his ear. When he finished, Jiroza said, "I will explain everything that transpired here later. For now, place this woman's body in the palanquin and have it taken to the fields."

As the two were talking, the two palanquin bearers returned. Jiroza thought this was perfect timing, and he instructed one of them, "I have a task that needs attending to, so go fetch another palanquin," and sent him off. He had the other bearer assist Kinosuke in placing Misao's body into the palanquin, and in time the second palanquin arrived, as requested. They put Kozue's body, which was lying at the top of the embankment, into the second palanquin.

6.21

"I apologize for burdening you with this, but they must be given a proper funeral," Jiroza said to Kinosuke, who nodded in agreement.

Kinosuke helped hoist up the palanquins, and they hurried off before dawn broke. Samezaya Jiroza watched them depart and murmured to himself, "I cannot leave this poor child to fend for himself. And I am certain the 'fiend' Misao spoke of must be *that* man..."

Chōbei the dreamer stood atop the embankment, holding an umbrella and a lantern, observing the scene below. Suspicious of what he saw, he descended the stairs. Jiroza heard the sound of his footsteps but pretended not to notice and continued walking, allowing Chōbei to follow him.

(6.21)

Suddenly, a rogue appeared, pushing his way out from among the grass of the embankment, sword drawn. Without a word, he struck at Chōbei, who jumped out of the way. In the glow of the lantern's light, he caught a quick glimpse of the rogue's face.

"You must be Enma no Kiroku! Fancy meeting you here!" Chōbei called out, throwing the lantern down and putting up his guard.

Kiroku retorted, "Chōbei, my grudge is upon you! I will take you apart and have Oroku as my wife. Say your prayers!" He swung at Chōbei, who parried the sword with his umbrella.

Jiroza stopped in his tracks for a while to watch the two fight. Beneath the dark sky on the cusp of dawn, the only light revealing the shapes of the fighters were the sparks of the blades crashing together.

Kiroku lunged, swinging his sword wildly. He mistook Jiroza for Chōbei and swung at him. However, Jiroza sidestepped, moving closer to Kiroku and slipping past him. Kiroku's blade cut through the air, and he lost his balance. Chōbei saw an opening, reached out, and grabbed the hair at the scruff of Kiroku's neck. Staggering, Chōbei pulled Kiroku back towards the lantern, and in the flickering candlelight, the three finally saw each other's faces. Suspicious of Jiroza, Chōbei and Kiroku surrounded him while brandishing their blades. Kiroku had a quick temper, so he attacked Jiroza without reservation. Chōbei struck the swishing blade out of the air and grabbed Kiroku's arm and twisted it.

(6.22)

In that moment, as the lantern's flame flickered out, Jiroza vanished without a trace. Kiroku tried to free his arm. As he flailed around, he knocked the lantern over, reigniting its flame. And there, in the rising smoke of the lantern, Jiroza could be seen, holding the crying baby, patting its back, and singing a lullaby. He exchanged a glance with the mystified Chōbei, and when the light of the lantern disappeared again, so did he.

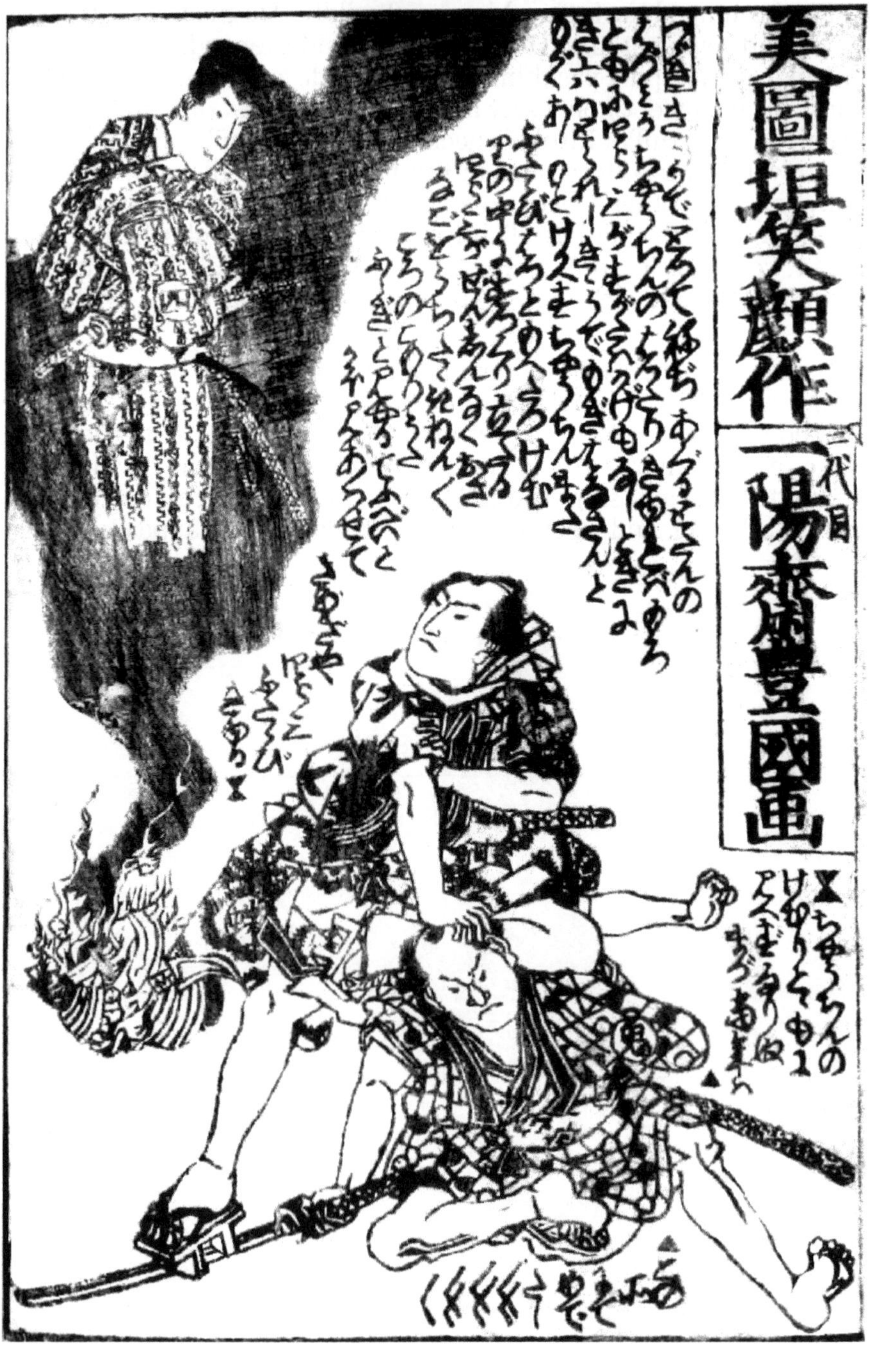

6.22

And thus, the tale concludes for this year.

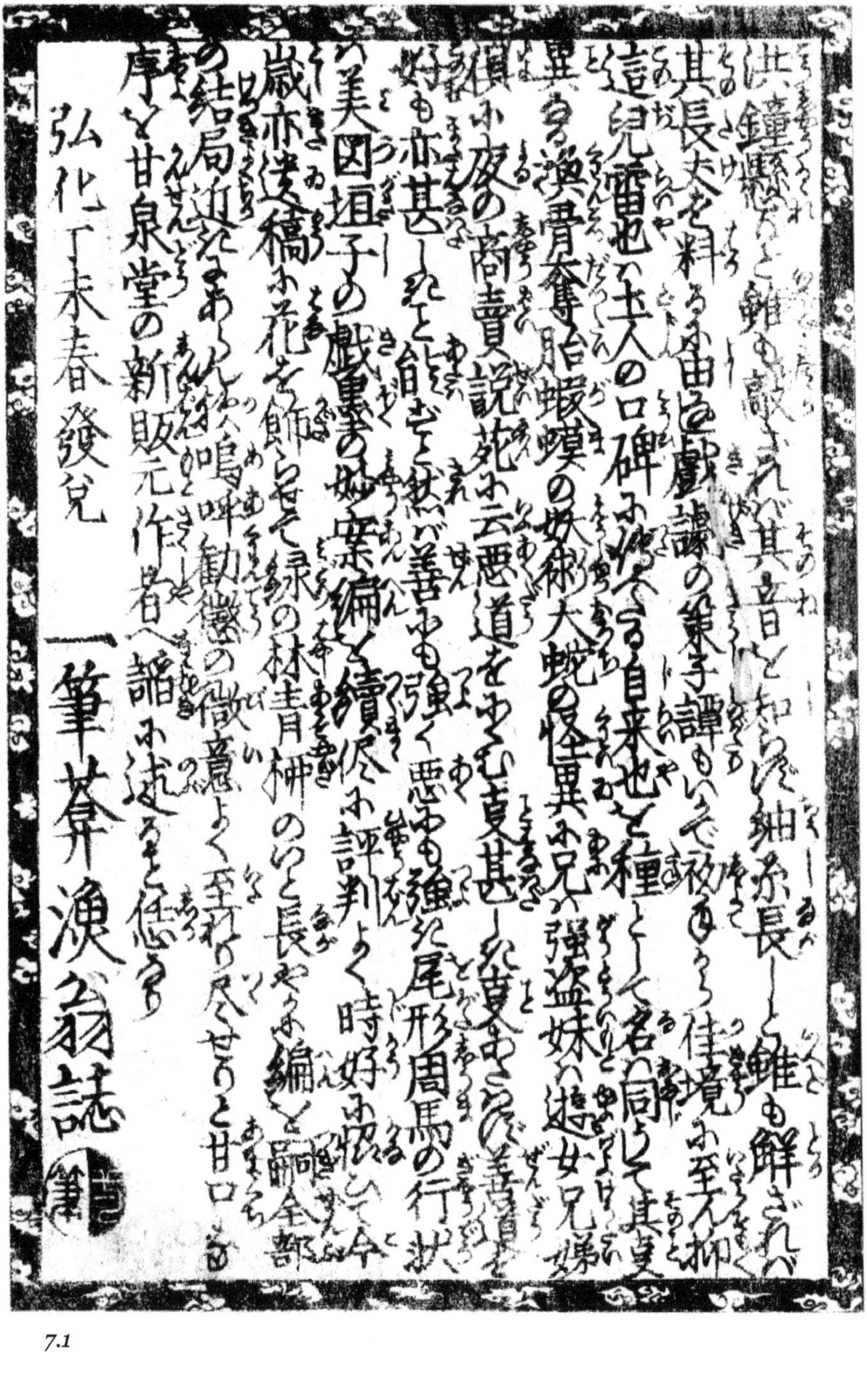

洪鐘懸ると雖も敲ざれば其音を知らず細亦長しと雖も鮮ざれば
其長丈を料るに由なし戯謔の稗子譚もいへで夜をふかす佳境に至る抑
這児雷也は古人の口碑に傳ふる自来也を種として名同して其実
異なる換骨奪胎蝦蟆の妖術大蛇の怪異に兄は強盗妹は遊女兄嫁
は貨小夜の商賣説苑に云悪道を求むる事甚しき者は亦其善道を
好も亦甚しと能くすと然ば善にも強く悪にも強き尾形周馬の行状は
美図垣子の戯墨の妙案編を續て尽に評判よく時好に恊ひて今
歳亦後編を稿に花を飾らぬ緑の林青柳のいと長き編を續で全部
の結局近きにあらん嗚呼勧懲の微意よく至れり尽せりと甘口なる
序を甘泉堂の新販元作者へ諂に流るを恐る

弘化丁未春發兌

一筆菴渙翁誌

7.1

Book 7

Although the grand bell hangs, if it is not struck, one remains unaware of its sound. Even if the silk thread is long, unless it is unraveled, one cannot measure its length. How can a dramatic narrative unfold from the opening to the climax? The Jiraiya of this tale takes its seed from the Chinese oral stories. Albeit the name is the same, it is a very different retelling. There is toad yōjutsu and monstrous snakes. The older brother is a bandit, the younger sister is a courtesan; both siblings engaged in the nighttime trade. As said in *Garden of Eloquence*, "He neither abhors the path of evil to an extreme degree, nor is he capable of loving the path of good to an extreme degree." However, following the ingenious schemes of Mizugaki's dramatic brush, Ogata Shūma is strong in both good and evil.

Continuously praised, this year I now adorn this posthumous work with flowers. A story, which has become a work of great length, like the weeping branches of willows in green groves. A story soon to be concluded, perhaps?

Alas! When this sweet-talking successor expresses his humble opinion that this story of rewarding good and admonishing evil leaves nothing to be desired, it is but flattery of the original author in this new publication from Kansendō publishing house.

Kōka era—Year of the Fire Sheep—Spring (1847)

Ippitsuan

7.2

Tagoto-hime, daughter of the Sarashina clan.

Leader of the bandits of Mount Kurohime, Jiraiya. Real name Ogata Shūma Hiroyuki.

7.3

Oroku, wife of Chōbei the dreamer, her comb aslant.
Takasago Yuminosuke the virtuous retainer.
Gōtekisai Muyami Gundazaemon, retainer to the Shōgun. Real name—Tatsumaki Arakurō.

7.4

Enma no Kiroku the evildoer.

Knight-errant Chōbei the dreamer.

Samezaya Jiroza.

Chōbei the dreamer took his name from the Butterfly Dream of *Zhuangzi*. A self-styled humanitarian delinquent, who cares not for good or evil but punishes the strong and rescues the weak, called a knight-errant with no regards for his own life.

7.5

Illustration showing the Sarashina clan preparing for its daughter to marry into the Tsukikage clan.

Part I

(7.5)
Sarashina Hangan Mitsuaki, lord of Shinano, and Tsukikage *Gunryō* Terutoki, lord of Echigo, were apt to war over border territories. They would amass soldiers and meet in battle, bringing much suffering to the people. In Kamakura, however, the clan that held the supreme administrative position of *Kanrei*, decreed the two clans had to reconcile through marriage. Thus, the Sarashina clan were to wed their daughter Tagoto-hime to Miyukinosuke, the son of the Tsukikage clan, aiming to ensure a long-lasting and peaceful relationship between the two clans. The Tsukikage clan sent numerous engagement gifts, and the Sarashina clan made the marriage preparations for Tagoto-hime.

They carefully selected the most auspicious day for the wedding and sent a marriage contract to Miyukinosuke. Tagoto-hime had her teeth blackened and her hair done up in the *marumage* to signify she was a married woman. Soon, she would depart for Echigo and needed to ensure she was fully prepared. She had already stocked up on clothes and belongings, but seeing it all piled up, she decided it still was not quite enough. Too many things were missing. To address this, she purchased new gold brocade and satin damask clothes and personal items. She prepared all manner of things until she felt it was just right. Relatives and friends of the family competed over who could give her the finest parting gift, including rolls of silk, cotton fabrics, decorative boxes, and incense burners. There was a double door cabinet for her books, a black lacquered shelving unit, and containers for her painted shells. They spared no efforts to make the preparations as outstanding as possible, and as the days went by, the presents kept coming. The accumulation of gifts grew to such an extent that all the things stacked up and filled a large banquet room, leaving very little space. The entire room was so bright and sparkly, that when people walked by, it was like seeing a room full of flowers. All anyone could talk about was this magnificent spectacle.

Within the household, farewell greeters arrived incessantly, and receptions took place every single day. Because of this, all the elderly ladies, maids, and various servants became even busier. While this was going on, all were anxious with anticipation and the number of men and women coming and going was a hundred-fold of what it usually was. From the liveliness and people laughing and calling out to each other, there was not a single quiet moment. The day of the bridal procession drew near, and the preparations were almost completed.

The hills of Kamakura on a starry and moonlit night were prosperous, like a place where trees of gold grow. The capital truly was wearing the colors of spring. Chōbei stood on Hanamizu Bridge, aptly named the "Bridge of Flower Waters," capturing the essence of the season. He had taken his name from the Butterfly Dream of *Zhuangzi*, which reflected his philosophical outlook on life. Chōbei, the self-appointed knight-errant of the area, commanded a devoted following of subordinates and loyalists. However, on a day now past, he had spent a festival fund on a loan which he intended to compensate for. Unbeknownst to Chōbei however, Enma no Kiroku had a lover's grudge against him and shamed him. As Kiroku relentlessly pursued him, Tsuruhashiya Kinosuke devised a plan. Kinosuke had secretly received one hundred ryō from Jiroza to give as Oroku's dowry which he used to save Chōbei from dishonor. But Kiroku clung to his grudge, secretly scheming for the perfect opportunity to strike back.

(7.6)

Oroku had shaved her eyebrows and was making her debut as a wife. Guests came in large numbers and celebratory saké was poured. Kiroku, aware of this festive occasion, believed it to be the perfect moment to exact revenge and humiliate Chōbei once again. As he pushed through the rope curtain with his head, the face that appeared was as bitter looking as Lord Enma himself, as if he had tasted powdered incense.

"Chōbei, are you in here?" he called out in a disrespectful tone.

"Ah, Enma no Kiroku! I was wondering who it might be. If you've come about the festival funds, then surely you have no further business with me. So, why are you here?"

"Why, you ask? Well, I have something I think you might want to hear."

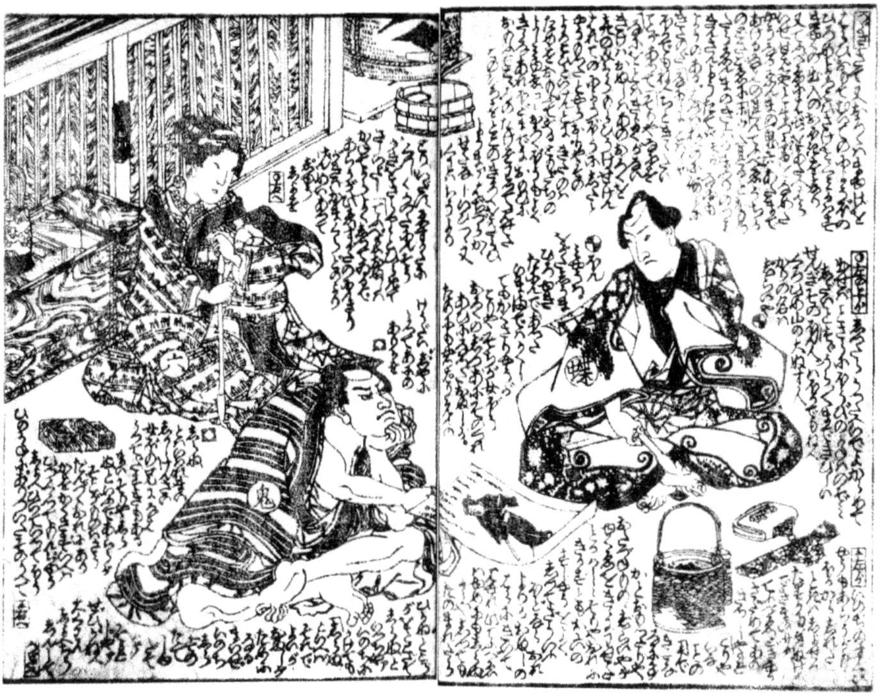

7.6

"And what might that be?" Chōbei inquired.

"Nothing pleasant, I can assure you. I am not here to argue against your happiness, even if it's obvious to everyone that you got Oroku as your wife through Kinosuke. I am here solely because I want what is best for you, my friend. Oroku, you should pay attention to this as well. I poured my heart out to you, Oroku, but you spurned me, a perfect lady-killer, and you shamed my face."

As he spoke, Kiroku extracted a meticulously detailed wanted poster from inside his kimono, unfolded it, and extended it forward.

"Chōbei, I suspect you already know, but this wanted poster carries the strictest order from the lord of Kamakura. If you know the whereabouts of the man on the poster, you must come forth and report it. You will be rewarded with as much gold as you desire if it leads to his capture. In every port and harbor they are searching for this man. He is none other than the thief of Mount Kurohime, known as Jiraiya, but his true name is Ogata Shūma Hiroyuki. There is no hiding it any longer. That man is Oroku's older brother. And since you are now married to Oroku, that makes him your brother-in-law. Surely, you cannot claim ignorance of his whereabouts. However, I suspect you won't want to put your wife's brother in ropes and hand him over either. Even if you do say you don't know where he is, you should listen to my advice. If you disclose Jiraiya's location to me, I will have him bound and dragged to the High Court in Kamakura. Once I have gotten the reward money, I might be able to save your life. However, should they learn about Jiraiya's

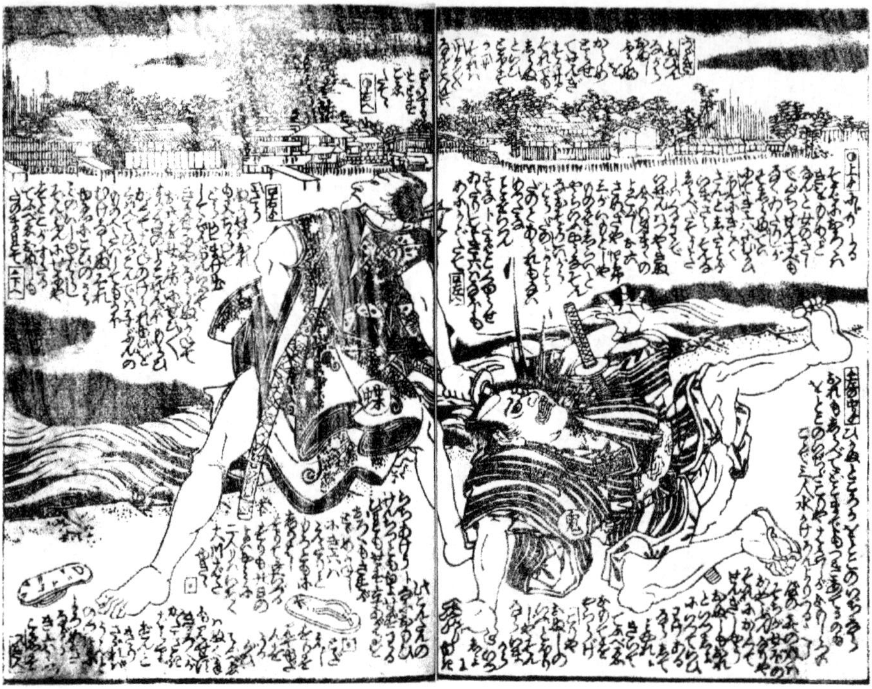

7.7

whereabouts from someone other than me, I won't be able to help you. Now, Chōbei, muster your courage and give me your answer!"

Chōbei said, "What a peculiar matter you've come here for. I was wondering what it might be, but to think you have come here to inquire about the whereabouts of the wanted Jiraiya? Hahaha! You don't need me to tell you this, but you know where Oroku comes from. So rather than asking me, maybe you should just ask your own belly for an answer. Not even in my wildest dreams do I know. But even if I did, I am a knight-errant. If I have been asked to do something, I cannot back down. Even if claiming ignorance risks my own life."

(7.7)

"If you insist you don't know, then so be it. But it won't bode well for you in the end, you reckless knight-errant. I guess there is nothing for it then. I will report you to the magistrate's office. And although it is regrettable, they will take both of you in for interrogation and torture. Do you still maintain that you don't know where Jiraiya is?"

"Well..."

"Hurry up and say your answer already!" bellowed Kiroku rudely, and he inched closer to Chōbei.

Beside them, Oroku was sitting and pondering what to do. Though it wasn't her place to interfere as a woman, she thought there was no other option. So, in a confused tone she turned to Kiroku and said, "Kiroku-san, I don't understand how you have reached such conclusions. I used to live in the pleasure district under the name Tsuyaginu. Now I am retired from that life, my hair done plain, and my name is Oroku. I am Samezaya Jiroza's younger sister, not some bandit or night burglar named Jirai or anything of the sort. Don't even say such extreme and unthinkable things."

Kiroku's eyes narrowed with anger. "If that is what you say, then you leave me no choice but to put it all out there and say everything! I have tried time and time again to make Oroku my wife, but she has rebuffed all my advances. If I step aside now, I won't be able to face my followers. I must get my vengeance on you and settle my grudge, otherwise it will tarnish my honor as a man!

"Chōbei, you say yourself that it is a man's nature to never go back on his word. I will continue investigating you to see how far this all goes, for that too is the nature of a man. How hilarious this is. Instead of the three of us sitting here, I should go question Tsuruhashiya Kinosuke. He is your wife's former employer. You should come with me, and then you can attempt to make your excuses."

Chōbei's expression softened, and he replied, "Indeed, we should. Let's go now together and sort all this mess out, so we can come to an agreement." What he was thinking was not clear, but he got up promptly without putting on a facade of toughness. Oroku could not stop them from going, so Kiroku also got up, hoisted the rear of his kimono, tucked it into his belt to make it easier to walk, and exited alongside Chōbei.

It was the twentieth day of the month, and the two of them hastened along the Ōkawa River, concealed by the darkness of night. When Chōbei saw the stream of people had died out, he waited for Kiroku to drop his guard. When the opportunity arose, Chōbei drew his sword without Kiroku seeing. With a swish, he cut into Kiroku's shoulder.

(7.8)

Wavering and struggling to remain upright, Kiroku mustered his voice, "Cowardly sneak attacks, Chōbei. Why won't you face me in a fair fight?" He put his hand on the hilt of his sword and tried drawing it, but his wound was too deep for him to overcome. Staggering, he continued, "How bitter this is. I suppose you are going to kill me now, Chōbei, leaving my grudge unresolved."

He gritted his teeth and opened his eyes wide, but his legs would not carry him, so he crawled and grasped at the empty air.

Chōbei kicked the man over and told him, "Kiroku, consider my words a final rite as you descend into the realm of the dead. Write them in the margins of the ledger where you track your travel expenses, and may Lord Enma, whom you share a name with, transcribe them into his book of sins! Jiraiya, the one depicted on your wanted poster, has entrusted someone precious to him into my care. I took his sister as my wife, but I will not let it be said we are a couple smitten by love. Until he achieves his great ambition, I will protect her with my life. This is my duty, and now that you know, you will only try to hinder me if I let you live. You might have been acting like you were love-struck and carrying

7.8

a lover's grudge, but I suspect you were asked by Gundazaemon to do this. If you truly hold a grudge against me, then go to hell, sacrifice your eyes and nose to the hag by the Sanzu River, beseech her to be your ally, and await my arrival!"

Chōbei adjusted the grip on his sword and ran Kiroku through, dealing the final blow. Without making a sound, Kiroku stopped breathing and died. Chōbei disposed of the corpse in the river, wiped the blood off his blade, and returned it to its sheath. He took a deep breath and exhaled. Then he hurried towards his home as the bells of temples tolled in the distance.

On a previous night, Jiroza had been traveling by the Hatchō embankment when, against all expectation, he came across an injured woman. She had entrusted her young child to Jiroza, and as if by fate, the child had taken to him and did not want to leave his side. He hired a wet nurse and would at the very least raise the child to make sure vengeance was exacted. He named the child Sutematsu, and despite Jiroza's ambitious nature, he harbored a deep affection for the endearing child.

During the day, he asked Kinosuke's wife to take care of Sutematsu, and during the night, he would hold him close to his chest as they slept. However, every night, at the third quarter hour of the ox,[1] Sutematsu

1 Around 02:00.

would crawl out of Jiroza's arms. With boundless energy, he played alone, laughing until dawn, only to return to Jiroza's embrace and fall back to sleep. Initially, Jiroza remained oblivious to these nocturnal escapades, but one night, he awoke suddenly. His vision was blurred from just having woken up, but there, close by the pillow, he saw Sutematsu playing by himself. Then, on the other side of the byōbu screen, he saw the figure of a woman sitting, drenched in blood and her hair in disarray. Jiroza understood what was happening, and in his heart, he started chanting the nembutsu prayer.

(7.9)

Jiroza imagined that in Sutematsu's eyes, the apparition must look like his departed mother Misao. Searching for her breast, Sutematsu went to her lap, and it looked just like a mother fawning on her child. While most people would have been terrified by this sight, Jiroza actually being the brave Jiraiya, remained unfazed and said, "The departed Misao's spirit must have been drawn here by her love, and now she wanders, trying to nurture and care for Sutematsu."

Tears trickled down Jiroza's face as he thought of the anguish Misao must have felt. Then he wiped away his tears and silently chanted out the nembutsu prayer.

"Namu Amida Butsu. Namu Amida Butsu."

As he chanted, the roosters crowed, and a new day dawned. Sutematsu crawled back inside Jiroza's night kimono and went to sleep again. As he did this, Misao's figure dissipated like smoke, leaving not a trace of its presence. It was said the spirit of the departed will not leave its home for forty-nine days after death. Misao's spirit, however, had been pulled by her love of her child to the house of a stranger where she now wandered pitifully.

Jiroza had borrowed a room in Tsuruhashiya Kinosuke's house and hid in one of the inner rooms, waiting for the time to come where he could carry out his ambitions. But as he waited, he chose to put on the guise of a champion of justice and had his underlings disguise themselves as hooligans working for Kinosuke. Together, they patrolled Kamakura, vigilantly observing and investigating the situation.

One of these men, Node no Sankichi, suddenly came running in a great hurry. When Jiroza saw him, he gathered with Kinosuke and his wife to hear what was happening. Gasping for breath, Sankichi delivered his report, "We secretly went to Ōgigayatsu and overheard that the daimyo of Echigo and Shinano are going to make peace with each other. A road is being constructed at the base of Mount Myōkō to expedite travel between the two regions. Soon, they will dispatch the marriage contracts and wedding presents, carried by Tagoto-hime, the daughter of the Sarashina clan, to Tsukikage Miyukinosuke of Echigo along that route! Master, you must act swiftly and go there. Gather the men, ambush the convoys and steal the shipment as it passes. Then take it to the mountain stronghold. The treasure obtained will provide essential funds for our military endeavors. Allow me to assist you in making the necessary preparations!"

7.9

Jiroza nodded, promptly got up, and said, "What fine work you have done. With such concise intelligence, I must depart immediately! Kinosuke, may I entrust Sutematsu's care to you and your wife while I am away?"

Osai, Kinosuke's wife, took care of Sutematsu, while Kinosuke helped with the preparations for the journey ahead. Then Kinosuke sent up a smoke signal and a great number of men assembled from various locations. In contrast to the wide-sleeved kimonos and three-shaku-long[2] obis they had worn to disguise themselves as townsfolk, they were now wearing breastplates and greaves. Eager and light-footed, they came brandishing their various weapons, calling out, "Master, we must act swiftly and prepare!"

(7.10)

Jiroza also swiftly changed out of his clothes and strapped on his chainmail, battle haori, vambraces, and greaves. Taking a seat on a folding stool, he checked the names of the men who had shown up. Before the dawn broke, he led his formidable host toward the mountain road on the border of Echigo and Shinano in a great hurry.

Sarashina Hangan Mitsuaki of Shinano had prepared a magnificent ceremonial kimono for sending Tagoto-hime to the neighboring

2 1 meter.

7.10

province. Because the journey was relatively short, on the day they were to leave he made sure the entire entourage consisted of women. He assembled them at Sakai River, which lay close to the border with Echigo, and no expense was spared in making it the most splendid sendoff. News of the sendoff spread, and men and women came running from nearby villages and areas to see the spectacle. The streets teemed with people, so the shops and merchants in the town made unexpected profits.

Seeing as it was a wedding procession of the Sarashina clan, Takasago Yuminosuke, being a long-standing retainer of the clan, was given full control of the event. His responsibility involved managing every aspect of the journey to the Tsukikage clan and ensuring the safety of the roads. Mitsuaki had given Yuminosuke the strictest orders to do a good job, so he had gone to Shinano ahead of the event to inspect the roads on the way. So, together with a small band of men, he headed for the foothills of Mount Myōkō.

This tale unfolds prior to the wedding, and the sequence of the illustrations may appear slightly jumbled. However, as you continue reading, the narrative will come together cohesively.

The *Kanrei* of Kamakura sought to enhance the martial skills of his warriors, thus appointing the rōnin Muyami Gundazaemon as a martial arts instructor with a generous salary. Under the pretense it was for the sake of a military drill, for teaching the lay of the land, or for traveling to gain skill in combat, he would go on inspections in neighboring provinces as he pleased. Accompanied by a couple of disciples, he also made his way to the borderlands of Echigo and Shinano.

(7.11)

The prominent Mount Myōkō straddles Echigo and Shinano with its cragged and steep slopes. During winter, the deep snow covered the roads, but from the end of spring until the end of summer, sometimes the start of autumn, it was a shortcut for travelers. Takasago Yuminosuke was in need of a shortcut while inspecting the main roads, so he clawed his way up the narrow paths.

On that particular day, the guide accompanying him, a logger, told him, "A while ago, there used to be a peculiar man named Senso Dōjin living on this mountain. There were many strange occurrences, because he could use toad yōjutsu. But the rulers of the mountain were two great serpents. Occasionally, people who made their living by making coal on the mountain would be devoured by them. As a result, loggers and mountain dwellers would never venture too far into the mountains. But somehow, one of the serpents died, leaving one alive. The survivor must be the male of the pair. People very rarely see it nowadays."

7.11

7.12

Part II

(7.12)

After hearing the logger's account, Yuminosuke remembered what he previously experienced on the mountain and ensured the logger that everything was fine. As they made their way farther up the mountain road, they heard voices from far behind them. It was two or three samurai heading up the same path. As the samurai drew closer, Yuminosuke turned back and saw something that startled him.

It was Tatsumaki Arakurō, the man who once served in the same house as Yuminosuke himself. His initial shock transformed into delight, and after he let them pass, Yuminosuke seized his spear and called out, "Well, well, if it isn't Tatsumaki Arakurō! Have you forgotten me already? Or were you planning on running again? Seven years ago, you killed my sister's father-in-law Himematsu Edanoshin. And because that apparently wasn't enough for you, you also murdered my brother-in-law Himematsu Sumatarō, before fleeing the house. Unfortunately, I was away on business in a distant land, serving my master, and was unable to be present. But here I stand, Takasago Yuminosuke—Sumatarō's elder brother-in-law! It must be ordained by the gods that I have been so fortunate as to meet you here in the mountains. Now, face me like a man!"

With a masterful hand, Yuminosuke thrust his spear forward, but the famous Gundazaemon evaded and grabbed the neck of the spear firmly.

"Don't make hasty mistakes! You have me confused for someone else. I am not this Tatsumaki, or whatever his name may be. I am on a journey to increase combative prowess. My name is Muyami Gundazaemon, a retainer of the Kanrei of Kamakura. I don't have any memory of ever killing someone, let alone being the target of a vendetta. Besides, I bet he isn't even my age."

(7.13)

"You might look a different age with your white hair, but your face, figure, and even your voice is without a doubt that of Arakurō. Perhaps you have altered your appearance with some kind of potion that turns hair white, haven't you? Now that I have seen through you, I suspect you are going to try to escape like a coward!"

Yuminosuke pulled his spear free and thrust it sharply forward again. Gundazaemon drew his sword. Sparks flew as the two engaged in fierce battle. Gundazaemon's two disciples also drew their swords and came to help him fight. Witnessing this, the mountain guide and Yuminosuke's companions grew terrified and hastily fled downhill. Yuminosuke fought all three adversaries without relenting or shrinking. Then, for some inexplicable reason, the two disciples froze, as if in shock. The adept Yuminosuke seized this moment to take them down and thrust his sharp spearhead at Gundazaemon, who struggled to defend himself and fell back.

After he managed to flee nearly one chō[3] into the shadowy depths of

3 109.09 meters.

7.13

the valley, he grabbed a small boulder to use as a hand-shield and mustered his courage. He cut off from the narrow path and went downhill, where he found himself in a place with no other paths or even a bridge to cross the valley. But there he saw a pine log, so massive that it would take two men to embrace it, which stretched over the narrow valley river, forming a one-way bridge. Gundazaemon thought himself lucky, but as he crossed the bridge, he also had to contend with Yuminosuke's spear. He was keeping an eye for openings so he could evade the spear, but Yuminosuke knew Gundazaemon could not keep it up much longer, so his attacks became more ferocious. Gundazaemon parried for dear life as the two stomped on the bridge, fighting.

Just then, something strange happened. The bridge, which had so far looked like an old tree, moved on its own, rocking from side to side as if pulled by some unseen force. Even in the midst of the fierce battle, Yuminosuke comprehended the situation and leapt to safety onto a nearby boulder. Seeing an opportunity to escape, Gundazaemon attempted to flee, but something materialized behind him—a pair of eyes gleaming like polished mirrors and a fiery tongue emitting a menacing crimson light, flickering in the air. The colossal serpent, as large as a small mountain, raised its head and devoured Gundazaemon in one swift gulp.

(7.14)

It looked like the snake was going to head into the mountains, and the slopes quaked and rumbled as it moved its body, which, until now,

7.14

Yuminosuke thought had been a bridge. At this sight, even Yuminosuke stood shocked and in awe. Leaning his spear against a rock, he stood motionless for a while as the snake made its way.

On the opposite side of the valley, a shadowy figure emerged. Though his face remained hidden, he called out, "Sir Takago, how rare and fortuitous it is that we should meet here! I have a most important message for you, but seeing the imminent danger you are facing, this does not seem to be the time for it, so I will keep quiet about it for now. Furthermore, even though it was only a small help, I was here from the beginning of the fight. The reason you could take down the two samurai who came to help so easily was because of my yōjutsu. As for the monstrous serpent, it is one half of a pair; I vanquished the female long ago. Now, the time has come for the second serpent to meet its doom! However, first and foremost, you must flee this place. Forget about Tatsumaki for now and make your way to the foot of the mountain before the serpent's poisonous mist engulfs you. It is only a small deed, but I will assist you, so you can escape this perilous situation. It is but a small gift from me to you, but please do not forget it. We shall meet again in due time, and when that happens, do not attempt to hinder my ambitions! Please, stay out of my path, valiant retainer! I shall return to share with you all that has befallen Sumatarō's mother and his wife, Misao, and I shall reveal my name as well. However, it is too dangerous to divulge more at this moment. Hurry, leave this place so that no harm befalls you!"

7.15

The voice echoed through the valley, and the figure rose up with the mist of the river and disappeared.

(7.15)

Without him knowing, Gōtekisai Muyami Gundazaemon had been swallowed by the great serpent. Now, he was inside the serpent's belly, where he would melt like he was made from snow and ice. Luckily for him, he had his sword, which he was using as a cane inside the serpent's belly. Although not by his design, the sword cut the serpent's belly open, slicing a hole in the snake seven or eight shaku long.[4] Plunging headfirst, he tumbled into the river below, where the water washed away the serpent's poison, saving his life.

Returning to the present...

In accordance with the strict order of the Kanrei in Kamakura, Miyukinosuke, the heir of Tsukikage Gunryō Terutoki of Echigo, was to take Tagoto-hime of the Sarashina clan as his bride. Miyukinosuke had chosen an auspicious day and made all preparations. When the day finally arrived, the cleaning and decoration of the mansion was carried out to its fullest extent, and in the evening, everything sparkled with the brightness of the finest weather. The golden screens shimmered, and the rows of lit candlesticks illuminated the surroundings as if it were noon, creating a dazzling sight.

4 2–2.5 meters.

7.16

On this day, the envoy of the Kamakura Kanrei, Hiki no Kurando, was expected to arrive, and it was decided the wedding banquet was to be provided with a gift of two thousand ryō of gold dust. This was all arranged discreetly ahead of time by Miyukinosuke as an invitation to the envoy.

The brave and loyal retainer, Takasago Yuminosuke, had been entrusted by Mitsuaki of the Sarashina clan to escort Tagoto-hime, and he was also awaiting the arrival of the envoy. Before long, a voice called out from the front of the mansion, announcing the envoy's arrival. Wearing long ceremonial robes with intricate fabric patterns and high shoulder pleats, Hiki no Kurando calmly followed his guide down the long hallway.

"Please, as the esteemed envoy, take the seat of honor," said the servant.

(7.16)

After the envoy leisurely sat down in the seat prepared for him, Tsukikage no Miyukinosuke bowed before him and spoke, "Honorable Lord Envoy, you have traveled long and endured much. To receive you is a gift from the Kanrei and it brings great honor and prestige to my household. I humbly request that you graciously accept this gift. It is beyond my imagination that someone as unworthy as I should be bestowed such honor as to marry Tagoto-hime, the daughter of Sarashina Hangan of our neighboring province. How great the happiness of my undeserving self is. Unfortunately, my father, Gunryō Terutoki, has fallen ill and I sincerely beg your esteemed forgiveness for his absence today." As he addressed the envoy, he bowed with both hands on the floor, showing the greatest respect.

Next, the Sarashina clan's retainer, Takasago Yuminosuke, who had been waiting in the background, addressed the envoy, "On this occasion, despite my incompetence, I have been given the honorable task of ensuring the safety of my master Mitsuaki's daughter as she enters her new family and brings peace. Nothing could bring more honor to my household than this. Hence, humbly standing here today, I extend my warm welcome to the esteemed envoy and present myself as a representative of my lord, though unworthy I may be. I kindly request your mediation as I fulfill this role on behalf of my lord." With utmost reverence, Yuminosuke delivered his respectful greeting, keeping his body low to the ground before respectfully retreating.

Hiki no Kurando straightened up and turned to Miyukinosuke. "I do not much enjoy being sent as an envoy. Nonetheless, I have come on orders from the Kanrei to ensure peace talks between the Sarashina and the Tsukikage clans. In order to tie long-lasting, friendly relations, I am to stand witness to the wedding of Miyukinosuke and Tagoto-hime. The Kanrei's plan is for them to bring tranquility to the land and lead their houses, and thus, on this night, on this auspicious day, they shall be joined in marriage. As for the gift of two thousand ryō of gold dust, the Kanrei has decreed that I shall take it into my possession. Furthermore, it has come to the Kanrei's attention that you have a precious treasure here in this house. Something called 'the moon-shaped seal' once used by the Ogata clan to command their armies. Additionally, there is the family tree of the Ogata lineage. Given the auspicious nature of today's event, I am under strict instructions to inspect these artifacts. I humbly request your compliance with this matter."

(7.17)

With a jolt, Miyukinosuke replied, "If it is the strict order of the Kanrei, I shall gladly permit your esteemed presence to examine the artifacts. However, it strikes me as odd that you should inspect the moon seal, an instrument of war, just now, during a wedding planned to quell the fighting with our neighbor and usher in peace. The family tree of the traitorous Ogata clan is useless to my clan, but these lands used to belong to Ogata Hirokado Hirozumi. When word spread in Kamakura of the Ogata clan's plans of revolt, being in the neighboring province, the Sarashina clan was dispatched. They attacked and tore down Ogata's castle, confiscated the two artifacts and sent them to the lord in Kamakura. Subsequently, my father, Tsukikage Terutoki, was bestowed the artifacts and an official title as lord of his lands as a reward for several generations of our family performing meritorious war service. Sarashina Hangan, however, bore a great resentment towards him over this, saying it was due to the war efforts of him, Mitsuaki, that Ogata Hirokado Hirozumi was destroyed, and that his grudge was now upon Terutoki for receiving this very land. Consequently, discord grew between our two houses and many wars were fought over border territories. To take those things out to look at them now, when we have

7.17

finally gathered to ensure peace, would be like sowing the seeds of the grudge all over again. Let us not muddy the clear water. After the wedding ceremony, I shall bring the artifacts to Kamakura myself. If you will but let the matter rest for tonight, I am certain there will be no unpleasantness at the celebration."

Kurando's eyes narrowed at this, and he answered, "As the envoy, I will not force you to let me see the artifacts. However, Miyukinosuke-dono, do you not think it to be disrespectful to go against the decree of the Kanrei? They are instruments of war, and ultimately you have fought border conflicts over them. If you were to show them to me it would be a different matter, but not having them on hand and saying you will give them to the Kanrei later, is tantamount to revealing your intentions to utilize the items to raise an army and rebel against our country. Is this what you intend to do?"

"I would never—"

"Are you going to let me see the items then?"

"Depending on the time and place, they can be quite ominous, which is why I initially declined. But if you insist, I shall see it done. Someone, go to the treasure hold and fetch the moon-shaped stamp and the Ogata family tree!" Miyukinosuke's words were sharp and loud.

Yuminosuke approached from the side. "The time has come for Tagoto-hime to arrive. Therefore, I implore you, Lord Envoy, to enjoy a cup of saké and postpone the viewing of the items until tomorrow. It surely won't cause any significant delay. Instead of those artifacts, I

7.18

have brought a humble item from the Sarashina clan's treasury. Please, honor us by inspecting it." Yuminosuke reached into his pocket and produced a lacquered *maki-e* medicine box. "This is the item that I hope the esteemed Lord Envoy will grant me the honor of seeing."

Yuminosuke pushed it in front of the envoy, who exclaimed, "Would you look at this! I remember this medicine box! At some point I gave it, along with some medicine, to a mountain brigand who was struck down by an illness on Shinano Road."

(7.18)

"You have come to us, like a morning star lily plucked on Mount Kurohime, but once the flower bloomed, it transformed into a tiger lily, and from the maw of the tiger sprang one of the Ogata!"

The envoy said, "And I thought you were akin to the *tametomo* lily—refined and elegant. But now you seem more like its common name, the *teppō* lily—the rifle lily, trying to get in my way. Have you forgotten the promise we made on Mount Myōkō? Why do you go against me, a vine that does not seek to compete with you? Are you turning my kindness into enmity out of loyalty or for your own sake?"

"I have feelings as well! However, human emotion and justice are not mutually exclusive! For the sake of my lord, I am willing to abandon even my own parents, forget my filial duty, and risk my life without hesitation. If I, the unwavering Yuminosuke, were to display any cowardice or reluctance to die, it would be a disgrace. Now, do not hide

7.19

your true name anymore and identify yourself! I suspected something like this might happen, so when we announced we were sending Tagoto-hime, I actually sent my daughter, Teruta, in her stead. The real Tagoto-hime has taken an alternate route and arrived at a different mansion. I am also aware that the Tagoto-hime who came in the palanquin is not the real Tagoto-hime. Along the way, your men stole the palanquin and placed an imposter inside, but I have already apprehended her. So, what do you think of my clever stratagem? With such a tactic incorporated into the present that you stole, even with yōjutsu, I doubt you can overcome the surprise. Now, men! Bring me the imposter! However, because I feel a debt to you which cannot be expressed in words, I will have her untied for now."

The sliding doors in the inner room opened and a single girl dressed like a princess came out. Her bonds were undone, and she was pushed beside them.

Then Yuminosuke spoke again, "What's the matter? No more bravado?"

Hiki no Kurando leapt to his feet and raised his voice. "I thought I was the one scheming, but it seems I was the one who fell for a scheme. Whatever shall I do? I had set my heart on getting the moon-shaped seal and the Ogata family tree so I could dispatch soldiers, raise an army against Echigo, and seek vengeance on the Sarashina clan. After all, I might be infamous under my alias Jiraiya, but my true identity is that of

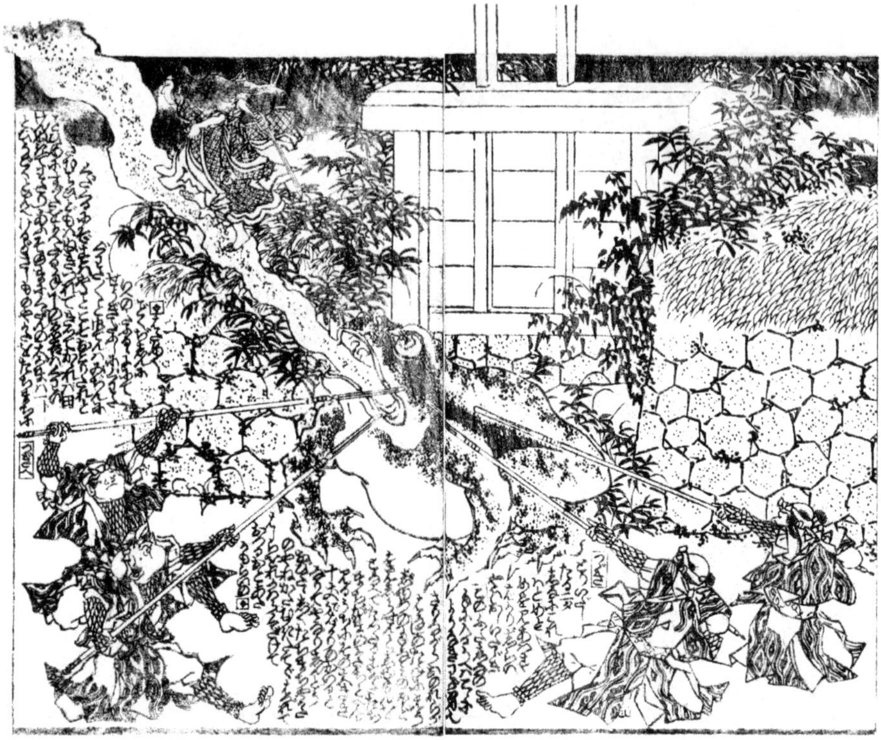

7.20

the last standing and forgotten son of Ogata Hirokado Hirozumi. I am Ogata Shūma Hiroyuki!"

(7.19)

Upon hearing this, Tsukikage Miyukinosuke erupted, "So you are Jiraiya Hiroyuki? Put him in ropes and send him to Kamakura!" However, he was interrupted when Yuminosuke signaled with a torch. From afar, a great host encircled the mansion, beating drums and gongs of war.

Jiraiya looked at the scene and remarked, "I suppose you prepared all these men to trap me. I infiltrated Kamakura and bided my time, waiting to resurrect the name of Ogata again from obscurity, raise an army, and march on Kamakura. For so long I wanted to pay tribute to my departed father Hirokado Hirozumi, but now my hopes are crushed. Without the moon-shaped seal, the armies of Echigo will never heed my command. Of course, I could have just used my yōjutsu to steal the two artifacts, but I wanted to ascertain the truth of everything. So, I assumed the guise of Hiki no Kurando and came here as an envoy. Without anyone knowing, I used my yōjutsu to steal the wedding gifts and kidnap who I thought was Tagoto-hime. However, it turns out, Yuminosuke, that it was actually your daughter. The woman I replaced her with is indeed none other than one of my subordinates named Ekichi. But, Yuminosuke, no matter how many men you call upon or what preparations you make to capture us, I would never fall prey to the petty tricks of someone like you. From the very start, Ekichi, who was being held inside the mansion, snuck into the treasury via my yōjutsu. Behold the stolen moon-shaped seal and the Ogata family tree!"

(7.20)

Ekichi pulled out the two artifacts from her pocket. They exchanged a knowing look, and Jiraiya took hold of the items.

"Now that I possess these two things, I have no more business here! And now, for the sake of you having something to talk about later, feast your eyes on the true power of yōjutsu!"

Jiraiya chanted a spell and transformed into a toad in the blink of an eye. The toad grew until it was ten jō.[5] The mansion groaned and trembled under its weight, shaking greatly. The roof started tilting, the joinery came undone, the columns snapped, and tiles fell from the roof with a clatter like thunder. Like falling shogi pieces, the mansion collapsed into splinters, resembling a house felled by an earthquake.

"We must be quick!" cried one samurai, and they pulled out their swords. But as they came to attack the toad, Ekichi, who had been disguised as Tagoto-hime, pulled out her daggers and met them in combat.

(7.21)

The colossal toad appeared poised to leap, but instead it pressed its belly on the already destroyed mansion, further flattening the wreckage. Miyukinosuke and Yuminosuke were nowhere to be seen, so the onlookers thought the two must have perished. Bewitched by the spectacle, the horde of men hesitated, stepping back. Then, an extraordinary occurrence unfolded. The toad, which was as big as a mountain, started shrinking. As it did, the mansion, which had looked like it was utterly ruined, reconstructed itself as if nothing had transpired. The men surrounding the mansion stood dumbfounded. Then, the toad jumped into the moat, swam through the water gate, and went to the front of the compound. The would-be captors waiting outside clamored as they readied their spears to strike the toad. But yet another peculiar event unfolded. A billow of five-colored smoke erupted from the toad's mouth. Jiraiya reappeared, and with the imposter Ekichi, he ran across the rainbow smoke and into the empty sky. As the men contemplated giving chase, the toad disappeared like snow before the rising sun, leaving the men bewildered.

On a previous night in Kamakura, Chōbei the dreamer had ended the life of Enma no Kiroku on the bank of Ōgawa River close by Hanamizu Bridge, without anyone knowing.[6] He had fled the scene and returned home, telling not a soul what happened. Not even his wife Oroku had he told, and he pretended to know nothing about the whole affair.

5 About 30 meters.

6 Most likely a reference to an area near present-day Nihonbashi in Tokyo.

7.21

However, in an unexpected turn of events, a group of constables from the magistrate's office stormed into his house, barging through the entrance and proclaiming, "You are under arrest!"

Chōbei did not lose his composure or put up his guard. He calmly asked, "What are you here to accuse me of?"

Before he could finish, the leader of the constables, Shikano Fuehachi, said in a crude voice, "What audacity to ask such a question! On the twentieth day of this month, under the cover of night, someone slew Kiroku by the Ōgawa River and cast his body into the water. However, it snagged on a weir and did not wash away. On the embankment, we found bloodstains, and among the blood was a sandal branded with the first kanji of your name, 蝶 (chō)! This is undeniable evidence of your guilt. Not only are you a murderer, but I also have trustworthy reports that you have been harboring the wanted criminal Jiraiya for a long time. No matter how you try to hide it or keep it secret, there is no escape. Put him in ropes!"

The men rushed at Chōbei, but for some reason he did not resist. He even willingly placed his hands behind his back, allowing them to be tied as if it were the most ordinary thing. With a look on their faces like they did a good job, the many constables stood him up, saying, "Get on your feet!"

Oroku, filled with anxiety, sobbed and pleaded with the men. "You are justified in suspecting Chōbei, but you don't need to tie him up. I am certain he doesn't have any intentions to try to run or hide. I am sorry for delaying you, but please listen to our defense."

"If he can provide a sound alibi, he will be freed of the ropes when we get to the magistrate's office. We are just constables who have come with orders to arrest him, so we cannot acquit him here. You are his wife, correct? Stay here and mind the fire." After saying this, they pulled him up and left.

Chōbei did not say a word. He closed his eyes and prepared for what was to come as he was pulled along behind Fuehachi towards the magistrate's office. Shortly after their departure, Tsuruhashiya Kinosuke came and spoke hectically. "I was a moment too late! But fear not, Oroku-san, I know everything that has happened. I will run after them to the magistrate's office and convince them to untie Chōbei. Until I've handled the situation and brought him home, you should focus your mind on something and not let your guard down. Perhaps you could organize your papers, letters, and writings to make sure you have everything?" With those words, Kinosuke ran off.

7.22

And so, Chōbei's life hangs in the balance. Jiraiya and Yuminosuke are caught by their sense of duty and obligation. And the son of Himamatsu Sumatarō, Sutematsu, must grow up and take revenge on Gundazaemon. Yet, dear readers, such a tale is too vast to be contained within this single installment, and I shall halt my brush for now. Before long, the next book will be written and published.

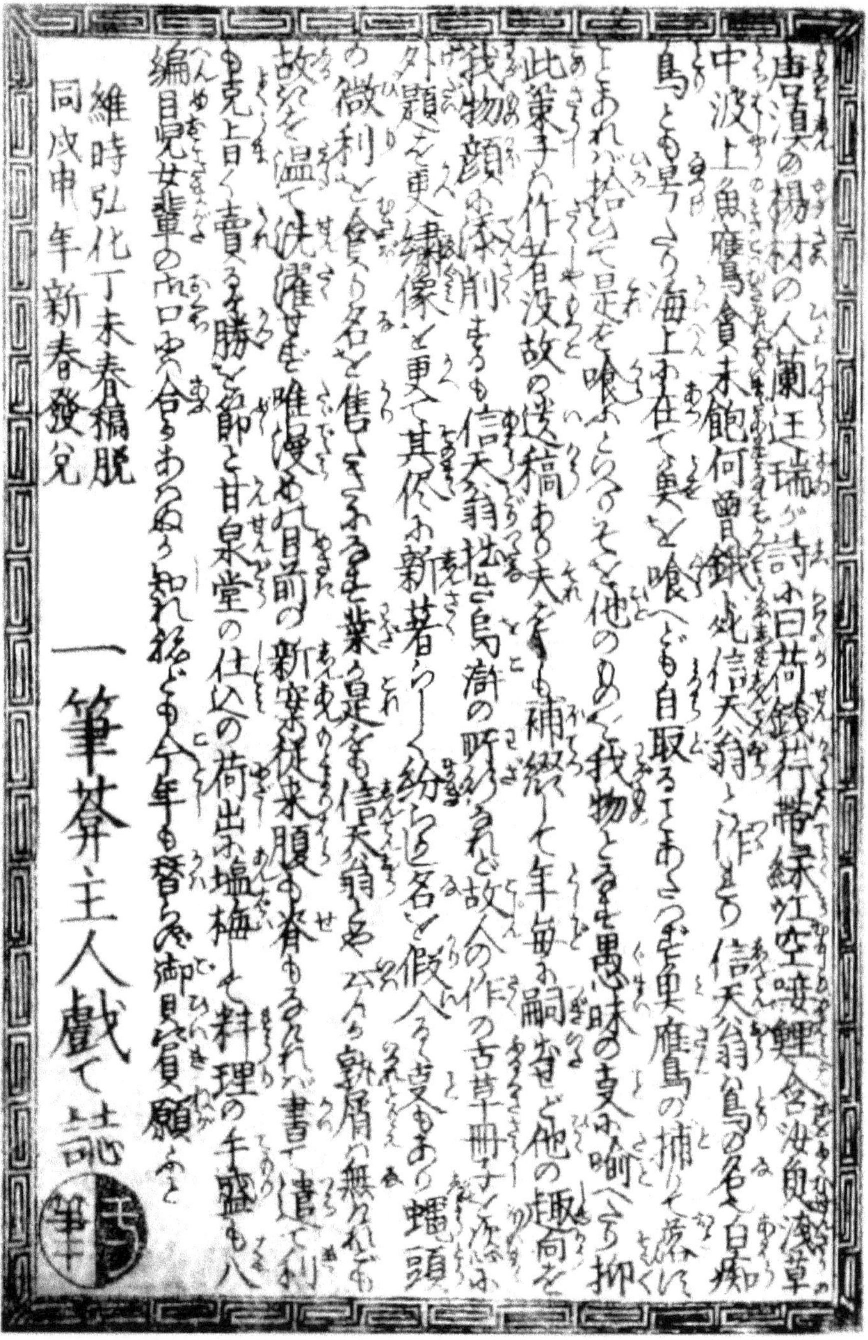

唐漢の楊材の人蘭廷瑞が詩に白荷銭杏帯緑江空唼鯉合没負濃草
中波上魚鷹鳥貪未飽何曽餓死信天翁と作れり信天翁は鳥の名で白痴
鳥とも号けり海上に在て魚を喰へども自取ることあたはず魚鷹鳥の捕りて落したる
をあれば拾ひて是を喰ふところをもて他のめぐみ我物とする愚昧の事に喩へて抑
此策主人作者没故の遺稿あるを夫をも補綴して年毎に嗣ながら他の趣向を
我物顔に添削すれども信天翁拙き鳥衛の呼ぶ名れど故人の作の古草冊すらに
外題を更へ繍像を更て其侭に新著らしく紛ら名を假へる事もあり蠅頭
の微利と会て名を售さるは業是をも信天翁と云べきか熟眉の無なれども
故きを温て洗濯せざ唯漫めれ目前の新案従来腹に脊もるれば書で遺て利
を見上旨く賣るを勝と節と甘泉堂の仕込の荷出に塩梅して料理の手盛も八
編目見女輩の口に合あるなきか知れねども今年も替らぬ御贔屓願ふと

一筆菴主人戯て誌

維時弘化丁未春稿脱
同戊申年新春發兌

8.1

Book 8

In the Yunnan province of China, a person named Lan Ting Rui from Yō penned the following poem:[1]

The leaves of the lotus and fringed water lily sit in the green river beneath the sky. The splashing carp and the snapping guppy coexist among the shallow reeds. Above the waves, the osprey flies greedily with no catch. How the albatross starves.

The albatross is also known by a different name: *ahōdori*—the idiot bird. It lives above the seas and eats fish, but it cannot catch them by itself. If an osprey catches a fish and drops it, the albatross picks it up and eats it. This serves as a metaphor for those foolish enough to claim another's possessions as their own.

This work is a posthumous manuscript left after the author's passing. In light of this, I supplement it and yet again this year, follow with another publication. However, altering the designs of others in such a manner, as if they were my own, is akin to behaving like an albatross. It may be a thoughtless and imprudent act, but regrettably, some individuals selfishly change the titles of old books by deceased authors, alter the images, and then try to pass it off as new work, while falsely putting their own name on it. Yearning for even the tiniest profit, akin to a fly's head, and seeking popularity, can it not be said that such individuals are also albatrosses?

Though there may not even be a scrap for chickens, I take these old, unwashed leftovers and reheat them, adding new, impulsive, and poorly thought-out ideas as I inherit and continue the writing. Whether or not it works and sells well will depend on the *katsuobushi* fish flakes and seasonings I add to the broth, already prepared by the Kansendō publishing house. I plate the eighth volume, not knowing if it will fit the tastes of the young boys and girls, and humbly ask for their patronage again this year.

Written: Kōka era—Year of the Fire Sheep—Spring (1847)
Published: Kōka era—Year of the Earth Monkey—New Year (1848)
Ippitsuan

On a summer night, what was said to be a human soul flying high through the skies, was in fact a flying toad.

In the *Baopuzi*, it is written that once a toad reaches a thousand years old, it grows horns on the top of its head. Crimson letters, known as *nikushi* for their auspiciousness, emerge on its stomach. Frequently consuming mountain spirits, the toad harnesses them for *senjutsu* hermit magic. It is said it can call forth fog, pray for rain, defeat warriors, and undo ropes that bind it. This is the thing known as toad yōjutsu. Chinese texts often depict toads transforming into humans.

Toads devour snakes. Ordinary toads also spray their urine on snakes, killing them and turning them into small insects to eat.

1 1528–1565 CE. Politician and scholar in Qing Dynasty. Wrote an entry in *Siku Quanshu* (*Complete Library of the Four Treasuries*) about albatrosses.

Consequently, despite snakes preying on frogs, they fear toads. The animal that appears in the three-way deadlock is not a toad, but a frog. It is said that slugs can also kill snakes. But they get devoured by toads. Hence, there seems to be no adversary capable of withstanding toad yōjutsu. Could this be the source of Jiraiya's exceptional courage?

Additional text: Fukitarō, male heir of Mochimaru.

8.2

Tagoto-hime, daughter of the Sarashina clan. Is actually Teruta, daughter of the brave retainer.

Bandit leader Jiraiya. Real name Ogata Shūma Hiroyuki.

8.3

Otsuna, a country girl on the Bandō Pilgrimage.

Yumeno Chōkichi.

Chōkichi heads out with captors to seize the leader of the bandits living in the Yamamon gate of Kokubunji Temple and making people suffer.

8.4

An image from the public display of the Kannon statue of Hase Temple in Kamakura.

Sekiya, a lady-in-waiting of the Tsukikage clan.

Many rōnin ask for pity from passersby to sustain them on their lives on the road, but this rōnin sits on the road, taking nothing. What he stands to gain from this will be explored in this volume.

Sign on ground: *Recently unemployed rōnin. Not asking for alms.*

Unnamed rōnin.

The brave and loyal retainer of the Sarashina clan, Takasago Yuminosuke.

8.5

Part I

(8.5)
Miyukinosuke, the heir to Tsukikage Gunryō Terutoki, and Tagoto-hime, the daughter of Sarashina Hangan Mitsuaki, were to be wed. The marriage contract was finalized, and an auspicious day for the event had been chosen. Tagoto-hime was to join Miyukinosuke in his new mansion, and because the news of the event spread so far, the Kanrei in Kamakura dispatched Hiki no Kurando as an envoy to receive tribute. However, Jiraiya had secretly caught wind of these plans. He disguised himself as a fake envoy and infiltrated the Tsukikage mansion. His subordinate Ekichi took the guise of Tagoto-hime, and Jiraiya had the wedding procession robbed of its gifts en route to the mansion. Not only that, he also planned for Ekichi to steal the Ogata family tree and the seal of the Tsukikage clan, which were hidden in the mansion. The scheme was meant to cause a great uproar, but the loyal Sarashina retainer Takasago Yuminosuke saw through Jiraiya's wicked plans. He had his own daughter, Teruta, masquerade as Tagoto-hime and sent her on the main road as part of the procession. Thanks to this, when the disguised Ekichi arrived at the new mansion and Jiraiya initiated his chaotic disturbance, the genuine wedding ceremony proceeded smoothly and without incident. The Kanrei clan in Kamakura and both the

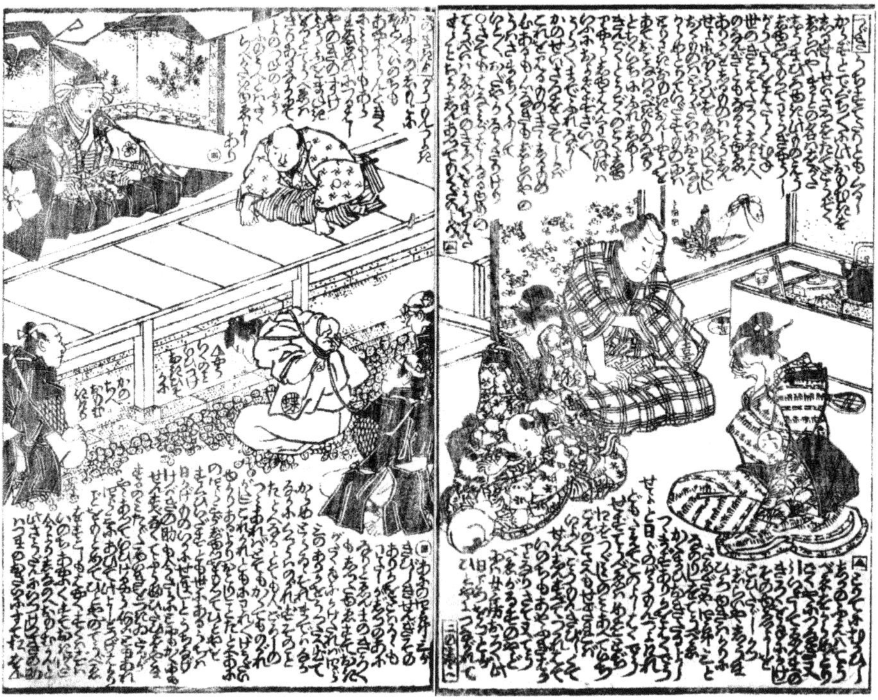

8.6

Tsukikage and Sarashina clans hailed Yuminosuke, recognizing that it was only possible due to his careful discretion, and they bestowed him with great rewards.

Tsukikage Terutoki and Sarashina Hangan Mitsuaki, choosing to see the whole affair as an eccentric curiosity, decided to forget about everything that happened. However, word had spread, and people said it was a disgrace for a warrior clan, so ignoring it proved to be difficult. Consequently, a messenger was dispatched to Kamakura to present a detailed account of how Jiraiya had to be punished. The Kanrei had grown weary of Jiraiya. The audacity and disrespect he had shown, disguising himself as Hiki no Kurando, whom he had sent as an envoy, was too much. Thus, the Kanrei issued a stern decree, demanding Jiraiya's immediate capture.

(8.6)

In an unparalleled vie to capture Jiraiya with ease, he had notices posted by every doorway, which read:

> *Wanted: The notorious outlaw Ogata Shūma Hiroyuki, also known as Jiraiya, is wanted for his use of yōjutsu to commit countless crimes. He has caused suffering to many and must be brought to justice. Anyone who knows of his whereabouts is urged to come forward and will be generously rewarded. Anyone found aiding or hiding Jiraiya will be considered an accomplice and will face punishment. The authorities offer a*

substantial reward for any information leading to the capture of this criminal and his associates.

The proclamation was meticulously drafted and disseminated extensively throughout the land. From the highest lords to the bustling harbors. Its presence pervaded far and wide, ensuring that both willing and unwilling eyes and ears fell upon its contents. Thus, the tidings of Jiraiya began to circulate, and his days of peace and quiet were over.

We return now to Chōbei the dreamer, who had killed Enma no Kiroku. A report had been filed with the steward of the area, who responded by sending Shikano Fuehachi to capture Chōbei and imprison him. Later, they dragged him out of his cell and questioned him about how he murdered Enma no Kiroku. Furthermore, they knew that he had been harboring Jiraiya Shūma Hiroyuki under the name Samezaya Jiroza, so for days they tortured him, trying to make him confess Jiraiya's whereabouts. The torture was brutal, but Chōbei never confessed to anything. He shut his eyes and kept silent, not uttering a single word. Eventually, the torture became so extreme that his body was close to giving up, and his life hung by a thread.

While Chōbei was imprisoned, his wife Oroku was left alone in the house. She heard he was being whipped and tortured, his very life in danger. She was beside herself and did not know what to do, so she called for counsel from Tsuruhashiya Kinosuke and his wife.

Oroku said, "As he is my husband, I have a duty towards Chōbei. However, our marriage is far from ordinary. My elder brother, Jiroza, is being hunted relentlessly and they are constantly searching for his whereabouts. After Enma no Kiroku found out that Jiroza is in fact my older brother, we could not let him be and had to eliminate him. Now they have Chōbei and are questioning him for the whereabouts of Jiroza. I fear he will never be able to escape his torment. Even if he manages to clear the charges related to Jiroza, he is still under suspicion for murder, which I don't think he can escape. All of this, just because he got involved with me and my brother. Even if Jiroza employs his *jutsu* to save Chōbei from jail, he would have to live the rest of his life in the shadows. What shall I do?" Then she wept.

Kinosuke sighed deeply and said nothing. Both he and Osai realized nothing could be done about the situation, so they sat with their brows in a furrow for a while. Eventually, Kinosuke said, "Be everything as it may, I will meet with Jiroza, tell him what has happened, and ask for his assistance. Chōbei's life hangs in the balance, and we must save him as soon as possible. We can't abandon him. I will leave for Shinano at once!" Having settled his mind on what he had to do, Chōbei entrusted Sutematsu to the care of his wife and set out for Shinano in secret.

8.7

(8.7)
Samezaya Jiroza, who was actually Ogata Shūma Hiroyuki, known by his alias Jiraiya, championed the weak and vanquished the mighty. Driven by an enduring ambition, he stole treasure from wealthy households, which he used to build up his military strength. He had amassed many followers, who awaited him in his fortress on Mount Kurohime. Some days prior, he infiltrated the mansion of Tsukikage Terutoki. There, he stole the moon-shaped seal used for army dispatches as well as the family tree of the Ogata clan. Now, he had set up a temporary residence for himself in the Kokubunji Temple in Echigo, where he bided his time. In the temple, he listened carefully to the comings and goings of the world, and he heard that the Kamakura Kanrei had issued a strict decree promising generous rewards to anyone who captured Jiraiya. Upon hearing the arrest order had also spread to the neighboring provinces, and that they were searching high and low for his whereabouts, Jiraiya thought to himself, "The moment is not yet ripe. Until the fervor surrounding me subsides, I shall seclude myself within my mountain stronghold, fortifying its defenses should any assailant dare to challenge me."

Meanwhile, when Jiraiya had disguised himself as the envoy of the Kanrei and infiltrated the mansion of the Tsukikage, he abducted Tagoto-hime and replaced her with Ekichi in disguise. Jiraiya thought everything had gone according to plan, but Yuminosuke had prepared for this, so the one Jiraiya kidnapped was in fact not Sarashina Tagoto-hime, but Yuminosuke's own daughter, Teruta.

Jiraiya thought to himself, "Regardless of her beauty, I mustn't entertain impure thoughts. My actions were solely driven by the need to obtain the two artifacts. However, if I keep Teruta here, it is inevitable that Yuminosuke's resourcefulness will get in my way again. And if I take this woman with me and shelter her in my mountain fortress, she will learn its location and it will surely bring disaster. Moreover, I cannot bring harm to an innocent soul. That would be an unforgivable cruelty. For now, I shall discreetly shelter her within the temple, awaiting the opportune moment to send her back."

And thus, the days passed, until Jiraiya decided it was time to send Teruta to Shinano. One evening, Jiraiya approached Teruta and said, "The reason you are here with me is not because I have an infatuation with Sarashina Hangan's daughter, Tagoto-hime. There is another reason, an aspiration I seek to fulfill, and your abduction was merely a means to that end. However, Yuminosuke-dono saw through my plans and had you change places with Tagoto-hime, resulting in you being the one kidnapped on the way to Echigo. Hence, you find yourself here with me. I understand your concerns about potential suspicions regarding your virtue after being held by bandits. So, tonight, I shall send you back to Shinano. In return, I implore you to convey to your father, Yuminosuke-dono, the thoughts occupying my mind."

Teruta, without a moment's hesitation, responded with unwavering resolve, "My father has known about you for a long time and speaks of you incessantly. That is precisely why he entrusted me to stand in for Tagoto-hime without your knowledge. I willingly came alone, fully prepared for whatever fate may befall me. Thus, I harbor no concerns. I took Tagoto-hime's place out of loyalty and have long ago steeled myself to face any cruelty or even death. If you understand that and still send me back, nothing could bring me greater joy. If there are any messages you wish me to convey to my father, speak them and spare no detail. I shall faithfully deliver your words, ensuring that not a single fragment is forgotten."

(8.8)

Jiraiya grinned and said, "All this time, I have hidden you away here in the Yamamon gate of the temple, which is by no means a proper home, yet you haven't been even the least bit daunted by the rough demeanor of my men. I would expect nothing less from Yuminosuke-dono's splendid daughter! A man couldn't hold a candle to your impressive samurai spirit! Now, the message you must convey to Yuminosuke pertains to your aunt, Misao-dono. Seeking revenge for her father-in-law and her husband on Tatsumaki Arakurō, she snuck into Kamakura under the guise of being a candy seller. Tatsumaki Arakurō was working as a fencing instructor under the name Gundazaemon. Unexpectedly, Misao-dono crossed paths with him outside the pleasure district. She thought she could finally fulfill her long-held desire, but unfortunately, he launched a counterattack. I stumbled upon her as I was passing by the embankment where she was tragically suffering from a deep wound she

8.8

had sustained. I couldn't abandon her, so I tended to her injuries. She looked at me and said just one thing: 'Please, take care of my child!' I thought it was so very heart-wrenching, so while tending to her I inquired what had happened. After telling me her tale, she passed away. I had her remains taken to a nearby temple, and I brought the child home with me. I cannot breastfeed him, but I have taken his upbringing upon myself.

"As I mentioned earlier, Misao was your father Yuminosuke-dono's younger sister. Long ago, Lord Sarashina entrusted your father with the task of assisting Misao-dono, relieving him of his duties for an extended period. Yuminosuke-dono was helping his sister find Arakurō, but the peace talks between Echigo and Shinano could not be left to anyone but him, so he was ordered to return. Although there is still no word of whether Arakurō has been eliminated or not, when the orphaned Sutematsu comes of age, I will guide him to exact vengeance upon Arakurō, avenging not only his parents but also his grandfather. To that end, I have concealed the orphaned boy in Kamakura alongside an elderly woman claiming to be Himamatsu Edanoshin-dono's wife, Kozue, and I am taking care of them. Sutematsu is your cousin, and I have taken pity on him. I am committed to seeing this through until the very end, fulfilling the wish entrusted to me by Misao-dono in her final moments. However, I am Jiraiya. I am infamous and a sinner, and to me, this vast world feels narrow, and I must navigate it with stealth. If I am unable to escape my destined fate and meet my demise before realizing my grand ambition, Sutematsu's whereabouts will be lost forever. I will not allow that to happen. Therefore, please relay everything I've shared with you to your father, the most loyal retainer."

After recounting the details of Misao's final moments to Teruta, Jiraiya said, "The night has grown late. I had considered having my men accompany you home. However, should you be stopped or questioned on the way, it will spell nothing but trouble for you. So instead, I shall prepare you an escort using my yōjutsu."

Standing up, Jiraiya folded some white paper that was on a nearby cosmetics cabinet. He chanted an incantation, and with each paper he tossed, it transformed instantaneously into a frog. In the blink of an eye, fifty frogs materialized, wriggling about until they assumed the forms of men and women dressed in various garments. Speaking in human language, they declared, "We stand at the ready!" and awaited Jiraiya's command.

Jiraiya inspected them. "You are to take this fair lady to her mansion and keep her safe from all harm along the way!"

The frogs confirmed the order and bowed deeply.

(8.9)

Then Jiraiya said to Teruta, "Oh yes, I forgot about something," and opened a box that was sitting next to him. From the box he pulled a *tanto* short sword and gave it to Teruta.

"I was entrusted with this tanto by Misao-dono on her deathbed, along with Sutematsu, as a memento of her. Please, deliver it to Yuminosuke-dono. Also, ensure you inform him that despite my bringing you into this temporary temple abode and spending days here with you, nothing inappropriate whatsoever has occurred. However, under no circumstances must you disclose the conversations I had with my men when they visited. Now, the time has come."

Teruta responded in agreement. She understood that Jiraiya's honor would not allow him to do anything inhuman, so she said her farewell and got up. The frogs, which were merely paper and had disguised themselves as humans, then carried her through the air and departed with her.

As Jiraiya saw the retinue off, a furrow appeared on his brow. He muttered to himself, "The hour of the boar has almost passed.[2] There is not a cloud in the sky and in the south a single star just fell, drawing its light across the heavens. This is a sign of some unknown calamity."

Gaze fixed on the sky, Jiraiya's attention was drawn to the distant sound of a temple bell. He counted the resonating chimes on his fingers—nine in total.

"How curious. It seems to be the hour of the rat, which is the first of the twelve zodiac animals and is considered the ruler of time. Due to their tendency to secretly hoard and bring items back to their nests, rats are often said to have the heart of a thief. As time passes, their families grow in the same way that my allies have increased. I believe this would be an ideal time for divination. However, a falling star to the south is an

2 21:00–23:00.

8.9

ill omen, indicating misfortune befalling one of my allies, and someone is likely suffering in prison. How ominous."

As Jiraiya stared at the sky, one of his petty thieves, Nobusuma Tenroku, came rushing before Jiraiya in a flurry of urgency. He knelt, put his hands on the ground and said, "We were left in Kamakura with instructions to keep an eye on things and report on both the good and the bad. Sire, after you left Kamakura for Shinano, Chōbei, the dreamer of Hanamizu Bridge, suddenly killed Enma no Kiroku. One of Enma's men discovered one of Chōbei's sandals at the crime scene and is using it as evidence to press charges against him. Shikano Fuehachi and a group of constables apprehended Chōbei, throwing him into prison where he is now being interrogated. Following the commotion caused by your impersonation as an envoy of the Kamakura Kanrei and your infiltration of the Tsukikage and Sarashina clans' wedding, the Kanrei has issued an order for your arrest. Your wanted poster is plastered on every street corner. There are proclamations, saying, in ink, that anyone who captures Jiraiya will be rewarded. Due to this, Chōbei's life is at risk. Despite Oroku-dono's attempts to conceal it, it seems like everyone and their mother already knows that Chōbei's wife is the sister of the bandit Jiraiya. Because of this connection, they do not care about the murder anymore. Every day, they torture Chōbei, attempting to force a confession revealing where you are hiding. Furthermore, Tsuruhashiya Kinosuke is taking care of Sutematsu and the elderly woman. It won't be long before they suspect him as well and capture him. You must leave this hideout immediately, fortify the stronghold on Mount Kurohime in Echigo, and prepare for war when the attackers come. We must act swiftly!" Nobusuma shot up from his knelt position.

(8.10)

But Jiraiya smiled and replied, "Nobusuma, you must be exhausted from your long and arduous journey. I had already deduced something like this must have happened. Because of his involvement with my sister and me, Chōbei-dono is suffering. I have even burdened Tsuruhashiya Kinosuke with the responsibility of caring for a young child and an elderly woman, despite having no relation to them. My impulsive actions have caused both of them problems, so I cannot simply abandon them now. Even if it means sacrificing my own ambition, I must take action. My honor compels me to intervene. If I do not save Chōbei now, my promises to him will have been worth no more than foam on the water. Now, what course of action shall I pursue?"

Even he, the stouthearted Jiraiya, found himself pondering, tilting his head and placing a hand on his chest as he sought a plan.

In the meantime, Teruta, the daughter of the loyal retainer, had boarded a palanquin and was making her way with her retinue. The retinue was in reality a great group of frogs, made of paper, which Jiraiya had enchanted with his yōjutsu, and the palanquin was really crafted from the leaves of a plantago plant. To all who saw them, it looked like a riveted palanquin with a fine escort going to Yuminosuke's mansion. However, to Jiraiya's eyes, they were nothing more than frogs. The frog entourage wasted no time carrying Teruta to Yuminosuke's mansion, where they safely delivered her.

The Kannon of Hasedera in Kamakura is renowned for its miraculous powers, attracting believers from all walks of life. Thus, it is always teeming with worshippers, lined up like the teeth on a comb. This year, the crowd was even more immense, as the Kannon statue was put on public display. Inside the temple precinct, there were equestrian performers, acrobats, strongmen, people selling curios and handiwork, animal fights, and for a coin one could see the sun goddess' forbidden cave. The temple grounds were packed with stalls, each trying to outdo the others, putting up the most flamboyant signs to try and stop temple-goers in their tracks. The air resonated with the cacophony of merchants, beggars, and festival drums, while the archery stalls resounded with twanging bows and the nembutsu prayer reverberated through accompanying gongs.

As a rare sight, among all this bustling revelry, there was a single beggar, who, for some peculiar reason, received nothing. His clothes stood out as they were quite fine, but he sat on a mat with his face hidden by a *tengai* basket hat. In front of him was a sign, which read: 'Recently unemployed rōnin. Not asking for alms.' Every day, he sat there, so the people could read his sign. Those with a little compassion furrowed

8.10

their brows in concern, and those without, chuckled as they walked by. Not looking back, they would quip, "What a strange rōnin. If he wanted to, he could go inside the temple, lie down and sleep. Instead he chooses to sit out here, without begging, on the street getting showered with sand and dust. What an incredibly peculiar inclination to have."

Among all the people, there was a katana merchant from Yukinoshita named Katanaya Hanshichi. He catered to various families with mansions in Kamakura, and so lived a prosperous life. With his wife, he had one daughter. Her name was Ohana, and this year she turned sixteen. She was as lovely as a flower bud in spring, and was known as Katanaya's enchanting daughter. Some households even expressed a willingness to offer great wealth to have Ohana as a court concubine. Numerous merchants, utilizing their connections, attempted to negotiate marriage proposals with those close to Ohana. Despite the persistent matchmaking efforts, Ohana was Hanshichi's only daughter, so whoever courted her would have to enter her household. After rejecting all who wanted to marry her, Ohana finally entered negotiations with a fitting man who could be the successor to the household. Once they had exchanged information about their social status and backgrounds, no obstacles were found, and they could finally exchange vows of matrimony.

However, an unfortunate turn of events occurred this year regarding tax payments, resulting in the prospective groom being assigned to a demanding task in a distant location until the following year. This unforeseen circumstance brought the long-awaited marriage plans to a standstill.

(8.11)

Meanwhile, Shikano Fuehachi, one of the constables serving the steward, at one time tried to catch a glimpse of Ohana. She had no interest in one of his standing, so when Fuehachi's superior, Yokoshima Guheida, had business with Hanshichi, Fuehachi secretly tried to leverage the steward's authority to make Ohana his wife. However, Hanshichi would not hear of it, as Ohana already had a fiancée. He also would not give her away to join a different family, leaving Fuehachi with no recourse.

So Fuehachi thought to himself, "If Ohana will not come to be my wife, I will speak my mind and my heart to her, persuading her sense of compassion. Then she will be mine," and bided his time for the right moment.

Coincidentally, on this day, Ohana had come to Hasedera Temple to offer prayers for her ailing mother. She had convinced her parents that now was the perfect time to visit the temple, so they allowed her to go, given she only went in order to give her most heartfelt prayers. Along with Ohana, they sent a male clerk from their store and a maidservant. They prepared to leave swiftly for Hasedera in the early morning, as it was likely to become rowdy after noon from all the visitors to the temple.

Someone must have informed Fuehachi about this beforehand, because he had arrived at Hasedera even before daybreak. He had gathered information about the tea house frequented by Katanaya Hanshichi and positioned himself there, waiting for Ohana's arrival. Because Fuehachi came so early, he grew tired from waiting and stretched as he sat on his stool in the tea house. There he caught sight of the nearby rōnin, holding a sign stating his disinterest in alms. This got Fuehachi interested, so he stood up, went over to the rōnin, and squatted beside him.

"You don't resemble a destitute rōnin. You're not asking for alms, so for what reason are you sitting out here?" Fuehachi inquired.

The rōnin replied, "You're being too loud. You must be Shikano Fuehachi-dono, right? I am hiding my face because I wish to remain anonymous. As for my purpose here, I am awaiting something. Like Jiang Ziya from the old tales, who fished with a barbless hook, I am biding my time for the perfect moment to set my plans in motion. I used to serve as a vassal of the Kanrei, but I have since resigned and embarked on a different path. Nothing for you to be suspicious about."

Fuehachi slapped his thigh and said, "Then tell me your name!"

However, the rōnin interrupted him and scanned their surroundings. "I am trying to be discreet, and I am completely dedicated to waiting here. I will tell you everything at a different time and place."

After hearing this, Fuehachi remembered his reason for being there. "In that case, let's meet later at a discreet location where no one can see us, and we can discuss matters in private," he said, and returned to the tea house.

8.11

8.12

Part II

(8.12)

Meanwhile, Ohana had finished praying to the Kannon statue, and on her way out from the temple she went inside the tea house to have a rest. Accompanying her was the maidservant, who prepared for their departure. The maidservant took out a mirror from her kimono and began touching up her face. Fuehachi saw this as his opportune moment and approached Ohana with a brisk stride.

"If it isn't Hanshichi-dono's daughter, Ohana-dono! I hope your pilgrimage to the Kannon was fulfilling. I have sent suitable marriage proposals over and over, asking if you would be my wife. Unfortunately, I have yet to receive a favorable response. Today, I came here for the display of the Kannon to pray for the success of my marriage proposal. That I have met you here on the way home must be by the grace of Kannon Bodhisattva. How grateful I am for Kannon's kindness." Fuehachi reached into his kimono and presented a letter to Ohana. "I have poured my heart into this letter. I pray that, as you cleanse your hands with the purifying water at the temple entrance, my feelings pour from the letter and into your heart."

Fuehachi's tone was very familiar, which caused Ohana to blush and hide her face. The clerk Jitsuemon intervened.

"Fuehachi-sama, what do you think you are doing, flirting like that with Hanshichi's young daughter? She already has a fiancée. If you were unaware, I suggest you speak to Hanshichi, and he will enlighten you. You must be intoxicated, acting like this in public!" said Jitsuemon, and pushed the letter back at Fuehachi.

Attempting to defuse the situation, Jitsuemon rose, ready to depart with Ohana. However, Fuehachi's expression quickly changed, and he seized the clerk by the sleeve.

"You're Hanshichi's clerk, so listen carefully! Even if I were merry from drink, I am not being rude. She is the daughter of a dear friend of mine, and I just came over to say hello because it is such a fortunate happenstance to meet here today. I simply wished to give her a letter expressing my deep emotions and seeking a response to a matter I asked her about long ago. Why should I hesitate to give my letter to someone I am so familiar with? Even if she does have a fiancée, I gave my proposal before that, so I could not know about this. So, shut up and go away!"

(8.13)

Fuehachi glared at Jitsuemon, who defiantly rebuked, "You dare approach, asking Hanshichi's *very* young daughter to give you an answer to a marriage proposal, hounding her with your meddlesome bargaining. What do you expect her to say? Your conduct is selfish and unbecoming of a samurai! After our visit to pray to Kannon today, you have the audacity to approach us on our way home with your insinuations. As Ohana's guardian, allowing such a travesty to occur is a grave dereliction of my duty, which is why I must reprimand you. Please, show some modicum of decency!"

8.13

Pressed by the sudden barrage, Fuehachi retorted, "I am a samurai, *manservant*! You cannot speak to me that way! I will strike you down before your insolent tongue can rest in your blabbing mouth, you impudent cur!"

With a resounding smack, Fuehachi struck Jitsuemon's forehead with his folding fan. The force of the blow was so strong that blood trickled from the wound, which proved to be too much for Jitsuemon to bear.

With a coarse and wavering voice, Jitsuemon said, "You were rude to a woman who is already spoken for, you acted like a drunkard and tried to pass it off as refinement, and when called out for your rudeness and carelessness, you struck me between the eyes and hurt me. Do you think you can get away with this, simply because you are a samurai? This will not stand! Now, Ohana-sama, let us hurry home, and then I will inform Yokoshima Guheida-sama of what has happened."

Jitsuemon tried standing up, but Fuehachi grabbed him and held him down. "For a mere townsman like yourself to be so rude to me, even if you do report it to Guheida-dono, I am certain he will dismiss it as a minor incident on my part. Now, prepare to face the consequences!" said Fuehachi and thrashed Jitsuemon with his fan.

Ohana and the maidservant were shocked by Fuehachi's behavior, and Ohana pleaded, "Please stay your hand. Do not be so short-tempered, Fuehachi-sama."

Fuehachi looked at Ohana's face as she tried to stop him, and smirked. "If you apologize to me, I might consider excusing the servant for his recklessness. Fret not. But instead of your words, you can take this letter and send me a favorable reply."

Ruthlessly and without consideration, he grabbed Ohana's hand and got close to her. She tried to jump away, but he grabbed her by the hip and said, "Now, now, don't play games like that."

A person emerged from behind a bamboo screen, grabbed Fuehachi's arm, and twisted it. "*Ow ow ow ow!*" Fuehachi cried out as he fell to the ground. The individual who had appeared, looked so gentle that they could have been either a man or a woman. And even though they were too old for it, their hair was done up like a wakashū, with bangs devoid of hair oil.

This person declared, "What do we have here? An older man like you, pulling at a young girl like her, and then bashing a servant? Furthermore, shamelessly insulting a committed woman in public! Such an ill-considered jest. Thinking you have the right to do what you want because of your swords. It seems you take pride in injustice and immorality. Well, I am in the market for a good fight, and I caught eye of the one you were peddling. I am Yumeno Chōkichi, the lazy brat who sees this floating world as nothing more than a dream. Now, Mr. Samurai-sama, I'll be your opponent! Get up and forfeit your life to me! Make sure the pin in your katana is fastened tight and come face me."

With a thud, Chōkichi sat down on a stool and looked around. Ohana and Jitsuemon had flown to their feet but were still lingering around, feeling indebted to Chōkichi but also wondering what might happen next.

"Do not concern yourselves with what will happen now. You best hurry along," Chōkichi said, urging them to depart with a glance.

Fuehachi, having landed on his back, rubbed his backside as he rose from the ground. "You are a street brawler I haven't seen before. I had good reason to be discussing with that girl. Why did you interfere?"

(8.14)

Fuehachi placed his hand on the hilt of his katana, to which Chōkichi replied in a nonchalant tone. "Oh, reaching for the stick you use to earn your living stipend, are you? Well, come and strike me if you believe you can. Right here," he taunted, slapping his own rear.

The mockery was too much for Fuehachi to stomach. He drew his katana and swung at Chōkichi. With a swift and well-trained motion, Chōkichi sidestepped Fuehachi, grabbed his arm and threw him. As Fuehachi attempted to rise, Chōkichi firmly held him down, pressing him beneath his knee.

"Now, hurry up and leave this place," Chōkichi instructed Ohana and her two servants. After Chōkichi made sure they left, he pulled Fuehachi up from the ground.

"Now, Fuehachi-dono or whatever your name may be. You might have met her once or twice before, but it is evident you barely know this girl. You can't simply approach her and her companions, attempting to forcefully win her over like some rutting deer. Nothing good is likely to come of this. Instead, how about I introduce you to some exquisite

8.14

ladies of the night for you to hold and sleep with? My treat. And in return, you listen to a small request I have?" Chōkichi proposed, his expression softening.

Fuehachi had learned the hard way what Chōkichi was capable of, so he knew better than to resist. Instead, Fuehachi brushed the dust off his clothes and answered in a friendly tone, "Let me hear what this request is then. I don't know if I can be of help, but I will do my best. I doubt it will be something I can't do, but I can't really say anything until I hear what it is."

Chōkichi laughed and replied, "Indeed! My request is none other than this... Recently, by order of the Kanrei, wanted posters of Jiraiya Hiroyuki have been posted everywhere. Well, I want to report I have learned where he is, and that I will catch him and collect the reward. Please, take me to the steward, so I can report this."

Fuehachi was taken aback. "With your skill, I have no doubt you could actually catch Jiraiya. But I am a constable, so I don't need to take you anywhere. Instead, you must lead me to his location, capture him, and present yourself as the informant to claim the reward you seek. However, Jiraiya possesses toad yōjutsu and can conceal his identity. I heard he commands a large force and has barricaded himself somewhere on Mount Kurohime, awaiting any attackers who might come. Capturing him would not be easy, not unless you attack with a sizeable force. So, what's your strategy for apprehending him?"

Chōkichi nodded and answered, "I have a plan to address that. Just take me to Yokoshima Guheida-dono, and I will explain everything in detail to him."

"Indeed, there are too many people to discuss this here. Let's make haste, and get you an audience with Yokoshima-dono," said Fuehachi, and quickly left with Chōkichi in tow.

The rōnin had been eavesdropping on the conversation, and now looked pensive. Someone resembling an express courier, with a letter container hanging from his neck, roamed the area, scanning his surroundings. He approached the rōnin discreetly and whispered into his ear. The rōnin opened the letter container and extracted a message.

"Well, well, a secret letter from Urafuji Saemon-dono. 'As we previously discussed, I intend to invade both Echigo and Shinano, and become the feudal lord of both lands. If circumstances permit and my men and horses are not too battle worn, I am prepared to continue into Sagami and Bōshū.[3] The preliminary plans have already been laid, but as you ruled in one of these places, you must know the shortcuts and ways to the fortresses amidst the passes and rivers. For now, continue gathering intelligence in Kamakura, enlist the aid of Jiraiya, and then come here as fast as you can.'"

When he finished reading every detail of the letter, the rōnin nodded to himself and said, "Aruhei-dono, thank you for bringing this from so far away. I have long been strategizing to forge an alliance with Jiraiya. However, since Jiraiya assumed the identity of the Kanrei's envoy, infiltrated the Tsukikage-Sarashina wedding in Echigo, and pilfered the moon-shaped seal for mobilizing armies, it is believed that he will strike from his mountain fortress.

(8.15)

"Rumor has it he is harbored within Mount Kurohime, and won't come anywhere near Kamakura now that he is so wanted. But this is difficult to verify. He is a rogue who can use yōjutsu at will. My scheme is to lure him to me. By disguising myself as a beggar who asks for nothing, I shall raise his suspicion to the point where he will be compelled to investigate. To ensure the success of this scheme, secrecy was paramount. This is the net that I have cast. Should my plan fail, I shall make haste to go to Mount Kurohime in search of him."

The rōnin then engaged in a lengthy private discussion with messenger Aruhei. Upon concluding their conversation, someone appeared from behind them, calling out, "You, suspicious rōnin! You are in league with Urafuji Saemon of Kai's rebellion! You are under arrest!"

Two men approached, one from the left and the other from the right. One attempted to tackle the rōnin but was thrown to the ground, while Aruhei pinned down the other when attacked. As the two men did their work, a voice suddenly called out, "Wait a moment, both of you!" Emerging from the shadows of a tree, a magnificent samurai stepped forward, his face concealed by a cloth. Amid throwing another attacker,

3 Current Yamanashi prefecture and southern Chiba, respectively.

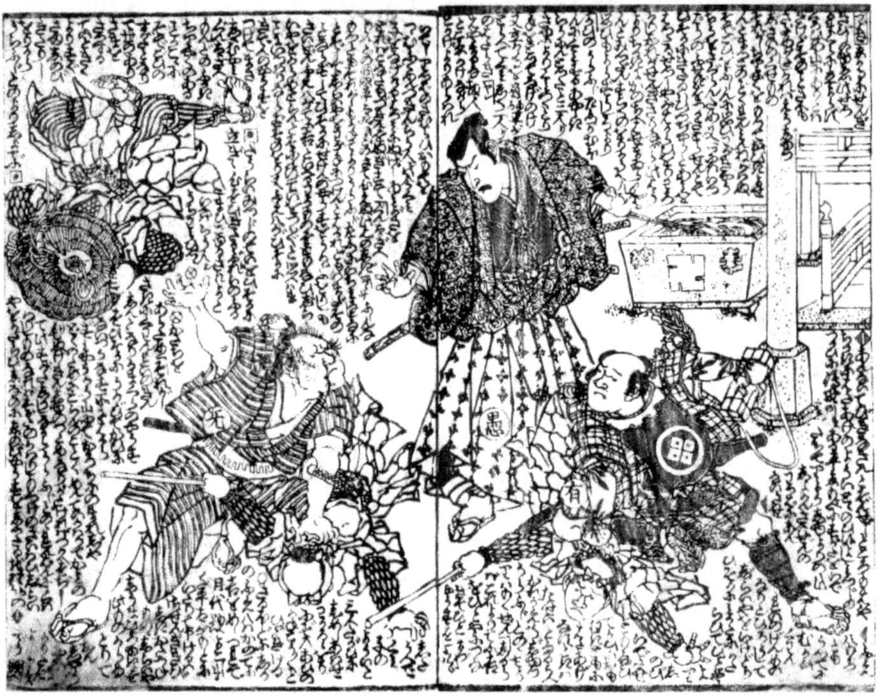

8.15

the rōnin inadvertently lost his basket hat. The samurai picked it up and called out, "Gundazaemon-dono!"

"Guheida-dono? I had no idea. What brings you here?" the rōnin exclaimed.

"I admit, my presence here may arouse suspicion. However, I too have long been an ally of Urafuji Saemon, and I also sought to recruit Jiraiya to our cause. Alas, I soon realized the futility of my efforts, so I disguised myself to walk freely and observe the world. Just now, I listened as Fuehachi talked with someone who calls himself Chōkichi. They left together, and it appears that Chōkichi is going to try to capture Jiraiya and bring him to justice. Fuehachi secretly told me about you. Lo and behold, it is really you, Muyami Gundazaemon-dono! When I heard you had a deep stratagem, observing the world dressed as a beggar, I snuck here as fast as I could. And just as I arrived, you received a letter from Urafuji-dono. I listened to the secret message and humbly beg your forgiveness for my intrusive actions."

The rōnin laughed and straightened up. "I was serving as the Kanrei's retainer, while also sending information to Kai about what was happening in Kamakura. However, I was suddenly swallowed by an enormous serpent on Mount Myōkō, and its poison did this to me. As you can see, I look very different, and my hair has fallen out. I couldn't keep up my position as an attendant, so I quit and became what you see now. Surprisingly, this misfortune has proven fortuitous, for it grants me the opportunity to converse with Jiraiya, infiltrate Shinano, familiarize myself with the terrain, and attempt to sway him to our cause. Shimano Aruhei, sent out as a secret messenger disguised as a servant, has brought me this letter from the feudal lord stating the preparations to raise the banners are almost finished. The young man from earlier will lead Fuehachi and attack Jiraiya, capturing him alive as per the Kanrei's strict orders. I will then secretly persuade him to be our ally and sneak him out of prison. Together, we shall journey to Kai. When the time to raise the banners comes, not only will we wield a formidable force, but we will also have Jiraiya's yōjutsu, and Urafuji-dono's victory will be close at hand."

"In that case, we should imprison Chōkichi now, see..."

"...who he is, and then prepare captors."

When the three finished conspiring, they went their separate ways, and the sound of the temple bell rang in the dusk.

Thus, Shikano Fuehachi brought Chōkichi before the steward, Yokoshima Guheida, and told him the person he had brought with him intended to capture the fiercely wanted Jiraiya Hiroyuki and collect the reward from the Kanrei.

(8.16)

After listening very carefully to Fuehachi's account, Guheida responded skeptically, "How exactly is it that you, who hasn't even shaved his bangs yet, intend to capture a rogue wielding strange yōjutsu—a feat not even the might of the Kanrei has been able to accomplish?"

Chōkichi dismissed his words and said, "If you think me so unreliable, by all means, prepare a large force of men and have them surround Jiraiya's hiding place. That way, regardless of what jutsu he uses, there will be nowhere for him to run. You should prepare as quickly as possible though, so I can guide you to him without further delay."

Chōkichi had done his best to urge Guheida, and after some time had passed, Guheida nodded and agreed, "Very well, I entrust this task to you. For now, we will confine you to the hold, but once we have made the necessary preparations, you may choose any armor and weapons you require."

This made Chōkichi rejoice and raised his spirits. He willingly allowed himself to be locked away in the hold, seemingly at ease as if nothing were amiss. Guheida then briefed the Kanrei on the situation, assembled a sizable contingent of men, and made the necessary arrangements for the journey to Jiraiya's hiding place, alongside Fuehachi.

Hearing the report from his subordinate, the thief Nobusuma Tenhachi, that Chōbei the dreamer was in dire trouble, Jiraiya was overcome with shock.[4] "It would be heartless to abandon someone I have a duty to save!" he exclaimed. He hopped on the back of a paper frog, which then flew through the air and brought him to Kamakura faster than the blink of

4 Previously, Tenhachi was Tenroku. A possible mistake by the author.

8.16

What is happening in the lower right picture will be explained in book nine.

an eye. First, he went to Chōbei's house to assess the situation there, but neither Oroku nor Kinosuke were present, so he proceeded to Kinosuke's house. There, he found only Osae, Kinosuke's wife, and Sutematsu.

True to what he had heard, when Jiraiya peered into the prison, he saw Chōbei, worn down from days of torture. His body was covered in festering wounds from being beaten with switches, and he was emaciated and feeble. He would surely perish if left for much longer under these conditions. Overwhelmed with pity, Jiraiya devised a plan to rescue Chōbei, nurse him, and restore his strength. Jiraiya cast a spell of invisibility on himself and infiltrated the prison. He snuck over to Chōbei's bedside, where the exhausted man lay prostrate, and gently awakened him. Then Jiraiya explained how he rushed to see him upon hearing what happened. Chōbei's face brightened with joy as he rose to his feet, expressing his gratitude for Jiraiya's kindness.

Then Chōbei said, "The reason I murdered Kiroku was not just to cover for Oroku. Kiroku suggested Oroku commit adultery with him, and his unrequited desires turned to resentment. Aware of Oroku's connection to you and Samezaya Jiroza being none other than Jiraiya Hiroyuki, he threatened to expose us to seek revenge. I couldn't let him go free, so I struck him down. Unfortunately, one of his wicked henchmen discovered one of my sandals at the scene—a sandal branded with the mark 蝶 (chō). They used it as evidence and reported me to the authorities. Now I am imprisoned, accused of murder and harboring a fugitive. Each day, they subject me to severe torture. Even if they break my bones and turn my flesh to paste, how could my pride as a man ever allow me to confess against you, my brother-in-law? My luck has run dry, and I will probably die from my next beating, but I have accepted my fate. However, your safety is of utmost importance and must be safeguarded. It is perilous for you to come here so casually."

Chōbei showed no hesitation in his words, leaving Jiraiya lauding the man's chivalrous spirit. Jiraiya then said, "When I rescued Fukitarō, my plan was to use an eagle to carry him and escape the ensuing consequences. However, if in rescuing you I was to merely use my yōjutsu to break the prison, it would only intensify the manhunt for you, and you would likely be recaptured. Hence, I have devised a different strategy—a clever ruse that will ensure your rescue soon enough."

With these words, Jiraiya retrieved an elixir from the medicine box on his hip. He rubbed it all over Chōbei's body and instructed him to put some in his mouth as well. In no time, Chōbei experienced a revitalization of spirit, forgot the unbearable pain inflicted upon him, and saw his wounds heal as if wiped away. It felt as though he had been reborn, and his will was strong.

(8.17)

Jiraiya heard more details about the situation from Chōbei, bid his farewell, and vanished, dispersing like a wisp of smoke.

Oroku wept after hearing the report that Chōbei had been imprisoned and was suffering brutal torture. Uncertain if Jiraiya was aware of the situation, Tsuruhashiya Kinosuke took matters into his own hands. Determined to find Jiraiya and seek his assistance in rescuing Chōbei using his extraordinary yōjutsu, Kinosuke hastened towards Mount Myōkō, situated on the border of Echigo and Shinano.

During his journey, Kinosuke encountered a day when he struggled to secure lodging, and as the sun set, he searched for a place to stay. Aluminous object streaked across the sky from the direction of Echigo, heading towards Kamakura. The people who saw this thought it a mysterious thing. Some believed it to be a *hitodama*, the wandering soul of a departed, while others thought it might be a *kanedama*, a golden spirit symbolizing good fortune. The rumor of it spread far, and discussions arose, debating whether it heralded an imminent natural disaster or served as a portent of both auspicious and ominous events. Reflecting upon it later, Kinosuke would come to the realization that it must not have been some flying object, but rather Jiraiya himself, using his yōjutsu to soar across the sky towards Kamakura, in order to see how Chōbei was doing.

Ohana, the daughter of Katanaya Hanshichi from Yukinoshita in Kamakura, was engaged to be married. It would be difficult for the groom

8.17

Left: This is Kamakura Right: This is Echigo

Aside: Sometimes frogs fly through the summer night sky, steamed by the heat of the season. As such, the toad has mystical powers, so it should not be considered strange that it can fly without wings.

to prepare the wedding by that year, but after Ohana's mother fell ill, her one wish was to witness her daughter's wedding before her passing. Hanshichi deeply sympathized and urged for the wedding to proceed. As Ohana's mother's condition worsened, Hanshichi relayed the situation to the intermediary, seeking to expedite the process. The other party agreed, they picked a date, and worked persistently to get everything ready in time.

Driven by filial devotion, Ohana placed her faith in the Hase Kannon, a Bodhisattva of mercy. She fervently prayed to the Kannon, offering ten years of her own lifespan in exchange for extending her mother's life by five years and curing her illness. Maybe it was because of Ohana's sincere heart, but her mother suddenly recovered, and Ohana praised and honored the Kannon Bodhisattva for its efficacy.

That being what it was, according to the agreement, the groom had already been welcomed in by his new family. He was very agreeable and did nothing to oppose his two in-laws. He worked hard on the family business, and he lived so peacefully with the couple that Hanshichi passed the headship of the family and his name to him. Thus, Hanshichi took a new name. The first character of the name consisted of the character 半 (han), like his previous name Hanshichi, and then he

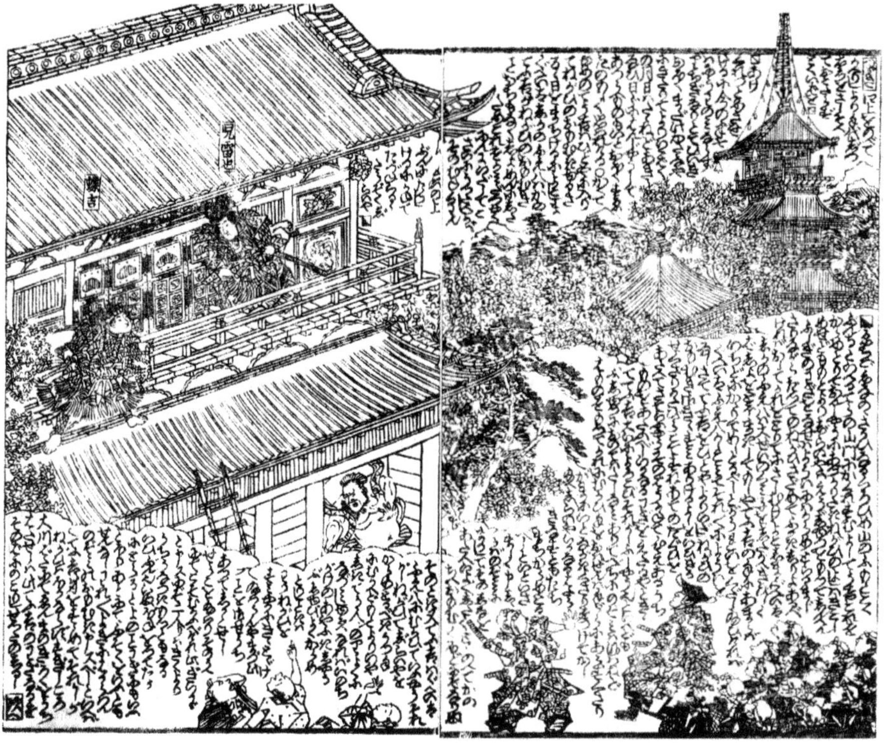

8.18

added a part that means person, making the first character 伴 (ban). Henceforth, he became known as Ban'emon. Together with Hanshichi, he went to all the mansions they dealt with, proclaiming, "This is my heir Hanshichi, and I hope you will continue doing your business with him as you have done with me."

(8.18)

Returning home, Hanshichi joined forces with his aide, Jitsuemon, and dedicated themselves tirelessly from dawn to dusk, diligently serving their clients. Hanshichi was not only agreeable but also loyal, which brought in many frequent customers. Although not much time had passed since he came to the katana shop, the business was booming with many customers asking for custom swords, and people thought Hanshichi to be a dependable man.

As Chōkichi was in jail awaiting the day when his request would be granted, Yokoshima Guheida and Shikano Fuehachi meticulously outlined Chōkichi's plea in a letter and presented it to a higher-ranking official. The thorough appeal reached all the way to a formal hearing with the Kanrei. It was revealed that the wanted bandit Jiraiya was hiding in the Yamamon gate of the Kokubunji Temple in the foothills of Mount Kurohime in the borderlands of Echigo and Shinano. Chōkichi intended to capture Jiraiya and claim the reward, but Jiraiya wielded yōjutsu and could work miraculous and mystical arts, so catching him would not be easy. However, Chōkichi must have taken this into consideration because he also requested that Yokoshima Guheida and Fuehachi be sent with a great host of constables and encircle the gate. This strategic move would ensure they would still have a chance to apprehend Jiraiya if Chōkichi alone fell short. Convinced, the Kanrei gave the order, and Guheida and Fuehachi made all the preparations, securing Chōkichi's release from prison and informing him of the Kanrei's approval.

Donning chainmail, vambraces, greaves, and other protective gear, they asked Chōkichi, "We said we would supply you with whatever weapons you are proficient with. What skill do you possess?"

Chōkichi beamed with joy and bravely exclaimed, "You could say I am not the most experienced person, but I am an accomplished martial artist, so I don't ask for anything in particular. However, since I will be up against someone with a sword, I can't rely solely on my skills and need to give Jiraiya a handicap. Please, lend me a chain sickle with an exceptionally long chain. With this weapon, I will eventually catch Jiraiya, no matter what tricks he employs."

Guheida and Fuehachi promptly provided him with the desired weapon, marking the completion of their preparations so they could set out for their destination.

Then Chōkichi said, "We are setting out to attack and capture Jiraiya on my request, but because I am used to the avarice of townsfolk, I have doubts you will fulfill my request promptly once I have successfully captured him. Since I'm risking my life, I must ensure you are fully aware of what my request is and have some proof that you will grant it. Only then can we proceed. What are your thoughts on this plan?"

Guheida and Fuehachi nodded and said, "You speak true. Like the proverb 'For the dog to have its prey stolen by the eagle after it has broken the bone' there would be little recourse for you, should we suddenly go back on our word. Rest assured we shall see it done, so tell us the details of your wish."

(8.19)

Chōkichi proceeded, "My request is as follows: I, Chōkichi, confess to being the one who killed Enma no Kiroku by the Ōgawa River some time ago. But the brand on the sandal you found on the scene was used as evidence to arrest Chōbei, who is innocent and not deserving of this disaster. This situation is deeply distressing, and I implore you to promptly pardon Chōbei, investigate the murder of Enma no Kiroku to reveal my true guilt, and then pardon me for the murder. If you grant me this, I ask for nothing else. I hope you can accept this request."

Guheida and Fuehachi looked at each other and considered for a while. Eventually, Guheida responded, "The arrest and imprisonment of Chōbei the dreamer was not solely due to the murder. Chōbei married Oroku, Jiraiya Hiroyuki's sister, and the couple harbored Jiraiya as he infiltrated Kamakura under the alias Samezaya Jiroza, allegedly gathering allies. He is by no means a simple rogue. Chōbei is no ordinary rogue. He is being tortured as an accomplice with knowledge of Jiraiya's

8.19

whereabouts. However, should you successfully capture Jiraiya, we will no longer have reason to investigate Chōbei. And if we can truly make clear that you were the one who committed the murder, I see no reason why Chōbei can't be pardoned. If it will ease your concerns, I shall provide you with a written pardon for Chōbei as the reward you requested."

Then Guheida had Fuehachi write a letter with the arrangements, which he handed to Chōkichi. Seeing the letter, Chōkichi could not contain his joy. "All right then! Let's get going!" he exclaimed in high spirits. The three courageously embarked on their journey. Wasting not a moment, they gathered the men and rushed towards the Kokubunji Temple in the foothills of Mount Kurohime.

The Kokubunji Temple in Echigo is a state-supported provincial temple. One of many, for every province throughout Japan has one Kokubunji branch temple. However, because of the tumultuous times of the world, and due to it being quite a large temple, the temple had fallen into disrepair. The Yamamon gate leaned precariously, covered in moss, while fallen tiles lay scattered on the ground. Bandits had taken it as their abode, but there was none to reign the bandits in. The temple was in a dilapidated state, so the head priest and the few monks lived together in the priest's private residence. It was the third month, the month of new life, and the sakura trees on the temple grounds were in full bloom, scattering their leaves. The scene resembled the untamed Shiga mountains, as if the trees themselves sought to conceal the ancient temple's imperfections.

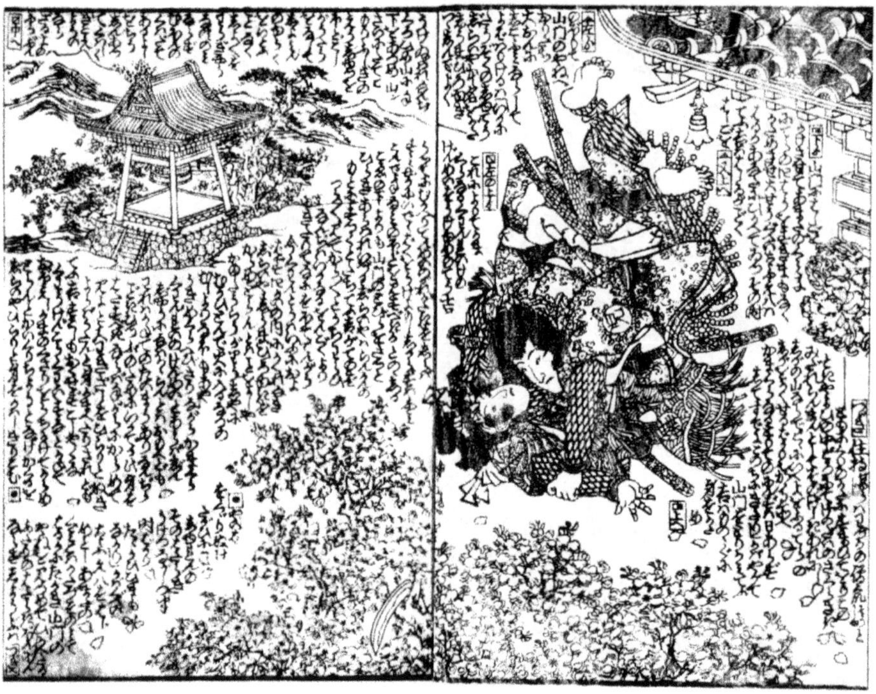

8.20

(8.20)

Before the break of dawn, numerous constables from Kamakura arrived and surrounded the Yamamon gate. Fully armed and armored, Chōkichi placed a ladder up against the Yamamon gate and instructed the men to surround the temple from all directions, leaving no gaps. Guheida, acting as commander, and Fuehachi had retreated far away. Then, as if running, Chōkichi ascended the ladder and reached the lower roof of the gate. There, he raised his leg like a sumo wrestler and delivered a resounding stomp. He called out:

"Hear me now, Jiraiya, leader of bandits, whose true name is Ogata Shūma Hiroyuki! You have amassed many men in your mountain fortress on Mount Kurohime. You wield eerie yōjutsu to commit banditry and you run rampant without any regard to the suffering of the common people. Not only that, but I have also heard detailed reports that you plot rebellion. The rumors surrounding you are grave indeed. Thus, I, Chōkichi, have received strict orders from the Kanrei of Kamakura to punish you! Your karma has finally caught up with you, and I demand that you surrender and face your shackles! If you do not, shall I then instead come in, and show you just what I am capable of?"

As Chōkichi's accusing voice reverberated, the sliding doors of the Yamamon gate flew open, and Jiraiya emerged, stepping onto the balustrade. He scrutinized Chōkichi and burst into boisterous laughter.

"From what distant province have you come to entertain us with such a joke? The fact that you want to capture me, Jiraiya Shūma Hiroyuki, now not just famous in the Kantō but throughout all the realms under heaven, is hilarious! You are akin to a praying mantis, brandishing its claws against a mighty cartwheel, or an insect in summer, foolishly flying into an open flame. You are like a blind man who fails to fear the unseen snake. Do you believe that, because it is the order of the Kamakura Kanrei, you can casually bind me with ropes? I have my own ambitions. How will you, oh rustic fool, accomplish such a feat? Let's see if your skills can truly capture me!"

Jiraiya drew his *ōwakizashi* sword and took a stance showing Chōkichi would be struck if he stepped any closer. But Chōkichi did not falter for a moment and called out, "Do not live to regret your impudent boasting!"

Chōkichi wielded the chain sickle he had prepared and slung it over his shoulders. Hauling it hand over hand, he hurled it at Jiraiya in an attempt to capture him. However, Jiraiya effortlessly sidestepped the chain, and Chōkichi evaded Jiraiya's blade. Their masterful work, evading and parrying, went on for an hour without pause. Guheida, Fuehachi, and the assembled men watched with bated breath, their eyes fixed on the roof of the towering Yamamon gate. The work of the two men was far beyond that of ordinary individuals.

(8.21)

Just as it looked like the duel would continue indefinitely, Chōkichi finally managed to tangle the chain of his sickle around Jiraiya's blade. He yanked the blade to the ground and, without any hesitation, grabbed onto Jiraiya to see who was the strongest. Everyone watching let out a gasp of surprise, but they were powerless to intervene. High above on the roof, the two adversaries grappled, entangling and disentangling, never yielding, challenging each other relentlessly. However, due to the uneven surface of the roof, they lost their footing. Jiraiya and Chōkichi tumbled over the edge as if descending a mountainside, their feet pointing skyward.

Guheida and the others ran towards them as they fell, screaming, "Oh no! They will be smashed to pieces and die. We must save them!"

However, Chōkichi's chain sickle had fallen and gotten tangled on the branches of a sakura tree growing below. He grabbed onto it, and the two plummeting men were stopped by the tree's branches, suspending them mid-air, writhing and squirming. The assembled men quickly procured several ladders, positioning them around the tree from all angles. Climbing up the ladders, they bound Jiraiya and Chōkichi tightly, securing them together.

With great effort, they lowered the two from the branches, untied the bundled rope, and attended to Chōkichi's needs, providing him with medicine and water. Jiraiya, on the other hand, was held down and had his hands and legs bound. They escorted him while surrounded by a multitude of men to the garden of the traveler's inn where they were staying.

Yokoshima Guheida and Shikano Fuehachi were jubilant, twitching at the nose with joy, and Chōkichi retired to a room to rest for a while.

From all the neighboring villages, men and women, young and old, came running like a landslide to see. They eagerly awaited to learn the

8.21

The explanation for this image is in book nine.

outcome of the battle, and when they finally saw Jiraiya was successfully captured, their voices erupted in praise, resounding through the air.

(8.22)

The joyous cheers echoed far and wide, and there was not a soul who did not commend the events that had unfolded. An express messenger was dispatched to Kamakura to recount the tale of how Jiraiya, who could deceive even an oni demon, had been apprehended thanks to the many hardships of Chōkichi. Should Jiraiya Hiroyuki use his yōjutsu to escape, they won't be able to capture him again. Aware of that, they bound him securely and arranged for a prison palanquin to confine him.

Guheida felt Chōkichi should be given a reward equivalent to no less than what he had asked for, and he remarked, "How did you come by such skill? Were you taught the martial arts by the *tengu* priest Sōjōbō of Mount Kurama? From now, we should call you Ushiwaka![5] If we were to recruit a formidable warrior like yourself, I doubt there would be anyone among the retainers of the Kanrei who could surpass you."

Every person who heard this shook with awe at Chōkichi's skill and their tongues fell silent in their mouths.

---

5 Ushiwaka is the childhood name of Minamoto no Yoshitsune, who is considered one of the greatest warriors of all time.

8.22

"They have successfully captured Jiraiya! Our wishes have been fulfilled! Hoorah! Hoorah! Hoorah! Hoorah! Hoorah! Hoorah! Hoorah!"
The events that unfolded thereafter will be described in detail in book nine.

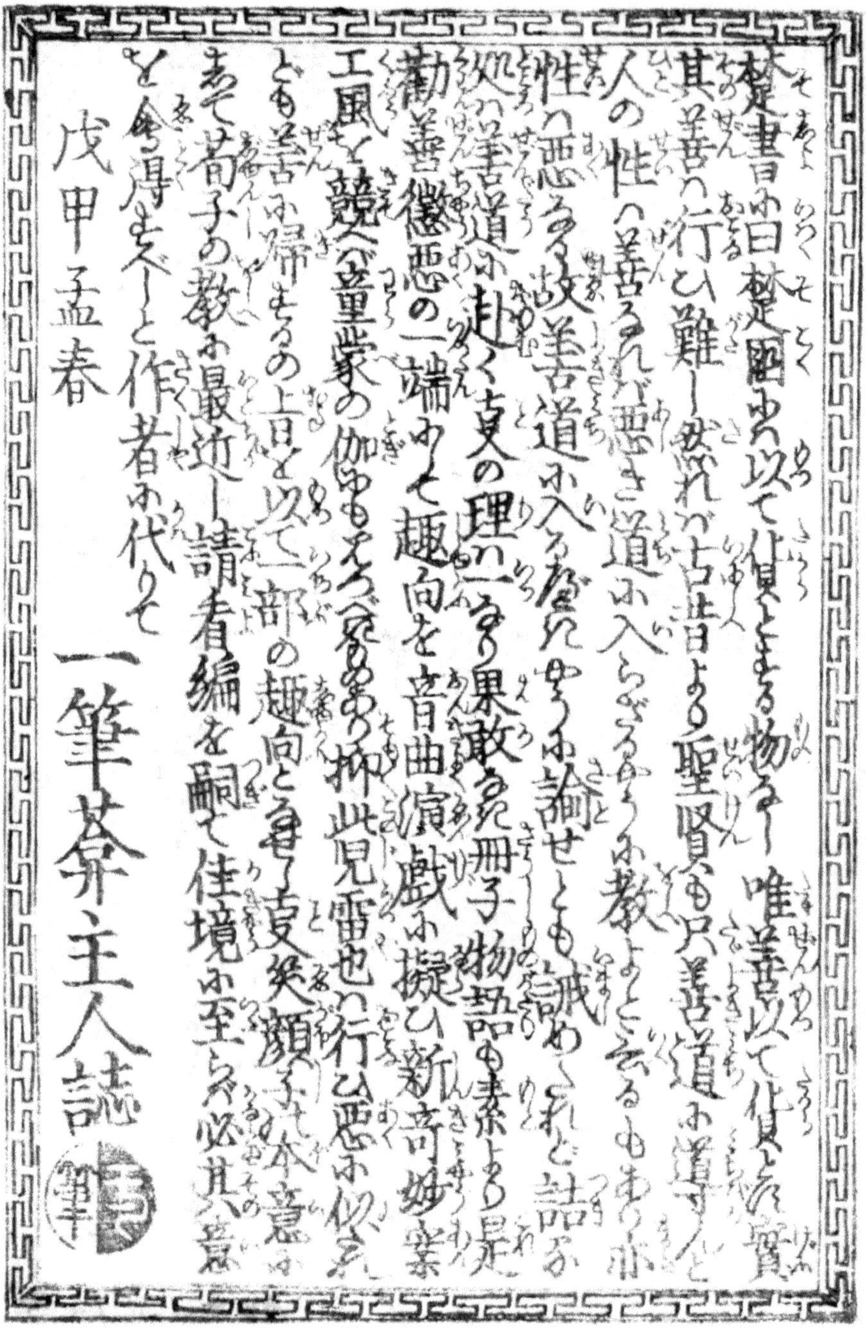
夫楚書に曰楚國ハ以て宝とする物なし唯善以て宝とす
其善ハ行ひ難し然れバ古昔より聖賢も只善道に導すと
人の性ハ善なれバ悪き道に入らざるやうに教よと云るも有り亦
性ハ悪なる故善道に入るなれバやうに諭せしも誡めくれど詰るか
処ハ善道に赴くも其の理ハ一なり果敢なき冊子物語も素より是
勧善懲悪の一端にて趣向を音曲演戯に擬ひ新奇妙案
工風を競ハば童蒙の伽にもなるべきなれバ抑此見雷也ハ行ひ悪に似たれ
ども善に帰するの上旨を以て一部の趣向となし且笑顔せし本意に
あらで荀子の教に最近し請看編を嗣て佳境に至らバ必其意
を会得すべしと作者に代りて
戊申孟春
一筆菴主人誌

9.1

Book 9

In the Chu writings, it is said that the only treasure in Chu is virtue. But being virtuous is difficult. So, from ancient times, even the sages and the wise have aimed only to guide towards the path of goodness, saying that human nature, if inherently good, should be taught not to tread the path of evil. Similarly, if human nature is inherently bad, the path of evil should be admonished, and they be guided towards the path of goodness. But ultimately, the reasoning behind embracing the path of goodness is the same.

Even in seemingly unambitious literary works and stories, this forms a part of encouraging virtue and disciplining vice. By imitating the style of musical performances, infusing novelty and strange yet skillful craftsmanship, there is something worth seeing even in children's tales.

Although Jiraiya may appear to be evil, his intention is to return to goodness. This plot is the original intention of Master Egao and is in line with the teaching of Xunzi. Upon continuing this compilation and reaching its climax, I will undoubtedly grasp its underlying meaning, on behalf of the author.

Year of the Earth Monkey—Spring (1848)

Ippitsuan

9.2

Ogata Shūma Hiroyuki, leader of the bandits of Mount Kurohime, alias Jiraiya.

Sutematsu, the only child of Himematsu Sumatarō.

In a later volume, a monstrous serpent will appear at the moon viewing pavilion of Sarashina Hangan in Shinano.

9.3

Ohana, the daughter of the katana merchant in Yukinoshita in Kamakura.

Through the connections of a matchmaker, Hanshichi and Ohana will inherit the katana trade.

The son-in-law for the katana merchant, Hanshichi.

Herbal rice cakes that make you think only of water shield.

—Shinmatsuan

9.4

Kintaga Detarō.[1]
Yamaneko Yanroku.
Neko Yamizō.
The girl Otsuna.
Inesaku of Nezumi-no-shuku.
Amenonaka Otashichi.

Upper right box:
Musasabi Tenhachi, leader of petty thieves.

1 The following unknown characters are stock characters often used in kabuki theater.

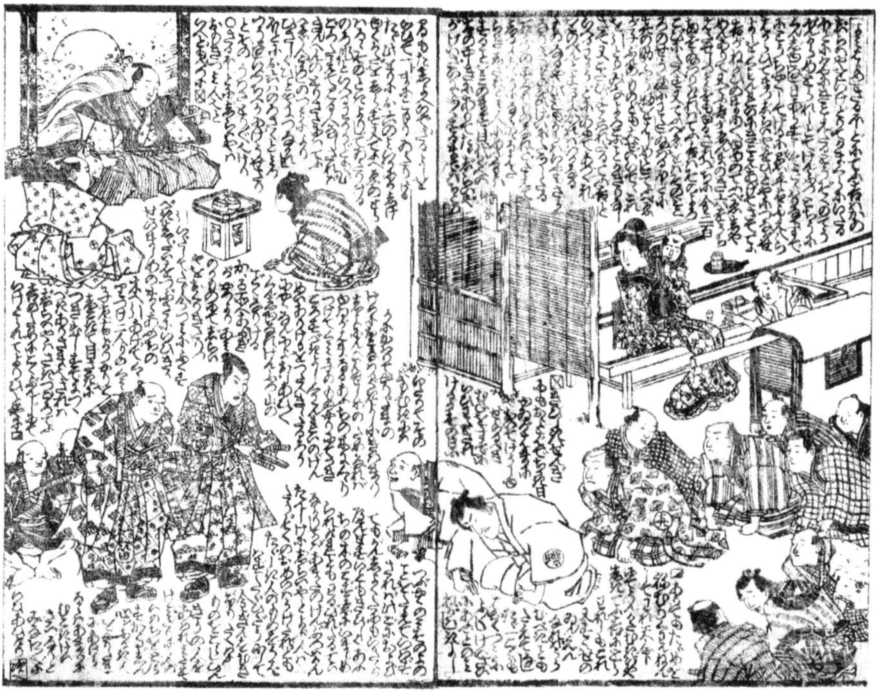

9.5

Part I

(9.5)
Chōkichi successfully captured Jiraiya alive, and as they made their way to Kamakura, word spread like wildfire. The news of the notorious bandit leader's capture drew crowds along the route, eager to catch a glimpse of the infamous man. Without encountering any obstacles, they reached Kamakura before daybreak. Guheida and Fuehachi immediately set about arranging Jiraiya's imprisonment. They recounted the entire story to the Kanrei. Considering Chōkichi's heartfelt request, the dreamer Chōbei was granted a pardon. Chōkichi himself received forgiveness for the crime of murdering Enma no Kiroku and was awarded two hundred ryō as an additional reward. His elation was impossible to conceal. When the local headman released Chōbei, the Kinosuke couple and a large group of Chōbei's loyal followers came out to welcome him with boundless joy.

Following his release, Chōbei wished to meet the young man called Chōkichi who had saved his life. He wanted to express his deep gratitude, see what kind of person he was, and of course, to befriend him. However, despite Chōkichi being an unparalleled and superior master of the martial arts, there were none around who knew him. Although he had performed an extraordinary feat, Chōkichi disliked meeting with people. He had secluded himself in a room in Guheida's mansion, refusing to go anywhere, even for a moment, until Jiraiya had served his sentence. However, at the same time, no matter who Chōbei asked, he could not find any information about Oroku's whereabouts. This had been the case since the time of Chōbei's arrest, and no one had seen the young man Norosaku either. Rumors circulated in the area, suggesting that after Chōbei's prolonged imprisonment for murder, Oroku had engaged in an affair with Norosaku and eloped.

Meanwhile, despite his heinous crimes, Jiraiya was not subjected to intense interrogation, as his captors had already been informed his head would be displayed on Yuigahama Beach in the coming days. When the day arrived there was a change in plans. It was decided that Jiraiya was to serve as an example for the people. Therefore, the Kanrei gave strict orders that Jiraiya was to be strung up on a bead-tree on Yuigahama Beach and stabbed to death by the constables. News of this punishment spread, drawing a curious crowd of old and young, men and women, eager to witness the spectacle as if it were a sightseeing excursion.

The procession began from Ōgigayatsu where Jiraiya was placed in a palanquin, which was covered with a net and transported. An announcement was made, that Jiraiya would now receive the punishment for his crimes. Still bound, he was strung up on the appointed bead-tree. Two men approached from both sides and slid spears through their hands, thrusting them in front of Jiraiya's eyes, indicating their readiness to pierce him. However, Jiraiya kept his eyes closed, just as he had done since his capture by Chōkichi at the Kokubunji Temple and during his time in prison. He embraced his fate, murmuring that even if his fortunes had shifted due to the intervention of fate, and even if he had fallen into the clutches of the detestable Chōkichi, he harbored no resentment. Believing it to be his karma from a past life, he wished to acknowledge his sins swiftly and face his punishment. Beyond these words, he remained silent. Even now, in his final moments, his countenance remained unchanged, displaying no signs of weakness.

The spectators who had gathered were astonished. Among them, some voiced their thoughts, saying, "Truly, this man named Jiraiya may bear the infamous title of a bandit, but he never stole from the righteous. He only punished those who coveted and amassed wealth through wicked means. He pitied and rescued the poor and never took someone's life rashly or selfishly. It is excessively cruel to subject a man of such deep honor to public display and execution."

(9.6)

However, there were others who held differing opinions, asserting, "He may present himself as honorable, but deep inside, he has been plotting rebellion. Word has it that he has been planning to disrupt the entire country. It is better to nip a problem in the bud than to struggle with an axe later, so it truly is a blessing from heaven that he has been caught so easily and can be punished today."

The guards, as well as the samurai who had come to inspect, said time was growing late and urged the proceedings on. Finally, the two

9.6

spears converged in front of Jiraiya's eyes, drawing a cross, and pulled back. In an instant, he was stabbed in the right side. The spear retracted, and then he was stabbed mercilessly from the left. Jiraiya endured around twenty stabs, yet he made no sound, and his countenance remained unchanged even as blood gushed like a cascading waterfall. It was a gruesome spectacle, one that nobody would wish to see. The onlookers were horrified. They swallowed hard and clenched their fists, murmuring, "Despite the agony he must be experiencing, he maintains such composure even while being mercilessly stabbed. Is he an illusion? A puppet? No human could endure this!" Finally, the two spears dealt the fatal blow. Jiraiya's breath ceased, his head slumped down, and thus he perished.

Yokoshima Guheida and Shikano Fuehachi, who had overseen the proceedings, wore expressions of satisfaction with a job well done as they departed. When they reported it was over, the Kanrei rewarded them generously and had all the wanted posters and signs promising rewards for capturing Jiraiya taken down. Everywhere, things quieted down again, and the talk about Jiraiya eventually stopped. Afterwards, Chōkichi bid farewell to Guheida, pocketed his reward, and departed from the mansion, embarking on a journey to unknown destinations.

Seemingly without Chōbei's knowledge, the man named Chōkichi had taken the blame for the murder and captured Jiraiya, ensuring Chōbei's

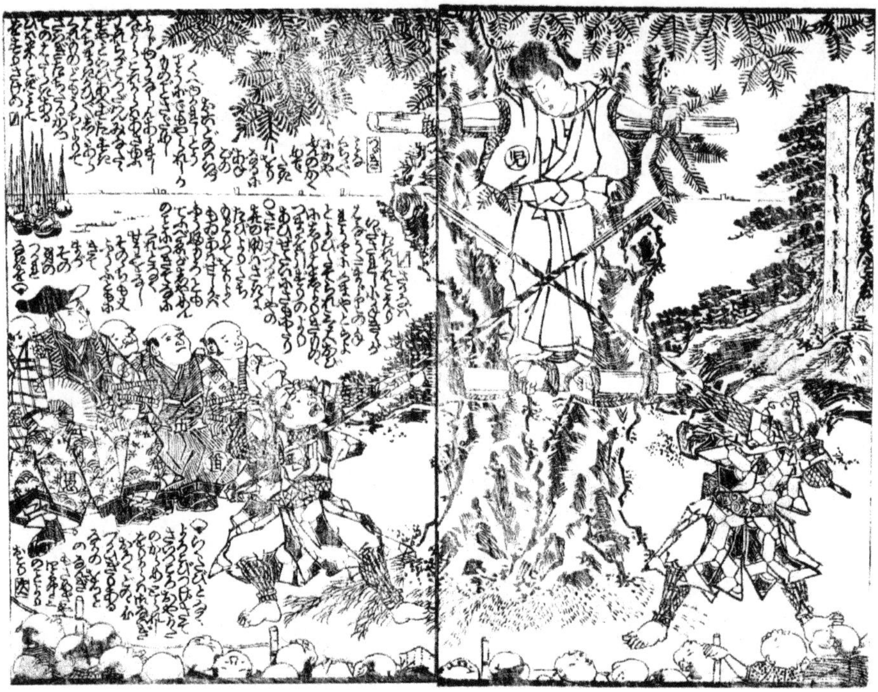

9.7

pardon. When he returned home to rest, Kinosuke, Osai, and his loyal followers rushed to his side, bearing food and drinks, celebrating his safe return.

(9.7)

The stream of well-wishers seemed endless, and they all clamored over each other, "Boss, while this fortunate incident has befallen you, where has big-sis Oroku-dono gone to? Has she gone to stay somewhere? Until things go back to normal around here, it is probably going to be very inconvenient for you, so we will help you day and night. Everyone, let's not stand around!"

They rolled up their sleeves, donned headbands, and rallied together. The boisterous group went to work. As some took charge of the kitchen, others washed rice, and some ground miso, while those skilled in cooking prepared snacks, all the while humming in harmony. Every brave and rowdy man was summoned, with their kimono skirts tucked up and lapels loosely hanging. It was as if a vibrant and bustling family had gathered.

Previously, Tsuruhashiya Kinosuke returned from his travels and happened to be present when Chōbei was granted his pardon. Alongside his wife, Kinosuke took care of Chōbei in various ways. After the festivities celebrating Chōbei's release, the couple came back to Chōbei's house, and told him how happy they were that he was not worn out.

9.8

Top right: Jiraiya returns to the mountain fortress with look-alike Jiraiya.

(9.8)

Then Kinosuke whispered to him, "When you were captured, your wife Oroku-dono came to me out of concern and said, 'The calamity that has befallen my husband, whom I have a duty towards, is due to him murdering Enma no Kiroku, which only happened because of Samezaya Jiroza, who is really Jiraiya. Because Jiraiya is my older brother, they will surely interrogate Chōbei for his whereabouts. Even if I must wear myself down to the bone, I will rescue my husband. If I cannot, there is no reason for me to live in this world anymore. However, should I harm myself or commit suicide, it will be of no help to my husband. And should I stay idle like this, my husband might succumb to the torture and his life end. If I start by finding my brother Jiraiya and tell him what has happened, he might be able to do something. What shall I do?' Oroku-dono cried while she said this to me.

"I couldn't provide her with any answers or solutions, so I immediately set off for Echigo. Along the way, there was a day when I was late in finding lodging. As I walked along the night road, a peculiar glowing object came flying by in the sky. I wondered if it was a spirit, perhaps the soul of the departed, or maybe a mystical kanedama. Sensing it could be a sign of fortune or an ill omen, I hastened my pace. When I reached the mountain fortress, I happened to meet Nobusuma Tenbachi. After I told him all that had happened, he said, 'Boss Jiraiya realized what calamity has struck in Kamakura and set out from here

9.9

in the evening. What you witnessed might have been Jiraiya, using his yōjutsu to fly through the sky.' When I heard this, I realized how pointless it had been for me to go see Jiraiya, because if Jiraiya had gone to Kamakura, then surely Chōbei would soon be rescued. So, I swiftly said goodbye and went home.

(9.9)

"However, along the way, I heard various rumors about a young man, a skilled martial artist, capturing Jiraiya alive at the Yamamon gate of the Kokubunji Temple. My heart was pounding in my chest, filled with worry about what was truly unfolding. Should it be true, there would be nothing to do in the face of such a disaster. From one thing to the next, it felt as if the hardships just kept being piled on top of one another, like an evil fate befalling Chōbei. Such thoughts weighed heavily on me, and upon my return, Oroku-dono was nowhere to be found. I do not lend my ears to idle rumors, but, as if to only make the mysterious circumstances even more suspicious, when I asked around, I heard that the young man Chōkichi had previously declared that he would capture Jiraiya if Chōbei was released. Upon further investigation, I learned that Jiraiya was to be punished on Yuigahama Beach, so I went there immediately. What I saw there gave me no reason to suspect it wasn'thim or that something was amiss. Can you shed any light on Oroku-dono's whereabouts and what has happened here?"

After hearing Kinosuke's tale, Chōbei nodded and looked around, scanning the room, for the walls had eyes and ears. Fortunately, there

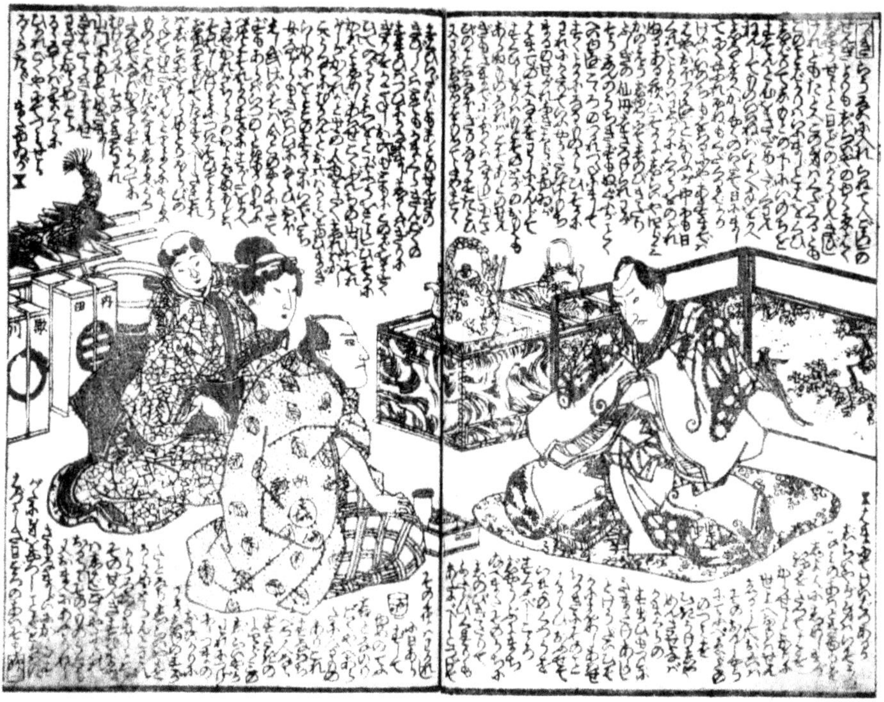

9.10

was no trace of human presence, so he leaned close to Kinosuke and quietly told him:

"I was thinking of telling you this a while ago already, but people have been coming and going from dawn till dusk, so there was no good time to tell you. Finally, today, I can reveal what has transpired.

(9.10)

"When I was captured by Shikano Fuehachi and imprisoned after being sold out by one of Kiroku's men, more so than being interrogated over the murder, I was viciously tortured daily to make me divulge Jiraiya's whereabouts. But even if they broke my body, I would not tell them anything, so I clenched my teeth and set my heart to die by the scourge. Because I had resigned myself to that fate and said nothing, they tried every tool in their arsenal, and every day their maltreatment grew more brutal. My flesh was torn, my bones shattered. There were moments when I believed my life would end without seeing the rising sun again, but even as dusk fell, there was no respite from the suffering. One night however, Jiraiya snuck into my cell using his yōjutsu. He gave me the most mysterious elixir, and all my wounds from the beatings healed. It was as if my injuries had been wiped away, and my fatigue disappeared completely.

"He spoke to me in secrecy, unveiling a plan: 'When I rescued Mochimaru Fukitarō from danger on the beach of Niigata by turning into an eagle, his offenses were so minor that it didn't provoke an extensive follow-up investigation. But this time, even if I can easily rescue you with my yōjutsu, the following search for you will be so severe that you will never be able to live anywhere near Kamakura again. Oroku and I have duty upon duty towards you, so we devised a way for you to escape your situation. I secretly arranged with her that I will let the common people find out that I am hiding in the Yamamon gate of the Kokubunji Temple. She will then do her hair up to appear as a man and come to take me down. Even though she is a woman, she still remembers the martial arts she has learned, and if ever there was a time to use it, this would be it. So, she will change her appearance and I will follow her like a shadow, so I may help her with my yōjutsu, should the need arise. Oroku will pretend to be consumed by greed, craving the reward money, and report her findings to the authorities. That should ensure that they will come after me. When the time comes, I will show them a most captivating spectacle at the Yamamon gate, deliberately allowing himself to be captured. They will then take me to Kamakura, and whether I be punished in prison or executed on the beach of Yuigahama, I will make them think Jiraiya has disappeared. Like the foam from the waves on the rocky shore. I will make them think the tree has been cut at its roots and the leaves have withered. That way, Oroku can take the sins of Chōbei-dono on herself, have you pardoned, and there will then be nothing hindering you from living in Kamakura. This is the scheme that we as siblings have worked out. Soon we shall make our plan come true and you will be saved from your suffering. Be assured and wait. I will sneak in soon and give you medicine again.'

"After telling me this, he left, and by the next day, another person by the name of Chōkichi had come into the prison. This was none other than my wife, Oroku, as Jiraiya had told me the night before.

(9.11)

"She cried and told me, 'For the time being, I have assumed the disguise of a wakashū and proclaimed that I will apprehend Jiraiya. Until they finish their deliberations, I'll be here in prison. I am filled with joy because I get to see you again, but I am sad and ashamed that I must talk with you in this unavoidable disguise. There is a front and a back to all things, and like the coursing Sanzu River in the netherworld, the heart is always changing, threatening to run out of love. But between us nothing has changed. I suffer in my heart, swearing to the gods and Buddhas and praying with all my sincerity that you may once again be able to go out into the world. Sharing my honest effort with you brings me comfort and sustains me. I have toiled and suffered, and my brother Jiraiya has done his best, yet it all ended up like this. It has come to the point where I even have to disguise as a man, and I can't face you. For now, just bear with it for a while longer and wait.'

"Luckily there was no one around, so we talked about many things. She said, 'Do not tell anyone what I have told you. Not even in your dreams,' and lay down to sleep. The next morning, she was called out and never returned to the prison. I had no way of knowing what fate befell her after that, so I worried alone, wrought with concern. One day, I overheard the guards conversing, mentioning the capture of Jiraiya by Chōkichi the dreamer and extolling his accomplishments.

9.11

9.12

Part II

(9.12)

"Even behind bars, I could infer what trouble Oroku must have been through. Before long, I was released, and upon learning that Jiraiya had been executed on Yuigahama Beach the day before, I secretly went to see for myself. The person there was not Jiraiya, but that Ekichi person. I thought it was very sad for him, but since there was no other way, I steeled my heart, said the nembutsu prayer for him, and returned home. Apropos, I do believe the thing you saw flying over the road to Echigo must have been Jiraiya on his way here, to sneak in and see me."

After finally sharing their hardships with each other, they let out a lamenting sigh. In a hushed voice, Chōbei then said to Kinosuke and his wife, "I pity Ekichi for having to stand in for Jiraiya at Yuigahama, but there was no other choice. Right now, however, the only thing I can worry about is where Oroku went after ending her ruse as Chōkichi."

Footsteps were then heard coming from the front of the house. Someone was coming inside, so the trio halted their conversation and turned to see who it might be. Accompanied by servants who placed a palanquin down, a figure silently entered. To their astonishment, it was none other than Jiraiya Shūma Hiroyuki, dressed in magnificent attire. Surprise painted their faces as Jiraiya closed the door and quietly took a seat, offering greetings to the three of them. They talked about all the troubles that had befallen them after Chōbei's unexpected peril, and Jiraiya informed Kinosuke that he had brought Oroku along. Despite Kinosuke's role in arranging their marriage, Oroku had to go into hiding once everything settled. Jiraiya mentioned she had shaved her eyebrows again, so she looked like a proper wife, but her hair still required some time to go back to normal. To Chōbei, Jiraiya also told every detail of what happened.

Jiraiya called for Oroku to step out of the palanquin right before a few of Kiroku's menacing henchmen, who had tailed the palanquin, appeared.

"This must be boss Kiroku-dono's vendetta of love!" they exclaimed, throwing open the blinds and attempting to seize the person inside. In a swift motion, Oroku dispatched two of them, sending them flying left and right. As they caught a glimpse of her face, they pleaded, "We made a mistake! Please let us go!" and hastily fled without looking back.

Jiraiya didn't spare a glance at the fight, instead turning to Chōbei and Kinosuke with joyous exultation that everyone emerged unharmed from their arduous ordeal. Ever thoughtful, Chōbei instructed his followers to promptly prepare food and drinks.

(9.13)

After reveling in merriment and drinks, Kinosuke asked in a hushed voice, "The astonishing performance by Chōkichi at the Kokubunji Temple on the Yamamon gate is on everyone's lips. Yet, only a select few are aware that Chōkichi is, in fact, Oroku-dono. How did you manage this?"

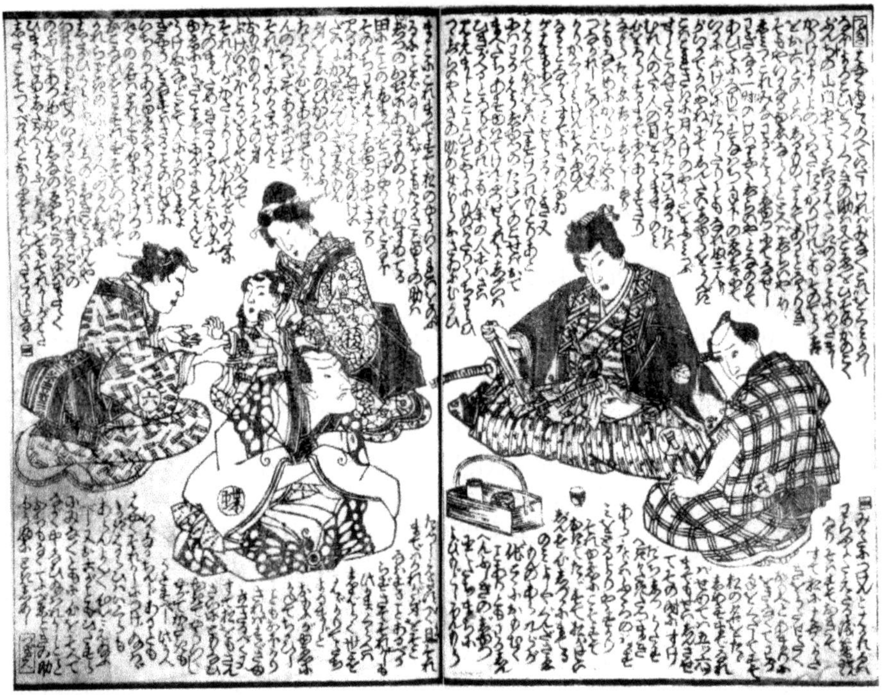

9.13

Jiraiya smiled and furtively said, "This is all part of a temporary plan I devised and executed with my yōjutsu. The one who called himself Jiraiya was in fact none other than my subordinate. No matter how skilled at martial arts the two are, they hardly know each other, so I thought they would be able to move more freely on the roof. As you know, previously when I played around and crushed the Tsukikage's mansion, that was nothing more than me pulling the wool over their eyes, so pulling off a trick like this wasn't much of a challenge. Nonetheless, I couldn't bear to see my subordinate eventually being caught, imprisoned, and subjected to suffering. Therefore, yesterday, during the planned execution at Yuigahama Beach, I employed another scheme and whisked them away. What remains there is a trick of my yōjutsu. If you visit tomorrow, you'll find that the body left behind is actually that of a frog, although I doubt ordinary people will be able to perceive it."

Jiraiya laughed and said to Kinosuke's wife, Osai, "I am truly at a loss for words to thank you for taking care of Sutematsu until now. Since Takasago Yuminosuke is his actual uncle, I should hand Sutematsu over to him. That's why I confided everything about Sutematsu to Yuminosuke's daughter, Teruta. However, when I used my yōjutsu to search for her later, I discovered the villainous Gundazaemon was hiding within the Hasedera Kannon Temple. There he plotted with Urafuji Saemon from Kai to start a rebellion. Gundazaemon, proud of his martial skills, believed I would seek him out and request him to be *my* ally. This was the ulterior motive for him putting on a strange act by not receiving alms from people. While I may carry the title of a bandit, I never forget to be gallant. As if I would ever follow the wiles of some vagrant like him and then take orders from the likes of Urafuji! Already now, they gather mercenaries in neighboring provinces, with intentions to invade and subdue Kai, Echigo, and Shinano. Urafuji doesn't realize that his plan to recruit me is a laughably shallow scheme.

"Setting that matter aside, I would like for Sutematsu to be able to take revenge soon, but he is still much too young. Even if I were to carry out the deed myself in his name, he should still be at least five or six years old. When the time comes, I will lend him my sword, and together we will dispatch the villain Tatsumaki Arakurō as effortlessly as catching a mouse in a bag. But until then, I will let the matter lie and wait quietly for Sutematsu to grow up. Even if Arakurō ventures to another province, with my mysterious and miraculous yōjutsu, I can summon him back instantly, and we can fulfill our ambitions. Until then, no harm should befall him.

"Be all of that as it may, I believe it's best if I refrain from visiting Kamakura for a while. Besides, I have so many other promises to fulfill, so I should leave here forthwith. I will bring Sutematsu with me to my mountain fortress, raise him, and in due time, we will seek his revenge. No matter what grave incident may occur, inform me immediately, and I will devise as many schemes as necessary. Remember this well. And please, ensure you all wholeheartedly take care of Oroku."

After delivering his lengthy and detailed explanation to Chōbei, Kinosuke, and Osai, Jiraiya said, "The evening has grown late, and I think our meeting has reached its end."

(9.14)

He bid his farewells, picked up Sutematsu, expressed his profound gratitude to Osai for her care, and stepped outside. Everyone gathered at the front gate to bid Jiraiya farewell as he soared into the sky, disappearing into the unknown.

After the feudal lord of Echigo, Tsukikage Miyukinosuke, had taken Tagoto-hime as his wife, the talks of their blissful married life spread far and wide. The Sarashina clan was also happy with the union, and both families were starting to flourish because of it, promising a bright future. They believed Tagoto-hime's unwavering faith in the Hasedera Kannon played a significant role in this. Thus, when they heard the Kannon would be on display, both families decided to send a servant on their behalf to pray for continued luck in the fortunes of war. The Sarashina clan chose to send Takasago Yuminosuke because of his experience with traveling, and because it was only due to his discretion that the trouble with Jiraiya during the wedding was settled without further incident. So, he was chosen as the emissary for the clan, given the offering for the Hasedera Kannon from Shinano, and set off to visit the Hasedera Temple.

9.14

The Kamakura Hasedera Kannon, the fourth Kannon on the Bandō Thirty-Three Kannon Pilgrimage, is a statue of worship standing two jō and six shaku tall.[2] Because its miracles are so wondrous, men and women coming to worship it never ends. Even more so now that the Buddha was on display, people came from near and far to form a connection with the Buddha, and both young and old kept pouring in to worship it. Furthermore, because it was already popular to go visit the Ise Grand Shrine without permission from one's parents, many girls and boys from the faraway countryside and mountains snuck out without telling their parents, just so they could visit this hallowed place.

In Kutsukake station town,[3] renowned by travelers as a place of refuge akin to their protective *ema* votive tablets, the inns flourished. Among all this prosperity, Inesaku, a rice seller who had recently come from elsewhere in Shinano, had opened the Nezumi-no-shuku inn. The god of fortune smiled upon the inn, and every day the business thrived beyond expectations, as guests looking for lodging never ceased.

One day, among all these travelers, a woman's palanquin arrived with a large retinue. The woman riding in the palanquin turned out to

2 About 8 meters.

3 No. 19 of 64 towns on Nakasendō Road, present day Karuizawa.

9.15

be Sekiya, a lady-in-waiting of the Tsukikage clan, so the whole inn was in a flurry. Inside, the men and women stirred, and ushered the visitor to a private room at the rear of the building. The innkeeper extended a warm welcome, demonstrating utmost respect to Sekiya. He also respectfully greeted her retinue and had them taken to a room reserved for warriors. As the group was of considerable size, the staff was making every effort to make their stay a pleasant one.

(9.15)

Meanwhile, Takasago Yuminosuke, a retainer of the Sarashina clan from Shinano, was also lodging at the same inn, so he came to greet Sekiya. Sharing a common journey to Kamakura, they decided to travel together, maintaining proper decorum by sleeping in separate quarters despite their shared accommodation. However, their numerous companions engaged in bathing, indulging in saké, and feasting heartily, causing the inn to bustle with activity on both its lower and upper floor.

After some time, the travelers finally entered the bedchambers and fell asleep. By then the hour of the boar[4] had already passed, and the travelers lay unconscious, tired from the day, snoring loudly. Seizing the opportunity, a back door slid open, allowing a group of thieves to sneak inside. They pilfered the belongings of the oblivious sleepers, breaking open the storeroom lock to retrieve chests filled with various tools, woven boxes of clothing,

4 21:00–23:00.

and other valuables. Then they tied it all up with rope and made two or three sizeable bundles and exchanged hushed whispers with one another. However, just as they had carried their loot to the entrance of the garden, the thief who was in the lead unexpectedly cried out, dropping his load. The abrupt sound awakened the inn's owner, Inesaku.

"Bandits have entered the house! Everyone, to arms!" Inesaku shouted, quickly lighting a lantern and grabbing a nearby stick. As he ran in the direction of the garden, the men awoken by the shock grabbed their weapons and cried out, "Bandits! Bandits!" as they also headed for the back door. The maidservants fetched metal pots and banged them fiercely, summoning not only the lodging travelers but also residents from nearby houses, wielding spades, hoes, and scythes. It was a wild and uncontrolled chaos. Amidst the commotion, Inesaku reached the garden first, only to find it eerily quiet, seemingly deserted. He murmured to himself, "Did the thieves get away already?" while raising his lantern to survey the surroundings. And then he saw something highly suspicious —a young maiden, her face appearing to be around fourteen or fifteen years old. She was standing before four burly men, glaring up at her, their hands bound tightly behind their backs, secured to a tree trunk.

(9.16)

"Stay calm. I have apprehended the thieves. You should ensure that all the travelers' luggage and your belongings are accounted for before we deal with them," the maiden said, but Inesaku still had not grasped the situation. He mistook the girl for one of the thieves, so he raised his stick and swung at her. The maiden swiftly sidestepped him, saying "Please, don't rush and get yourself injured now. I am not a thief!" She snatched the stick from Inesaku's hands and grabbed him so he could not move and would not get hurt.

Inesaku finally comprehended what was happening and looked at the maiden, saying, "I let you stay at the inn for free because you are on the Bandō Pilgrimage. What exactly transpired here?" After he asked this, the maiden released her grip on Inesaku's arms. The people of the neighborhood came running with lanterns, torches, and stokers, which they held out towards the maiden, surrounding her and peering at her face.

Unfazed, the maiden spoke with utmost grace, "Your suspicion is not unwarranted, but I am merely another lodger. In the evening, there were so many travelers, and even the kitchen was in disarray, so I chose to go into the woodshed over there to sleep alone. Around the third quarter of the hour of the ox, I noticed some people sneaking in through the back door. I peeked from the shed to see what was going on, and there I saw people carrying things away. I realized they must be thieves, so I took a rope from inside the shed and went out to the back gate where I waited for them to come out. I managed to apprehend them without much trouble. Just as I was about to wake

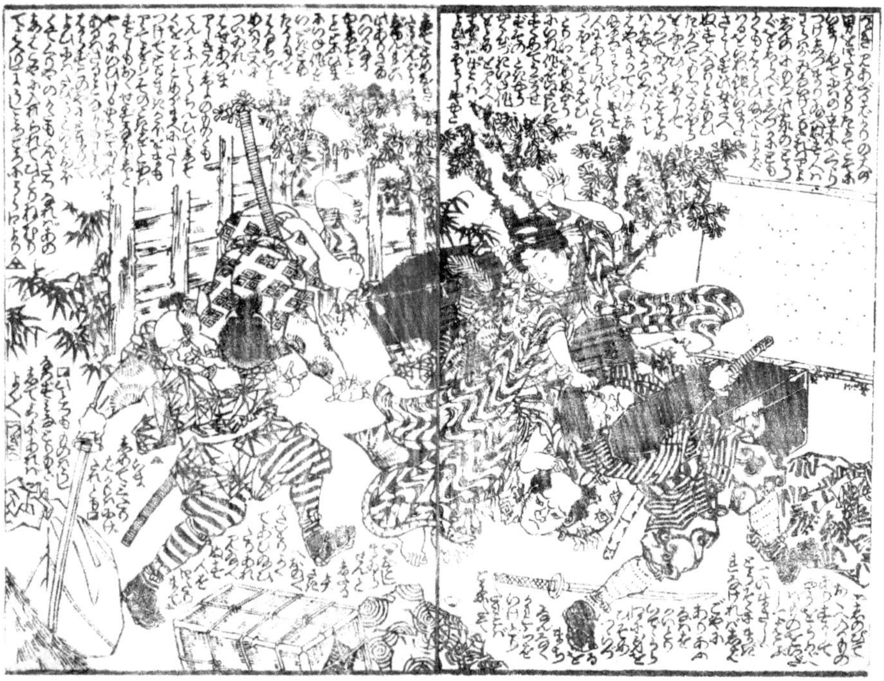

9.16

all of you and seek your assistance, you all woke simultaneously with impeccable timing. Look, there are the four thieves that I tied up. Another three got away, but you did not lose anything. I made sure to take everything back, but please give it an extra look to make sure everything is there."

(9.17)

She brushed the dust off her clothes, and with a calm and unflustered complexion, she looked around at the crowd as if nothing was out of the ordinary.

Some were shocked and scared of her, saying, "How can this be? This girl cannot be human. She must be a tengu in disguise or something of the like."

After a while, the people engaged in a heated debate about what should be done. Some argued for beating the tied-up thieves as a form of punishment, while others advocated for taking them to the High Court for judgment and imprisonment.

Amidst the clamor and disagreement, the maiden interjected. "If they had taken away even a single thing, it goes without saying that we ought to take the four of them to the High Court for questioning. However, since nothing was lost, there is still a chance for them to find redemption. I am on the Bandō Pilgrimage, so I do not wish to commit any sins. You should reprimand them for what they have done, and then release them. What do you all think?" she said, doing her best to convince them.

9.17

Having always been frank and compassionate, Inesaku spoke up, "You speak the truth, and I would not feel comfortable for my house to have to be the plaintiff against these four men. I think we should follow your suggestion." He convinced the other people who were there, and they untied the thieves to let them go.

Following this, the people who had initially been shocked and frightened of the young pilgrim's tremendous strength, now impressed by her skills, were invited inside one of the rooms of the house. Inside, they eagerly surrounded her, bombarding her with questions. Where was she from? How old was she? What should they call her?

(9.18)

Blushing, the maiden, still in her youth, replied, "For doing such a small thing, I feel embarrassed for getting such praise. I was born in Etchū province,[5] and my name is Tsuna. When I was young, I was separated from my parents, and I was brought up in my aunt's house in the countryside. From a young age, I possessed strength, and I always assisted the men with their work. I wanted to contribute to my caregivers and not be a burden. This year marks my sixteenth spring, and with the Kannon-sama of Hasedera in Kamakura on display, I embarked on the Bandō Thirty-Three Kannon Pilgrimage to pray for my deceased parents' happiness in the next world. I am just a tomboy who doesn't know how scary it is to travel alone on unknown roads, but you gave me free lodging on my pilgrimage tonight.

5 Present day Toyama.

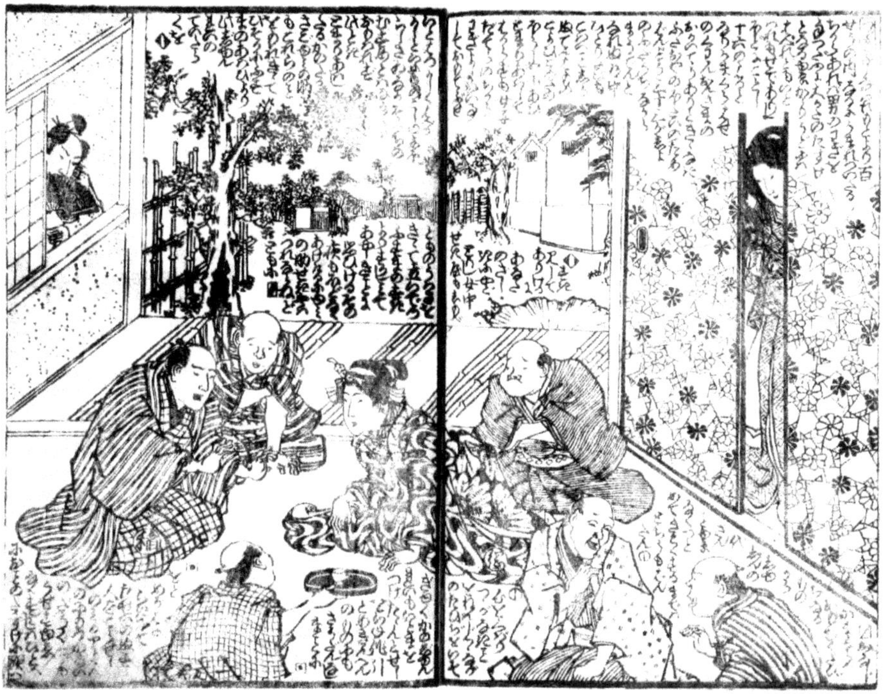

9.18

Without thinking, I went and performed a feat of strength so unbefitting of a girl while staying here. I am embarrassed for doing something so strange that I just want to hide my face." Her meek and gentle demeanor made it difficult to believe that she was truly brought up in the countryside.

Meanwhile, Takasago Yuminosuke, who was also staying at the inn, overheard the conversation and discreetly peered through a gap in the sliding door, stealing a glimpse of the maiden's predicament. Sekiya, the lady-in-waiting who was staying in the parlor room next door, heard from her servants what was going on. She rose from her seat and, like Yuminosuke, peered through a crevice in the sliding doors, finding the scene most peculiar. It was not long before the night dawned, and although Yuminosuke and Sekiya were not a company, they hurried on the long road to Kamakura. Since they traveled alongside each other on the road to Kamakura as surrogates for their masters, they could ensure mutual protection on the road until they made it back to their respective homelands after fulfilling their duties.

The pilgrim also said her goodbyes, but when she arose, Inesaku held her back, saying "I talked with the neighbors, and thanks to the help of you, a maiden, a large group of thieves were reprimanded, and not even one piece of the travelers' luggage or the house's belongings were lost. We wish to express our sincerest gratitude to you for your help, but rather than giving a lone traveling girl something she doesn't need, take this, and use it for replacing your straw sandals." Inesaku took out one ryō to give to her.

9.19

Text in box: Jiraiya using his frog yōjutsu to keep an eye on the strange events in Kamakura.

(9.19)

However, the young girl politely refused, explaining, "I appreciate the gesture, but you let me stay at the inn for free and took care of me. I cannot accept a reward simply for being present last night and driving away the thieves. On the contrary, when one is traveling alone, carrying money might make the road more arduous. I will be more at ease, standing in gates and receiving alms in my ladle."

She pushed the money back, but Inesaku and all the others did their best to convince her, saying, "Even if it is such a small amount, you still refuse? Please, just accept it as a token of our appreciation."

The maiden could not possibly decline the offer again, and eventually accepted the reward. Then she faced everyone and said, "My intention is to visit the renowned Kannon of Hasedera in Kamakura and offer a votive slip, as I have heard of its prosperity and magnificence. I also plan to visit other spiritual sites and shrines, but being alone without friends or acquaintances, I have no place to stay. Undertaking such a journey to the temple from a distant province is no easy task. Thus, I humbly request that if anyone among you has a friend or acquaintance in Kamakura, could you kindly write them a letter on my behalf, asking if I may stay with them for a while? This would be an even greater blessing to me than receiving money. I know it sounds like the saying,

'To be so spoiled as to ask to be carried when offered to be shouldered', but it is the only favor I will ever ask of you."

Rubbing her hands together in a gesture resembling a plea for alms, the people unanimously agreed. "If that is the case, Master Inesaku should have plenty of connections. Inesaku, write a letter for her."

Inesaku accepted. "That I can do with ease! In Yukinoshita in Kamakura there is a katana merchant named Katanaya Ban'emon. He has a daughter named Ohana, and her husband Hanshichi recently married into her family. Hanshichi originally hails from Nezumi-no-shuku in Sarashina and is the son of someone named Mochimaru, who was my previous master. He was supposed to inherit the family business, but he met with various disasters and the headship of the family was instead given to me. In order to have a friend in Kamakura, I acted as a go-between with the Katanaya family for them to take him in, and recently he was married into their household. His original name was Fukitarō, but now he is Katanaya Hanshichi. He is as dear and close to me as if he were my own son, so I will draft an introduction letter to him immediately."

Shortly after, Inesaku handed the letter to Otsuna, who received it with reverence. "With this letter, there is nothing I could wish for more. So please, allow me to exchange it for the money you bestowed on me already," she said, returning the money. Otsuna then bid her farewells and set off on her journey.

(9.20)
Now the story takes us back to Kamakura.

Previously, Shikano Fuehachi had made advances towards Ohana, the daughter of the katana merchant, but Chōkichi had put him in his place. Since then, against all expectations, Chōkichi had captured Jiraiya alive. For that deed, he and Fuehachi had been rewarded by the Kanrei. Fuehachi and Guheida had both been commended for their work and were in high spirits. However, Fuehachi couldn't shake his thoughts about Ohana. He considered trying to use his position to appeal to her, but he knew she had a husband named Hanshichi, so he secretly sent her letters and asked people who were familiar with her to act as intermediaries. His infatuation consumed him, and Ohana had to do her best for no one to find out about it.

One day, however, the Katanayas' pet Japanese chin dog was running wild in the parlor with an extremely long letter in its mouth. An apprentice named Nagamatsu came running and tried to take the letter from the dog, but it refused to let go, tearing the paper in the process. Coincidentally, Hanshichi entered the room and inquired Nagamatsu about the commotion.

"It is a letter that Fuehachi-sama asked me to deliver to Ohana-sama," answered the boy. Without hesitation, Hanshichi collected the torn pieces of the letter and read the outrageous content written on them. Ohana casually entered the room, and Hanshichi called out to

9.20

her, showing her the letter. She knew she could not hide from Fuehachi's unwanted infatuation anymore, so she told Hanshichi everything about how Fuehachi had approached her at the roadside tea shop by Hasedera, saying all manner of things, including how it had ended. Hanshichi did not lend his ear any further, but instead went in secret to Jitsuemon, the head clerk, to ensure the news would not reach his father-in-law, Ban'emon. He confided in Jitsuemon, explaining what transpired. The clerk told him how, some time ago, he had gone together with Ohana to worship at the Hasedera Kannon, how Fuehachi had beat him, and how he had secretly reported Fuehachi's behavior to his superior, Yokoshima Guheida, to have him reprimanded. The gift of sweets and drinking money Jitsuemon brought Guheida were well spent, because Guheida, who had no interest in lustful things, later admonished Fuehachi most severely. When Hanshichi learned the details of the scolding, he and Jitsuemon shared a laugh over Fuehachi's incorrigible behavior.

Having been so severely reprimanded, Fuehachi harbored a deep grudge, and he wanted to clear it by somehow getting rid of Hanshichi. He conspired with some unsavory characters, discussing plans to wait for Hanshichi to leave home, ambush him as he returned home at night, and then beat him to teach him a lesson. So, they lay in wait, ready to spring their perilous trap.

(9.21)

Eventually a day came when Katanaya Hanshichi had gone to a mansion on business. By the time he made his way home, it was night. He

9.21

was hurrying for an inn in Yukinoshita, going along the bank of the Nameri River all alone, when he bumped into a group of rough looking men by accident. They hurled insults at him, and despite Hanshichi's profuse apologies, the scoundrels refused to listen, vowing to beat him senseless. Just as Hanshichi was about to attempt an escape, Shikano Fuehachi appeared.

Fuehachi exclaimed, "So you are that Hanshichi who married into Katanaya Ban'emon's family and took my beloved Ohana? Ohana is also obsessed with me, her feelings as deep as the Nameri River. Yet she is trapped in a fate that is poorer than not even having three cups of rice bran. She is forced to endure being married to a husband who is as insistent as the smell of pickled *takuan* radish left over summer, and about as limp as one too! Because you were jealous of our love, you wanted to shame me and had Yokoshima reprimand me, leaving visible wounds on my head and making me lose heart. To repay the favor, Ohana has asked me to ambush you today on the way back from the mansion, beat you to death, and toss you into Nameri River. That is how it will be. Now, say your nembutsu prayer!" Fuehachi kicked Hanshichi to the ground and stomped on him.

The ruffians rushed at Hanshichi from the sides, but a maiden pilgrim on the Bandō Pilgrimage happened upon the scene and witnessed the commotion. Without hesitation, she broke in between the ruffians, blocking their way and stopping them. Then she called out, "I don't know what is going on here, but you're treating that defenseless man with violence, and I demand that you stop!"

“What do you think you’re doing?” called out one of the ruffians, grabbing her in an attempt to remove her. But the pilgrim grabbed his arm, twisted it, and forced him to the ground. The two others rolled up their sleeves and lunged at her. The pilgrim grabbed them and pulled them down, placing them on the ground next to the first attacker.

(9.22)

With ease, she grabbed a nearby rice mortar and slammed it down on top of the three men with a resounding thud. Shikano Fuehachi, terrified by the maiden’s unexpected display of strength, attempted to flee. But in his cowardice, the maiden seized his dominant arm and twisted it. All four men were now immobilized and could only squirm around in a state of panic. It was a most pleasing sight to behold. Hanshichi finally got up, brushed the dust from his clothes, straightened his collar, and stood dumbfounded by the unknown maiden’s mysterious strength.

The true nature of this maiden, whether she is good or evil, will be revealed through a perilous event involving the lady-in-waiting, Sekiya. Also, in the upcoming book, Jiraiya having Sutematsu take revenge on Arakurō, as well as Jiraiya going to work with taking down Urafuji Saemon of Kai, will unfold.

This graphic novel has evolved into a story much longer than what was first intended. Thus, many children may find it difficult to understand and get tired of reading it. However, in the end, I will explain the meaning of rewarding good and punishing evil in detail and reveal the author’s true intentions. Therefore, I hope that each volume will be read carefully and receive high praise.

9.22

To be continued...

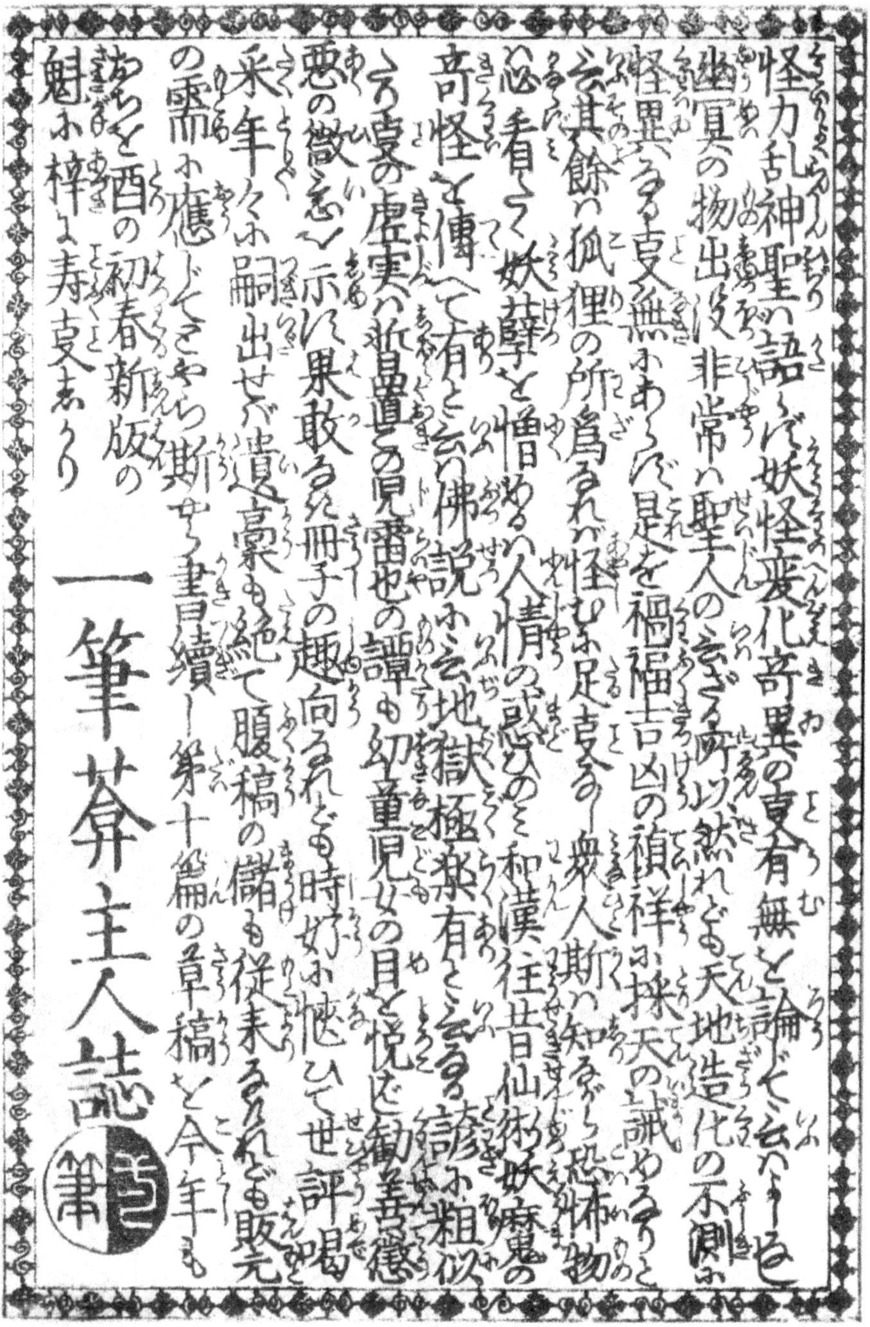
怪力乱神聖ハ語らず妖怪変化奇異の事有無を論ぜず云ハざるも
幽冥の物出没非常ハ聖人の言ざる所以然れども天地造化の不測ニ
怪異なる事無ニあらず是を禍福吉凶の禎祥ニ採天の誡めなりと
云其餘ハ狐狸の所為なれバ怪むニ足ざる事なり衆人斯ハ知ながら恐怖物
ハ恐れ看てハ妖孽を憎めるハ人情の惑ひのミ和漢往昔仙術妖魔の
奇怪を傳へて有と云ハ佛説ニ云地獄極楽有と云るも諺ニ粗似
たる事の虚実ハ新旧道との見當也の譚も幼童児女の目を悦バし勧善懲
悪の微意を示し果敢なき冊子の趣向なれども時好ニ愜ひて世評過
釆年々ニ嗣出せバ遺豪も絶て腹稿の備も従来なれども販元
の需ニ應じてさやら斯せず重續し第十編の草稿を今年も
読らを酉の初春新版の
魁ニ梓よ寿事志かり
一筆菴主人誌

10.1

Book 10

Do not speak of mysterious strength, chaotic deities, or the sacred; it is futile to discuss the existence or non-existence of supernatural beings and strange occurrences. The reason for the extraordinary emergence and disappearance in the mysterious realm lies in the words unspoken by the wise. However, there is nothing truly strange in the unpredictable course of the creation of heaven and earth. There is only fortune and misfortune, good and bad omens, and it is all said to be the punishment of heaven.

As for the rest, attributing everything to the deeds of foxes and tanuki is an inadequate explanation. Although people are aware of this, the fear of the unknown compels them to investigate it, and the ensuing hatred towards mysterious beings is merely a confusion of human emotions. Stories of the supernatural, handed down in both Japanese and Chinese traditions, speak of mysterious immortals, magic, and demons. These stories are similar to the proverbs in the Buddhist teachings of hell and paradise. But for now, let us set aside the distinction between truth and fiction.

Jiraiya's story delights the eyes of children and youths, revealing a subtle encouragement of virtue and punishment of vice. Though it continues to be released with acclaim year after year, the original manuscripts have ceased, and the stock of unpublished ideas remains unchanged. Nevertheless, responding to the demands of the publishers, I carry on with some writing that is neither here nor there. This year, the draft of the tenth book is being printed, commemorating the beginning of the new edition in the early spring of the Year of the Rooster (1849).

Ippitsuan

10.2

Jiraiya—Ogata Shūma Hiroyuki.

Terukage's fortress on Mount Kurokoma being destroyed in the flames of war.

Urafuji Saemon Terukage, the country samurai of Mount Kurokoma in Kai.

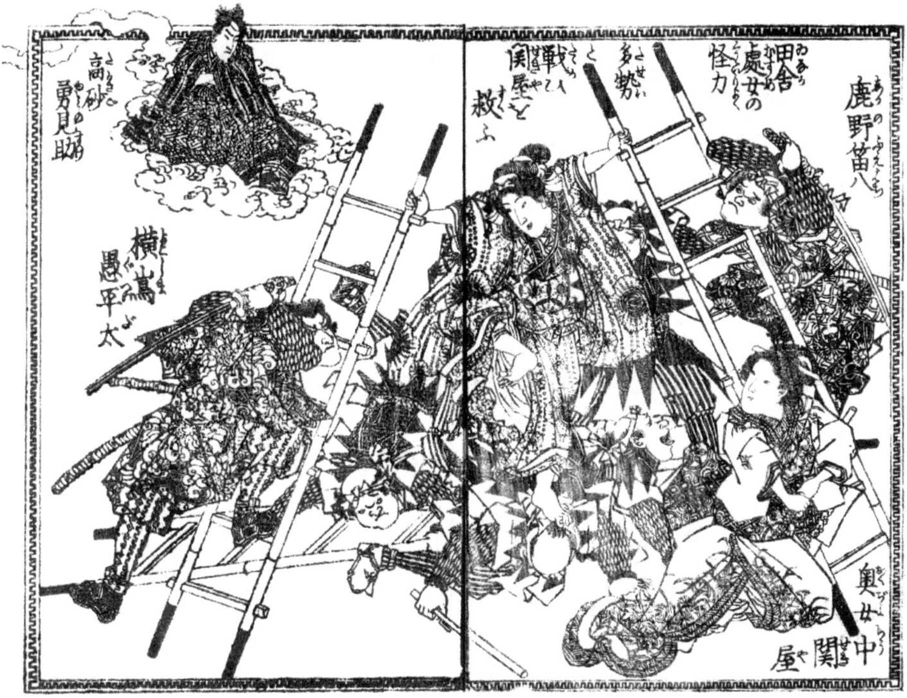

10.3

Shikano Fuehachi.

Lady-in-waiting, Sekiya.

The country girl with monstrous strength, fighting many to save Sekiya.

Yokoshima Guheida.

Takasago Yuminosuke.

10.4

Left side:

Upper square:

The young girl from Konoha Village in Etchū receives teaching in senjutsu.

The sage Katsuyu.

Lower square: In the hidden dwelling of Jiraiya on Mount Kurohime, Ayame bit Jiraiya's darling Tagane to death and was put down by Jiraiya's own hand. Her heart ablaze with the flames of jealousy, Ayame's vengeful *onryō* spirit has appeared in the form of a monstrous serpent, to bring her malice down on Jiraiya for stabbing her chest with his blade of wrath. But this yōkai apparition, driven by evil desires, was given enlightenment by the arts of the hermit Katsuyu, and her grudge was lifted.

Right side:

Ohana, daughter of the katana merchant in Yukinoshita in Kamakura.

In the evening, while my feelings burn brighter than fireflies, is it that the light is invisible, or is it that person who remains indifferent?
—Kokin Wakashū: "Love II"

10.5

Upper-left corner: Urafuji Saemon Terukage's fortress on Mount Kurokoma.

Center box: The story now splits in two.

Part I

(10.5)

Previously, Shikano Fuehachi had pressured Ohana to become his mistress, as if he was a buck in heat. He gathered a group of thugs on the banks of the Nameri River, and when Hanshichi unsuspectingly passed by, they attacked him. However, just as they were about to beat Hanshichi, a young maiden pilgrim appeared out of nowhere. She possessed extraordinary strength and bravery, which made Fuehachi and his cronies scatter and flee.

Hanshichi rejoiced and asked the maiden, "Who are you? A kami? A Buddha? A glorious savior? Your strength is a rare sight. I doubt there are any humans, let alone women, that are as strong as you. Even here in the dim light of dusk, I see that you wear the clothes of a pilgrim. Would you tell me where you hail from and where you are lodging?"

With a smile, the girl replied, "I am from Etchū and am currently on the Bandō Pilgrimage, leaving votive slips at the temples of the Kannon. I am also searching for someone. I have never been here in Kamakura before, so I don't know my way and haven't been able to find any lodging. I am on my way to a place called Yukinoshita Village to find a man named Katanaya Hanshichi."

Hanshichi was taken aback and exclaimed, "I am that Hanshichi! Why are you looking for me?"

Equally surprised, the girl said, "What fortuitous happenstance for me to have spotted you here. Although I didn't understand the situation completely, when I saw you in distress, it seemed as if you were simply engaging in playful banter, so it was fortunate that I drove away those thugs. You really are Hanshichi-sama?" Overflowing with joy, she swiftly reached into her kimono and retrieved the introduction letter from Inesaku in Kutsukake. "Everything is explained in this letter," she said, handing it to Hanshichi.

Hanshichi carefully accepted the letter, opened the envelope, and held it up in the moonlight. At first, he looked shocked, then moved, and after he had quickly skimmed the outline of the letter, he rolled it back up and put it in his kimono.

"Be that as it may, we are standing in the middle of the road. Come with me to my home. Once you have settled down you can tell me all the details. It is not far from here." Hanshichi led the way to Yukinoshita, while enquiring about Inesaku's well-being in Kutsukake.

In the foothills of Mount Kurokoma in Kai province,[1] the clan of Urafuji Saemon Terukage had been exercising its authority on the neighboring districts for generations. Urafuji was a renowned country samurai, and he had a large cavalry at his disposal. His personality was one of wiles, cunning, and evil desires. Although he had no noteworthy military exploits, and through his long-lasting presence in the region, he had earned the people's respect. He had an ego like that of an eagle, thinking itself the mightiest bird in the sky and never looking up. Like a rich man always wanting more, he devised wicked strategies that were the teachings of war. His ultimate plan was an audacious rebellion aimed at seizing more land and territories. When the opportune moment arose, he would incite an uprising, and bring the neighboring lands to heel with the edge of his sword. To foster his army, he would often recruit rōnin who were skilled in the martial arts, providing them with stipends in the area.

With this goal in mind, Urafuji Saemon reached out to Muyami Gundazaemon through a letter, forging an alliance with him. Gundazaemon, whose real name was Tatsumaki Arakurō, was a crafty person, who until recently had served close to the Kanrei in Kamakura. Under the pretext of a border dispute, Urafuji plotted to gather his co-conspirators for his rebellion, and when the time was right, in one fell swoop he would attack the neighboring lands. Urgently, he summoned Gundazaemon to join his war council through a letter.

During the council, Urafuji said, "If we can secure the infamous Jiraiya Shūma Hiroyuki as our ally, there is no doubt we will easily gain victory. How goes this endeavor?"

1 Present day Mount Kurodake.

10.6

(10.6)

Gundazaemon answered, "While it is true that I possess the ability to achieve this, as you already know, Jiraiya is renowned for his mysterious and otherworldly toad jutsu. He acts according to his own will and has his own plans, so he is not one to follow the commands of others. However, I have no doubt that my martial prowess surpasses his. If I can but meet him once and give him a taste of my swordsmanship, I am certain he will submit and become our ally. I will not rest until I've settled this matter."

His confident response pleased Urafuji. "If we follow your plan and gain him as an ally, he will be worth more than a thousand soldiers. Nothing would bring me more joy than this! Persuade him to sign a pledge of loyalty to me, and any reward you desire will be granted!"

They continued their secret council for several hours, followed by a grand banquet. Gundazaemon remained in the mountain fortress for a period of time before eventually returning to Kamakura.

While that happened, the lady-in-waiting, Sekiya, and her extensive entourage set out from the inn in Kamakura towards Echigo in the early hours of the morning. Tagoto-hime, the wife of Tsukikage Gunryō Terutoki from Echigo, had entrusted Sekiya with a mission to pray for continued fortune in war at the Kannon of Hasedera which was on display. Sekiya had given the many offerings she was entrusted with, and her duty was now complete. As the entourage was making its way through the footpaths of the rice fields, a large number of samurai suddenly appeared from under a cluster of trees. Seeing the flashing lights from the swords they were brandishing, Sekiya's servants panicked, abandoning the palanquin and fleeing in all directions. The foot soldiers grabbed the hilts of their swords, halted, and drew steel.

"Rioters! Why have you insolent knaves set your eyes on this woman's palanquin? If you have a valid reason, say it quick!" a foot soldier bellowed.

(10.7)

The group of rogues spoke, "We have no reason to disclose our hidden intentions to the likes of you. However, if you're worried about your reputation being tarnished by being robbed, we'll enlighten you. So, listen carefully! Urafuji Saemon Terukage-sama of Mount Kurokoma in Kai has long ago set his heart on that woman. He had a famous matchmaker go and suggest a marriage to her parents, but he was rejected. Call it the stubbornness of a warrior, but when he heard she was made a lady-in-waiting to the Tsukikage clan in Echigo, he decided to bide his time and steal her away and ravage her if that was what it would take to fulfill his desires. Long has he waited, and now that she returns from Kamakura, he secretly asked us to steal her along with her palanquin and deliver her to him. Too bad for you that you fell into our trap. If you say you won't hand her over because of your honor or any other drivel, we will part your heads from your bodies. If you value your lives, get lost, and be quick about it!"

The rogues furrowed their brows at the foot soldiers who stood firm. For even if his stipend is no more than a single cup of rice, a samurai is a samurai. They brandished their blades, showing that, by their katana, they would not hand over anything. They fought as hard as they could. After the battle concluded, Yokoshima Guheida and Shikano Fuehachi commanded their accompanying thugs to pick up the palanquin and take it with them. Sekiya, who overheard everything, loosened her self-defense sword from its sheath and prepared to jump out of the palanquin. At that moment, a young girl, no more than sixteen years old, decided that she could no longer bear to stand idle. She burst in between the gleaming swords of the crowd, seizing two ladders that happened to be nearby. Without uttering a word, she effortlessly swung the ladders around such enormous momentum that everyone retreated, fell to the sides, were knocked down, or crawled away in fear. None could stand against her.

When Fuehachi saw her, he burst out, "Ah! It's that little bitch of a pilgrim who caught me off guard at Nameri River last evening! Jump her all at once and catch her!" he ordered.

"Aye!" responded the men before coming at her from all sides. The girl paid them no heed, kicking them over, trampling them underfoot, throwing them aside as one would a handful of pebbles. This was too much for Guheida and Fuehachi, who turned tail without as much as a glance in the direction of the palanquin carrying Sekiya.

10.7

With no other attendants remaining, the girl approached the palanquin and said, "I may not fully understand the situation, but I am your friend. The rogues I chased off will surely be back, so let's go to my lodging for now."

She grabbed the end of the pole of the palanquin, put her shoulder to it, and without as much as changing her expression, picked up the palanquin and calmly walked through the crowd that had gathered to witness the confrontation. Onlookers were shocked and frightened by the girl, who appeared to be no more than sixteen or seventeen years old, with a face so exquisitely beautiful that some believed she must be a tengu in disguise. Their hairs stood on end as they stood in awe and disbelief.

And so, Otsuna effortlessly carried Sekiya's palanquin and gently set it down by the katana shop in Yukinoshita. She then opened the palanquin door and said to Sekiya, "It must be uncomfortable sitting inside that narrow palanquin for so long. You must be exasperated by now. This is where I am staying, and the owner is a friend of mine. You can rest easy here. All the people who were with you seem to have scattered and run off somewhere, but I suspect they should gather here before long. Now, please," and led Sekiya inside.

Ban'emon and Hanshichi eagerly inquired about what transpired, and Otsuna shared the story with them, providing a rough account of the events. Ban'emon, witnessing Otsuna's remarkable strength firsthand, finally realized that the tale of Hanshichi being rescued by

10.8

Otsuna from the ordeal orchestrated by Fuehachi was not a fabrication, and for a while he was left astounded.

(10.8)

Concurrently, the retainer of the Sarashina clan of Shinano, Takasago Yuminosuke, carried a present from his lord to the Kamakura Kanrei with great care, which he discreetly presented to the Kanrei. Afterwards, he went to Hasedera Temple on behalf of his lord to leave a prayer and was planning to depart on the same day. However, he heard various rumors about a troubled lady traveler and the involvement of a suspicious young girl. He wondered about the well-being of Sekiya, the envoy of the Tsukikage clan, whom he had last seen when they stayed at the same inn in Kutsukake. Since parting ways with her in Kutsukake he had not met her, so his wondering changed to worry. However, since witnessing the young girl's incredible bravado at the inn, he guessed that maybe Sekiya had met with her again, and that the girl had miraculously rescued her. He took note of the rumors and was soon on his way to Yuminoshita. Upon reaching the katana shop, he inquired at the door and was ushered inside. When he saw Sekiya again, he expressed how happy he was to see that she was unharmed.

Otsuna then approached Ban'emon and his family, kneeling before them, and spoke, "These two honorable individuals stayed at the rice merchant Inesaku-dono's inn in Kutsukake in Shinano during their

10.9

Top middle: Etchū Mount Tate Hell Valley illustration.

Middle: Mountain of blades.

Left: Lake of blood hell

Right: The realm of Shura demons.

Lower-right box: The dead who died untimely at the sword, suffering the hands of the Shura, asking for Otsuna to help them with her strength, begging her to take their revenge in the world of the living, clear their grudges, and let them ascend to Buddhahood, lamenting as they cry tears of blood.

journey to this area. On the same night, I too found lodging there as a pilgrim. In the middle of the night, a large group of thieves made their way inside, but I beat them back. Because none of Inesaku-dono's valuables were stolen, he rewarded me with this letter. These two also stayed at the same inn and can confirm everything that happened, proving that I am not making this up."

Takasago Yuminosuke and Sekiya applauded Otsuna for yet again ensuring their safety with her monstrous strength. When Ban'emon heard all this, deep in his heart he started to fear the mysterious girl.

Yuminosuke then asked Otsuna, "Why are you, so young and on your own, on a pilgrimage on a road you are not familiar with? I would like to hear the reason behind this."

Otsuna responded without hesitation, "Your suspicion is well-founded. I hail from a place called Konoha Village in the foothills of Mount Tate in Etchū province. I am the daughter of a poor rice farming family in the countryside, descended from Saburō Yoshihiro, the third son of the Ogata clan. Unfortunately, my parents passed away, and I was left with no one to rely on. Then, on a mysterious night, an old man came to my house. He taught me martial arts and bestowed upon me the mystical teachings of the water. This year, when I turned sixteen, the old man finally revealed something to me.

(10.9)

"He said, 'Your parents, the rice farmers, were sorrowful for not having a child, so they made vows to the Tateyama Gongen deity on Mount Tate in order to be given a child. The exact moment you were born, was the year of the Metal Monkey,[2] and there is a saying that children born in the year of the Metal Monkey will have the heart of a thief. This troubled your parents greatly. They thought bearing a child, whom they unfortunately knew would be despised and hated by the world, must be some sort of curse from a previous life. They dreaded and feared, hoping that you would at least not be born a man. But your destiny is beyond the comprehension of ordinary people. You were born to take a famous gallant as your husband and make your name known. However, if you do not win honor first, you cannot expect to wed a great gallant. For these purposes, you were born with natural beauty surpassing others, and it is why you have such strength. Lastly, my real name is Katsuyu, and I am a slug spirit who has lived for many years in the Hell Valley of Mount Tate. I was ordered by the god of the mountain to raise and guide you. And now, seeing as you have mastered martial arts and the way of the water, the time has come. With haste, journey through the provinces, become the wife of a gallant whose name is known under all of heaven, and make your fame!'

(10.10)

"After he said this, he disappeared as if he had never existed. I knew I had to go, so I informed the village head that I wished to embark on the Bandō Pilgrimage to help my parents in the next life. I bid farewell to everyone and set out alone, seeking the guidance of the god of marriage to lead me to my destiny. That is all there is to my story."

Sekiya and Yuminosuke thought the story of her prominence was most peculiar, and they halfway believed her, yet also halfway doubted her. For a while, everyone sat silently exchanging looks, but then Yuminosuke slid closer to Otsuna and said, "Hearing your story makes me think of an idea. You should go to my homeland. You need to marry a gallant like no other in the world, correct? Right now, there is such an unparalleled gallant, from the same clan as you even. His name is Ogata Shūma Hiroyuki, also known by his alias Jiraiya. Not only does he possess unmatched wisdom and courage, but he can also wield toad yōjutsu to do whatever he wants under the heavens. That being said, he also suffers the stigma of being called a bandit. Knowing this, what do you think?"

(10.11)

After pondering for a moment, Otsuna replied, "Granted, it is what I was told by the old man Katsuyu, but he never said anything about me

---

2 1380, 1440, 1500, or 1560 CE during the Muromachi period.

10.10

being related to the person. Surely, you must have heard of someone else out there."

Yuminosuke nodded. "There are two other individuals who possess courageous valor that is not inferior to Jiraiya. I suspect you shall learn of them in due time. But for now, leave that matter to me and come with me to Shinano," he said in a kind and guiding tone.

Time passed with their discussion, and Sekiya's servants finally arrived at the katana shop. They gathered Sekiya's luggage, inquired about her well-being, and excitedly shared stories of Otsuna's extraordinary deeds.

Subsequently, Yuminosuke joined with Sekiya, with assurances of her safety during their journey to Shinano. They bid farewell to the katana merchant family, made a promise with Otsuna that she would join them later, and embarked.

10.11

10.12

Upper-right: In Jiraiya's mountain fortress, Sutematsu is afraid and will not stop crying. Could this perhaps mean that the revenge of the ghosts of the Himematsu clan is at close hand?

Part II

(10.12)

Elsewhere, Urafuji Saemon Terukage of Kai plotted rebellion within his mountain fortress on Mount Kurokoma, accompanied by his mercenaries. He held a military council on how to attack the neighboring provinces, and had called for Muyami Gundazaemon, who was known for his skills in the military arts, to join him in the fortress.

Urafuji instructed Gundazaemon, "Talk with the crafty Yokoshima Guheida and Shikano Fuehachi in Kamakura and figure out a way to make Jiraiya my ally."

Gundazaemon, speaking loudly and boastfully, replied, "When it comes to martial arts, I am confident that I can rival Jiraiya or anyone else. However, he is versed in yōjutsu and can perform bizarre things. That is why I have yet to approach him. But this time, I will make him kneel before us and carry out our plan!" Upon making this bold promise, he added, "For now, I will return to Kamakura and inform Yokoshima and Shikano about the situation and discuss what to do." With that, Gundazaemon bid farewell and left Mount Kurokoma.

And so, Gundazaemon departed from Kai. Before the day was over, he was in Sagami province. He tried to make it back to Kamakura on the same day, but took longer on the roads than he had planned. When he arrived in the outskirts of Ōiso, it was already past the hour of the dog[3] and there was no lodging to be had in the towns or villages. Considering his options, he came across a foreboding straw-thatched hermitage. After hearing the sound of a wooden fish gong used in Buddhist rituals and spotting the faint glow of a lamp inside, he decided to spend the night there before entering Kamakura early the next morning. He called out at its wicker gate. The owner, a nun around thirty years old, came out.

"Is it rain or is it hail that the wind is blowing through the pines? To this humble hermitage where none other comes to visit, to whom do I have the honor of welcoming?" she inquired.

(10.13)

Gundazaemon answered in his kindest voice, "I am a traveler who seems to have lost his way a bit and ended up being too late to find lodging. If you let me stay the night, I will reward you handsomely."

The owner of the hermitage nodded and said, "That is an easy request, but as you see, this is but a thatched hermit's dwelling. There is no food to offer you and no sliding doors to close at night. If this is not too disagreeable, you are welcome to stay until morning."

Gundazaemon replied happily, "As long as I can stay until daybreak, I wish for nothing else. I have a box of food with me. Now, please excuse my intrusion," and stepped inside.

Resting at the hearth, he took off his straw sandals, and wrung out the moisture. The nun poured him some lukewarm tea and said, "Relax and rest. I will be chanting sutras now, so please pardon me for a while."

---

3 19:00–21:00.

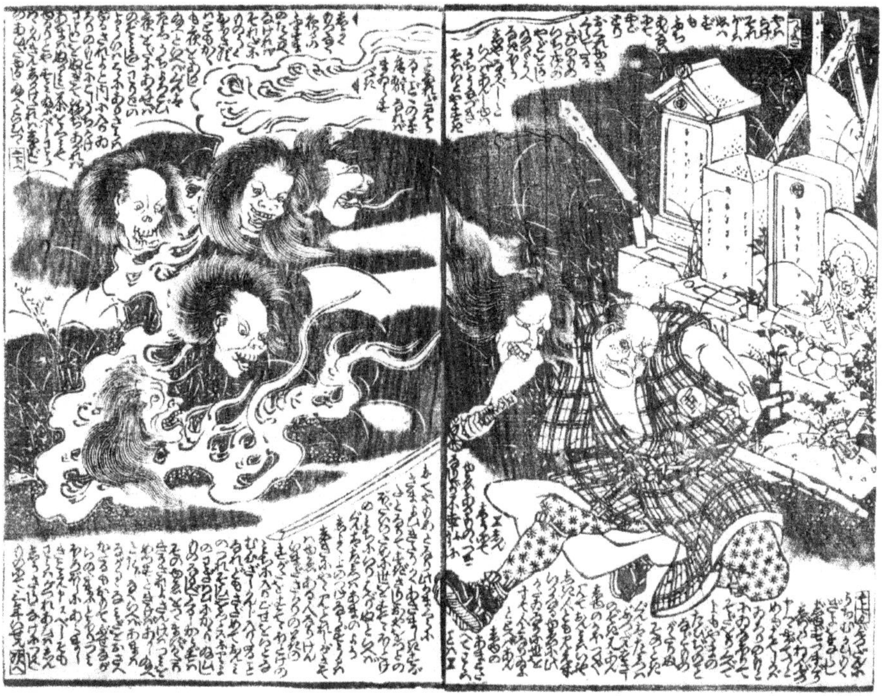

10.13

She went to the Buddhist altar, and as she struck the fish gong and ran the prayer beads through her fingers, she chanted the nembutsu prayer. After finishing, she returned to the hearth and threw some broken brushwood in the fire, and they talked about travels and the roads of the world.

At that time, Gundazaemon stared at the Buddhist altar and then studied the nun's face closely.

"You don't seem like a suspicious person. How did you end up renouncing the world and residing in such a remote place?"

In response to his question, the nun replied, "I was the wife of a man who had connections with Shinano, but due to an ill fate I became a widow. I wandered to Kamakura and became the humble figure you see before you now. For the sake of my dead parents and husband, I cut my ties with the secular world and embraced the path of the Buddha."

Gundazaemon found the nun's looks uncommonly fair, and was captivated by her. In a straightforward manner, he said, "I see that you have a compelling reason. I am impressed that a beautiful flower like yourself, yet to fully bloom, has forsaken everything to follow the Buddhist path and conduct rituals for the afterlife. However, there must be a reason why your husband met such an unforeseen tragedy. Share with me the full story without hesitation. Confession, they say, absolves one of sin, so bring everything to light."

(10.14)

The nun held back her tears. "I must conceal my face in embarrassment as I disclose this, for you are right—to vanquish sin, one

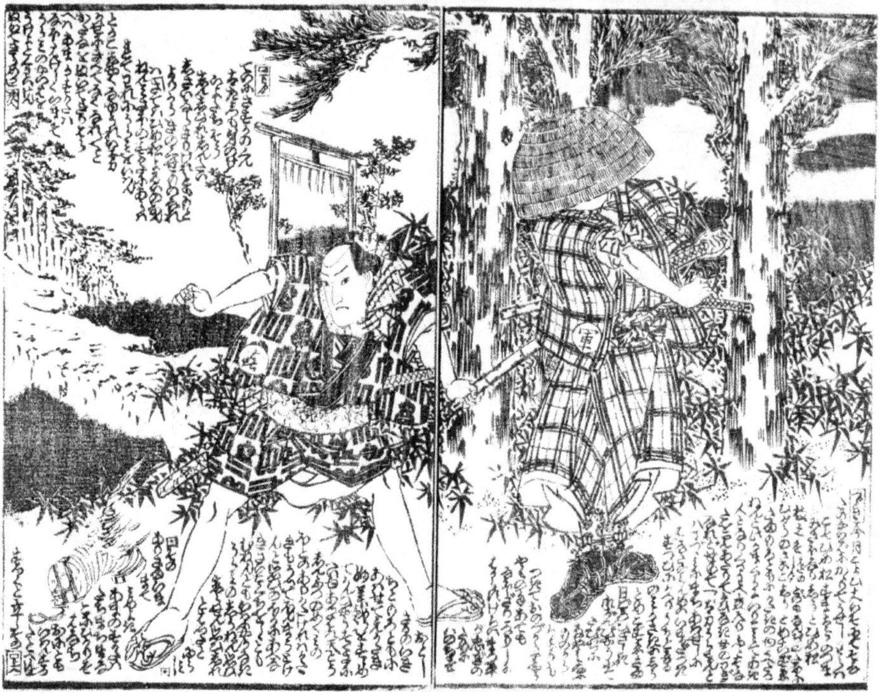

10.14

must reveal everything. The man I was married to, was a retainer of the Sarashina clan in Shinano, and three years ago, in this month, on this very night, he met with *your* blade in Ōiso and perished. I am Misao, wife of Himematsu Sumatarō! Even my father-in-law, Himematsu Edanoshin, met an untimely demise at your hands. Together with my mother-in-law, Kozue, I came to Kamakura in search of our sworn enemy. Disguising myself as a merchant, I entered the pleasure district where I caught sight of you. Unfortunately, I am a woman, but I wanted to at least land one hit on you with my sword. So, I waited at the Hatchō embankment, but it seems your fate was not yet at its end, and you countered me. But before that, you ended my mother-in-law, Kozue. She had been suffering from an eye disease for a long time on the road, and when we ran out of funds, we neglected to take care of her and give her medicine. Unbeknownst to us, our retainer Matsuhei, out of loyalty, took his own life and, combining his blood with that of our pet monkey, created an elixir of great rarity. It immediately cured Kozue's illness. We thanked all the kami and Buddhas for their blessing. However, just as we thought we were on the brink of vengeance, we met a wretched end. Words cannot describe the depth of regret and bitterness resulting from my unyielding grudge against you. But I will make you understand. Know my grudge!"

While glaring at him, the nun, who had previously appeared beautiful, began to undergo a transformation. Her eyes glowed, and her form shifted into that of an oni. With a sudden leap to her feet, she left

10.15

Sekiya presents her lady with a souvenir from Hasedera Temple in Kamakura. "A Fragrance of Kaori." The new face whitening powder from Ippitsu'an, with pure gold and musk.

Gundazaemon momentarily frozen, his body paralyzed and the hairs on his arms standing on end. Nevertheless, he remained a fearless villain.

"So, the lingering hatred of the Himematsu family has taken the guise of Misao to vent its grudge against me. You impudent ghost! Feel the wind of my sword and be gone!" declared Gundazaemon. Drawing his sword, he swung at the nun. Her form only grew more ferocious, and she revealed a gleaming dagger.

(10.15)

It was time for Gundazaemon to experience the blade of her resentment. The nun leapt at him, but he swung again and cut into her with his sword. Yet, she clung to the blade, as if embracing it, and did not let it go. When Gundazaemon finally managed to throw her off, he delivered the final blow, decapitating her with a single stroke. Or so it would seem, but the head floated around. Then, the heads of Edanoshin, Sumatarō, Kozue, and Matsuhei also appeared, and whirled through the air.

"Arakurō, you shall know our hatred! Come to the realm of the dead!" they cried out, and Misao's head bit down on Gundazaemon's upper-right arm. He tried to cut at it, but it would not let go. The excruciating pain waned his strength. Recoiling, he fell backward onto the ground.

The mysterious demonic lights ascended into the sky, vanishing from sight, their cackling laughter blending with the darkness. The straw-thatched hermitage dissolved without a trace, leaving Gundazaemon standing bewildered in an empty, grassy field.

"This must be the place where Misao and her mother-in-law were buried after I killed them on my way home from the pleasure district. Their spirits must have been trapped in the netherworld, unable to move on, lingering in their vengeful grudge against me. Laudable tenacity, I must admit. However, in the realm of the living, the dead stand no chance against me. Such pitiful souls," Gundazaemon mused to himself with a chuckle. "Or perhaps this hermitage I sought for lodging was merely the work of a mischievous fox or tanuki. How peculiar."

With that, he brushed off the dirt from his clothes and, as he stood up, he heard the sound of someone near at hand. In the light of a lantern, Gundazaemon saw what looked like Matsuhei, Himematsu's manservant. To avoid being recognized, he crouched down and tossed a stone, extinguishing the lantern's flame, then swiftly passed by the holder, disappearing into the darkness.

(10.16)

Sekiya, the lady-in-waiting of the Tsukikage clan, had met with an unforeseen peril in Kamakura, but was saved by the pilgrim Otsuna. She was then taken to the residence of the katana merchant, Ban'emon, in Yukinoshita. Hearing rumors about the incident, Takasago Yuminosuke, a retainer of the Sarashina clan, met with Sekiya and ensured her safety. After having marveled at Otsuna's bravery and strength, Yuminosuke expressed his concern for Sekiya's future travels and decided to accompany her. Together, they reached Shinano unharmed and had an audience with the master Miyukinosuke and Tagoto-hime, recounting the events. The couple were surprised when they heard of the pilgrim Otsuna's astounding feats and praised her. They also thanked Sekiya for fulfilling her duty of visiting the temple on their behalf, and for bringing souvenirs from the trip.

Upon receiving a detailed report of the incident, Tsukikage Terutoki, the lord and father of Miyukinosuke, was infuriated by the unjust actions of Urafuji Saemon and the wicked deeds of Yokoshima Guheida and Shikano Fuehachi. He commended Otsuna and dispatched two of his most trusted men, along with numerous gifts, to Ban'emon's residence in Yukinoshita. They were tasked with bringing Otsuna back to Tsukikage Terutoki's domain.

Unbeknownst to him, Muyami Gundazaemon had passed over the graves of Kozue, Misao, and Matsuhei among the villages of Ōiso. Their vengeful onryō spirits had deceived him and tormented him throughout the night. Furthermore, someone who looked like Matsuhei had shown

10.16

up, looking like he wanted to question Gundazaemon. Following this, Gundazaemon hurried to Yokoshima Guheida's house during the night. There, he first shared the news from Kōshū and then told about the unexpected and otherworldly event that happened to him in the eerie graveyard. Gundazaemon recalled where Misao's head had bitten him on the upper arm, and the pain grew to be unbearable. In a short time, it developed into a large lump, which swelled into something akin to a human head. When Guheida and Fuehachi saw this, they panicked and called a doctor. The doctor tried all kinds of medicine, but unfortunately the lump grew even more, showing no signs of healing. However, the medicine dulled the pain, so the brave Gundazaemon ignored the lump and shifted the topic. He reached into his breast pocket to retrieve the letter from Urafuji so he could hand it over, but found nothing.

"I must have dropped it in the graveyard in the night. But I still have my handkerchief for some reason. How odd," Gundazaemon remarked. He undid his belt and shook his clothes in search of the letter, but still found nothing. Gundazaemon was quite drunk from the saké Guheida provided, so he did not mind the letter being gone. Instead, he told Yokoshima and Shikano about Urafuji Saemon's plans for rebellion and had them agree to it. Together, they focused on devising a way to make Jiraiya Shūma Hiroyuki their ally.

10.17

(10.17)
Previous to this, Tsuruhashiya Kinosuke had come to Yukinoshita because Hanshichi Fukitarō had something to tell him in secret. However, since Kinosuke couldn't openly reveal his long-standing friendship with Jiraiya, he had to feign ignorance about their connection. Similarly, Oroku, Chōbei's wife, who was also linked to Jiraiya, had to keep it a secret, so Katanaya Ban'emon knew nothing of this. Instead, Ban'emon told them of Otsuna's mysterious courage and strength, mentioning that she seemed to want to meet Jiraiya. Hearing this, Hanshichi said nothing, but signaled Kinosuke with his eyes and whispered to him, "This young pilgrim may be the strongest person in the world, but being a woman, she may not be suitable to assist Jiraiya. However, we should first send him a message, so he doesn't waste his time with it. He needs to know the details of this matter as soon as possible."

When they finished their discreet discussion, Kinosuke understood what he had to do and departed. On his way back to Ōiso, he happened upon a suspicious person who looked like a rōnin. The rōnin had seemed frightened of him, and as they passed each other, the rōnin inexplicably threw a rock, extinguishing Kinosuke's lantern. In the darkness, Kinosuke felt a letter with his foot and picked it up. He could not see the name of the recipient on it, so he put it into his breast pocket and headed to Chōbei's house. There he explained what happened, and they secretly discussed dispatching an express messenger to Mount Kurohime. Kinosuke then took out the letter he had picked up on the road, opened it, and discovered that it lacked a recipient name. It did, however, reveal plans of rebellion, emphasizing the time being right and the need to gather an army. This being a very suspicious and important matter, Chōbei and Kinosuke furrowed their brows and discussed the contents of the letter.

When Jiraiya Shūma Hiroyuki of Mount Kurohime in Shinshū was executed on the beach of Yuigahama in Kamakura, he used his yōjutsu to escape. Afterwards, he retreated to his mountain fortress in Shinshū and refrained from returning to his dwelling in Kamakura. One night, while engrossed in reading a book under the lamplight, and with Sutematsu sleeping by his side, Jiraiya lost track of time. At this late time, the child burst into weeping as if plagued by a dreadful nightmare. Jiraiya picked him up and tried everything to console him. Although Sutematsu had never before yearned for his mother, he cried out, "Mother! Mother!" as if chasing after her in his dream.

Jiraiya found this to be peculiar and pondered, "It was on this month and night that Sutematsu's mother, Misao, and grandmother, Kozue, were struck down in a counterattack by Gundazaemon on the Hatchō embankment. I happened to be passing by and saw an injured woman who asked me to take care of her orphaned son. It has already been three years since then. The reason Sutematsu is now filled with fear and longing for his departed mother on this particular night might be due to a dream guiding him to Gundazaemon's whereabouts in Kamakura, urging him to seek revenge."

Then Jiraiya chanted an incantation to himself, gathered his toads, and divined the signs. It was as he thought. The fiendish Gundazaemon's fate was sealed.

(10.18)

Jiraiya saw Gundazaemon suffered from some mysterious ailment and thought, "I have patiently waited for Sutematsu to grow older so that I can assist him in seeking vengeance. I had intended to wait a little longer, but it appears the time has come. We shall travel forthwith to Kamakura and get satisfaction." As he awaited the break of dawn, Jiraiya made the travel preparations for their journey.

In the house of Katanaya Ban'emon in Yukinoshita, Kamakura, a pilgrim named Otsuna had arrived with a letter of introduction from the inn owner, Inesaku, in the Kutsukakejuku post town. By a stroke of luck, she had come across Sekiya, who was visiting temples on behalf of the Tsukikage clan. Sekiya was in peril when she met her, and Otsuna had displayed great courage and strength. The rumor of this spread all over Kamakura, and now there were daily crowds gathering outside the

10.18

Katanaya house, hoping to see Otsuna. The samurai families sent messengers to inquire about it without end. Ban'emon's business always depended on him going with Hanshichi to the mansions, but now they were constantly followed by people wanting to see Otsuna no matter where they went.

Otsuna, deeply troubled by all this, said to Ban'emon and Hanshichi, "I had no option but to use my strength, but I am truly sorry for becoming so famous. I only came here to the Katanaya house by a fortuitous connection in order to have a place to rest. But now that things have turned out like this, I cannot stay. I will proceed with the Bandō Pilgrimage, and when I come back, I shall consider my next steps."

Otsuna thanked them for having been so blessed as to get to know them, said her goodbyes, and yet again set out on the road.

Meanwhile, Hanshichi, Chōbei, and Kinosuke planned together and sent word about Otsuna to Jiraiya, but they also wanted to be straightforward about their intentions to Otsuna. Unfortunately, it was a well-kept secret from Ban'emon and his wife that they were long-standing friends of Jiraiya, so it was difficult to do anything to stop the young maiden. All they could do was hope everything would turn out all right on its own accord.

Jiraiya Hiroyuki with Sutematsu arrived in Kamakura before the day was over. There, he met with Chōbei, Kinosuke, and Hanshichi and told them, "Last night, after Sutematsu was tormented by a nightmare,

I used my jutsu to divine the future and saw Muyami Gundazaemon's destiny is at its end. He is already suffering from some strange illness, so I promptly came with Sutematsu."

They were all taken aback when they heard this, and Kinosuke remarked, "I had no idea you possessed such an ability. On another note, there was an outstandingly strong and brave woman named Otsuna staying at Hanshichi's place. We thought that if we could make her your ally, she could be helpful, and we also learned she is searching for a famous gallant. We wanted to inform you about her, so we sent an express courier, but I guess you passed him on the way. I know it is by no means the first time you have done something like this, but to be able to ascertain what has happened here, and then come so speedily...your jutsu really is extraordinary." He stopped for a moment before continuing, "Today is the third year after you came upon the murdered old lady and Misao-dono, when you were undercover as Samezaya Jiroza. Yesterday was their death anniversary, and I sent a small offering to Muenji, the temple of the unknown, so they could do Buddhist memorial services and put flowers and incense up for them.

(10.19)

"On that night, on my way back from Yukinoshita as I passed by the graves where we buried their bodies at the side of the road, I saw a suspicious looking rōnin. He seemed to recognize me or mistook me for someone and feared me. I stopped without thinking about it, and then he threw a rock at my lantern, extinguishing it, before fleeing. It was there that I stumbled upon this letter. Although I do not know its intended recipient, it might hold a clue regarding Gundazaemon, the target of Sutematsu's pursuit."

He reached into his breast pocket and pulled out the letter. Jiraiya took it, opened it, and when he finished reading it, he clapped his hands in astonishment. "This must be a letter from Urafuji Saemon, the country samurai on Mount Kurokoma in Kai, whom I've heard about! I had already figured out he had talked with Gundazaemon about making me his ally and that he was planning a rebellion. But this letter confirms an imminent battle, and Urafuji is trying to inform his allies here in Kamakura. Gundazaemon must have been carrying this letter from Mount Kurokoma, and then happened to cross paths with you. This is quite a vital piece in their secret plans."

After discussing this with Chōbei and Kinosuke, Hanshichi finally told Jiraiya all the details about Otsuna. In response, Jiraiya remarked, "When I was flying through the sky with my yōjutsu on the way here, I spotted a peculiar young woman riding what seemed like a small boat going against the current in the Tonegawa River. However, I was in a hurry to come here so I did not stop to investigate any further. That must have been this Otsuna you speak of. I guess she has left the area."

Hanshichi agreed and said quietly, "She performed extraordinary feats that garnered her widespread attention, but she disliked the notoriety, and desired to leave the day before yesterday. There was nothing we could do to stop her, so we let her leave as she wished. Her

10.19

Bottom right corner: In the next volume you can read about Sutematsu's sorrowful goodbye, as he bids farewell to the toads he grew attached to over time.

ability to traverse the water suggests another master of some mystical yōjutsu. She did indeed tell us she was trained in martial arts by Katsuyu, the slug hermit of Mount Tate in Etchū. She is truly an enigmatic woman."

Jiraiya's ability to discern connections was nearly uncanny. After contemplating the information he had just received, he remarked, "It would appear this Otsuna's destiny is entwined with my own, but the time is still too early for that destiny to be fulfilled. However, the time for our encounter should not be too distant. She must be some remnant of an ancestor in the Ogata clan."

After Muyami Gundazaemon remembered the distressful meeting with the specters outside Ōiso, where the ghost of Misao had bitten down on his right upper arm, an unusual tumor developed there. It gradually expanded in size until it was as large as a human head, causing unbearable pain day and night. In his anguish and torment, Gundazaemon became unhinged, babbling incoherently about his wicked deeds like a madman. He had quite lost his mind, making a racket, and it was too much for Guheida, who had him hidden away in a separate room. However, the servants took delight in imitating

Gundazaemon's deranged ramblings, laughing loudly and speaking ill of him. Who exactly said it is unclear, but it eventually reached the ears of the magistrate Hatamori Daizen.

Hatamori Daizen had long despised Yokoshima Guheida for his wickedness, and he also heard about the foul deeds of the underling, Shikano Fuehachi. Fuehachi had reportedly said indecent things to Ohana, the daughter of Katanaya, and by Urafuji Saemon's request, he tried to kidnap Sekiya, who went to Hasedera Temple to worship on behalf of her master. Upon learning this, Hatamori Daizen dispatched a spy to investigate further. At that same time, Tsuruhashiya Kinosuke of Ōiso quietly delivered a suspicious letter to Hatamori Daizen's office, which Kinosuke happened upon by chance. After reporting the contents of the letter to the Kanrei, Hatamori Daizen was issued with a strict order to capture Yokoshima Guheida and Shikano Fuehachi and subject them to severe interrogation. Under the unbearable pain, the two confessed, divulging all the information they possessed.

During Guheida and Shinano's arrest, Gundazaemon was still locked away in his room, suffering from his ailment. He had managed to slightly regain some of his senses and was startled by the commotion. While still wearing only his nightgown, he escaped into the garden and scaled the wall. His plan was to escape to Inamuragasaki Village, but his body was weak from his condition, and he quickly became exhausted. He stopped and sat down at the root of a tree for a while to catch his breath. As he sat there, a remarkable samurai, clad in travel clothes, emerged from the shadows of the trees. He exuded gallantry and dignity, yet also warmth and gentleness.

(10.20)

"Tatsumaki Arakurō, also known as Muyami Gundazaemon. I hold no grudge or resentment against you. Although we have unknowingly met on several occasions in various places, I have never had a reason to introduce myself. Nonetheless, even though we have not been on friendly terms with each other, I already know your name. I am certain you have heard of Ogata Shūma Hiroyuki, also known as Jiraiya, who is famous throughout all of Japan. Well, he is none other than me. Due to unforeseen circumstances today, I have been awaiting you here for quite some time. I have long ago guessed you were tasked by Urafuji Saemon of Mount Kurokoma in Kai to recruit me as his ally for his plans of rebellion. I might be an infamous and dirty bandit, but I have my own long-held and deep desires. Why would I take orders from Urafuji, who is practically no more than a mere rat? In my mountain fortress I have swarms of subordinates just as capable as him. Furthermore, Urafuji Saemon is cruel and rapacious, he excels and takes pride in making the people suffer, and he is a selfish menace. The frog in the well knows nothing of the sea, and the bat in the village without birds believes itself to be the only creature that flies. Urafuji has no compassion or benevolence in his heart. When those who he seeks as allies come face to face with his true nature, they will turn their backs on him, and his ambitions will remain unfulfilled. Your plan to carry out his schemes,

10.20

alongside his comrades Yokoshima and Shikano, is as futile as trying to steal the magical orb from the clasp of a dragon's claws! You are doing nothing but throwing your life away. But let us set that aside for now. There is something else I must convey to you.

"Three years ago, one night while returning from the Ōiso pleasure district, I passed by the Hatchō embankment. It was there that I encountered a wounded woman who implored me to care for a young boy. He was the orphaned son of Himematsu Sumatarō, who served the Sarashina clan in Shinano. Sumatarō's father, Edanoshin, met an unexpected and unnatural death, and Sumatarō became entangled in your avarice. You killed him for it. Seeking vengeance, his elderly mother, wife, and servant Matsuhei came to Ōiso, where they happened upon you. The old mother and Misao waited at the top of the embankment for you and announced themselves as they attacked. Unfortunately, the women were countered by you, and in her final moments, Misao caught eye of me and requested, 'Have this child avenge us!' In her suffering, she entrusted me with these words. The futility and pity of the situation struck me deeply. Despite being a woman, because she was born into a warrior family, she resolved to avenge her father-in-law and her husband. I understood how frustrated she must have been, not being able to get satisfaction, and I swore on my katana that I would help. I picked up the boy, named him Sutematsu, and raised him as my own. It has come to my knowledge that, on this very month, marking the third year since those events, you were afflicted by a mysterious illness. Now, while you still have some life in you, Sutematsu will present himself, kill you, and exact revenge for his clan. This will clear all attachments of those in the future, and my efforts will not have been in vain. For this purpose, I have brought him here with me.

(10.21)

"However, Sutematsu is barely four years old and not yet fit for a duel. Hence, Kinosuke and Chōbei, who have helped in his upbringing, will support him. Those two have enough resentment towards you for a sword each, and they already await you here. Now, face them in honest combat! I will observe from here."

Jiraiya calmly stepped back, and Gundazaemon jumped to his feet. Cackling, he exclaimed, "So, you are Jiraiya Shūma Hiroyuki? And you brought some backup in the form of these unrelated individuals? The people of the Himematsu, I had valid reasons for their demise. Even if their deaths were pitiful, I could not allow them to live. Misao's dying request for you to take in a child whom you neither know nor have ever seen before, raising him to seek revenge and attempting to pacify the clan's obsessive bloodlust, is nothing more than feigned virtue and none of your concern! You are a bandit who roams the lands and should be more concerned with stealing money than getting vengeance. Are you a drunken madman? But if this is truly your desire, then it is most unfortunate, for I, Gundazaemon, will reduce you to mere rust on my blade. Bring out your backup and face me with all three swords!"

As Gundazaemon called out, he stood firm, loosening his katana in its sheath and glaring about for his opponents. He emanated an aura of true bravery and invincibility, making it difficult to underestimate him.

Kinosuke and Chōbei appeared alongside Sutematsu. Drawing their katana, they advanced toward Gundazaemon, who understood the gravity of the situation and also unsheathed his sword. Just as the clash of blades was about to commence, an intense surge of pain coursed through Gundazaemon's tumor, rendering his body numb and hindering his movements. His two opponents realized his swordplay was in shambles due to pain, so they piled on the attacks. Gundazaemon cried out in anguish, unable to withstand the onslaught, and collapsed. Kinosuke picked up Sutematsu, straddled on top of the prostrated Gundazaemon, and together they gripped the katana for the finishing blow. With a forceful thrust, they drove the sword through their enemy's chest. The young child, still barely able to speak, proclaimed, "Let that be a lesson to you!" and pushed the blade in as hard as he possibly could, ending Gundazaemon's life. Kinosuke set down Sutematsu and chopped Gundazaemon's head off. Then he took out tablets with the posthumous Buddhist names of the Himematsus and washed the head in a nearby stream. Together, they all performed a service for the dead, chanting the nembutsu prayer many times over.

10.21

Now that Sutematsu had finally gotten satisfaction, a report was given to the local magistrate, who bolted to the scene. Kinosuke and Chōbei recounted the entire event, laying bare every detail, yet the magistrate Hatamori Daizen had Sutematsu, Kinosuke, and Chōbei taken to the village head for the time being. Then he sent a messenger to the Sarashina clan in Shinano to seek further information. The true extent of Tatsumaki Arakurō's heinous deeds came to light, and upon learning the entire Himematsu clan had fallen victim to Tatsumaki's hands, Hatamori regarded the actions of Chōbei and Kinosuke, mere townsfolk, as rare and commendable. As an official reward, he gave each of them ten blue strings of coins, each worth one thousand mon, and gave them a stern command to raise Sutematsu and show him affection.[4] With gratitude, they accepted the rewards, marking the end of their vendetta without any further incidents.

Meanwhile, Jiraiya had concealed himself from the world and snuck into a room detached from Chōbei's main house. Upon hearing how things worked out, he reflected, "As we exacted our revenge, the tumor on Arakurō Gundazaemon's upper arm, which resembled a human head and formed not only by Misao's hatred but also the vengeful onryō spirits of the Himematsu clan, mysteriously vanished without a trace, dissipating like morning mist before the sun. It must be a sign that the timing was right for our vengeance.

4 Strings of coins were an official reward. Each blue string was worth 1000 mon, roughly weighing 3.75 kilos each.

(10.22)

Now assistance from the Sarashina is sure to come, so it will be inconvenient if I depart before all matters are fully resolved." And so, Jiraiya hid away in Chōbei's home and waited.

Sarashina Hangan Mitsuaki of Shinano heard that his loyal retainer Takasago Yuminosuke's sister, Misao, who had married the heir of Himematsu Edanoshin, Sumatarō, had set out to avenge the deaths of her father-in-law and husband. After having traveled through the lands, she met with a counterattack in Kamakura, and her orphaned son was left in the care of two townsmen in Kamakura. Upon hearing from the Shōgun that the boy, a mere four years old, had exacted revenge and settled the vendetta, Mitsuaki told Yuminosuke, "We cannot abandon Sutematsu in such circumstances. We must reward the two townspeople generously and bring the child back to us, lest the people become discontent."

Yuminosuke understood his orders and dispatched two trusted samurai to Kamakura. They presented themselves before the Kanrei's Board of Inquiry to plead their case, and gave Chōbei and Kinosuke many gifts to thank them for taking care of Sutematsu so far.

"It is only because of the distance between the lands that this matter has remained unknown to us," they said, apologizing for the oversight. Then they told their order to take Sutematsu back with them immediately. They were very grateful for the compassion of Kinosuke and Chōbei.

10.22

From here, the official meeting between Yuminosuke and Jiraiya, as well as what will happen to Sutematsu, will follow in book eleven. For now, this marks the end of this volume.

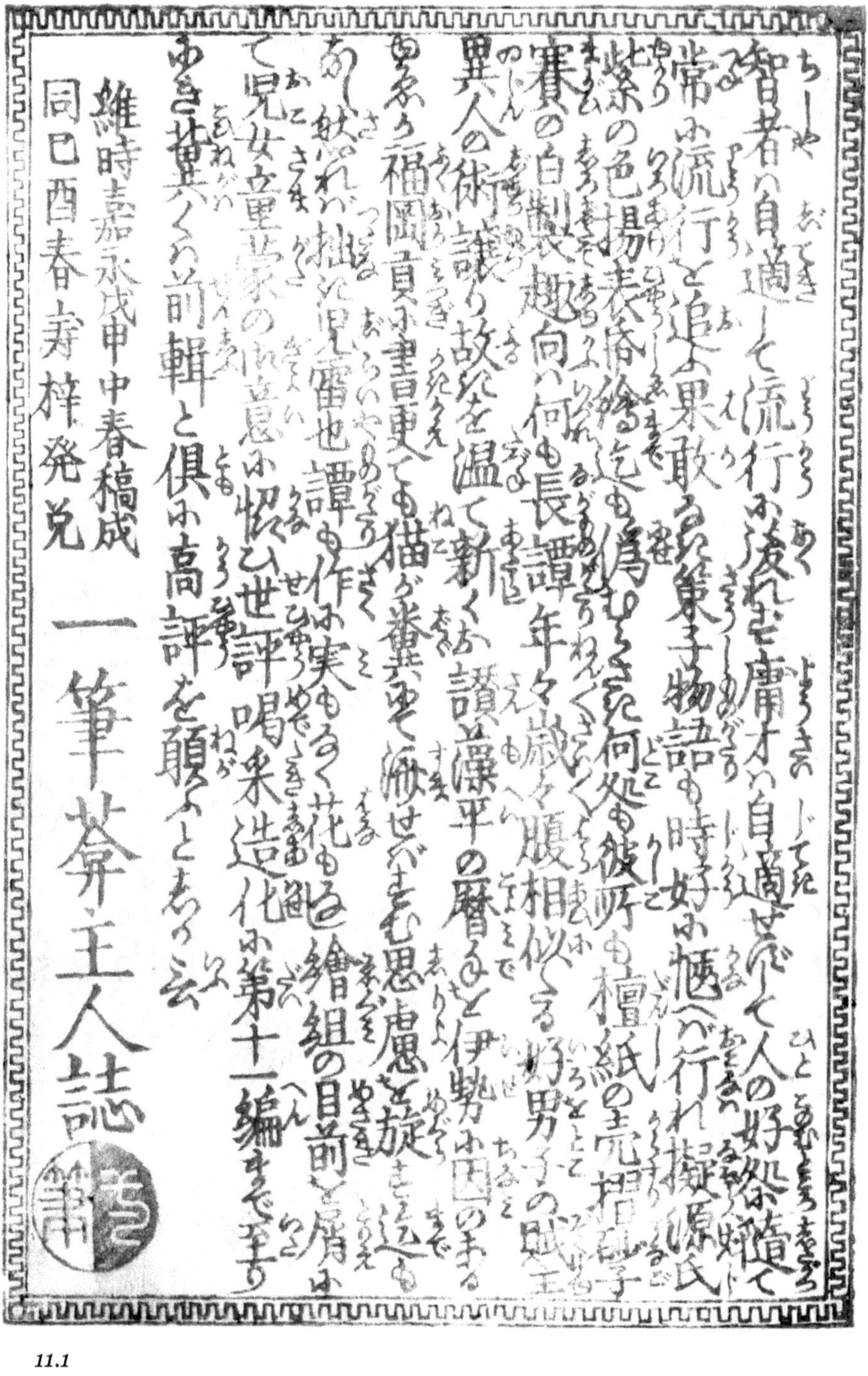

智者ハ自適して流行ニ後れど庸才ハ自適せずして人の好所ニ随て
る常ニ流行を追ふ果敢なる草子物語も時の好ニ随へバ行れ擬源氏
紫の色揚表紙絵を艶もあらバ何処も彼所も檀紙の売揃子
賽の白製趣向ハ何も長譚年々歳々腹相似たる好男子の賊主
異人の術譲り故を温て新くなる讃藻平の暦ると伊勢ニ因のまる
自多き福圏貢ニ書目更ても猫が養異して厭世バまも思慮を旋きに返も
あし然れバ拙ハ児雷也譚も作ニ実もなく花もなき繪組の目前を肩ニ
て児女童蒙の慰ニ怡び世評喝采造化ニ第十一編まで至り
ゆき並く前輯と倶ニ高評を願ふとなん云
維時嘉永戊申中春稿成
同己酉春寿梓発兌
一筆菴主人誌

11.1

Book 11

The wise pursue their own path without being swayed by passing trends. People of mediocre talents, on the other hand, conform to the popular tastes, always trailing the latest fashions. Even a vain venture into storytelling, when timed well, can be well-received. Like *The Rustic Genji*, imitating *The Tale of Genji*, its cover illustrations are in vivid purple on fine white paper.

This story is also a long tale, and through the years, the protagonist bandit leader using strange jutsu, has been a lady-killer like Prince Genji.

Reheating old leftovers and making them new, like taking the calendar maker Osan Mohei from *Tales of Five Lecherous Women* and replacing him with Fukuoka Mitsuki from *A Song from Ise of Love and Swords* because of some connection to Ise, is like a cat defecating. It does not require much thought.

Thus, I hope that the tale of Jiraiya, with neither substance nor bloom, its illustrations like trash before one's eyes, aligns with the wishes of young readers as it has now reached its eleventh volume. I wish for high praise alongside the previous installments and favorable a reception.

Written: Kaei era—Year of the Earth Monkey (1848)
Published: Kaei era—Year of the Earth Rooster (1849)
Ippitsuan

11.2

Left side: Jiraiya of Mount Kurohime in Shinano—Ogata Shūma Hiroyuki.

Top-right square: Bitei, the woman sage of Hell Valley on Mount Tate in Etchū.

Bottom-right square, continuing into left side of page: The snake eating frog—a type of toad.

In the *Honzō Kōmoku* it is said that the snake-eating frog is a large toad, adept at consuming snakes. It rarely fails when it pursues a snake. By skillfully manipulating the snake's tail for a long time, the frog brings about the death of the snake. After losing a few segments from its tail, the snake's flesh is soon consumed. In the *Bunshi Shūryaku*, it is mentioned that the snake-eating frog is a kind of toad that can eat snakes.

In works like the *Jibun Ruijū* and the *Tōba Shūchū* there is mention of the so-called "three-way deadlock" which includes the toad, centipede, and snake. None of these three creatures moves when confronted by the others, as they are all fearful of being consumed. The record does not include information about the slug.

In the current common understanding, the three-way deadlock is considered to be the snake, frog, and slug. According to the *Honzō Kōmoku*, there is evidence of the snake-eating frog fearing centipedes and slugs. In the *Gozasso*, there is mention of dragons fearing centipedes. The truth of this matter is still unknown.[1]

1 This entire text is copied from *Wakan Sansai Zue* book 54, the section on "Hebikuikaeru".

11.3

Fearless young men could not compare, as there is nothing unfamiliar to her in the realm of martial arts. A master of the mystic and trained in the ways of the water, she traverses the waves without a boat. Having received these mysterious techniques from the slug hermit Katsuyu Dōjin, she became a formidable, brave warrior. Thus, beneath the light of the moon, her destiny of love was foretold, and she became like the demon wife of a fierce god.

Tsunade, wife of Ogata Hiroyuki.
Mijin Kotsuhei Tanenashi.
Onibi of the rainy night.
Yokutsura Rinhei.

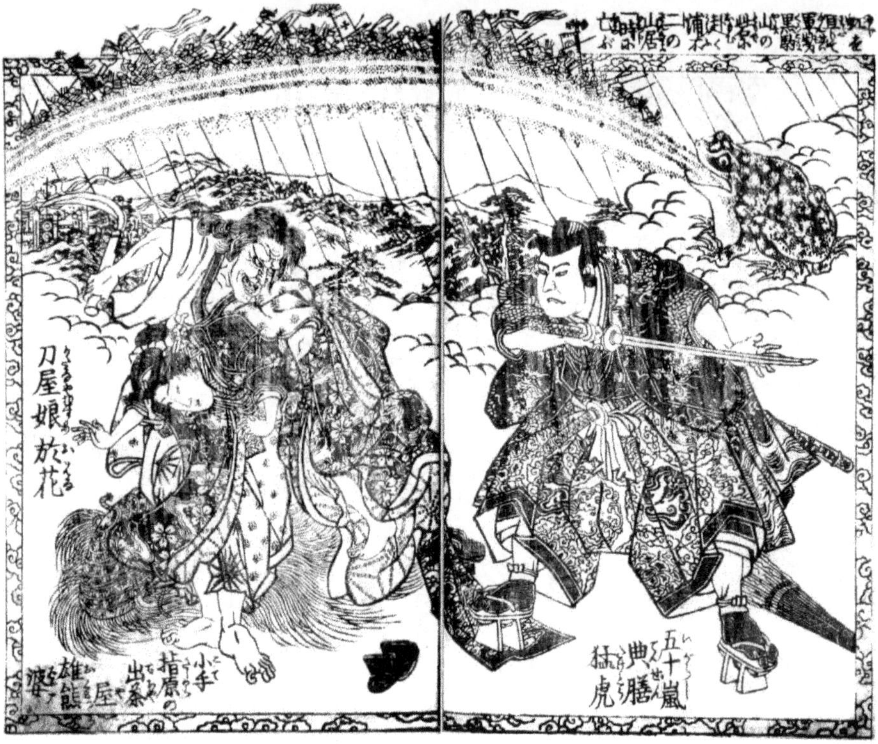

11.4

An army marches over a rainbow to the stronghold on Mount Kurokoma. Urafuji's mountain retreat falls in a moment.

Igarashi Tenzen Taketora.
Ohana, daughter of the katana merchant.
A greedy hag of Dechaya in the fields of Kotesashi.[2]

2 An area in southern Saitama.

11.5

Part I

(11.5)
Tatsumaki Arakurō had murdered the father and son of the Himematsu, retainers of Sarashina Hangan Mitsuaki, the feudal lord of Shinano. He then changed his name to Muyami Gundazaemon, became a retainer of the Kamakura Kanryō, and caused the death of the father's wife Kozue, Misao, and the servant Matsuhei. During a journey to the neighboring lands to hone his martial arts, he unwittingly found himself devoured by a colossal serpent, which altered his appearance. Because of this, he had no choice but to yet again become a masterless rōnin and allied himself with Urafuji Saemon of Mount Kurokoma in the province of Kai, who was plotting rebellion.

However, the heavens, having witnessed his years of atrocious acts, could no longer tolerate his wickedness. At Inamuragasaki, Sutematsu, a mere four-year-old, with the aid of Chōbei, Kinosuke, and backed by Jiraiya, exacted revenge upon him for the murder of his parents. When the Shōgun inquired about this to the Sarashina clan, they confirmed what had been reported. Thus, it was decreed that Kinosuke and Chōbei were to be rewarded, and they were to shower Sutematsu with love.

News of the revenge spread far and wide, and messages from both major and minor feudal lords working in Kamakura came pouring in, offering to hire the young Sutematsu. When the Sarashina clan learned of this, since the Himematsus were originally their retainers, the clan decisively summoned Sutematsu to restore him as the rightful heir to his family name. Luckily, Takasago Yuminosuke was related to Sutematsu by power of his sister's marriage. Upon being given the order, Yuminosuke dispatched two of his own retainers, Asuwa Hibanda and Fukai Chinonai, to go to Kamakura with a host of men. There, they were to summon Sutematsu and give gifts for Kinosuke and Chōbei. Because Jiraiya had always thought this was how it should be, he stayed in one of the inner rooms of Chōbei's home, waiting for the situation to stabilize. Upon their arrival in Kamakura, Hibanda and Chinonai met with Chōbei and Kinosuke, telling them all the circumstances of why they had traveled a long way to escort Sutematsu. They also carried a message with the same information for the Kanrei, which they intended to deliver soon.

It was difficult for Jiraiya to let Sutematsu go, but since it was very difficult for him to enter and exit Kamakura, he had no choice but to remain in hiding, unable to make his presence known. Consequently, he discussed the matter in secret with his comrades, concluding that the best course of action would be to have Chōbei hand over Sutematsu cleanly and by the book, as he had been the one outwardly caring for the child for an extended period. Kinosuke and his wife, on the other hand, would accompany the entourage on the journey to Shinano. With haste, they made the necessary travel arrangements, and soon Chinonai, Hibanda, and their men departed from Kamakura, arriving in the vicinity of Bunbaigawara in Musashi before long.[3]

(11.6)

Without notice, a whirlwind blustered around them, snapping trees and sending sand and stone flying through the air. The sky darkened with clouds, resembling the darkest of nights, and the door to Sutematsu's palanquin blew open. From within the billowing clouds emerged a colossal toad which snatched Sutematsu before flying into the unknown. Hibanda and Chinonai stood flabbergasted, as if they had just had a tatami pulled from beneath their feet.

Around the same time, Kinosuke and his wife caught up with the retinue. Having been roughly ten chō behind on the road,[4] they had not witnessed the whirlwind. However, upon finally chasing down the group, they inquired about Sutematsu. When they heard of the boy's abduction by a yōkai to whereabouts unknown, they fell silent for a moment, overwhelmed by a mixture of shock and sorrow.

With no recourse available to them, Hibanda and Chinonai gnashed their teeth and looked to the skies. "We were entrusted with escorting Sutematsu. How can we return home brazenly unaffected, when he has been taken by a yōkai on our watch? Our destinies end here. We should cut open our bellies and die!"

Witnessing their resolve, Kinosuke stepped in to stop them. "As mere townspeople, we understand it may be impudent of us to speak

3 Current Bubaigawara area in Saitama. Musashi is present day Tokyo and Saitama.

4 About 1 kilometer.

11.6

thus, and you are justified in dismissing our words. However, as the saying goes: 'Sometimes, you need to consult even your knees.' So I beseech you to still your hearts and lend me your ears. If you take your honorable lives and disappear like the mists of the rainy season on the plains of Musashi, only your sorrowful corpses will return to Shinano. There is still no knowing if Sutematsu will appear and return on his own. You have not seen his body, nor do you know his whereabouts, or whether he is alive or dead. First, you should ascertain where he went. If we still remain uncertain of his condition, though we may be insufficient, my wife and I will accompany you to Shinano as witnesses and explain everything that transpired. However, should our best efforts fail to provide a satisfactory explanation and your lord be displeased, it may still lead to disastrous consequences. For now, though, we implore you to heed our plan."

The couple did their best to persuade the two men, and after a while changed their minds, agreeing to follow Kinosuke's counsel. They gathered their men and stayed in the area for a while, scouring for Sutematsu's whereabouts. Yet, with no leads to guide them, they embarked on the journey back to Shinano, disheartened and powerless.

Now the tale returns to the young Otsuna. She had been staying as a pilgrim in the house of Katanaya Ban'emon in Yukinoshita, Kamakura,

11.7

and had happened upon Sekiya in a dire situation. Without thinking, Otsuna had displayed her power and became the talk of the town, making her continued stay impossible.

(11.7)

Consequently, she left Yukinoshita and embarked on a journey to Shinano. Hastening along the road, she found herself in the plains of Musashi. There, she approached a lone house, extending her ladle and requesting alms for her pilgrimage. A woman in her thirties came out of the house clutching a handful of wheat. She gave Otsuna a look, taking in her appearance and garments.

"Pilgrim, are there any fellow pilgrims with you, dear girl? You are so young. And your looks! Why is someone as uncommonly lovely as you traveling as a pilgrim? If you don't mind, I would like to hear this," said the woman kindly.

Otsuna replied, "Because of my age, wherever I go, I am met with suspicion and questions. I am originally from the area around Mount Tate in Etchū, born into a worthless peasant family. Sadly, my parents fell ill and passed away unexpectedly. I have no other relatives to rely on, so I chose to go on the Bandō Pilgrimage to pray for my parents in the afterlife. I sold what little of a house I had, and once I had enough travel money, I left my homeland behind, relying on alms as I traveled through the country. If only I could find someone with whom I could live, I would gladly seek apprenticeship or serve as a live-in maid, content to spend my days. Alas, I am but a wanderer, lost and alone on these endless roads. Such is the sum of my story."

The owner of the house smiled. "The sun is already going into the west, and it is a long way to the next village with an inn. You may spend the night here. I will give you lodging as alms."

Overjoyed, Otsuna said, "If you let me stay here all night, I wonder what merit it will bring you," and thanked her host respectfully.

"Well then, come inside already," said the woman with kind hospitality. "Take off your straw sandals and your gaiters. Sit near the hearth, stretch your legs, relax and heal your fatigue. I don't have much in terms of an evening meal, but I will give you what I have."

Otsuna did as she was told, removed her sleeveless *oizuri* pilgrim's overcoat, and fixed her belt. Then, without reserve and feeling at home, she rested from the fatigue of the road.

As the day grew into night, the lantern came on, and they had the evening meal. Afterwards, the owner of the house and Otsuna sat by the hearth, breaking brushwood for the fire while they talked about everything and nothing. As they talked, Otsuna saw no signs of a man living in the house. This seemed a bit odd to her, so she said to the owner, "You really are tough, living all alone out here in this lonesome house, not getting lonely," and laughed.

The mistress of the house also smiled. "I thought I would only stay here once in a while, but as the days and years have passed, I enjoy the tempests that blow through the pine trees, the moonlight leaking through the eaves, the wind in the silvergrass, and sounds of the insects. It makes me feel at ease. At times I also rent out the house to travelers, but my husband is making his living in the mountains, so he is rarely home, and I have nights where I am alone. Oh my, the temple bell just struck the first strike of the night. You can sleep by this bamboo folding screen. Tomorrow, get up at your own pace, and when you have finished your breakfast, you should be quiet as you leave. Now, chop-chop," she said, and took out some futons.

(11.8)

When she did this, the futon made a shining cleaver knife fall from the closet. Surprised, Otsuna said, "What is this cleaver?" and tried to pick it up, but the mistress would not let her have it, and snatched it from the floor.

As she held the knife in a backhand grip, she said, "I was hoping to do this after the night had grown later, but I guess I might as well tell you the story of this knife since it fell out on its own. This blade is for making sure peregrine travelers who come to stay here do not return home alive. You are a pilgrim so you should have some travel funds with you, even if just a little. Do exactly as I say, and I will take you to Koigakubo and make some money off you. If you utter as much as a peep against me, this knife will pay your stomach a visit and I'll sell your liver as medicine! It is a blood-soaked job, and I thought I'd let you sleep first, so I didn't say anything. But taking the money from travelers staying here in exchange for their lives is my trade! For when people

11.8

talk about the demonic will-o'-wisp fires of the fields of Musashi, they talk of me, Onibi! But now, will it be your life, or will you come with me to Koigakubo to be sold when morning comes? What is your answer?" Onibi's expression changed, and her hair stood on end.

Otsuna intentionally shuddered and trembled as she said, "To think that the lone house in Musashi they say is the home to an oni demon that will not let you return alive was here! Woe is me, a Bandō pilgrim scared for her life and with no one to turn to! I will give you all my travel money, if you will but spare my life." She pulled out the wallet in her breast pocket with both hands. "Please, take this and let me go!"

She opened the wallet, revealing fifty ryō in koban. When Onibi saw the coins, shining like yellow mountain roses, she exclaimed with an air of shock, "What an unfittingly large sum of travel money for a pilgrim. This will do in exchange for your life."

Consumed by her greed, the mistress of the house then put the knife down beside her. Her avaricious heart convinced her that she had won the money and could now do as she pleased, so she moved for the wallet. Without a moment's delay, Otsuna grabbed Onibi and pushed her down, twisting both her arms behind her back. Onibi was skilled at fighting and would not let Otsuna have her way, but although she struggled, there was no way she could ever match the pilgrim's strength. All she could do was squirm in vain and with regret under Otsuna's knee.

Otsuna laughed, grabbed a rope next to her, and tied Onibi up

11.9

tightly. Then she roused the lantern, faced Onibi, and said, “Unlike what you thought, I am not some weak woman you can treat like a child. I saw through what you were all about and deliberately showed you the money in my wallet. Now, you’re going to have to add your profits to my fifty ryō and make it a hundred! You must have money from all those innocent travelers you killed. Tell me and hide nothing! I will take it as a pilgrim and give it as offerings at the temples. Now, I am going to squash you and kill you without using a blade!”

Otsuna stepped into the garden and picked up a large stepping stone the size of a rice bale like it was nothing. Then she went and held the stone over Onibi’s head, ready to crush her at any moment. Onibi panicked, her teeth clattering from fear and her face turning as pale as if she were already dead. She trembled and apologized, “You must be a tengu or a mountain god or the spirit of Mount Togakushi itself! Please, I beg you, spare my life! I have money saved up. You can have it all. Please forgive me!”

(11.9)

Even though her teeth clattered with fear, she still managed to slowly edge herself over next to the hearth. She extended her foot and reached the signal she had set up to call her allies. When she pulled down the bamboo pothook over the hearth, an unexpected gunpowder signal went off from the roof of the house. Immediately, five or six wild and heavily armed men emerged from the floor, throwing aside the tatami mats. They saw Otsuna and were surprised. As they looked around the room to see if there were any male travelers with her, Otsuna threw the stepping stone into the garden with such force that it made a great tremor as it buried itself halfway into the ground. Even these fiendish men were completely horrified by the gentle-looking girl's unexpected valor. They exchanged looks amongst themselves, and none dared strike at Otsuna.

Still tied up and lying next to the hearth, Onibi said with a trembling voice, "This young lady pilgrim has appeared to punish us for our evil deeds and sins, and she must certainly be a god of teaching! You should not think any crude thoughts."

Then Onibi told the men what happened, after which Otsuna spoke in a soft tone, "I am neither a tengu nor a god, but I am someone who wants something from you. But before I tell you the specifics of what I want, I shall show you what I am capable of." She got up, went to the half-buried boulder, and without any difficulty, she picked it up like it was lighter than a brazier and easily carried it back to the hearth. "Since I am a woman, I cannot carry a blade, but if I have something heavy close to me, be it rock or metal, I have been trained so I can crush anyone who turns a blade on me. Is it for this purpose that you have put the rock here as a stoop?"

The men all replied at once, "No, that stepping stone must weigh a good hundred kan.[5] No one has ever been able to even wiggle it by their own strength."

Otsuna again held the stone lightly in her hands. "Then I shall hand it to you, and you can put it back where it belongs," she said, and held it out like it weighed nothing, sending all the men sprawling to the floor with shock.

Otsuna hurled the stone back in the yard, making an impact like an earthquake. No one said anything, as they were stunned by her sheer power. Otsuna undid Onibi's ropes, sat down, and took out a scroll from within her breast pocket.

"If you have truly surrendered to me, then pledge yourself in blood on this scroll and become my subordinates. What say you?" she pressed with determination.

Onibi and the five bandits prostrated themselves and declared together, "Though we may not comprehend the reason behind it, we cannot defy your command. We will follow you!"

Otsuna then sat back down in the seat of honor in the room. "I have a long-held ambition, and this is the signature scroll I use to sometimes gather compatriots. Show you will join me by signing your names and sealing it with your blood. If you do not do this, I cannot rest easily here for even one night. Will you comply?"

She opened the scroll and pushed it forward. Without hesitation, Onibi and the rugged men signed their names and sealed it with their blood. Then they said, "We are, from this moment forth, your sworn subjects. We pray to the gods and swear to the Buddhas we shall not deceive you. Reveal your plans and desires so that we may understand them."

---

5 1 kan = 3.75 kilos.

11.10

Text in box: Sutematsu enjoying and playing with paper frogs. Jiraiya hands Sutematsu over to Yuminosuke and returns to Mount Kurohime.

Otsuna straightened up and told them, "My wish is none other than this... On Mount Tate in Etchū, I encountered a divine being known as Katsuyu Sennin, the slug hermit. He told me, 'You have a destiny with the man who is hailed as a gallant beneath the heavens. You must travel the nearby lands and gather people. The roads will be arduous and there will be many who are greedy and unjust. You must punish them and spread their wealth to benefit the people.' Though I am but a young girl, these are the words of the gods. I shall punish the unjust and the greedy, guiding them onto the right path and aiding the impoverished. This is the holy vow that I am trying to fulfill. Seeing as tonight we have sealed our bond, I shall give you some money for drinking."

(11.10)

Otsuna took out money from her wallet and gave each of the six people five koban coins. Ecstatic with joy, they warmed up their homemade saké and roasted pheasant meat on skewers, which they offered to Otsuna. They decided it was now time to tell her about the leader. Among the five men, their leader was called Horikane no Itoroku, who appeared to be Onibi's husband. The rest were named Shinozuka Rikurō, Kuryū no Shirō, Hatano Saburō, and Watari no Gorō. Together, they were known as the Four Heavenly Kings of Itoroku of Musashi. They had many comrades who had infiltrated the neighboring provinces, and so had additional support to call upon, should they need it. Otsuna decided to stay in the area, investigate the surrounding villages, and make plans. Before the sun had risen, she departed from the house to begin her investigations.

At the same time, Jiraiya Shūma Hiroyuki of Mount Kurohime had kidnapped Sutematsu in Bunbaigawara in Musashi and brought him along to the mountain fortress. When his subordinates and Sutematsu's wet nurse made sure the boy was safe, all rejoiced and became high spirited. With Sutematsu by his side, Jiraiya addressed the wet nurse who had cared for him.

"Although being so very young, the time became ripe and Sutematsu finally took revenge for his parents. A considerable number of people have been dispatched from Shinano to take him back, both to resume his service to the Sarashina clan and to restore his house. However, I wanted him to bid a proper farewell to all the people here in the mountain fortress whom he has grown fond of during his stay. So, I secretly stole him away as he was being escorted back to Shinano. Tonight, he will stay here, but tomorrow I will take him back to Shinano. I ask that you all fill your cups for a farewell toast. Although you may meet him again in the future, let us bid him a proper farewell."

Following Jiraiya's words, the men prepared food and drinks, and a farewell feast commenced. Nonetheless, the wet nurse was especially sad to part with Sutematsu, and the little toads that Sutematsu had played with and become friends with, must have heard and understood what was going on. They were jumping all over the floor, crying and lamenting, looking as if they were sorry to part with him. Jiraiya himself was also deeply moved and mourned in silence.

The next morning, Jiraiya assembled a group of his followers to pose as a samurai retinue. They carried palanquins, spears, and crates on carrying poles, attired in *hakama* and haori suitable for travel. Placing Sutematsu in a palanquin, they embarked on their journey to Sarashina in Shinano.

And so, Jiraiya arrived in Shinano before the day was over. He made his way to Takasago Yuminosuke's mansion and humbly requested entry at the gate. He told them he was Ogata Shūma Hiroyuki from Mount Kurohime, and that he would like to see the master of the house if at home. He explained that he underwent a long journey just for this purpose. When the receiving samurai heard the name Ogata Shūma, they immediately recognized him as the infamous bandit Jiraiya. Without delay, they informed Yuminosuke, who welcomed Jiraiya into the parlor room. Finally, the two men met and exchanged greetings, with Jiraiya respectfully approaching Yuminosuke on his knees.

(11.11)

"The reason I am paying you this unannounced visit is none other than this. A long time ago now, while I roamed Kamakura, I came upon your sister Misao and her mother-in-law Kozue. They had been lying in wait for the fiend Gundazaemon at the Hatchō embankment. They announced their revenge on him, but sadly, because they were but weak women and no match for him, he cut them down in a counterattack. At that point, I happened to be passing by, and the wounded Misao called me to a halt. She told me what happened and single-mindedly asked me to take care of her young child. The woman had poured all her heart into her attack, but to no avail. She had been countered and I found her story so very pitiful, so I accepted her plea and picked up the boy. Then I said to her, 'I have no relation or connection to you, but I have understood your situation. Your wounds are grave, so I am unsure if medical care will help you. I will take care of this child, tell your older brother Yuminosuke-dono what has happened, and will have the child take his revenge and bring you satisfaction. Now, rest easy, and enter nirvana. Namu Amida Butsu.' I said the nembutsu prayer to soothe her, and then she passed away.

"Luckily, as I wondered what to do about her body, two men called Tsuruhashi Kinosuke and Chōbei happened to pass by. I entrusted them with the burial of Lady Kozue and Misao-dono, and they buried them at the temple of the unknown, giving the ladies a kind funeral service. Afterwards, Kinosuke's wife breastfed the boy and took care of him, and since we did not know his given name, I named him Sutematsu and raised him as my own. However, because I am who I am, I face many perils, which I shall not tell you about, and he grew much faster than a boy of his age should. Even at three years old, he possessed the appearance and intelligence of a five or six-year-old. He took to me immediately, and I engaged a wet nurse and took Sutematsu with me to my mountain fortress on Mount Kurohime, where I showered him with all my love.

"However, earlier this year, I experienced a peculiar dream, telling me of the villain Tatsumaki Arakurō, who had fallen victim to a mysterious illness, altering his appearance. The dream guided me to journey to Kamakura, where Arakurō's destiny would reach its end. Simultaneously, it became apparent that Arakurō was conspiring with Urafuji Saemon of Kai to incite rebellion. The other accomplices, Yokoshima Guheida and Shikano Fuehachi, were imprisoned under the strict orders of the Kanrei. Initially, I wanted to wait for the boy to grow up before having him take his revenge and quell the bloodthirst of those departed, but since there was a risk of Arakurō also being captured, we were pressed for time. I had to ask Kinosuke and Chōbei to help him get vengeance. Since Sutematsu is still so young, they helped him hold the blade and deliver the final blow. In a symbolic act, they offered Arakurō's head to the spirit tablets of Sutematsu's parents, granting Sutematsu the merit of fulfilling Misao-dono's request. With Misao-dono's request fulfilled, there is no longer a reason for Sutematsu to stay in my mountain fortress. Hence, I have brought the young boy here today to hand him over to you. These are the circumstances that compelled me to pay this unannounced visit."

Yuminosuke listened to Jiraiya's tale from start to finish and felt his deep compassion. Then he said, "You took upon yourself the request of someone you are not even related to by blood and raised an orphan who was only three or four years old. You even have such a kind heart that you helped him get satisfaction. I have no words to express my gratitude to you."

As Yuminosuke arranged for drinks and food to be brought out, Jiraiya went to the palanquin, retrieved Sutematsu, and presented him before Yuminosuke.

"From this moment on, you shall live here. The future of the Himematsu house will now pass to you," said Jiraiya, and introduced Sutematsu to Yuminosuke. Although only being four years old, the boy was outstandingly tall and had an air of maturity about him. Today was the first time Yuminosuke ever saw his younger sister Misao's only remnant.

11.11

11.12

Part II

(11.12)

With sincerity, Yuminosuke openly shared his story of shame and remorse to his visitors. “I have been hopeless, wanting to help my sister get satisfaction and wasting so much time. Yet, Jiraiya, who bears no blood relation to us, raised Misao’s orphaned son and fulfilled her long-held desire. It makes me regret the pointless things I did before. And alas, poor Matsuhei the servant! I knew him as his master when he served in the Himematsu household. Even if he were but a servant, he joined the vendetta due to his loyalty. To obtain a cure for Kozue’s eye disease, he took his own life and even sacrificed the life of the monkey he had tamed. This all became the catalyst for the disaster that was to come. One could argue it was only due to Kozue’s eyes being cured that they were struck down in a counterattack. Seen from that perspective, Matsuhei threw away his life for merit but died like a dog. All military fortune must have left him and both the kami and the Buddhas must have abandoned him. As for myself, I spent years traversing the lands incognito, with neither victory nor merit to show for it. Now, compared to your noble deeds, my futile pursuits as a warrior for my sister seem utterly foolish. I am consumed by shame!”

Jiraiya responded, “A long time ago now, when the Sarashina Hangan and the Tsukikage Gunryō were to have their wedding in this very house, I disguised as an envoy of the Kanrei of Kamakura, stole the princess, and secretly sent someone else in her stead. The imposter snuck into the mansion and stole the Ogata family tree along with the seal to deploy the armies. Motivated by my ambitions, I resorted to a dishonorable and momentary strategy. However, you spared the imposter’s life, allowing her to escape. Today, I offer Sutematsu as a token of gratitude for that mercy. And what’s more, at that time, the person I thought was the princess was actually your daughter. I am astounded by your perceptiveness, as you had already discerned my intentions beforehand. It is one of the reasons I ensured the safe return of your daughter.

(11.13)

“Because of our complicated history, we have alternated between friends and foes with bows drawn and trained on each other. Yet, we have never had any resentment or grudge against the other, so I suggest we reconcile. Though I am unworthy, and my name has been sullied as the leader of mountain bandits, this is but a temporary state. Before long, I plan to rise up so that I may stand shoulder to shoulder with ordinary people. Until then, please do try to discern what measures I am going to take.”

After discussing their own faults, they apologized to each other.

Then Yuminosuke said, “I had no idea about this connection, so when we got the message from Kamakura, by order of my lord I sent Fukai Chinonai and Asuwa Hiban with a large party of men to escort Sutematsu. It is fortunate that you brought Sutematsu here before they returned.”

11.13

After saying this, he had his daughter Teruta bring the drinks and food and make Jiraiya feel welcome. Afterwards, she called Sutematsu to her and treated him kindly and amused him.

Now we return to the pilgrim Otsuna, who had stayed a rainy night in the house of Onibi in the plains of Musashi, where she subjugated a group of mountain bandits. Inquiring about the area, Otsuna learned there was a wealthy man in a village called Kogane. He hoarded a substantial treasure, but had taken every possible precaution to safeguard it, so the bandits could not easily get to it. The rich man was named Yokutsura Rinhei and he had not a shred of compassion in his heart. Through unjust means, he had done his utmost to gather money, but his wife and child left the world before him, so he had nothing to look forward to. He was never satisfied, and was so miserly that he would even burn his nail trimmings for lamp wicks. After the bandits told Otsuna everything, she devised a plan with Itoroku, Onibi, and their henchmen, and together they set out unto the plains of Musashi towards Kogane Village.

During the journey, Otsuna suddenly felt an extreme pain in her chest and chose to rest next to a Kōshin pillar.[6] As she tried alleviating

6 Kōshin faith is the belief in Shōmen Kongō who stops the three monkeys from reporting someone's bad deeds while they sleep. Usually adorned with the three monkeys.

the pressing feeling on her chest, a man of almost sixty was passing by. He stared at Otsuna as she was struggling with her sudden ailment. Although dressed as a pilgrim, she was a girl of no more than sixteen or seventeen. And her features were so lovely it could not be put into words. The man stood still, taken in by wondering how such a beautiful young girl could be a pilgrim.

Otsuna massaged her chest and spoke with a pained voice, exaggerating her discomfort, "I suddenly felt a tightness in my chest, and the pain became unbearable. I cannot possibly take another step. Please, if you have any medicine on you, could you spare me some?" She looked up at the man with a face like cherry blossoms in the rain, so beautiful that it sent shivers down his spine. As he became steadily infatuated with Otsuna, he rummaged around in the satchel at his hip.

"You are in luck, for I am carrying medicine with me here. Now, swallow this," he said, offering some medicine. She took it gladly, poured it in her mouth, and swallowed. But she still looked like she was in the grips of pain, so the man slowly edged closer, took her in his arms and sat her up. Then he rubbed her back and padded her chest, and after a while her discomfort subsided. Grateful for his kindness, Otsuna expressed her gratitude.

(11.14)

The man was happy and said, "I am Rinhei, from Kogane Village just over yonder. I don't expect there will be anyone to take care of you where you are going, should you be troubled again. For now, you should come to my house and rest for a while. And if you have any travel companions, they are welcome too. I will provide food and a place where they can rest without reserve."

Delighted, Otsuna replied, "I am traveling alone without any comrades. If it's not too much trouble, I would be grateful to stay with you briefly and find some rest. Thanks to your medicine, my chest has opened up and I can walk calmly again, so I ask you to please walk with me."

"In that case, I shall lead you," said Rinhei with a giddy smile on his face, and he guided Otsuna along the way.

Before long, they arrived at Rinhei's house. As Otsuna said that her affliction had more or less subsided, luck would have it that bath water had just been heated. Rinhei gave some instructions to his servants and offered Otsuna to take a bath.

As Otsuna bathed, Rinhei thought to himself, "My departed daughter was also eighteen years old, and now that I think about her, I realize that the pilgrim's build and face look very much like hers. Maybe I should adopt her as my daughter and raise her here in my home."

Rinhei retrieved some clothes belonging to his departed daughter and asked Otsuna to change into them. Otsuna was already born beautiful, but the clothes she changed into fit her so well that she was a hundred times more stunning than before. Rinhei was so happy that he ordered the maids to make a feast to celebrate Otsuna. They engaged in lively conversations about worldly matters late into the night. Eventually, Rinhei, thoroughly intoxicated, retired to his bedchamber to rest.

11.14

That night, in his drunken state, Rinhei called Otsuna to his bedside and made many indecent remarks. However, Otsuna did not do as he said and dealt with him adeptly. Rinhei finally decided that he would violate her, so he grabbed her hand and tried to pull her under his covers.

Otsuna grabbed his arm firmly and said, "I can allow your ill-natured jokes, but for you to try and violate me is crossing the line."

The firm grip left Rinhei's arm numb, and the pain coupled with being overpowered by a woman made him lose his nerve and sobered him up. Otsuna took her belt, tied Rinhei up securely, and as if she had given a signal, the doors to the garden opened. A large number of bandits stormed inside. The men and women in the house awoke from the noise and came out, but Otsuna tied up every last one of them.

(11.15)

Then, she turned to Rinhei and declared, "I've heard rumors of your vast treasure hidden in this house, so I purposefully pretended to be having a heart episode. My apparent illness made you lower your guard, and I got into your house. However, I am no bandit. You might not know of me, but I disguise myself as a pauper and capture those who by injustice and inhumanity gather treasure and make the common people suffer. I am Tsunade, the mountain sorceress, and on behalf of heaven I carryout teachings like the Kannon of Great Mercy! Tonight, I will have my followers take all the treasure in your storehouse and give it to the surrounding villages. Give me the key to the storehouse and take me to it!"

11.15

Shocked, Rinhei rolled out of his futon and cried out, "So, you are a bandit! No matter how much you make me suffer, I will not surrender my treasure. Sound the alarm, my servants! Call for the villagers!"

There was indeed a bell to sound the alarm in case of emergency, but all the staff of the house had been tied up and they could not move. All they could do was look on in silence. Otsuna issued a command to her followers, and they gave Rinhei a severe beating. Unable to stand the pain, Rinhei revealed the location of the storehouse key. Onibi, the female bandit of the Musashi plains, Horikane Itoroku, and the four bandits known as the Four Heavenly Kings—Kuryū, Shinozuka, Hatano, and Watari—all assembled, and they had their many accomplices light torches and open the storehouse, from which they carried out many gold coffers which they prepared for transport. Afterwards, they went to the kitchen, where they roused the fire and warmed tea. They pulled out the rice bucket and rummaged through the cupboard.

"Such a cheapskate for a rich man!" one of them exclaimed. "If he doesn't want to eat anything, that's his business, but he doesn't even have pickled takuan horseradish! If that be the case, let's just eat the miso pickled eggplant and gourd together with some rice with hot water."

One of the more thoughtful bandits then found a saké jar. With a ladle, he distributed the saké in teacups. The bandits then ate all the rice in the sizeable rice bucket, leaving nothing behind, and drank all the saké.

11.16

"We are already full from eating rations, so taking any more will just be casting shame on Rinhei. Let's hurry and leave before the night dawns," said the bandits. Pleased with their triumph, they took as much treasure as they desired and departed.

Otsuna had been giving the orders from start to finish, and now she said to Rinhei, "Tonight, we have plundered and taken the treasure you spent years accumulating. It may appear as though we have strayed from the righteous path, but I have grand ambitions and intend to return the money in due course. When that time comes, we shall meet again." With that, she got up, took off the clothes she had been given, and changed into her previous pilgrim attire. Though she appeared as a simple country girl, she possessed unknown strength and wisdom. Everyone held their breath at the sight of her, and in silence, she left with her subordinates.

(11.16)

Thus, Rinhei's servants remained bound until dawn broke. When people from the neighborhood awoke and arrived, they were shocked by what they saw. They untied and did away with the ropes, took care of the servants, and a report was filed with the local magistrate, Mijin Kotsuhei.

Shocked, Kotsuhei gritted his teeth and said, "This must be the work of some cursed bandits! If necessary, I shall split the grass to find them, hand them over to Kamakura, and have them executed!" He gathered his men, divided them into groups, and dispatched them to nearby villages and areas to investigate Otsuna's whereabouts.

Meanwhile, Otsuna had sent Onibi and Itoroku running ahead of her. She took her straw hat, threw it into the Karasu River, and stepped onto it. As if she walked on flat ground, she calmly rode the currents down river, and before long, she arrived near Onibi's house in the Musashi plains. Neither Itoroku nor any of his bandits had reached the house yet, so Otsuna thought they must be delayed by the heavy load they were carrying.

We now return to Jiraiya of Mount Kurohime. After handing Sutematsu over to Yuminosuke, he returned to his home. On further thought, he realized Chōbei and Kinosuke should be informed of the events. Using his yōjutsu, he departed from the mountain and set out on the Shinshū Road towards Kamakura. Along the way, Jiraiya encountered Kinosuke and his wife. He informed them about Sutematsu and discreetly asked them to relay the message to Hibanda and Chinonai. Kinosuke understood and passed the knowledge on to the two men, who were both extremely happy to hear the news, but also dumbfounded and fearful at the miraculous and uncanny Jiraiya.

Kinosuke and his wife would go with the two samurai to the Sarashina clan and explain all that had happened, and it was by no fault of Chinonai and Hibanda.

(11.17)

Jiraiya, on the other hand, continued his journey to Kamakura, bidding farewell to Kinosuke and his wife as they departed for Shinano.

Meanwhile, the magistrate of Musashi, Mijin Kotsuhei, diligently investigated Otsuna's whereabouts. He received information from an informant stating a suspicious female pilgrim had been sighted in the Ōmiya area. Acting upon this tip, Kotsuhei gathered his deputies and went to Ōmiya to investigate. One night, Kotsuhei rested for a while in the sacred Myōjin Forest, when a suspicious woman wearing a straw hat and coat walked past the torii gate.[7] Kotsuhei grabbed his javelin and thrust it at her, but she dodged, grabbing the javelin at the neck and tried to take it away from him. Just then, a samurai came, obstructing their fight. The three maneuvered around each other equally, but carried by the impetus of the fight, Kotsuhei's spear struck a nearby hinoki tree, creating sparks that illuminated their faces. The other two vanished without a trace, leaving Kotsuhei shocked and bewildered.

Back in fortress on Mount Kurohime, Jiraiya had returned from Kamakura. One day, while resting from the trip, he had an idea and

7 The Myōjin Forest is most likely the forest belonging to Hikawa Jinja Shrine.

11.17

summoned a large number of his men. He told them, "While I have been considering my fortunes lately, I have received news that I must soon start making plans for battle. These days, either the time to carry out my ambitions will come, or the lord of Kamakura will send a great host to capture us here in the mountain fortress. There is no way of knowing which will come first. Therefore, I need all the men I have scattered across the neighboring provinces to gather here as quickly as possible."

Musasabi Tenbachi,[8] understanding the urgency, sent out a notice in secret, calling on all the underlings. The bandits who lived across the provinces all rallied to Jiraiya's side.

(11.18)

In a strange twist of fate, Jiraiya had encountered a suspicious woman in the sacred Myōjin Forest on a previous night. Since then, his heart had been melancholic, completely incapable of forgetting the woman, whose face and figure he had but caught the faintest glimpse of. Jiraiya was perplexed by his own emotions.

However, in the early hours of this particular night, whether it was real or a dream, a snake, one také long[9] appeared at Jiraiya's bedside. Gripped in its jaws was the head of a woman, which looked freshly severed. The snake emanated a deep resentment towards Jiraiya, but he was unmatched in bravery, so he did not show any indication of fear. When

8 Previously Musasabi's name was Nobusuma.

9 3.03 meters.

11.18

he steeled his gaze, he recognized the head as that of Tagane, who died years ago when Ayame, mad with jealousy, had bitten the woman to death.

"Is this snake the grudge of the jealous Ayame? How many years have passed since then? Is it due to my own uncertainties that this long-past event manifests before my eyes tonight? How uncanny," pondered Jiraiya, bravely holding firm as he glared at the snake.

Suddenly, the snake spoke with a human voice. "It is natural to suspect a grudge long gone, because long ago, Ayame proved no match for you and met her demise. She departed this world consumed by jealous hatred, yet her vengeful soul could not find peace. It transformed into this snake, and her malice towards Tagane-dono prevented both of them from reaching Buddhahood. Every day was torturous, and my spirit wandered the space between life, death, and rebirth, thinking of placing a grudge on you as well.

(11.19)

"However, your bravery is too overpowering, so I could not even approach you. As the months and years passed, I eventually wandered into Hell Valley on Mount Tate in Etchū, where the hermit Katsuyu imparted teachings to me. It revealed your destined path, where you will encounter a woman fated to be your wife since a previous life. So, I gave up on you, made a connection with the Buddha, and was told I will leave this plain of existence and be reborn in paradise and attain

11.19

Nirvana. Although pitiful, I have appeared in this borrowed form to atone for the sake of my future. With this, my grudge shall be lifted, but I am forced to appear in this embarrassing snake-form to expiate my sins. Now, I can be at peace."

As the snake uttered these words, a five-colored smoke enveloped it and the head of Tagane, transforming into the shape of a Buddha. However, Jiraiya remained skeptical, doubting whether this apparition was merely a manifestation of his inner turmoil, and he kept his eyes fixed on the apparition.

(11.20)

The bell struck seven or eight times with a tremendous toll, awakening Jiraiya. Convinced that it must have been only a fanciful dream, appearing before him for a fleeting moment, he thought, "Yet, the words spoken by the apparition linger in my mind, mentioning the attainment of Buddhahood through the teachings of a hermit named Katsuyu, unknown to me, from Mount Tate in Etchū. My thoughts are in turmoil, contemplating whether it was a dream or a revelation. Although I hold no romantic feelings for her, the image of the woman that flickered before my eyes remains unforgettable. There must be a reason behind this." As Jiraiya ruminated on these thoughts, his doubts and suspicions only deepened.

11.20

Signpost: Border of the territory of Shinano. | Border of Kai.

Takasago Yuminosuke, the courageous retainer of the Sarashina clan of Shinshū, had received the orphaned boy Sutematsu from Jiraiya and made a report of what happened to his lord Mitsuaki. However, Jiraiya had mysteriously arrived together with Sutematsu before the return of Hibanda and Chinonai, who he had sent to Kamakura to escort the boy. Jiraiya's yōjutsu had furrowed many brows. Afterwards, Hibanda and Chinonai arrived together with Kinosuke and his wife. They told Yuminosuke how a violent wind kidnapped Sutematsu in Bunbaigawara, leaving no trace of where he was taken. Kinosuke then explained how he came all this way to stand witness. Yuminosuke reassured them, explaining how Jiraiya came on a previous day and delivered Sutematsu unharmed. He rewarded Kinosuke greatly and they all breathed a sigh of relief.

Meanwhile, reports continued to surface from commoners, saying Urafuji Saemon, the ruler of Mount Kurokoma in Kai, and his allies were absorbed in schemes of invasion. The Sarashina clan sent soldiers to the borders of its territory as a precaution, and Takasago Yuminosuke went on an inspection tour of the territorial borders. He went to the village heads, reminding and ordering them not to falter in sending men to guard the border.

(11.21)

As he was going around the villages, he came across a lone female pilgrim on the road. Upon closer inspection, Yuminosuke recognized

11.21

Top-left box: In the next book, you can see how the Sarashina clan sends Teruta as a messenger to inquire about the safety of the wife of the Tsukikage clan, who is suffering from a mysterious illness.

her as none other than Otsuna, whom he had previously conversed with at Katanaya Ban'emon's house in Yukinoshita in Kamakura.

"Hey, pilgrim! Have you forgotten me?" he called out, stopping her in her tracks.

The pilgrim smiled at him and knelt on the ground. "My lord, thank you for recognizing me. I also remember you, but I was afraid it would be rude of me to speak out, so I refrained from saying anything. I am actually trying to find your mansion, so it's incredibly fortunate that we meet here on the way! It truly makes me happy beyond words." She bowed deeply until her forehead touched the ground.

Yuminosuke returned a smile and said, "I am equally delighted! However, as I am currently on official business, I hesitate to accompany you to my residence. Fortunately, it is nearby, so you should be able to find it easily."

Yuminosuke kindly provided her with directions to the mansion, and they continued on their separate paths. In volume twelve, you shall know more of Otsuna's good and evil.

(11.22)

A suspicious ghostly air rises from the Tsukikage clan's mansion.

Some time ago, the Tsukikage clan of Echigo sent Sekiya, a lady-in-waiting, to Hasedera Temple to offer prayers on their behalf. Along the way, she encountered a dangerous situation but was saved by Otsuna. When Sekiya told her master what happened, he said, "This Otsuna does indeed possess a mysterious strength. We shall send for her and give her a stipend," and had a quick-witted samurai go to Kamakura. Unfortunately, he had no strategy and relied only on rumors, so he was unable to locate Otsuna, and returned disappointed and empty-handed, unable to accomplish his goal.

11.22

What happened afterwards with the Tsukikage, the Sarashina, Jiraiya, Otsuna, and Sutematsu, will be told in books twelve and thirteen.

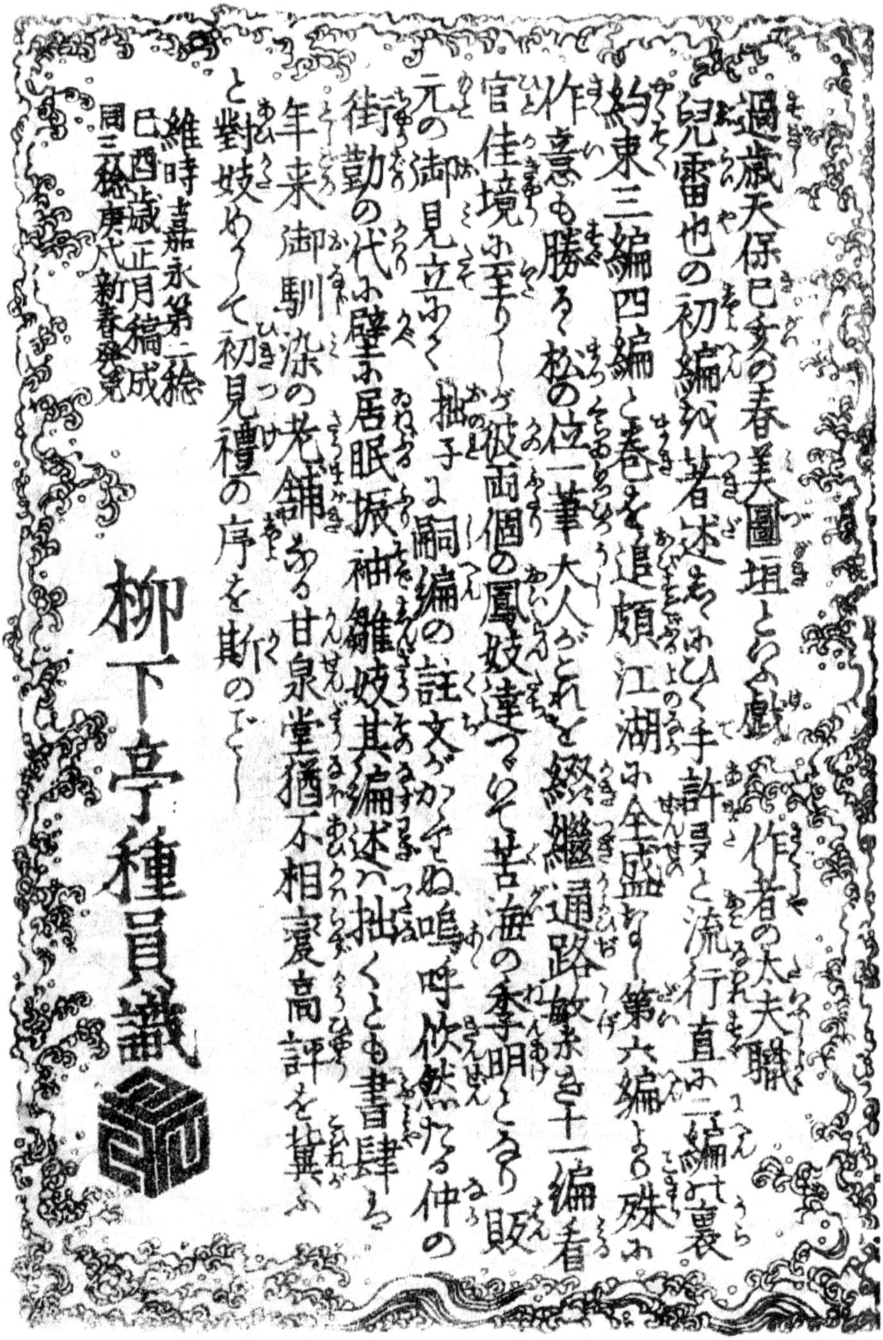
過歳天保巳亥の春美圖垣とふ戯作者の大夫職
兒雷也の初編を著述して手許多と流行直に二編は裏
約束三編四編と巻を追頗江湖に全盛なす第六編より殊に
作意も勝る松の位一筆大人がこれを総繼通路なき十一編看
官佳境に至りしが彼両個の鳳妓達ぞそ苦海の季明となり販
元の御見立にて拙子は嗣編の註文ながつぬ嗚呼依然たる仲の
街勤の代に壁に居眠振袖雛妓其編述へ拙くとも書肆は
年来御馴染の老舗なる甘泉堂猶不相変高評を冀ふ
と對妓めして初見禮の序を斯のごとし
維時嘉永第二稔
巳酉歳正月稿成
同三稔庚戌新春発兌
柳下亭種員識

12.1

Book 12

Previously, in spring of the Earth Boar year in the Tenpō era, Mizugaki, the *gesaku* writer akin to a *taifushoku* courtesan,[1] penned the first book of Jiraiya. It was in such great demand, that he was immediately given an offer for a second book, which was followed by a third and a fourth. From the sixth book, the writer Ippitsu Ushi, a *matsu-no-kurai*[2] brimming with creative ideas, took over. He kept going until book eleven, the tale reaching a climax for the readers.

However, these two *oiran*[3] reached the end of their contract with this world, so the publisher went to select a new courtesan, and I received an order for this follow-up volume. I, a *suigi* apprentice *geisha*, who, instead of working in the lively town, only naps in her long-sleeved *furisode* kimono. Albeit this book is clumsy, Kansendō is a long-established and well-known publishing house, and like the first courtesy greeting of a new courtesan, I pray this book meets continued high praise.

Written: Kaei 2—Year of the Earth Rooster—New Year (1849)
Published: Kaei 3—Year of the Iron Dog—Spring (1850)
Ryūkatei Tanekazu

1 A term for a courtesan of the highest rank idolized in Edo period society.

2 A different term for a courtesan of the highest rank. Also an idol of the Edo period.

3 Blanket term for the highest-ranking courtesans.

12.2

The heroine Tsunade. Later to become Jiraiya's wife.

Emiwaka the trainee monk of the Yoneyama Temple. Later becoming Orochimaru, the pirate leader of Mount Mano on Sado Island.

Jiraiya, Ogata Hiroyuki.

12.3

Hamaogi Rokusaburō, retainer of the Tsukikage clan.
Shikano Fuehachi.
The cormorant fisher and raftsman have names which you will learn in book thirteen.
The Fubuki Katatsuki tea container, a precious treasure of the Sarashina clan.
The Katsuyumaru tanto.
Mijin Kotsuhei.
Nunobiki Road.
Tamagawa Village.

A weir burning from the ambition of the cormorant that does not swallow it quarry.

—Shin Kikaku

12.4

The lay Buddhist pilgrim Jōun, real name Jiraiya.
The demon hag Okowa.
Okowa's daughter Kosono.

12.5

Part I

(12.5)
We begin this book with a different tale. In the Kubiki area of Echigo, in a place called Sekita Village,[4] there lived a country samurai named Matsuzaki Shirōdayū. He was a virtuoso with the bow and many, even from the Tsukikage Ryōshū's domain, were his disciples. He had a single male heir named Tamanosuke. Because Tamanosuke was fair looking and bore no signs of being born in the deep countryside, when he finally came of age, courters came from far and wide, asking if they could send their daughters to be his wife. However, Shirōdayū thought, "Tamanosuke's mother has left this world already, and I am getting old. So, unless a potential suitor possesses beauty that matches Tamanosuke and the ability to manage the household, he should not marry her." As a result, Tamanosuke remained without a wife.

Close to Sekita Village there lay a lake called Aoyagi Pond.[5] It was not particularly expansive, but its depths remained a mystery. The people there believed some creature ruled the lake, so they feared the watery abyss. Curiously however, since the age of twelve or thirteen, Tamanosuke had visited the lake every day to fish. His father and the

4 Present day Itakuraku Sekida.

5 Present day Boga Pond.

people tried to stop him, saying, "Something rules that lake, and it is feared by all. Just getting close to the lake is bad enough, but fishing in it is too dangerous. Stop it at once!" Yet, even though Tamanosuke was born with a mild disposition, no matter how many times people expressed this opinion to him, they did nothing to actually stop him, so he simply ignored them and continued his fishing excursions.

One day at the height of autumn, when Tamanosuke was eighteen years old, he had his manservant Hosaku carry a bamboo container with saké and went with him to Aoyagi Pond. He fished as he would usually do, but on that day the catch was so plentiful that he kept on fishing, not noticing that the sun went down. It wasn't until the mountain temple bell reverberated across the lake that he finally noticed the time and began packing up his fishing gear. As he was making ready to go home, the harvest moon rose above the mountain ridges, its light reflecting in the lake, and the insects chirped in the tall grass. The scene compelled him to open the saké container. He drank together with Hosaku and had a merry time. During which, an enchanting maiden no older than sixteen came out of nowhere and stood beside them.

"Two gentlemen pouring saké by themselves is such a lonely sight to behold. May I pour for you?" she seductively proposed, her intent to assist them apparent.

The two men thought nothing of it, and Tamanosuke said happily, "You have come at a good time. But forgive my curiosity, I haven't seen you around here before. From where do you hail?"

The maiden responded with a smile, "My name is Mokuzu, and not long ago, my mother and I arrived here from the capital." She revealed nothing else, choosing instead to sit down next to Tamanosuke.

(12.6)

She was very attentive at pouring saké for them, and before long, Hosaku became quite intoxicated. Stumbling into the grass, he collapsed and passed out, snoring loudly.

Sensing an opportune moment, the maiden spoke in a bashful tone, "I suspect you have not noticed, but I have observed you every day, reflected in the lake. There has been no one with whom I could share my longings, and even in my dreams I have not been able to forget about you. That's why I came here today. If you find me pitiable, I implore you to grant me your love, if only for this single night." With a sorrowful gaze, she drew closer to Tamanosuke.

He found himself entranced. The sails of his heart were filled with the winds of love, and hidden from prying eyes upon grassy pillows, they shared a profound affection, deeper than the depths of Aoyagi Pond.

Surprised at how much time had passed, Tamanosuke shook his manservant awake. Then, with his heart filled from the sorrow of parting, he returned home. From that moment, rumors spread like wildfire, leaving no one unaware that the maiden would secretly visit Tamanosuke's bedchamber every night.

Eventually when spring came around, Tamanosuke fell ill to an unknown sickness. As the months went by, his body grew frail and weak,

12.6

and he looked like he would not survive. Nevertheless, the woman continued her nightly visits like it was the first night for her to do so. People knew of these secret visits and started to find the whole thing very suspicious. Thus, they reported it to his father, Shirōdayū. Astonished by the revelation, he confronted his son about the matter, but Tamanosuke remained silent.

So Shirōdayū thought, "I will see through these nocturnal rendezvous and ascertain who the woman really is," and kept a prying eye out close to Tamanosuke's room late in the night. As the rumors suggested, a solitary maiden slipped into his son's chamber, engaging in hushed conversations.

When he listened carefully, Shirōdayū could hear Tamanosuke's voice, saying, "My father knows of us and has questioned me about you."

The maiden expressed her lament, pleading with utmost sincerity, "I am already carrying your child, and soon, when the month passes, I will give birth. You should come live together with me and the child in my home."

(12.7)

When Shirōdayū finished listening to all of this, he thought to himself, "This is indeed suspicious. I must find out where she goes," and made sure that he was well hidden. Just then, the rooster crowed, startling the two inside the bedchamber. Promising she would come back again the following night, the woman stepped down into the garden and left. Shirōdayū tailed her in secret. Eventually, she reached Aoyagi

12.7

Pond, and there, she disappeared from sight as if erased from existence. Shirōdayū observed all that unfolded very carefully, thinking to himself, "There is no doubt she is some sort of apparition." He returned home, prepared his bow and *hikime* arrows made for exorcizing malevolent spirits, and waited through the day that was dawning.

When the night again grew late, Shirōdayū verified the time, armed himself with his bow and arrows, and resumed his watch. Just as before, the apparition snuck into Tamanosuke's bedroom, engaging in whispered conversations. However, something felt different from the previous night. As the third quarter of the hour of the ox approached,[6] the apparition departed, making her way back to the lake.

"Before the night is over, we shall see if my suspicions are correct," thought Shirōdayū as he trailed her, constantly keeping her in his sights. Upon reaching the shore of the lake, Shirōdayū prayed to the kami and the buddhas, nocked an arrow on his bow, drew, and let loose. True to his aim, the arrow struck its mark flawlessly. The night sky cleared inexplicably, and moonbeams illuminated the surroundings.

(12.8)

However, a solitary cloud still lingered, obscuring a particular area of the sky. It rose up, ominous and dark, as the mountains trembled and echoed with a roar. Shirōdayū readied a second arrow, took aim at a part of the cloud that could conceal a woman, and released. Again,

6 About 02:00.

12.8

Top-right: Tamanosuke drowns himself in Aoyagi Pond.

the arrow hit its target unerringly. As the night gradually transformed into day, he surveyed the lake's surface, now stained crimson. Drifting amidst the water was a fearsome snake, impaled by an arrow through its neck and another deeply embedded in its left eye. Shirōdayū wanted to quickly inform people of what happened, so he gathered his servants and the villagers. When they saw the scene, there was none who was not impressed with Shirōdayū's archery skills.

He was determined to retrieve the serpent from the lake for closer examination. With the assistance of the young and courageous, they successfully pulled the serpent out of the water. Its body was at least two také long[7] and as thick as an old pine tree. They wondered how many years it must have been living in the lake for it to grow so enormous. Furthermore, when they looked at its belly, it appeared as if it had swallowed something. Shirōdayū had a hunch about its contents and commanded, "Someone, cut the belly open so we may see what is inside," but none volunteered to do it. They all tried to pass the responsibility to the person next to them, when finally, Hosaku, who had always come with Tamanosuke to the lake to fish, stepped forward and declared, "I will do it." Hosaku pulled out his hatchet and cut an opening about two shaku long[8] below the snake's throat, where

7 About 6 meters.

8 About 60 centimeters.

it looked like the snake had swallowed something. Inside the snake's womb lay a child.

Hosaku pulled it out and held it up to look at it. There was no doubt that it was a human child. Except, scales seemed to grow from its shoulders down its back. Its birth cries were loud, and everyone looked on in amazement. Shirōdayū, however, was lost in painful and wretched thoughts. "It is as the apparition said last night. This must be Tamanosuke's offspring. If this child reaches adulthood, it will probably bring untold calamities. I must kill it."

"Hand over the child. I will kill it and dispose of it," said Shirōdayū and tried to seize the infant. Until that moment, Hosaku had cradled the newborn without any particular attachment. However, at that instant, a single wisp of white smoke emerged from the serpent's lifeless mouth. In a silent and imperceptible manner, it drifted into Hosaku's chest. Though unseen by all and unnoticed by Hosaku himself, a shiver ran through his body, causing his hair to stand on end. Mysteriously, as he looked at the newborn, he began to pity it.

Hosaku pushed away the hand of his master who tried to take the child, and tears welled in his eyes. He pleaded, "Even if this child came from the belly of a serpent, just look at it! It looks no different from a human. What curse could possibly befall us if we allow it to live?" Refusing to let go of the child, Hosaku carried it home with him. Seeing his steadfast conviction, Shirōdayū realized there was nothing he could do and abandoned killing the baby. It was the serpent's grudge, which had entered Hosaku's being, compelling him to save the infant. In due course, the serpent's curse would be fulfilled.

Following this, Shirōdayū told the villagers to burn the serpent's corpse and dispose of it. He made sure none would speak to Tamanosuke about what happened. However, unbeknownst to Shirōdayū, someone told his son anyway. Upon learning the truth, Tamanosuke lost all will to live and secretly slipped out of the house that very night, making his way to Aoyagi Pond where he drowned himself. Shirōdayū and his family were consumed by immense grief, as it became clear their efforts had been in vain. Eventually, with tears streaming down their faces, they recovered Tamanosuke's lifeless body from the pond and sent it off for cremation.

Meanwhile, Hosaku harbored sympathy for the infant boy, and cared for him as if he were his own. He named the child Tamakichi, arranged for a wet nurse, and raised him diligently. Tamakichi quickly grew intelligent and was the spitting image of Tamanosuke, which caused Shirōdayū to eventually lose the desire to kill him. He thought of Tamakichi as the only legacy of his son, and when he looked at him, he saw him as a reminder to forget his sorrows.

And so, spring turned to autumn, and when Tamakichi turned five, he possessed incredible strength. He was as tall as a normal ten-year-old, and had a resolute spirit. Shirōdayū contemplated, "To ensure my son's well-being in the afterlife, it is best for him to enter a monastery to make sure the serpent's evil is eradicated from him."

12.9

He decided to make it so, and as luck would have it, he was very good friends with the head priest of Yoneyama Temple in the same area.[9] Shirōdayū went and said to the priest in a frank manner, "When this boy grows up, you must let him become a monk in your temple." Then he sent Hosaku together with Tamakichi to the temple, where the head priest took them in. The head priest initiated the young boy as a trainee monk and bestowed upon him a new name: Emiwaka, meaning "the smiling youth". However, those who were aware of Emiwaka's true lineage secretly referred to him by a different name: Hebiwaka, meaning "the young snake".

(12.9)
A decade passed like a fleeting dream, and when Emiwaka reached the age of sixteen, his behavior took a dark turn. He found great pleasure in theft and not only targeted his fellow monks but also the priests themselves. This misconduct led everyone in the temple to desire his capture and reprimanding, but Emiwaka possessed formidable strength, so there was none in the temple who could stand up to him. The head priest was at his wits' end, so he called on Hosaku in secret and implored him to reprimand Emiwaka.

Hosaku, deeply saddened by the situation, called Emiwaka to seek refuge under the shade of a tree. Tears welled up in his eyes as he said,

9 Real place. Nothing left but a ruin now.

"Because your ancestry is not like anyone else's, I have kept this truth from you. But it is time for you to know your true birth story." He recounted the story of Tamanosuke, the serpent, Shirōdayū shooting the serpent, and how he himself had cut open its belly and pulled out Emiwaka long ago. He continued, "Because of your origin, Shirōdayū-dono sincerely wanted you to become a monk. However, you have not followed his commands and only grown worse by the day. Perhaps, it is because you possess a dreadful soul, inheriting the malevolent spirit of a snake. I implore you, mend your heart and choose goodness!"

Upon hearing the truth and Hosaku's reproach, Emiwaka's countenance changed. His eyes ran red with blood and his breath became like fire. "I have heard that people call me 'Hebiwaka' in the shadows, so I had a feeling there was a reason like this. But now that I hear it is actually so, I have no intention to remain a monk. Instead, I will embrace my mother's legacy and harbor wicked thoughts of devouring humans. I shall unleash chaos, commit every vile act imaginable, and inflict suffering upon all. First on my list is Shirōdayū, the bane of my mother. I will break into the Matsuzaki house, tear him apart, and feast upon his liver. Then, I will annihilate every last person there until none remain!" Emiwaka sprung to his feet, consumed by insane wrath.

(12.10)

Hosaku exclaimed in shock, "For your heart to have grown so terrifying, your parentage has finally become obvious. There is no other option now. Rather than allowing you to commit such abhorrent acts against humanity, I must take your life!" He seized an axe that lay nearby, raised it, and swung it toward Emiwaka.

With the agility of a bird, Emiwaka evaded the blow and sneered, "Such a feeble move! I shall start my rampage with a bloodbath, killing you as an offering to my mother!" Tearing the axe from the man's grasp, he plunged it into Hosaku's shoulder, causing blood to spew forth like a cloud.

The people in the temple who witnessed the scene panicked and criedout, "Emiwaka has gone mad! He must be captured and restrained!" Although they attempted to subdue him, they were no match for his strength and fury.

One astute monk recognized that the only way to stand a chance against Emiwaka was through sheer numbers. He rushed to the belfry, intending to ring the bell and summon help from the nearby village. When Emiwaka saw this, he bellowed furiously, "You won't be ringing that bell!" He grabbed the monk and hurled him from the belfry. Then, with both hands, he yanked the bell free, raised it high above his head, and tossed it into the crowd. Shaking off and kicking those who tried to restrain him, Emiwaka then left to Sekita Village.

After rampaging through the Yoneyama Temple and leaving in a rage, Emiwaka finally arrived in Sekita Village around the third quarter of the hour of the ox.[10] After seeing that the main gate to the Matsuzaki house was locked up tight, he picked up a nearby boulder and threw it at

10 About 02:00.

12.10

Top-left box: Sado Island

the gate. The gate bolt shattered, and the doors swung open. Emiwaka stormed inside, immediately setting his eyes on a groggy manservant who had been awakened by the commotion. Without hesitation, Emiwaka lunged at the servant, ripping off his head and discarding it. Then he ran into the entrance hall of the house, and all who he saw, be they men or women, he either stomped or bit to death.

Despite Shirōdayū's bedroom being secluded at the rear of the house, shielding him from the sounds from the rest of the building, he heard the disturbance and was about to get up to investigate. However, Emiwaka already loomed over him. In his hands was a stone wash basin that he had picked up in the garden.

"You killed my serpent mother with your arrow. Now you shall experience her wrath!" Emiwaka declared, as he brought down the washbasin upon Shirōdayū, ending the man's life pitifully before he could even raise his voice. "That felt good, but I am still not satisfied," Emiwaka cursed, and he stormed out through the front gate in a fit of fury.

The people of the village finally heard about what was happening and came running from all directions, shouting, "Kill him! Capture him!"

Undeterred, Emiwaka charged into the crowd, scattering them with his immense strength. By the dim light of dawn, he reached the seaside, with a multitude of people still in close pursuit.

In the distance, Emiwaka caught sight of a single fishing boat amid the waves with someone who had gone out to fish during the night. When he noticed the boat was rowing towards his location, he dove into the sea and swam towards the boat. Perplexed, the captain of the vessel hesitated to allow Emiwaka aboard, raising his oar in defense. Swiftly evading the strike, Emiwaka seized the oar and deftly leapt onto the boat. He grabbed the fisherman by the scruff of his neck and unceremoniously tossed him into the water.

(12.11)

As the pursuing crowd anxiously cried out, "Don't let him escape!" the rhythmic stroke of the oars carried Emiwaka to the faraway island of Sado.

When Emiwaka successfully crossed the sea to Sado Island, he made a secret refuge for himself. His extraordinary strength attracted numerous bandits to join him, and he adopted a new name, Orochimaru, meaning "The Serpent". With his gang, they targeted merchant ships, cargo vessels, and ships laden with valuable goods. Boarding these vessels, they plundered their treasures. On occasion, they would venture ashore, breaking into affluent homes to rob them. Furthermore, Orochimaru had inherited the wicked nature of the snake, and his carnal desires were bottomless. When he saw a good-looking woman, he would abduct her and take her to his mountain hideout. His exploitative and selfish behavior inflicted suffering upon many.

The lords of various domains issued orders for his capture, but Emiwaka proved elusive. He would disappear into the mountains or take refuge on a ship at sea, constantly changing his whereabouts and working from an unfixed location. Hunting him down became a futile endeavor, and he wreaked havoc wherever he pleased.

Orochimaru crossed over to Sado Island the same year that Jiraiya left Nezumi-no-shuku in Shinano.

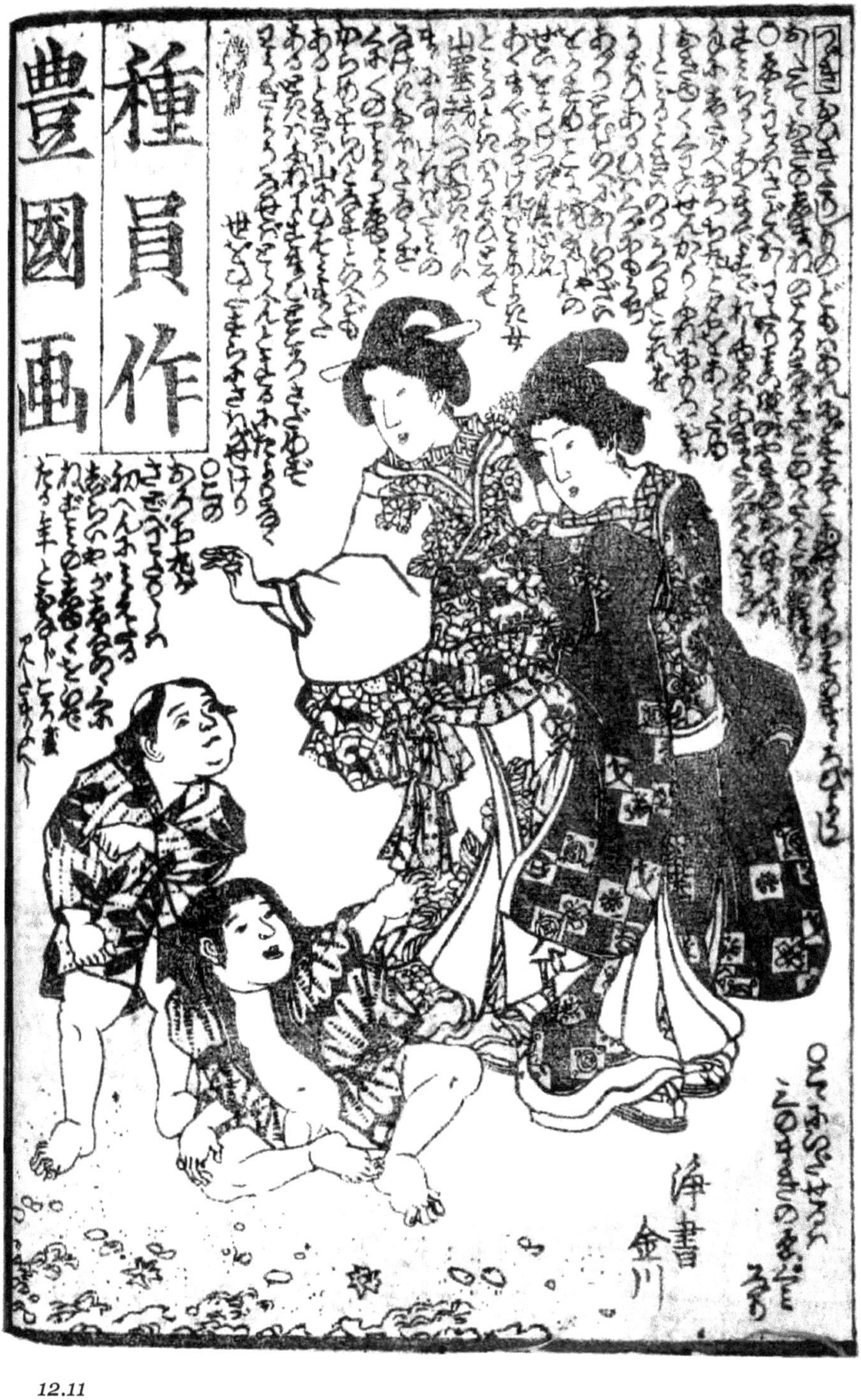

12.11

12.12

Part II

(12.12)

Previously, Tagoto-hime, the daughter of the Sarashina clan, had married into the Tsukikage clan, and she was very intimate with her husband Miyukinosuke Takanao. Because their mansion was not far from the seaside, which there was none of in Tagoto-hime's homeland Shinano, the couple frequently went to the beach close by for outings. In spring, they would hunt for cherry blossoms by Nagamine,[11] and in autumn, they would host moon viewing parties in Mitachi manor.[12] Whether catching fireflies in the evening or witnessing the beauty of snow in the morning, they invited many companions to join in their merriment, evoking envy from those who witnessed their harmonious relationship. Even commoners would remark, "Be it their looks or their relationship, they are such a fitting couple."

Today was the start of the third month, and the couple had brought a large group with them to the seashore in Nozumi for a seashell hunt during the low tide.[13] They put up a curtain around the beach, with the ladies-in-waiting collecting shells together with the couple and indulging in a day of amusement. Unbeknownst to them, Orochimaru, formerly Emiwaka, had taken refuge on Mount Mano in Sado, engaging in all manner of wicked acts. He had received information that the Miyukinosuke couple would be enjoying themselves on this very beach today.

"I think I will give that family a look, and when the opportunity arises, I shall step in and do my work," thought Orochimaru. He disguised a small boat with straw mats, making it appear as though it belonged to a fisherman venturing into the waves offshore.

(12.13)

From within the boat, he covertly observed the events unfolding on the beach. Born with the vile nature of a snake, his carnal desires were insatiable, and when he saw Tagoto-hime surrounded by her ladies-in-waiting on the beach, he instantly fell for her.

"What a beauty!" Orochimaru thought with excitement. "I can't imagine there are any other women in this world as exquisite as her. I must abduct her and take her to my hideout, where I can have my way with her."

Silently, he went ashore, but the number of samurai guards protecting her prevented him from finding an opportune moment to snatch her. He hesitated for a moment, and as sunset was imminent, one from the retinue said, "It is time to return to the manor." With palanquins encircled by guards on all sides, the party began their journey back to the manor. Orochimaru stood there, stunned, like he just had something taken from out of his hands. Then he followed the palanquins to see where they were going. Lost in thought, Orochimaru suddenly heard a voice calling out from behind him.

---

11 Area in Niigata City, previously by the water.

12 Also read as Odate. Currently in Joetsu City.

13 Present day Nozumi Beach.

12.13

"Halt, you abominable scoundrel! I know you have set your heart on the feudal lord's wife Tagoto-hime!"

Orochimaru turned around in surprise and saw a samurai who had managed to sneak up on him. He was finely dressed, and his face was concealed beneath a wide-brimmed straw hat. Orochimaru said, "Impressive work uncovering my dubious motives. Unfortunately for you though, you might be an obstacle later, so I cannot let you live," and lunged at the samurai.

"Don't act hastily! There is a matter that I must discuss with you," exclaimed the samurai, stopping Orochimaru in his tracks. Looking around cautiously, he whispered to Orochimaru in a low voice:

"I am Igarashi Tenzen Taketora, a retainer of the Tsukikage clan. For years, I have harbored a desire to overthrow Miyukinosuke and claim the Tsukikage lands for myself. Despite my careful planning, I have struggled to find reliable allies, and an old fart named Hamaogi Naminoshin has hindered my progress at every turn, so I have not achieved anything yet. However, I recently heard rumors about a bandit named Orochimaru residing on Mount Mano in Sado Island. It is said that he possesses unmatched strength and commands many followers. I thought if I could recruit him as an ally, I would have no need to seek others. Therefore, I sneaked over to Sado where I found out you would be on this beach today. I hid myself here in this grove, hoping to be able to meet with you. I have been watching since the start and based on how intently you were looking at Tagoto-hime, I surmised that you had fallen for her. If you join forces with me and eliminate Miyukinosuke, not

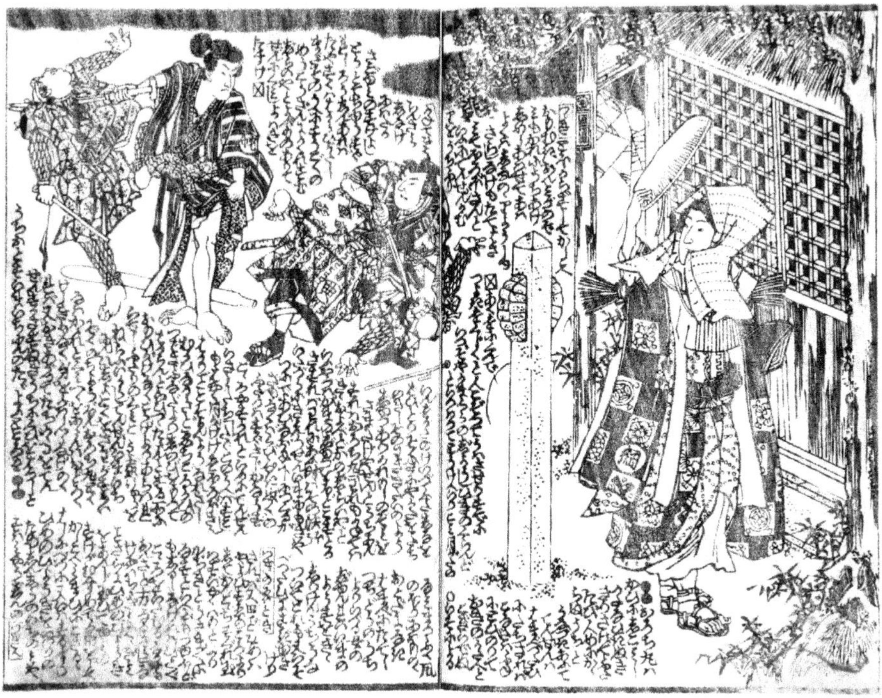

12.14

only will we get Tagoto-hime, but all of Echigo will fall into our hands! Then you and I can split the land between us and rule. What say you?"

Hearing Tenzen's persuasive words, Orochimaru smiled and replied, "You have indeed thought this through. It is clear we should become allies. Let us unite and strategize. Additionally, I have already established correspondence with Urafuji Saemon Terukage, who is currently barricaded on Mount Kurokoma in Kai. Before long, he shall be heading in this direction. By informing him of your ambitions, we can conspire together and launch a synchronized attack on the rulers of Shinano—the Sarashina clan—and bring about their downfall."

(12.14)

Tenzen shook his head. "You may have heard that the Sarashina clan is supported by the wise and valiant retainer Takasago Yuminosuke. He will be most difficult to deal with. And furthermore, hidden on Mount Myōkō in the same land, lives the man named Jiraiya. It is said that he fights on the side of justice, aiding the weak, admonishing evil, and crushing the strong. Some time ago, he disguised himself as Hiki no Kurando and infiltrated the Tsukikage mansion, where he stole the crescent-moon-shaped seal and the Ogata family tree. Then he escaped in an instance with miraculous yōjutsu. If he decides to get in the way of our plans—"

Orochimaru interrupted Tenzen's worries. "I have already heard all of this, but this Jiraiya character is supposed to use toad magic, right?

In that case, when he faces me, he won't be able to use his magics at all. If he were to face me now, he would have no choice but to become my subordinate or have his head torn off. You can rest assured."

This encouraged Tenzen, who arose while saying, "Then we have not a moment to waste. It is vital that we make our plans to destroy the Tsukikage clan. The scull and the paddle shall carry us like wings from Echigo to Sado, where we will make our secret plans."

Two constables appeared unexpectedly from the shade of the trees.

"Igarashi Tenzen! You are under arrest for plotting against the house of our master. And you, Orochimaru, you are under arrest for leading pirates and causing trouble in various provinces. Prepare to be restrained!" they declared, attempting to apprehend both Tenzen and Orochimaru. However, showing no sign of shock, they dodged the constables, and threw them to the ground. When one of the constables regained his footing, Tenzen drew his sword in one fluid motion, slicing the man's throat. The remaining constable faltered, and Orochimaru drew the sword he had hidden in his oar and cut him down. Before anyone else saw them, the two nodded to each other, and Tenzen left along the coast while Orochimaru jumped in his boat and rowed out to sea.

The beach was silent save for the sound of the waves on the shore and the wind in the pine trees. From out of a wayside shrine that stood close to the beach, a solitary female pilgrim appeared. She nodded once, as if she had heard everything, and departed along the shoreline.

Returning to Tagoto-hime, at around the end of the third month, she had not been feeling well. She started with medicine and had even tried incantations and prayers, but there was no indication that her health was getting better. Everyone was deeply worried about her, and even her honorable father and mother in her hometown were disturbed by her illness. In response, Yuminosuke sent his daughter, Teruta, to visit Tagoto-hime at her sickbed, bearing a message:

(12.15)

"To pray for the princess's recovery, we arranged for a priest at Suwamyōji Shrine, the most esteemed shrine in Shinano, to perform a *kagura* ritual. The female shaman who performed the purification rites became possessed and spoke this omen: 'The illness is caused by the wrath of a specter. As it is caused by an enamored apparition, no physician will be able to heal it. If you wish to avoid an all-encompassing disaster, you must place a renowned and unmatched sword next to her pillow for protection. Do this, and she will make an immediate recovery.'"

After Teruta relayed this, Miyukinosuke said, "These are distressing tidings indeed. However, fortunately, our household possesses an illustrious sword passed down through generations. It is a tanto shortsword forged by none other than the progenitor of the katana—the smith Amakuni of Yamato himself. The blade's temper is naturally reminiscent of a slug, which has earned it the name Katsuyumaru.

12.15

Recently, I wished to have it sharpened, and I heard of a townsman in Yukinoshita in Kamakura named Ban'emon who deals with swords and is a virtuoso sword sharpener. I had Katsuyumaru sent to him a while ago. The day it is scheduled to be finished is almost here. We must send for it immediately, and have it protect Tagoto's bedroom. Please relay this to Tagoto's parents in whatever manner you deem fitting."

Teruta, now granted permission to move freely, stepped back and shared all the inquiries from Tagoto-hime's mother with the lady-in-waiting Sekiya. Later, on the same day, she headed back to Shinano.

Miyukinosuke then summoned the aging retainer, Hamaogi Naminoshin, whose family had served his for generations, and instructed him, "Previously I sent the tanto Katsuyumaru to Katanaya Ban'emon in Kamakura to have it sharpened. Go quickly and retrieve it."

(12.16)

Naminoshin respectfully complied, returning home to swiftly make the necessary arrangements before setting off for Kamakura. He traveled day and night until he finally reached Yukinoshita, where he met with Katanaya Ban'emon. Naminoshin explained, "The reason I have come so abruptly is because an urgent need has arisen. I need to take the tanto back."

When Naminoshin had told all the details, Ban'emon replied, "Because it is so close to the deadline, I have finished sharpening the blade already. Please, give it a look." He brought out the tanto and placed it before Naminoshin.

12.16

Katsuyu means slug. Because this word will be appearing a lot in the text to come, please remember this.

He took it in his hand, held it up, and removed the scabbard. It had indeed been sharpened to perfection. Impressed, Naminoshin praised Ban'emon and generously compensated him for his work, as had been agreed upon. That night, He stayed at Ban'emon's house, where he was warmly welcomed by Ban'emon, his son-in-law Hanshichi, and his daughter Ohana.

When the next day dawned, he bid farewell to Ban'emon and his family and set out from Kamakura, heading for the roads that would take him towards his home in Echigo. However, while crossing the Shinano hill, situated on the border of Musashi and Sagami, came two women's palanquins from afar. They were escorted by a samurai clad in travel clothes and a considerable retinue. They were headed towards Naminoshin, and when they passed him, the samurai called out, "I apologize for the sudden inquiry, but are you perhaps from the Hamaogi clan, serving Tsukikage-dono, the ruler of Echigo? I ask because I am Kitafuki Kazahira, and I serve Sarashina, the feudal lord of Shinano."

Naminoshin stopped in his tracks at this. "Indeed, you are correct. I am Hamaogi Naminoshin, a retainer of Tsukikage. For what purpose are you traveling through these parts?"

When he asked this, the doors of the two palanquins were lifted and two women stepped out. One was a white-haired, elderly lady, and the

12.17

Signpost: North is the land of Musashi. | South is the land of Sagami.

other was a beautiful young woman of barely twenty. Kazahira led the two women over to Naminoshin and explained, "This is Iwane, a senior lady-in-waiting of Tsukikage. The maiden is Teruta-dono, the daughter of Takasago Yuminosuke, the chief retainer of the Sarashina clan. She was recently sent on a formal visit to your homeland. We have come across you here, because we are en route to Kamakura to meet with you. Because the lady of your house is burdened with an illness that grows worse by the day, in order to pray for her swift recovery, we have most sincerely asked and received permission from Tsukikage-dono to take the Katsuyumaru tanto, bring it to Suwa, and have a seventeen-day long kagura dance ritual performed. This was already the wish of Tagoto-hime's honorable father and mother, but if we were to wait for you to return home with the tanto from Kamakura, it might be too late. Hence, we requested a letter of approval from the Tsukikage clan to retrieve the tanto directly from you. Teruta-dono bears the responsibility of acquiring the tanto, accompanied by the lady-in-waiting Iwane, acting as her aid, and myself, serving as her bodyguard."

(12.17)

Upon concluding his explanation, Kazahira turned to Teruta, who presented a letter from Tsukikage-dono with great reverence. She handed it over and Naminoshin inspected it closely. It had the clear brushwork of the scribe of the Tsukikage, which Naminoshin was well-accustomed to, as well as the lord's seal. He rolled the letter up, put it away, and said, "Since you have brought this as proof, I cannot doubt you. However, if I could receive a letter from envoy Teruta herself stating, 'I take responsibility for Katsuyumaru,' it would be all the safer."

Without delay, the senior lady-in-waiting produced a travel inkstone, and Teruta wrote the letter, handing it to Naminoshin. After reading it, he handed Katsuyumaru to Teruta. After bidding their farewells, he continued his journey on the roads to Echigo, while the other three hastened into the hills towards Suwa.

In a secluded thicket in Hodogaya, Musashi, a rōnin wearing a straw hat came face to face with the lady-in-waiting and the young girl. Speaking covertly, he said to them, "Well done, you two. You looked just like an old lady-in-waiting, and you performed just like Teruta. No one suspected you were imposters. Even the samurai of the Tsukikage clan thought you were real and handed over the tanto. Here is the payment for your labors."

The aging woman took the money the rōnin held out, opened the paper it was wrapped in, and made a disgruntled look. "This is only tenryō. We didn't risk our lives for pocket change!" she exclaimed, flinging the money back at the rōnin.

The rōnin's face flushed with anger. "You were the ones who decided on ten ryō in our original agreement! And now you complain after finishing the job? Are you trying to blackmail me?"

"How dare you accuse me of blackmail! It is atrocious that you try to pay us with pocket change like this after knowing that we worked like dogs! Perhaps you are driven by greed, thinking you can claim this valuable Katsuyumaru tanto, which can fetch a tremendous price. Or maybe we are in the wrong for demanding more after receiving our initial payment. However, listen closely to this first. If you chose to tell us you won't give more, then we might just go to the Tsukikage clan and tell them that this whole thing was a scam.

(12.18)

"But why stop there? We know that you are a samurai known as the useless Mijin Kotsuhei, who served as a magistrate in Kamakura until the news broke that you were abusing the commoners. Then it was curtain call for you in Kamakura, and now you stand here, all shabby looking. We only took this job because we learned that Terukage Urafuji Saemon of Mount Kurokoma offered you one hundred ryō to acquire Katsuyumaru. And he was instructed to retrieve it by a man named Igarashi Tenzen, who serves as a retainer for the Tsukikage clan. We don't even need to bother with going all the way to far-off Echigo. We can go to nearby Kamakura and report it to the magistrate's office of the Kanrei himself. So, what will it be?"

Unyielding in her demands, she did not budge the slightest. Recognizing there was no other choice, Kotsuhei reluctantly produced the additional money. The exchange for the tanto was over in an instant, and as he tucked away the tanto into his breast pocket, he tightened the string on his straw hat and hurried away from the scene.

12.18

The daughter saw him off, and then, with tears in her eyes, she turned to the old woman and said, "I know what we are doing is wrong, but I am willing to be your accomplice in these dreadful scams because you are my mother. Once we have earned enough, I would like to change my ways and travel through this floating world on the straight and narrow. However, I also have one more wish. My older sister, Ayame-sama, met her end due to the bandit Jiraiya in Echigo, and I want to avenge her."

The old woman nodded. "And you followed me without objection. I have done so many wicked things, people now speak of me as Okowa the demon. Even if I know that what we are doing is evil, it is my destiny, and I cannot stop now. It is a result of my karma. Listen closely now, as I tell you my tale of remorse. When I was still young, I met with a man in secret and had a son with him. Then I went to Kamakura without my parents knowing, and thirty years later, I married and gave birth to Ayame and you. Shortly after, my husband left this world, and because you were so young, Kosono, I sold you in the capital to be a *shirabyōshi* dancer. Your older sister, Ayame, went to work as a woman of the night in the Kumadeya house in Niigata in Echigo, where she suddenly vanished. Upon asking around, I slowly discovered she had been kidnapped by a bandit named Jiraiya and taken to his mountain fortress on Mount Myōkō. There, I heard she was eventually murdered by him, suffering a miserable death. When you became of age and returned to me, you learned of Ayame's fate and said you wanted to avenge her. I also desired revenge, so we traveled through the lands, but Jiraiya commands mysterious forces, so we still

12.19

Text on curtain: Nunobiki Shinmei Shrine.

haven't found out where he is. But we have the determination of women possessed, so we will have our revenge."

Kosono cheered up and said, "Mother, even if this is how you feel, it doesn't mean we cannot cease our wicked ways. And if we can meet with my older brother, whom you gave away when he was little, we can ask him to join us on our vendetta."

The temple bells chimed, signaling the sunset.

Okowa got up and said, "Let us continue this conversation at our lodging for tonight. Come," she urged, pulling Kosono along towards a nearby village.

The infamous 'Okowa the demon' was in fact none other than the demonic hag who had previously attempted to murder the widows Himematsu Kozue and Misao, along with their servant Matsuhei, after offering them lodging in a village at the base of the Usui Pass.

(12.19)
In the foothills of Mount Nunobiki, along the Tama River in Musashi, stood a splendid and solitary shrine. When evening fell, a crowd of locals came, carrying a six-legged chest, led by a Shinto priest. Their footsteps halted as they reached their destination, and they raised the curtain at the entrance of the shrine to place the chest inside. Then the

headman stepped forward and said, "Well done, everyone. Well done. Just like we do every year, tomorrow we shall have a festival in honor of the kami, Amaterasu, enshrined here in Nunobiki Shinmei Shrine. The kagura dance ritual will commence at the seventh bell of the morning.[14] In preparation for this occasion, we have stored the ceremonial attire in this chest. However, leaving it unguarded would be unwise. Is there anyone willing to stay and watch over it?"

One person stepped forward and suggested, "Instead of choosing someone, shouldn't it be the priest's duty to guard the chest?"

Rather than shaking his bells, like priests usually do, the priest instead shook his head and said, "Lately, this area has become quite perilous. Even though this shrine is splendid, I have no desire to remain alone here and become a potential offering for boars, wolves, or serpents. Thank the gods that it is already the darkest time of night. Any potential passerby wouldn't know there is something within the shrine, so they wouldn't be inclined to take it. Now, let's be off!" Then they all departed, going towards their homes with the priest walking in front.

In the dead of midnight, a lone samurai appeared from upstream. He paused, gazed at the shrine, and thought to himself, "How unfortunate that it is already pitch-black tonight. The river rocks are too treacherous to walk on, so I might as well stay at this shrine until dawn."

Sitting down on the porch of the shrine, he took out his fire-striker, lit his pipe, and puffed on it. Then he gathered some leaves from around the shrine and kindled a campfire. Another samurai saw the light of the fire from downstream and approached.

"Apologies for the sudden intrusion, but remember to keep an eye on that fire," the second samurai said, stepping closer to the campfire and surprising the first samurai.

"Mijin Kotsuhei-dono! What brings you here?" exclaimed the first samurai.

(12.20)

"And what about you, Shikano Fuehachi? Fancy running into you here, of all places!" said Kotsuhei as he recognized the other's face in the firelight.

Kotsuhei surveyed their surroundings and remarked, "I heard a rumor that you and Yokoshima Guheida were arrested by Hatamori Daizen and imprisoned in Kamakura. However, it seems you managed to escape. Where have you been all this time?"

Shikano Fuehachi responded, "It is as you say. On a stormy night, I broke out of prison and fled from Kamakura. I snuck to the land of Kai where I stayed with Urafuji, a country samurai from Kurokoma. But to my regret, I learned he is a short-tempered man who quickly took to lambasting me like I was nothing but trash. However, I knew that Urafuji was in possession of a special tea container, the Fubuki Katatsuki, dearly treasured by the Sarashina clan. Long ago, the container was entrusted to Himematsu Sumatarō in Ōiso, but he was killed and had the container stolen by Tatsumaki Arakurō. Last

14 03:00.

12.20

year, however, going by the name Gundazaemon, he was killed at Inamuragasaki by Sutematsu. Before that, though, he managed to sell the container to Urafuji for gold, which is how it came into Urafuji's possession. Seeking retribution against Urafuji, I stole it from him. Now, I am here because I intend to return the tea container to Shinano, expose Urafuji's wicked deeds, and seek their forgiveness. In return, I will ask them to help me resume my service under the Kanrei."

Kotsuhei shook his head and said, "Such prudence is unlike you. I, on the other hand, was chastised by that bumbling idiot of a Kanrei and made into a rōnin. Just as I had no idea what to do from there, I received a secret letter from Igarashi Tenzen Taketora, a retainer of the Tsukikage clan, asking Urafuji for a favor. Due to an illness that Tagoto-hime has contracted, they require the tanto called Katsuyumaru, which was being carried back from Kamakura by a man named Hamaogi Naminoshin. Along the way, I cleverly swindled it from him and have it with me now. I'm on my way to bring it back to Kai, where I will be rewarded by both Urafuji and Igarashi to my heart's content. I urge you to reconsider your actions and accompany me to Kai. However, if you refuse, I will simply take the tea container from you and present it as a special gift."

Fuehachi smiled wryly at Kotsuhei's pressing words. "No, no. It is you who should hand over that tanto to me. I will bring it to the Tsukikage clan and be rewarded by both Echigo and Shinano."

Kotsuhei deftly evaded Fuehachi's attempt to reach into his breast pocket, guard raised. "You really are like a buck in heat, Fuehachi. Only,

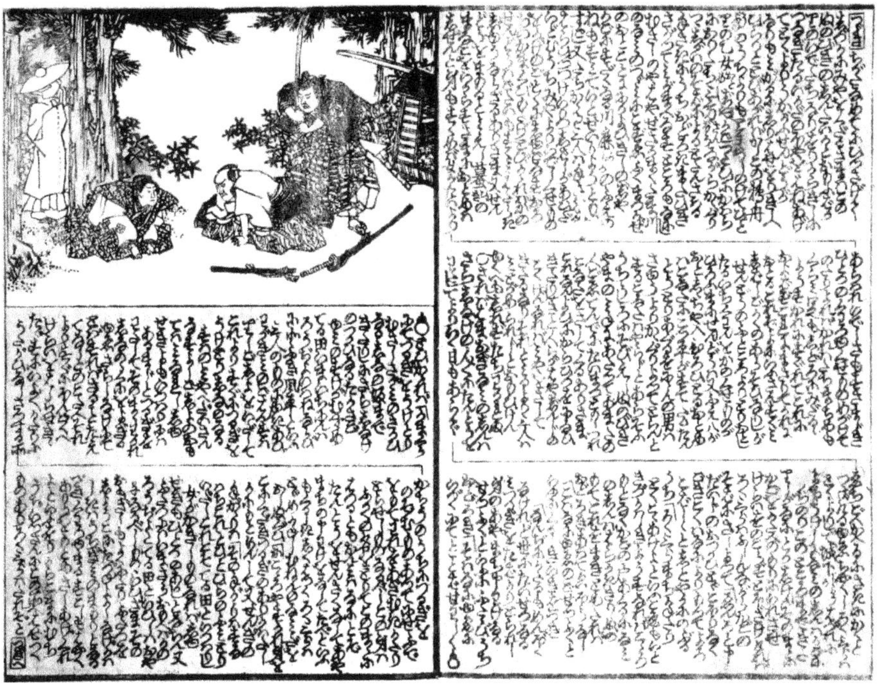

12.21

instead of being on the look for a mate, you are possessed by greed! I'll kill you!" he exclaimed and swung his sword at Fuehachi, who leapt backwards and drew his own sword.

"I hope you are prepared to die, useless Mijin Kotsuhei!"

The two fought ruthlessly, both receiving deep cuts. When Kotsuhei stumbled over a rock, Fuehachi seized the opportunity and delivered the killing blow. Fuehachi then fumbled around for the tanto and the tea container which had fallen on the ground. From beyond the curtain hanging over the door of the ancient shrine, a gleaming blade thrust out and pierced Fuehachi's ribcage. With nothing but a single grunt, Fuehachi collapsed to the ground. Emerging from behind the torn white fabric of the curtain was a figure adorned in a fine silk *happi* coat, crimson wide-legged hakama pants, and a celestial crown.

(12.21)

Gripping the bloodied sword in his right hand, the figure descended slowly from the shrine. It looked exactly like it could have been the very god of the Nunobiki Shrine itself. At that same moment, the woven reed covers on a raft moored by the shore of the river flew up, and someone resembling a boatman nimbly leapt ashore, his kimono tucked into his belt to free his legs. Simultaneously, a maiden emerged from a cormorant fishing boat, pushing aside the straw mat roof, and disembarked onto shore. All three individuals stepped onto the dry riverbed which ran along the rocky stone wall of the stream and started rummaging around. As they approached the two corpses, their hands touched, causing all three to fly back in shock and assume defensive positions.

In Musashi, renowned for its turbulent rapids, flows the Tama River. Its waves beat like a hand drum, and the sound of the wind that blew through the tops of the pine trees was like the strings of a koto. The chirping of the *kajiki* frogs among the rocks of the stone wall was clear and serene, creating a scene of utmost tranquility.

Brushing off their hands, the three individuals scrutinized one another, searching for weaknesses and issuing silent challenges. A great serpent appeared, protecting the rogue who had stepped out of the shrine like it were his shadow. The serpent reared its head and struck towards the boatman, who froze and became unable to move freely. In response, a toad materialized, guarding the boatman, while its fierce gaze left the maiden paralyzed. From the maiden's body, an enormous slug appeared, fixating its gaze on the rogue figure and drawing closer. This immediately made the rogue dizzy and his legs faltered beneath him. Even if one of them was stronger than another, they could not compete with the remainder. Even if they could win against one, they would lose to the other. It was a true three-way deadlock.

For a brief moment, the battle remained evenly matched, until the boatman accidentally dropped a scroll from his breast pocket. Seizing the opportunity, the rogue snatched up the scroll, prompting the boatman to retrieve the tea container dropped by Fuehachi. The maiden, meanwhile, picked up the tanto that Kotsuhei had dropped, but the two men seized it from either side, engaging in a fierce struggle, none wanting to let go of the tanto.

From the peak of Mount Nunobiki looming behind them, the voices of a large group of people echoed. They carried lit torches and marched directly towards where the three were fighting. It was the villagers who had brought the chest to the shrine in the evening, aiming for the shrine as it was time to start the ritual. When the three combatants saw this, they each thought they did not want to get questioned. Without a trace, they abandoned the fight and vanished.

Not many days after having handed the tanto over to the people sent by the Sarashina clan, Hamaogi Naminoshin returned to Echigo. His son, Rokusaburō, was waiting outside the castle to greet him for a while, as news of his return had already been received. However, when the palanquin carrying Naminoshin arrived, for some unknown reason, it continued into a forest next to the castle, leaving all the retainers far behind. Suspicious of this unusual behavior, Rokusaburō approached the palanquin.

"It brings me great joy that you have returned safely from your long journey," he greeted respectfully.

Naminoshin replied, "Rokusaburō, I apologize for having kept you waiting. Now, hurry up and open this thing."

The sound of his father's voice made Rokusaburō nervous, so he opened the palanquin door without any hesitation. Inside, he discovered Naminoshin with his stomach cut open and wrapped in fabric to stem the bleeding. Shocked, Rokusaburō desperately tried to assist his father.

"What has happened? Why have you resorted to committing seppuku?" Rokusaburō asked.

With a pained breath, Naminoshin answered, "I am ashamed to tell you, but I was scammed out of the all-important sword. To atone for my mistake, I chose to commit seppuku."

Rokusaburō's shock deepened, and he questioned anxiously, "What do you mean? When did this happen?"

Despite causing him great suffering to speak, Naminoshin replied, "I had gone to Kamakura and retrieved the sword, and when I arrived on Shinano hill, which lies on the border of Musashi and Sagami, I met with three people who were sent as envoys for the Shinano clan. Teruta, the daughter of Takasago Yuminosuke, a senior lady-in-waiting named Iwane, and Kitafuki Kazahira. They presented a letter bearing my lord's seal, saying that they were to take the sword immediately and bring it to the shrine in Suwa in Shinano, to pray on behalf of the Sarashina clan. The handwriting on the letter seemed familiar, leading me to believe it was genuine. Thus, I entrusted them with the sword and departed. However, as I was passing through Shinano, I went to the Sarashina clan to ask what had happened, and they assured me that they did not know of what I spoke. I immediately sent a retainer running to Echigo to ascertain the truth, and all doubts that I had been deceived disappeared. There must be someone among the retainers who wants the sword, and they forged the letter to deceive me and swindle me out of the sword. I have tarnished my name, and this is the consequence. But you, you must search out the sword and make amends for my mistake."

Rokusaburō wiped away his uncontrollable tears of regret and vowed, "Rest assured. Even if I must grind my body to dust, I will seek out the whereabouts of the sword! Have you uncovered any leads during your investigation?"

"This is the only clue I have," he said, taking out a single letter. "If this is indeed written by the woman who masqueraded as Teruta, then the writing style might provide a lead. Now that I think about it, another lead could also be the old woman who was with the one pretending to be Teruta. They spoke and resembled each other so closely that they must be mother and daughter. You must uncover their true identities. However, what is most lamentable is Katsuyumaru, which was meant to protect our lady. You must find it without delay and deliver it to her!"

As he said this, a rider approached, whipping his horse at a furious speed. Rokusaburō called out to inquire about the rider's identity, and saw that it was none other than Igarashi Tenzen.

(12.22)

After confirming what he saw, Tenzen nimbly leapt from his horse and scowled at Naminoshin. "We have apprehended your subordinates, had them tell us everything that happened, and reported it to the lord.

What a fool you are for losing the sword! You should be hanged, but you have managed to commit seppuku on your own. I will have your head and show it to the lord!"

Without waiting, he sliced off Naminoshin's head with a swish and tied it to his saddle. When he made ready to depart, Rokusaburō cried and implored, "You were right to punish him for making such an inexcusable mistake, but please, I beg of you, let me dispose of his head together with the body to not separate the two. Please, find the mercy to let me have the head."

Tenzen kicked the head back to Rokusaburō with a resounding thud. "One who committed the grave offense of losing his lord's treasure does not deserve a proper burial! His body should be cast away in an abandoned field for kites and crows to feast upon. That would be a good example of what happens to those who are disloyal! I should unleash divine retribution upon you as well, but I will spare you and condemn you to exile. Now, I must hasten to the castle!" With those words, he swiftly mounted his horse and rode back to the keep.

Rokusaburō, at a loss, said to himself, "My father's head was cut off right before my eyes, and all I could do was watch like a shameless and spineless cur. Fortune has forsaken me, and the quest for the treasure seems bleak. I shall follow my father into the realm of the underworld."

With his decision made, Rokusaburō loosened his kimono, baring his torso. He was on the brink of committing seppuku when a Buddhist monk on the path to enlightenment, who had been listening from the shadows of a nearby tree, rushed forward.

"Do not be rash! I have something I must tell you," cried the monk, grabbing Rokusaburō's hand and stopping his blade.

12.22

What the Buddhist practitioner had to say to Rokusaburō, will be unveiled in book thirteen.

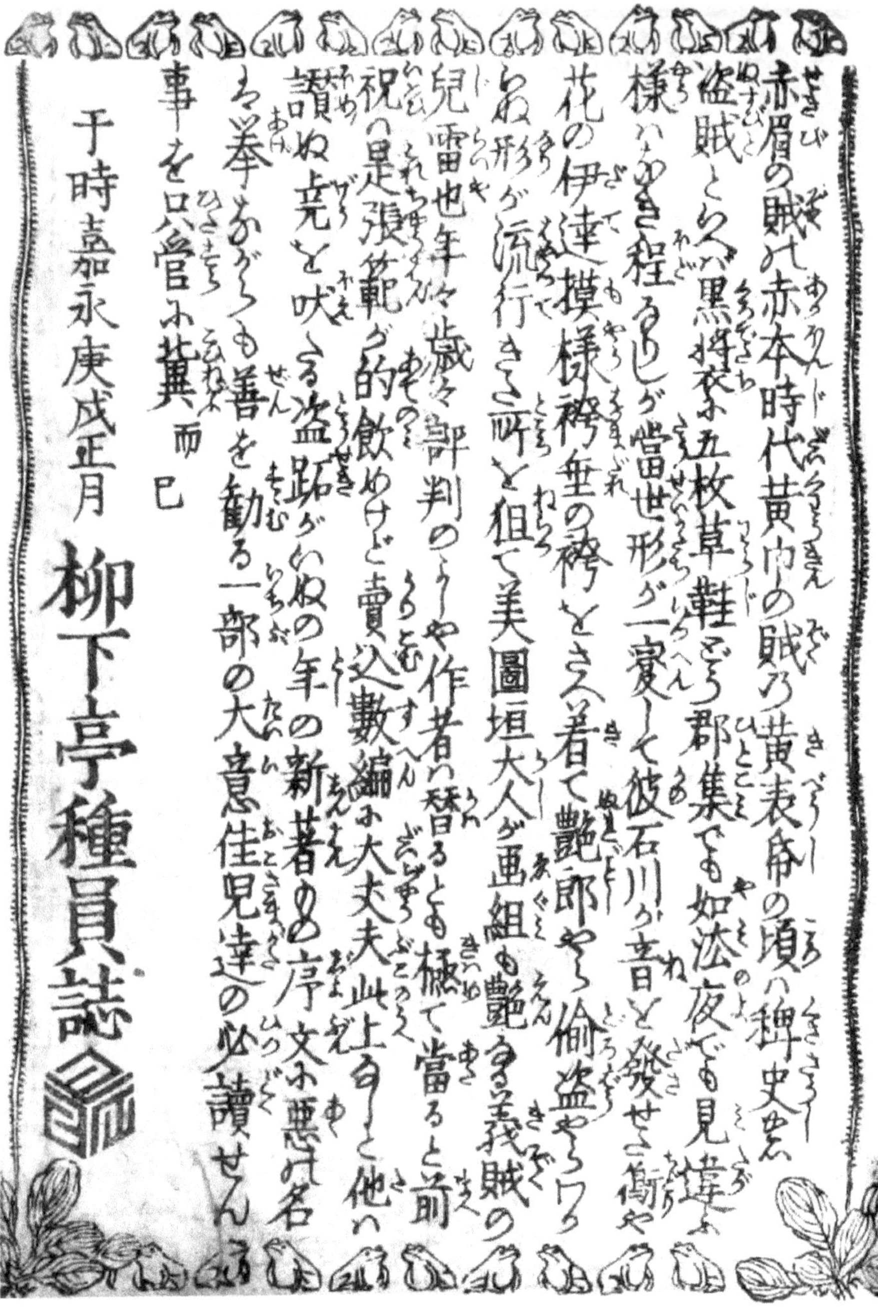
赤眉の賊ハ赤本時代黄巾の賊ハ黄表帋の頃ハ稗史出ん
盗賊とハ久しく黒将ならず五枚草鞋ごろ郡集でも如法夜でも見違ふ
模様いかき程るとしが當世形が一変して彼石川が音と發せし衛や
花の伊達摸様袴垂の袴とさへ着て艶郎やら偸盗やらワろ
扮形が流行きし所を狙て美圖垣大人が画組も艶なる義賊の
兒雷也年々歳々評判のよしや作者ハ替るとも極て當ると前
祝の是張範ぐ的飲ぬけど賣込數編ふ大丈夫此上ゟと他ハ
讃ぬ尭を吠る盗跖がいぬの年の新著の序文ふ悪の名
ある挙なからも善を勸る一部の大意佳兒達の必讀せん
事を只管ふ冀而已
于時嘉永庚戌正月
柳下亭種員誌

13.1

Book 13

When mentioning outlaws from historically inspired tales, such as the *Red Eyebrow Bandits* during the era of the red-backed *akabon* books, or the *Yellow Turban Bandits* from the time of the yellow-backed kibyōshi books, they were all clad in black and with thick straw sandals. They were indistinguishable from any ordinary person or ruffian. But these days, they are often depicted wearing hakama pants with plover birds or flowery *date* style patterns, as if they were wearing the flashy hakama of Hakamadare himself. It has become impossible to tell Casanovas from outlaws. Taking advantage of this trend, Mister Mizugaki depicted Jiraiya as a gallant and gentleman thief. Over the years, even with the authors changing, the reviews have been good, but prematurely celebrating great sales would be like imitating the bandit Chōhan. The night before a great heist, he drank for as much money as he would make from the heist itself, and on the next day was defeated by Ushiwakamaru while nursing a hangover. Others praise only sales, saying there is nothing above this.

A dog knows not good from evil. If raised by a thief, it would bark at even the emperor if he were a stranger to its master. In this year of the Dog, a new author writes this foreword, one intention being touting evil while promoting good. All I pray for is for this book to become a must-read for fine young readers.

Kaei era—Year of the Iron Dog—New Year (1851)

Ryūkatei Tanekazu

13.2

Gisuke, fisherman from Nadachi in Echigo and younger brother of Hosaku who worked for the Matsuzaki family.

Orochimaru, pirate leader.

Otoma, wet-nurse for Sutematsu and Gisuke's wife.

13.3

A bandit fight between the subordinates of the two leaders. Jiraiya's men are marked with a frog. Orochimaru's men are marked with a triangle.

Jiraiya.
[Frog] Kukami no Kazahei.
[Frog] Sakatake no Fushihachi.
[Frog] Kusauzu Aburoku.
[Frog] Kitafuki Kanzō.

Orochimaru.
[Triangle] Suteikari Sunahachi.
[Triangle] Tobinori Futatarō.
[Triangle] Washisaki Tsumeroku.
[Triangle] Tsukahara Dōkurō.

13.4

The fake Jiraiya Ogata Hiroyuki. Actually Orochimaru's henchman and petty thief Jimoguri Kuroyasha.

From the *Eikyūhyakushū*:
I can neither stand nor sit,
If I could but touch your sleeve,
Even after three thousand years have passed,
It would surely become a peach.

—Minamoto no Toshiyori

Bitei the sage—Taoist immortal of Mount Tate in Etchū.
The heroine Tsunade.

13.5

Part I

(13.5)
And so, the story continues.

Hamaogi Rokusaburō found himself in utter despair, and just as he was about to end himself, someone ran from the shadow of a nearby grove and stopped his hand. Startled at first, when Rokusaburō looked closer, he saw it was an elegant lay monk, with clear skin and prominent eyebrows.

The monk said to Rokusaburō, "I understand why you would want to commit suicide together with your father. His sudden act of seppuku and the loss of the treasure have brought upon you immense hardships. However, if you were to meet your end now, who would search for the treasure and clear your father's name? Even in the old writings, does it not say that dying is the easy path? Still your heart, for I have an idea. It is not as if you have absolutely no leads regarding the lost tanto."

The monk's words gave Rokusaburō pause. With great reverence, Rokusaburō thanked him, saying, "Truly, your lesson is most welcome and has deeply resonated within my heart. However, may I inquire, honorable monk, from where do you come, showing such profound kindness? And secondly, how did you come upon the idea of the tanto's whereabouts? I would like to know where it is."

The monk answered Rokusaburō's hectic questions, "I dwell beneath the trees, sleeping upon the rocks. I have let go of this world and have no fixed abode or house. Concerning my lead on the blade, in secret, I recently overheard something on the banks of the Tama River in the land of Musashi. Supposedly, that man named Igarashi Tenzen, who decapitated your honorable father just now, asked Urafuji Saemon Terukage of Mount Kurokoma in Kai to help him get the tanto. Urafuji Saemon, in turn, entrusted Mijin Kotsuhei, whom he was harboring at the time, with the task. Kotsuhei then had some women be his accomplices and tricked Naminoshin out of the sword. Afterwards, he told a man named Fuehachi, who was his comrade, what happened. Fuehachi fought Kotsuhei over the treasure, and as they fought, someone killed them. He dropped the treasure, but because the incident occurred during the pitch-black of night, I am not sure exactly what happened to it, only that it passed into someone else's hands. If you start an investigation of Tenzen now and he finds out, even if through insinuation, it will likely bring trouble your way. Instead, focus on discovering the whereabouts of his two accomplices. Once you have cleared your father's grudge, you can proceed with searching for the treasure and reinstate your house. This would be the most filial way to honor your departed father. Do not act on impulse."

The monk's words carried kindness and persuasion, causing Rokusaburō to reconsider his earlier resolve to die. "I will do as you say and halt my death, seek out the two women, and make every effort to investigate the whereabouts of the tanto. And what about you, honorable monk? Where will you go from here? And if you don't mind, I would like to know your name." Rokusaburō pulled on the monk's sleeve as he asked.

(13.6)

The monk nodded and said, "My name is Jōun. Today my walking staff has led me here to Echigo. Tomorrow, I shall journey to Tsukushi for further ascetic training.[1] I am a wandering monk. Just like the water and the clouds, you can never know where I will go. If fate wills it, we shall meet again." With that, he shook his sleeve free and departed for unknown destinations.

Rokusaburō lingered for a while, looking in the direction the monk had gone, feeling sad at their parting. The many retainers, who had been waiting at a distance, approached him, and Rokusaburō recounted the events. Together, they then picked up the father's body and left with heavy hearts.

One day, Hanshichi, the son-in-law of Katanaya Ban'emon from Yukinoshita in Kamakura, paid a visit to Chōbei the dreamer's house. He had something he needed to tell Chōbei and his wife in private. As he had his meeting with them, Tsuruhashiya Kinosuke also arrived, carrying a secret letter, making it a well-timed gathering.

1 Chikuzen and Chikugo, which is present day Fukuoka, where Jiraiya's family ruled.

13.6

Hanshichi told them, "Lately, I've been hearing rumors and talks from people all across the land. They say Jiraiya-dono has gathered a considerable following and is going around the country, breaking into the homes of wealthy families, stealing their treasures, killing people, and even kidnapping beautiful women. Rumor has it, he causes so much suffering for the people that the stewards and the magistrates have received official claims against him. But Jiraiya-dono is an honorable man and would never take a person's life without proper cause. I took it upon myself to inquire further as to the reason for these rumors and have come here to discuss this matter with you."

Upon hearing this, Kinosuke knelt closer and said, "I, too, have come here today due to the prevalence of these rumors. Chōbei-dono, I wanted to inform you and your wife about this and see if you have any insights into the origin of these rumors."

Oroku and Chōbei exchanged glances before Chōbei replied, "We have also heard the rumors and don't believe them. As you said, Jiraiya-dono would never engage in such immoral acts. There must be an ulterior motive behind these rumors. I firmly believe that someone is impersonating Jiraiya and committing these vile deeds. In the end, I think that, rather than contemplating, sitting idly here where it's safe, we should seek out Jiraiya-dono, and capture the rogue pretending to be him. Therefore, I intend to embark on a journey soon. During my absence, I entrust the two of you to take care of everything."

Hanshichi and Kinosuke were both elated to hear this and exclaimed, "As always, you are so very chivalrous, Chōbei! Don't worry about

13.7

what happens here after you leave. The two of us will not let anything untoward happen on our watch."

Because Jiraiya was Oroku's brother and she had a duty towards him, Oroku was very happy knowing her husband was so reliable and committed to finding her brother.

(13.7)

Before long, Chōbei made the necessary travel arrangements. First, he would head to Mount Kurohime in Shinano, where his subordinates would investigate Jiraiya's whereabouts. From there, he would have them go around the lands in search of him. Once the preparations were complete, Chōbei bid his farewells and departed from Kamakura.

After parting ways with Rokusaburō, Jōun, the traveling lay monk, ventured into the land of Kōzuke[2] with the intention of paying his respects to Mount Myōgi. However, as he ascended the mountain, he lost his way and wandered deep into the wilderness. The sun had already set, so he climbed up a ridge in hopes of spotting a house where he could spend the night. As he looked down, he spotted what looked like a firelight on the opposite side of the valley, which he set his sights on. Upon arrival, he discovered a person who had kindled a campfire in front of an old shrine.

2 Present day Gunma.

Jōun thought, "I guess I shall stay here for the night." He approached the man and said, "I am a traveling monk who seems to have lost his way. I would like to spend the night here at this shrine. Would you mind sharing your fire with me?" As Jōun got closer, he saw that the man was rather tall, had a dark complexion, and looked like a very imposing and skilled warrior.

Sitting together by the campfire, the two exchanged tales of their respective journeys. The warrior scrutinized the traveling monk and remarked, "Now that I look at you, you don't have even the slightest inkling of fear about you, despite being lost so deep in the mountains. And your appearance and physique tell me you are no ordinary person. How come someone like you has chosen to give up on this fun and interesting world to do something as tedious as joining the monkhood?"

The warrior's question was arrogant and haughty, but Jōun smiled and replied, "You are correct in your assessment. However, no matter what someone like me does, overcoming the floating world is difficult. At least by joining the monkhood, I hope that my life in the next world will be a little easier, which is why I have embraced the way of the Buddha."

The warrior laughed at him and said, "Your spinelessness is the reason why you will die never having learned of all the many pleasures of this world. What a poor lot in life you have! If you were to change your heart now and become my follower, your hemp clothes could be replaced with lavish brocade. Your hands, which you've used to beg for rice in gates, shall be filled with money. You could indulge in the embrace of as many beautiful women as your heart desires. Instead of some distant future, there is wealth and paradise to be had in this world. Is this not a sect you'd like to join?" His suggestion pressed the monk to concede.

With a trembling voice, Jōun replied, "In this world governed by law and dharma, I cannot accept such an offer. But tell me, you wouldn't happen to be a bandit leader, would you?"

(13.8)

"Indeed, it is as you have guessed. I am, in fact, a bandit leader. I am certain you must have heard of me. I go by the name Jiraiya, though my true identity is Ogata Hiroyuki. Now, prostrate yourself and bow to me three times and worship me as your god, and you shall know such pleasures of the flesh!"

Stunned, Jōun said, "You must be Jiraiya-dono, whom I have heard so much about! Please forgive this foolish monk and indulge me with one question. I heard that you have miraculous powers. That you can take the heavens and the earth and stuff them in a pot, or that you can travel over a thousand ri as your heart desires. If these tales hold truth, could you please demonstrate your magic to me?"

Jōun asked with utmost reverence, and the warrior replied, "Indeed, you are correct, and I can easily perform such feats thanks to my toad yōjutsu. However, setting aside these extreme displays of my mysterious power, let me instead summon colossal toads right here where we stand. That should put some wonderment in your eyes!" With

13.8

these words, he began chanting a spell and gesturing with his hands, forming intricate seals. From among the dense bamboo grass and the shadows of the trees, numerous gigantic toads stealthily crept out.

At that time, the flickering light of the campfire illuminated the toads, and Jōun saw they were not real toads, but men in costumes. Finding this to be rather amusing, he remarked, "Just as the rumors described, what an astounding demonstration of miraculous powers. Now that we are on the subject, I too know a little bit of magic. It pales in comparison to the uncanny and eerie spectacle you have just shown me, but as an expression of gratitude for allowing me to witness it, I could showcase my limited skills if you wish."

Seating himself upon a large boulder, the warrior responded with a smirk, "What kind of magic do you know? Demonstrate your abilities, and I shall observe. Be quick and perform your little magic!"

"In that case, since you employed your miraculous power to summon toads in our midst, I shall copy you and conjure forth a frog. Behold!" Declaring this, he promptly rolled up his sleeves and straightened his back. Then he started chanting a spell and tying seals with his hands in prayer.

The mountains and valleys began to tremble, and the ancient shrine next to them started to shift. As the shifting became perceptible to the naked eye, the shrine toppled forward, transforming into an enormous frog that assumed a protective stance beside the monk.

Jiraiya, dumbfounded, struggled to find his words for a moment. Then, he said, "If you knew such extraordinary yōjutsu all along, you

13.9

Along the bottom, from right to left: Sado Island, Izumozaki, Shiiya, Yoneyama, Imamachi.

must have been just humoring me up until now, using sly words and making a fool out of me. All so you could perform this conjuring and try to break my spirit! Who exactly are you? Tell me your real name!"

(13.9)

The warrior's words were demanding, to which the monk gave a little smile and responded, "Aren't you one to ask? I had no intention of revealing my name to the likes of you. However, now, I shall share it with you as the people tell it, like a legendary tale. So, listen up! They say that I can take the heavens and the earth and stuff them in a pot, and that I can travel over a thousand ri as my heart desires. Even the most fearsome demon god trembles in my presence when I am angered, and my smile inspires adoration in young children, making them my devoted followers. My name resonates louder than the thunder of the gods, and it is known far and wide. Even you must have heard of such a man from Mount Kurohime in Echigo. My true name is Ogata Hiroyuki, but you might know me better as Jiraiya! Now, prostrate yourself and bow to me three times and worship me as your god." With these words, he cast aside his monk's hood and rose with such intensity, that he looked like he could crush an army of a million horsemen. The real Jiraiya spoke once more, "I have heard tales of a rogue who has been masquerading under my name for a while now, wreaking havoc, harming people, and stealing their treasures. Thus, I disguised myself and went on a journey across the lands, in the hopes that I could catch him. And now, unexpectedly, I find you here today. Pray tell, who exactly are you?"

The man's face grew pale. Although he trembled, he quickly responded to conceal his hesitation. "I am a subordinate of the pirate leader called Orochimaru, who lives on Mount Mano. My name is Jimoguri Kuroyasha. Because you are so well known, I would attack your good reputation by using your name, threaten the common folk, and do all the wicked deeds I could think of. It is truly fortuitous that our paths have crossed, for by killing you, I can rightfully claim the title of Jiraiya. Get him, men!"

At his command, the bandits who had so far disguised themselves as toads leapt to their feet, drawing their swords. They aimed their weapons at Jiraiya and attacked. Jiraiya countered, seizing his assailants, and smashing them against the rocks or kicking them down into the valley, killing every single one of them. While this was happening, Kuroyasha snuck around Jiraiya to attack from behind, but Jiraiya evaded his attack. With a resounding clash, Kuroyasha's blade struck the ground and slipped from his grasp. When he tried to run, Jiraiya grabbed him by the scruff of his neck and immobilized him.

"I could squash you under my foot right now as easily as a toad swallows a mosquito. However, I have heard a rumor that this Orochimaru, whom you lot look up to and call leader, aspires to take my mountain fortress from me. I want you to go back to Mount Mano and tell him this: 'The fox who covets the tiger's den shall not see his dreams fulfilled.' Now, I will use my magic to carry you there." Jiraiya hoisted Kuroyasha into the air and placed him atop the back of the frog. A fierce wind erupted, and dark clouds enveloped the frog, lifting them up in the sky as they soared northward.

In the port town of Nadachi, in the Kubiki province of Echigo, there was a fisherman named Gisuke. Originally, he was a servant of Matsuzaki Shirōdaifu from the same province, and the younger brother of Hosaku, who had been killed by Orochimaru. Gisuke and his brother hailed from a long line of servants to the Matsuzaki family. However, because of an abundance of youthful energy, Gisuke fell in love with a kitchen girl named Otoma, and they exchanged vows with each other. When their relationship was discovered, Shirōdaifu discussed the matter with Hosaku, and not only did Shirōdaifu tell the young couple to get married, but he also gave them some money and released them from their duties for the time being. The two sadly left the house of their lord, which they were so accustomed to, and went to Otoma's hometown of Nadachi. There, Gisuke became a fisherman and Otoma became a weaver.

(13.10)

The couple lived a harmonious life until they heard that Emiwaka's stay at Yoneyama had been ineffective. Emiwaka had killed not only

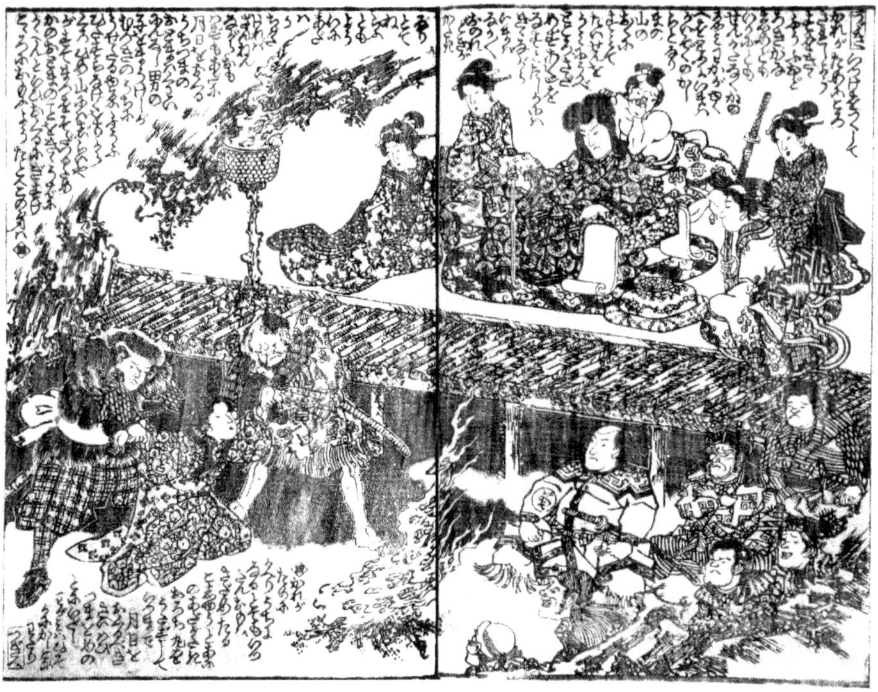

13.10

Gisuke's brother but also their old lord and the entire household. They were overwhelmed with shock and grief, but there was nothing they could do. They sought information about Emiwaka's whereabouts, only to discover he had become a pirate leader, dwelling deep within Mount Mano and commanding a formidable ship at sea, making him untraceable. They heard he committed all manner of evil deeds, and realized exacting vengeance against him in their present circumstances would prove exceedingly challenging. They were so taken up by their grudge, that many moons passed without them noticing, and Otoma became pregnant. She gave birth to a boy, but sadly, they lost him when he was only just into his diapers, plunging them into despair. During this period, Jiraiya, caring for Sutematsu atop Mount Kurohime, learned of Otoma and her situation. He had sent them a message, asking Otoma to come be Sutematsu's wet nurse.

Gisuke contemplated, "Even if I were to risk my life and confront Orochimaru, how much time must pass before I can avenge my lord and brother, as I have fervently desired? It is a stroke of luck that my wife can go as a wet nurse, allowing me to secretly travel across the sea, become Orochimaru's subordinate, patiently awaiting the opportune moment to kill him, and clear my long-held grudge."

(13.11)

His mind was made up on the plan, and once Otoma had been sent to Jiraiya's mountain fortress to be a wet nurse, Gisuke secretly went to

Mount Mano, becoming Orochimaru's follower, vigilantly monitoring his every move.

Meanwhile, Otoma was in Jiraiya's mountain fortress, taking good care of Sutematsu. After three years, under the protection of Jiraiya, and with the help of Chōbei the dreamer and Kinosuke, Sutematsu avenged his parents and his grandparents by killing Tatsumaki Arakurō, also known as Gundazaemon, at Yuigahama. Subsequently, Sutematsu was sent to Yuminosuke, and although it hurt Otoma deeply to say goodbye to him, she eventually left Sutematsu and the fortress, returning to her hometown of Nadachi. Once there, she found that Gisuke was not at home. When she asked the people in the neighborhood, no one knew where he was. Devastated, Otoma embarked on a quest to uncover the truth of his whereabouts.

The nefarious acts of Orochimaru of Mount Mano had steadily escalated, and he would often roam the lands, pillaging and killing people. To make matters worse, he brazenly conspired with Urafuji Saemon of Mount Kurokoma in Kai and Igarashi Tenzen, a retainer of the Tsukikage clan in Echigo, with the aim of toppling the Sarashina and Tsukikage clans, and, if all went according to plan, even destroying the Kamakura Kanrei. However, he lived on a faraway island, so it was difficult for him to carry out any such plans. Therefore, he set his heart on taking Mount Kurohime, which sat on the border of Shinano and Echigo and housed Jiraiya's mountain fortress, to build his own stronghold there. But Jiraiya's military prowess was well honed, leaving no openings. He had also placed sentinels at the foot of Mount Kurohime, who knew the checkpoints along the roads well. They thwarted any attempts to approach the mountain for investigation. However, because he was unaware of these lookouts, Orochimaru sent underlings to sneak into the mountain on many occasions, and they always returned in vain.

However, one day, Orochimaru was presented with a woman in her thirties who was bound and brought before him. The men who delivered her were clamoring, saying, "By your command, we made numerous attempts to catch a glimpse of that devilish Jiraiya's mountain fortress on Mount Kurohime. Alas, they are too vigilant, and we can't get close. We have tried all kinds of tricks, and at long last, luck has favored us. We heard about this woman, who happened to be a wet nurse to some child named Sutematsu, whom Jiraiya picked up in Ōiso. Until recently, she resided within the mountain fortress. However, she recently returned to her hometown of Nadachi. When we heard where she lived, we caught her and brought her here. If you interrogate her, there is no doubt that she possesses at least a general understanding of Mount Kurohime." They looked triumphant as they conveyed their great news.

Otoma, having overheard the bandits and comprehending the purpose behind her being taken to this place, trembled in fear. However, when she looked around, she saw something unexpected. Among the gaggle of underlings, she saw her husband Gisuke, whom she had been seeking for months. She was stunned and thought it might just be a dream.

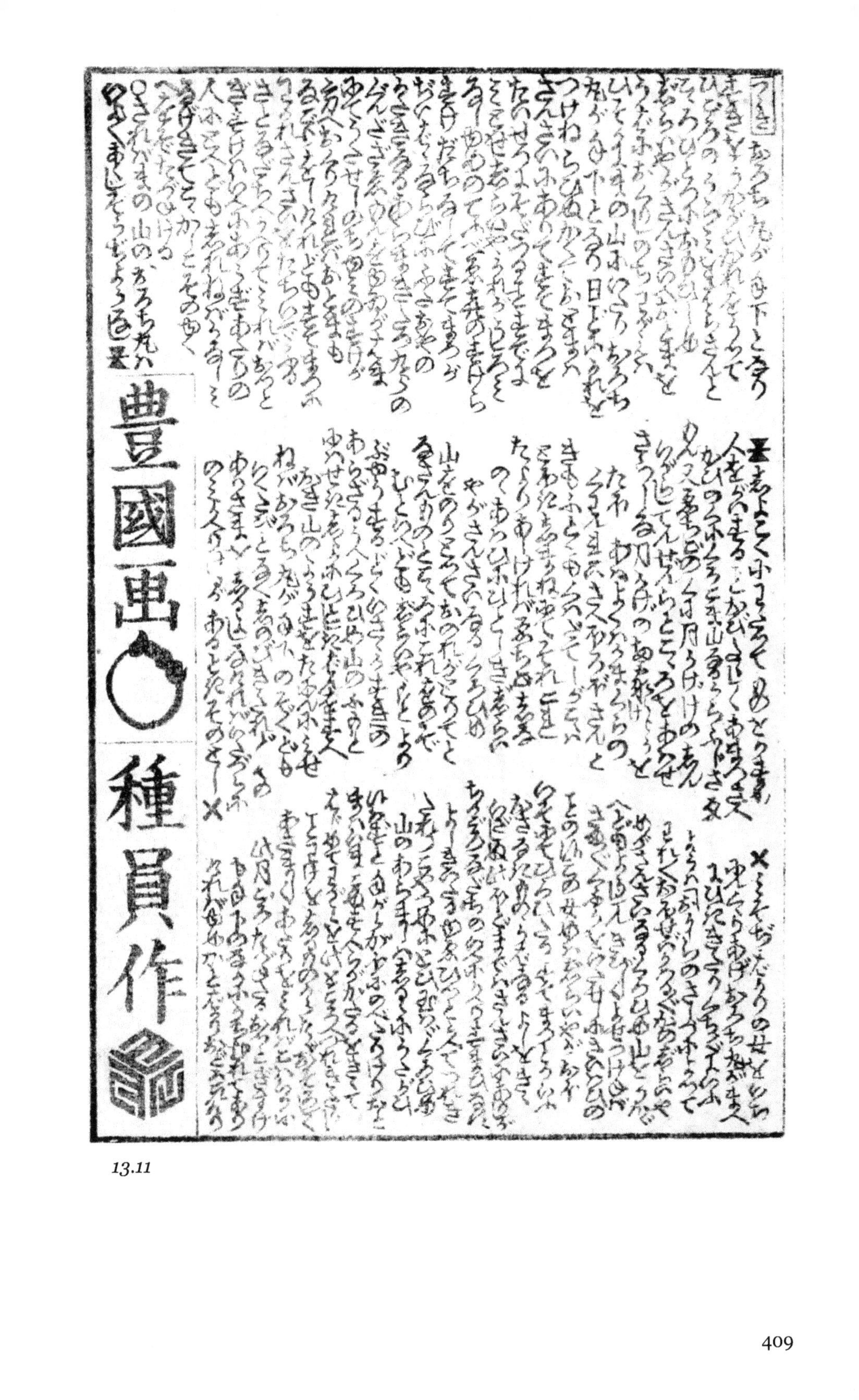

豊國画

種員作

13.11

13.12

Part II

(13.12)

When Otoma caught sight of her long-sought husband among the crowd of bandits, she wanted to call out to him. But, Gisuke signaled her with his eyes, telling her to keep quiet. Otoma understood that there must be a good reason for Gisuke to be there, so she suppressed the fluttering of her heart and tried to appear composed.

After hearing the report from his subordinates, Orochimaru grinned and said, "Well done, men! Now, interrogate the woman about Mount Kurohime immediately!" Then he called over the numerous women he had abducted to pour him saké, indulging in a feast as he watched the interrogation.

The men tried all manner of things to press Otoma about Mount Kurohime. However, she had always been a virtuous woman, and her time spent on the mountain had shown her Jiraiya's compassion. She simply replied, "I have never been to that place, so no matter how much you ask, I won't have anything to tell you." Despite their many attempts to intimidate her, she said nothing.

The bandits grew weary from the questioning, and when it looked like there was nothing left for them to try, Orochimaru, who had always been short tempered, furiously hissed, "What a loathsome woman you are! I guess I will have to question you myself. Then we'll see if you won't start talking."

When Gisuke saw Orochimaru getting up, he stepped forward and said, "Your anger is justified, but judging by this woman's demeanor, I do not believe she will speak even if force is used. Allow me to handle her for now. By morning, I will extract the truth and report it to you, my liege."

After some further discussion, Gisuke finally managed to convince Orochimaru, who said, "In that case, I shall leave her to you. But to make sure she doesn't escape, confine her in the holding cell until dawn!"

Gisuke accepted the orders, pulled Otoma along, and pushed her into a cell made between the boulders.

(13.13)

The night grew late, and when it seemed like it was about the third quarter of the hour of the ox,[3] Gisuke silently went to the cell. He pushed open the latticework bars and freed Otoma, but she said nothing. For a while, she allowed her husband to guide her, until she finally broke down in tears of anger and despair.

Gisuke guessed what was on her heart and said, "Your resentment towards me is justified, but I have come to this island with the purpose of avenging our former master and my elder brother by killing their bane, Orochimaru." His words were soft as he told the details of his intentions, adding, "Let us both sneak into Orochimaru's bedchamber and have our satisfaction. What say you to that?"

Otoma rejoiced, eagerly accepting the sword her husband handed her. Stealthily, they crept toward Orochimaru's bedside.

3 About 02:00.

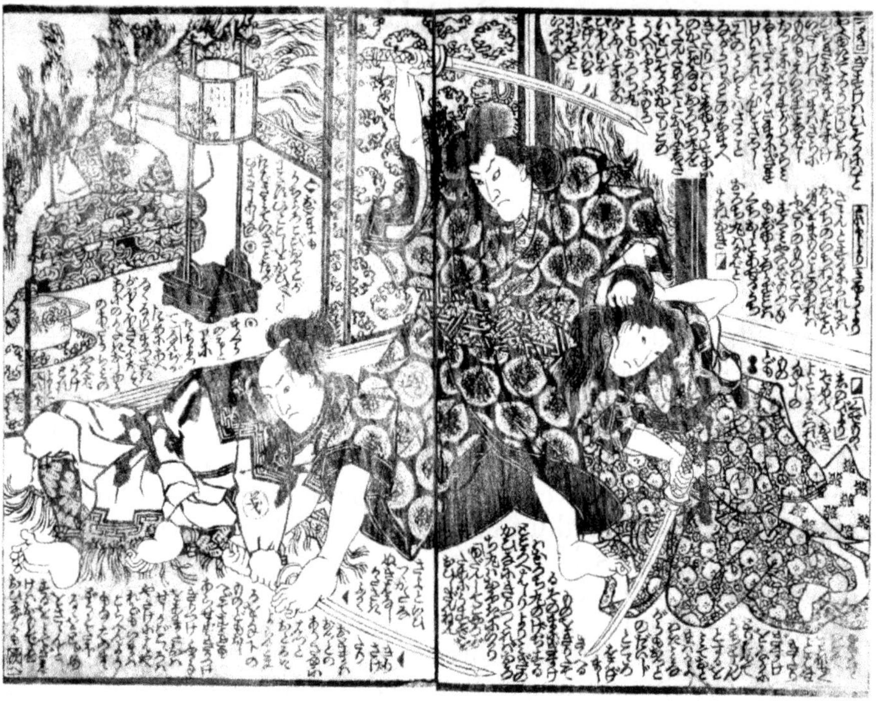

13.13

"I am the servant of Matsuzaki and the younger brother of Hosaku, who suffered greatly because of you. Take these blades of hatred and the vengeance of my older brother and our former lord!" declared Gisuke, as they lunged at Orochimaru from both sides to stab him.

However, Orochimaru was followed by the singular mind of the serpent which protected him. The couple found themselves instantly paralyzed, unable to move their sword-wielding hands, and they became consumed by bitterness and panic.

Orochimaru sprang to his feet and shouted, "It seems two tricksters have snuck in! Everyone, get up!" His underlings swiftly responded to his call, swarming around Gisuke, attempting to overpower him. Witnessing this, Otoma, despite her frailty, could not bear to see harm befall her beloved husband. Fueled by her emotions, Otoma slashed at one of the men blocking her husband's path, and Gisuke used the opening to dash at where Orochimaru was giving his orders, striking Orochimaru's right upper arm.

Infuriated, Orochimaru exclaimed, "How annoying! I let my guard down and this one manages to graze me!" Drawing his sword, he delivered a deep cut into Gisuke's shoulder. Shocked at what had just happened to her husband, Otoma tried to get closer, but Orochimaru's minions blocked her way. The sword slashes rained down on her without pause and she sustained many heavy injuries. Even though her heart was ablaze with eagerness, it was impossible for her to withstand the onslaught and she collapsed with a thud. Although severely wounded himself, when Gisuke saw someone step over to give Otoma the final blow, he used his sword as a cane to pull himself up and staggered over towards his wife to save her. Orochimaru kicked him over and stabbed him just above the knee. Then, he commanded his men to cease their attacks.

(13.14)
"Men! Do not kill them right away! They had the audacity to seek vengeance on me and even managed to hurt me. As retribution, I will torture them to death myself and get satisfaction!" As he said this, Orochimaru pulled out his sword lodged in Gisuke's thigh. He proceeded to sever both of Gisuke's arms and then ran his sword through Otoma's chest. Watching the couple suffer, a look of great pleasure spread across his face. However, as their breaths weakened, he decided to let them rest. Gripping their hair, Orochimaru dragged them towards the garden of the house. There, in a most cold-blooded display, he killed them both with a single sword stroke and flung them into the valley deep below.

Orochimaru cackled and peered down the valley he had thrown the two into. A fierce mountain wind blew, and from the bottom of the valley, two orbs of blueish *onibi* fire fluttered and rose up, flying towards him. However, Orochimaru was bold and fearless, so he swung his sword at the onibi. Perhaps frightened by his bravado, the orbs flew off towards the south. Strangely, upon seeing this, Orochimaru was unable to shake off an unsettling chill spreading through his body. He grew aware of the pain from the wound Gisuke had caused him earlier, so he got some medicine and applied various treatments to it.

We now return to the heroine, Otsuna, who had previously reunited with Takasago Yuminosuke on the border of Kai and Shinano. After they had parted, she traveled through various lands. Whenever she heard about a sacred Buddhist site, she would visit to respectfully pray for her parents in the next life. When she heard of a prominent kami, she would go to pray for her own current life, hoping to meet her destined husband as foretold by the immortal on Mount Tate. As she was traveling, the death anniversary of her parents drew close. She decided in her heart to return to her hometown, visit her parents' graves, perform Buddhist rites for them, and then resume her wanderings. Around autumn that year, she arrived in Konoha Village at the foot of Mount Tate in Etchū, where the village head and all the people of the neighborhood were happy to see that she was safe and sound. Everyone extended their warm hospitality, inviting her from one home to another.

Otsuna spent some days recovering from the fatigue from her travels, and before long, the death anniversary of her parents arrived. With deep reverence, she conducted the Buddhist rituals and invited all the villagers to her home. She entertained her guests, and the atmosphere brimmed with joy and mirth. Some shared tales of Otsuna's parents, the Tasakus, while others asked Otsuna for tales from her travels. They had a grand time, but when the evening grew late, the guests thanked Otsuna for the night and went back to their homes.

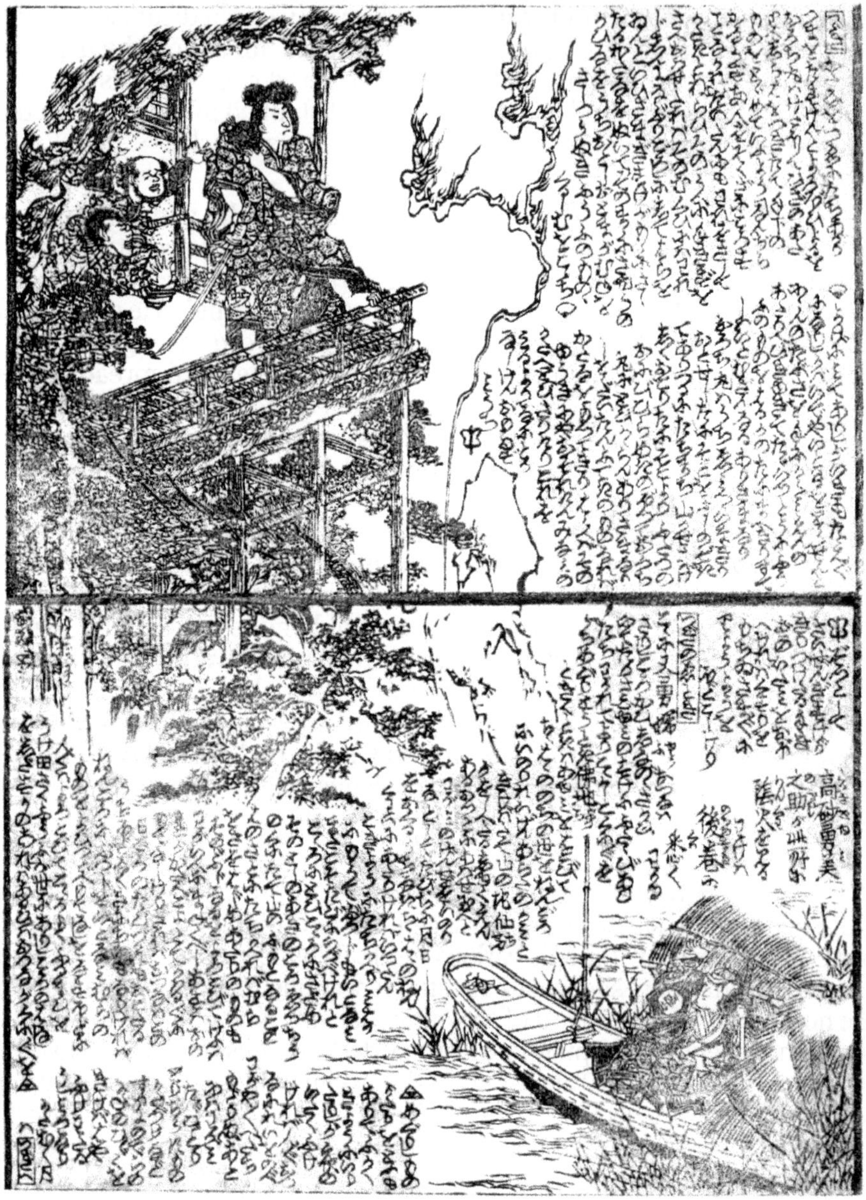

13.14

How Takasago Yuminosuke was in this place to see the ghostly fire orbs will be explained in a later book.

13.15

(13.15)

Afterwards, when she was alone and picking up the mess from the party, she heard the bell of the countryside temple. It was the third quarter of the hour of the ox. The moon, setting in the west, cast its light through the window, illuminating everything as if it were midday. The white bush clovers of the garden were blooming full and wild, and dew lay heavily on the flowers. The chirping insects were serene, and when Otsuna stilled her heart, she could feel the melancholic beauty of nature's impermanence. She went to the window to gaze at the moonlight and thought about all that had passed and all yet to come.

"I have followed the instructions given to me by the old man who long ago gave me nightly lessons in martial arts and the way of the water. I have toured through the lands searching for the one I have been fated to be with from a previous life. Yet, none have made me believe they were the one. I wonder how my end will come, as I pass the days and months in vain like this?" As she sat with her thoughts, she felt the passing nature of autumn even more keenly. Her heart was fierce, but it was, after all, the ephemeral heart of a woman, and she fell into despair. Nevertheless, she regained her composure and thought, "What foolish thoughts for me to have. Doubting the honorable elder's words like this is nothing short of profanity. All that remains is to simply pray for the grace of the kami and the Buddha." Then she knelt in worship towards the moonlit peak of Mount Tate and prayed, "I am but the offspring of

13.16

my parents, sworn to the kami of Mount Tate. I humbly seek protection, that my path may be guided and safeguarded."

After praying for some time, Otsuna gazed into the distance and saw something uncanny. Atop Mount Tate's very peak, she spotted a figure resembling a human. As she fixed her eyes on it, something, perhaps made of mist or even the rainbow itself, suddenly stretched out from the peak like a bridge. Step by step, it closed the distance to Otsuna's house, and then a young and charming boy walked fearlessly across it. He came before her and said, "I have come on behalf of my master, who has something to tell you. You must follow me back to meet her."

(13.16)

The boy grabbed Otsuna's hand in such an inviting way that she followed him without any thought of where they were going. They crossed over the bridge that elevated into the clouds, and there, high above the towering and jagged boulders, by the trunk of an ancient pine tree, a person was resting.

The boy guided Otsuna over to the person and took his place by her side. As Otsuna observed the figure, she beheld a lady like no other she had encountered. Adorned with a jade hairpin and donning brocade sleeves, she was so beautiful that even flowers would be ashamed of themselves. The lady raised the fan she held and, with a smile on her face, she beckoned Otsuna.

"I have summoned you here because I have something I wish to tell you. Your birth was unlike any other in this world. You are destined to find a man of exceptional courage and wit, to rescue people from calamity, exact vengeance, and achieve fame throughout the world. And yet, your heavenly ordained destiny still has not unfolded. You must leave your hometown behind once again and embark on a journey through the lands. During one of your travels, the day will come when you meet the one who is meant to be your husband. However, if your meeting does not unfold exactly as destined, you must leave him there, and before long you will meet him again."

Otsuna listened respectfully to the lady's guidance, and with great joy she said, "I wonder, who might such a gracious being as you be, who bestows such abundant blessings as this invaluable lesson to someone like me? And who might this man be, who is destined to be my husband? If I may ask, would you please tell me these things?"

"I am Bitei, an earthly immortal who has resided in the valleys of Mount Tate for many years. I cannot disclose the name of your future husband. However, if you depart from your hometown at the beginning of this winter and venture beyond the northern shores, you will find him in the greatest peril of his life. There, with the item you have acquired along your journey, you shall ward off disaster and be rewarded in remarkable ways. Beyond that, I cannot tell you any further without danger of upsetting the natural order of the universe."

(13.17)

Having concluded her words, Bitei gestured for the boy who had guided Otsuna earlier, and the boy understood. He led Otsuna back across the bridge, and even though it looked very far away, before long, she arrived at the gate of her house. She wanted to thank the boy, but he was nowhere to be seen. As she thought to look for him, the bell of daybreak resounded in her ears, waking her up and dispelling the dream. Left with an unshakeable eerie feeling, Otsuna gazed toward Mount Tate, where a few moonbeams still lingered. There, on the summit, she clearly and vividly saw the immortal Bitei, whom she had met in her dream. Yet, as a morning gale blew through the branches of the trees, Bitei vanished.

Otsuna respected the guidance given to her in the revelation by the female hermit, and for some time, she stayed in her home. As autumn drew to a close, the winter rains of the middle of the tenth month started falling. It was then that Otsuna thought to herself, "The time foretold by the immortal maiden must be upon me. The northern sea must be in Echigo, so that is where I shall go," and made up her resolve to leave.

Despite thinking it would not be the same as when she traveled as a pilgrim, going from one journey to the next, Otsuna still got her overcoat and her ladle and made various other traveling preparations. She said her goodbyes to the villagers. Under the autumn sky and with her garden full of withered branches, Otsuna left the village of Konoha behind her.

First, Otsuna wanted to go pay her respects on Mount Tate and pray for her safety, so she climbed the mountain and worshipped at the shrine of the mountain deity at the top. However, once there, she remembered Bitei had told her that she lived among the valleys of the

13.17

mountain. Thus, Otsuna trekked around the mountain until she came to Hell Valley, a place surrounded by many rumors. As she reached the valley, even though the sun was still high in the sky, it suddenly became pitch-dark all around her, causing her to lose her way. She waited for a moment, when a man and a woman, both completely pale, came out of the gloom of the valley. They stood rather far from where Otsuna was, with a sad look, like they had something they wanted to say to her.

Finding the two to be quite eerie, Otsuna called out, "You both appear far from ordinary. If this is the doing of mischievous foxes or tanuki attempting to deceive a young girl, I will not tolerate it. However, if you have something to say, come closer and say it quickly!" Her tone was scolding, showing no trace of fear, and the two finally raised their heads.

(13.18)

The man spoke first, "We have long known that you, who is braver than any man, would venture to this place. Although we no longer possess physical forms in this world, we have manifested in order to meet you. As a precaution, please refrain from coming any closer, as there is a risk you have a blade in your possession. We were once a couple who lived in Nadachi in Echigo, where I fished off the shore and made my living. My name is Gisuke, and my wife is Otoma. To avenge our former master, Matsuzaki Shirōdaifu-dono, and my older brother, Hosaku, we crossed the waters to kill the pirate named Orochi, who lives on Mount Mano. It was, however, a heartbreakingly futile

13.18

endeavor. Because he was born of the great serpent that lived in Aoyagi Pond in Echigo, he proved too cunning for us and killed us both."

After her husband's account, Otoma wiped away her tears and continued, "From now, your destiny shall become deeply entwined with a man named Jiraiya. I served as a wet nurse for him for nearly three years in his mountain fortress, caring for a boy named Sutematsu. Jiraiya found him in Ōiso, and he is the forgotten heir of Himematsu-dono, a close retainer of the Sarashina clan. Because of the time we spent together, I cannot deny my attachment to the boy. We are sharing this information because Orochimaru fears Katsuyu, your protector, and we seek to borrow your strength."

Gisuke said, "Not only that, Orochimaru also deeply desires Jiraiya-dono's fortress on Mount Kurohime and is making evil plots to steal it from him. It probably won't be long before Jiraiya-dono will face a great peril. When that time comes, you must rescue him, and if the opportunity arises, kill our nemesis and clear our grudge. We failed to achieve our goal, falling victim to our enemy's blade, and in departing this world, we found ourselves trapped in the sinful depths of Hell Valley, haunted by the scenes of our demise. Please, have mercy on our tormented souls!"

After hearing their tale, Otsuna said in a kind and respectful tone, "You have materialized here in order to tell me the wishes of your two departed souls. Since your message aligns with the maiden's prophecy, you can rest easy. I will take down your foe, Orochimaru, and clear your grudge. Now, let go of your malicious thoughts and attain Nirvana."

13.19

(13.19)

A look of tranquility spread across the faces of the two spirits. As they disappeared, what had looked like the dark of night lifted and the rays of the sun reached into the valley again. Mystified, Otsuna thought to herself, "I suppose this means that the man the maiden said I will marry is this Jiraiya I've heard about." Armed with this realization, she descended towards the foothills of the mountain.

A while ago, Hamaogi Rokusaburō had attempted to kill himself, but was stopped by a lay monk, who convinced him to abandon the idea. Afterwards, Rokusaburō collected the body of his father and took it to the temple his family belonged to. Together with his mother, Asaka, he left Echigo.

Meanwhile, however, Igarashi Tenzen Taketora thought, "If Rokusaburō does a thorough investigation into the Katsuyumaru tanto, the wrongdoings I have committed might come into light." Thus, he schemed and told his closest retainers to make the Rokusaburō and Asaka disappear along the road. Unbeknownst to him though, Rokusaburō was already searching for the two women his father had mentioned, hoping it might uncover Tenzen's crimes and naturally lead him to the treasured tanto. Having a keen sense of piety towards his parents, Rokusaburō took great care of his mother on their journey.

Tenzen's retainers gave chase for Rokusaburō and his mother, eventually reaching the Karasu River in Kōzuke province. There, they asked the vagrants and the boat captains to join them in a fight and kill Rokusaburō and his mother. When the retainers showed them their reward, albeit a rather small one, the miscreants accepted the offer and lay in wait for the two travelers to show up. When Rokusaburō and his mother finally arrived, the men surrounded them, and it appeared they might attack at any moment. Because his old mother was with him, Rokusaburō apologized and tried to diffuse the situation without violence. However, just as the men were about to take advantage of Rokusaburō's bowing and give him a thrashing, Chōbei the dreamer appeared. He had been on his way to Echigo after having left Kamakura in search of Jiraiya when he came upon the scene. Unable to stop himself, Chōbei jumped in between the pack of scoundrels, throwing and scattering them. Intimidated by Chōbei's might, both the miscreants and Tenzen's retainers beat a hasty retreat.

Rokusaburō and Asaka were so happy they thought they might be dreaming, and thanked Chōbei deeply for having come to their rescue. Chōbei, thanking the stars that he had not arrived a moment later, kindly said, "From now on, please, be more careful towards your destination," and left them, going on a different road.

Since long ago, Jiraiya had a heartfelt wish to revive the Ogata clan. For this reason, he came to believe that by doing meritorious deeds for the Kanrei, he might redeem the name of his father, Ogata Saemon Hirozumi. It was during this time that he learned about Urafuji Saemon of Kai, a country samurai who seemed to be defying Kamakura and had established a fortress on Mount Kurokoma, where he had barricaded himself. Jiraiya saw an opportunity to subdue Urafuji Saemon, reveal his true intentions to the Kanrei, and possibly fulfill his wish. Thus, he disguised himself and went to investigate the area close to Mount Kurokoma, where he quite unexpectedly stumbled on the Sarashina clan's treasured Fubuki Katatsuki tea container on the banks of the Tama River.

"This must be the tea container that was lost when Sutematsu's father, Sumatarō, was murdered in Ōiso. If that is the case, I must send it to Takasago Yuminosuke quickly, so it may be used in our efforts to restore the Himematsu clan," thought Jiraiya, and he composed a letter for Yuminosuke. In it, he detailed how the container was sent to Urafuji Saemon Terukage by Tatsumaki Arakurō, hidden by Urafuji, and how a man named Shikano Fuehachi had stolen it when he escaped from Mount Kurokoma. Jiraiya also shared that he had heard the story from Fuehachi's talk with Mijin Kotsuhei, and that the tea container had fallen into his possession by sheer happenstance.

(13.20)

Jiraiya then sent the letter, along with the tea container, to Yuminosuke, who was with the Sarashina clan. Yuminosuke was exalted

13.20

Bottom-right: This picture is for the text on the page after the next one.

to no end and thought, "That Jiraiya, chivalrous as always! It is inconceivable for him not to be rewarded for this." He retold all these circumstances to his lord, Sarashina Mitsuaki-dono, who was elated that the tea container, a treasure of his family, had finally returned after all this time. "With this, I see no reason why Sutematsu cannot take over the headship of his family once he becomes of age," said Mitsuaki-dono, granting approval.

Previously, both the Sarashina and Tsukikage clans had received an unofficial message from the Kanrei, urging them to destroy the pirate Orochimaru and Urafuji Saemon. Following this, Yuminosuke had discreetly gone to Sado Island to see what was happening there. Afterwards, he carefully considered the best course of action, persuaded his lord Mitsuaki to talk with the Kanrei, and before long, they received a letter of pardon, saying, "If Jiraiya can accomplish the worthy deed of eliminating Orochimaru and Urafuji, he shall be excused of his sins and be allowed to reestablish his clan."

Yuminosuke took the letter with him and went to Mount Kurohime in secret, where he announced himself. Luckily, Jiraiya had returned to the fortress, so Yuminosuke could meet with him immediately. First, Yuminosuke thanked Jiraiya deeply for helping Sutematsu by sending

13.21

In box: This picture belongs in book fourteen. The reason it is here is to inform the reader of the exciting story that will come, and it is nothing but a silly idea by the author.

the tea container. Then, he presented the pardon from the Kanrei and said, "You have probably already heard about this, but there is a pirate leader called Orochimaru, whose atrocities have escalated greatly. He is in cahoots with Urafuji Terukage, and they are supposedly eyeing even Kamakura. If you can kill them and quell their rebellion, not only will your name be cleared, but the Ogata family can also be remade. Should you wish for it, the combined forces of the Sarashina and Tsukikage clans will be sent out to fight alongside you."

The ecstatic Jiraiya said, "This is exactly what I had hoped for! I already heard this Orochimaru wants my fortress here on Mount Kurohime, which I was intending to let him have. I thank you for this great boon!" Jiraiya then took the pardon into his possession, and both of them were in high spirits as they strategized on how to take down Orochimaru and Urafuji. Afterwards, Yuminosuke left and returned home.

(13.22)
Urafuji Saemon Terukage of Mount Kurokoma had been asked by Igarashi Tenzen, a retainer of the Tsukikage clan, to steal a tanto that Hamaogi Naminoshin was carrying home from Kamakura. Urafuji had

in turn given the task to Mijin Kotsuhei, whom he was sheltering at the time, and planned to make Kotsuhei trick Naminoshin out of the blade. However, Kotsuhei never returned after that. When he later heard that Kotsuhei had died on the banks of Tama River alongside Fuehachi, who had stolen his tea container and ran away, he was shocked. He had entrusted the man with a significant sum of money to recruit co-conspirators, and now he wondered if Kotsuhei had been killed for the money. Or maybe, he had been killed after he had already obtained the tanto? Without knowing what happened, he had no way to investigate where the two valuables had disappeared to.

As if that wasn't enough, he also heard a rumor that forces were moving to attack his fortress to take it, so he could not rest easy. He traveled to Echigo in secret, where he met with Igarashi Tenzen. Just as they were preparing to cross the sea to reach Mount Mano, they learned Orochimaru's mothership was stationed at Niigata port. They slipped to Niigata to see Orochimaru and disclosed everything.

Orochimaru's response was devoid of astonishment. "When I went to the shrine in Nunobiki, I heard about the two treasures. One day, I will get them and give them to you. Moreover, if anyone dares to attack your fortress on Mount Kurokoma, I will come to your rescue."

Relieved, Tenzen and Urafuji could finally discuss their nefarious plans. Afterwards, the two bid their farewells and went home.

Some time ago, Orochimaru had become furious when his subordinate, Jimoguri Kuroyasha, had been strongly reprimanded by Jiraiya. He also deeply desired Jiraiya's fortress on Mount Kurohime, and wanted to destroy Jiraiya at all costs. So, he sent shinobi to keep an eye on Jiraiya's comings and goings. One day, the shinobi came back and reported, "We have learned all of that scum's movements. Around the middle of this month, he will go to the capital. After leaving Mount Kurohime, his route will take him to Etchū."

Elated, Orochimaru danced with joy, saying, "Excellent discovery! I already have a plan for how to take him out!" He then left for the shore of Ichifuri in Echigo, which was said to be the most dangerous pass in all the northern territories. The cliffs were called different names, such as *Oyashirazu*—the family splitter, because parents would be separated from their children while hurrying to escape the waves. Or, *Komagaeshi*—the horse flipper, because horses were apt to fall from the rocky slopes.

There, he made his men hide among the rocks and instructed them, "As soon as you spot Jiraiya, unleash all your arquebuses. We shall also scatter landmines everywhere, so that if he manages to evade you, he'll be blown to bits!"

Orochimaru's plans covered every contingency, and it seemed Jiraiya would be in danger even if he used a technique to soar through the air.

13.22

What will Orochimaru do to Jiraiya, and what will be the heroine Otsuna's role? All will be revealed at the start of book fourteen.

14.1

Book 14

The mountain known as Kurohime is situated in both Shinano and Echigo. Furthermore, they are not too distant from each other. In Shinano, its foothills reach the lake of the Akagawa River in the Minochi area, stretching all the way to the Daimyōjin Pass in the Kubiki area in Echigo. The nearest post station in that region is Sekikawa. Additionally, the Kurohime mountain of Echigo is also located in the Kariba area of Echigo. If one goes to Yatsuishi Peak of Mount Matsu in Kariba, it is no more than ten ri away.[1] The place that Jiraiya has made his mountain hideout in these books is none other than Mount Kurohime of Echigo. While explaining the geography of Echigo, the story becomes somewhat muddled and lost.

And now, this book sees the story at the perilous *Oyashirazu* or *Komagaeshi*. The coast is hit by great waves, but the omens are good. Watch, as the deadly battle for the treasures unfolds on the shore of Ichifuri!

Kaei era—Year of the Iron Dog—New Year (1851)
Ryūkatei Tanekazu

Also on page:
Dobiroku, nephew of Ban'emon the katana merchant.
Sutematsu, the lone child of Himematsu Sumatarō.

1 About 39 kilometers.

14.2

Just fluttering about,
Is it merely playing,
The autumn butterfly?

—Amamugi

Also on page:
Jiraiya.
Hamaogi Rokusaburō.
Igarashi Tenzen.

14.3

Evening flowers
Jyanosuke the drinker
Resenting the bell.

—Tsunenori[2]

Also on page:
Sekiya, lady-in-waiting of the Tsukikage clan.
Kosono, daughter of Okowa.
Tsunade.

2 The haiku is by Tanaka Tsunenori. It references the name "Jyanosuke", the first kanji meaning "snake". This name is itself a reference to Tsunenori, who was nicknamed Jyanosuke after writing a poetry collection with this in the title. Jyanosuke is furthermore a nickname given to heavy drinkers, as it references the legend of the god Susano'o no Mikoto killing the serpent Yamata no Orochi by getting it drunk and cutting off its heads. Thus, the poem references the poet, as well as painting a scene of a flower viewing party, where the bell rings in the night and a drunkard gets disgruntled that the party is now over.

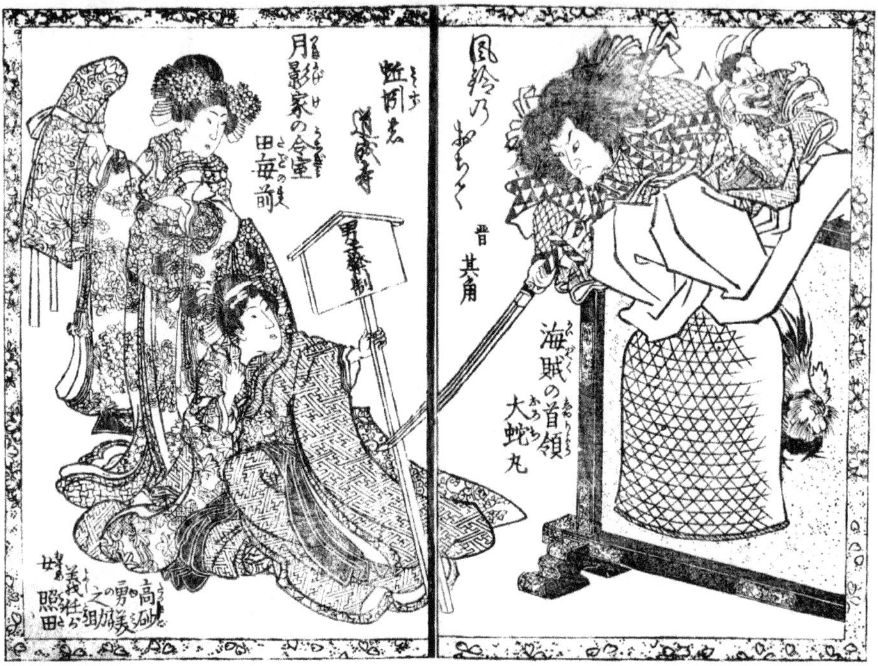

14.4

The fallen wind chime
Like the bell of Dōjōji
To the earth worm.

—Shin Kikaku[3]

Also on page:
Orochimaru, the pirate leader.
Tagoto-hime, wife of Tsukikage.
Teruta, daughter the brave retainer Takasago Yuminosuke.
Sign: No men allowed.

3 The poem references the Noh play *Dōjōji Temple*, which features Kiyohime—a woman who turns into a serpent from unrequited love, wraps herself around a temple bell hiding the man she is in love with, and then burns him alive inside the bell. Shin Kikaku is a penname of Takarai Kikaku.

14.5

Part I

(14.5)
The coast of Ichifuri in the Kubiki area of Echigo lies at the very western end of this country, very close to Etchū. Before it stretches the azure sea, with waves the color of both the water and the skies. Behind it looms steep mountain paths, not easily traversed by either man or horse. Moreover, when the northern winds rage, enormous waves pound the shore, reaching far up on the cliffs, beating even the boulders to pieces. Travelers who come and go there are all terrified of it. When the waves hit the shore like that, travelers hide in caves on the cliffside, waiting and observing for the moment the waves withdraw before they run for the next cave. Truly, it is the most perilous place in all the northern territories, and its ominous names like Oyashirazu and Komagaeshi are befitting.

It was the start of winter, a period often called "the small spring lull" because the weather becomes surprisingly calm. On this day, even these typically fierce seas were as flat as tatami mats, and as far as the eye could see, there was not even the shadow of waves. A lone *Boronji* monk in travel attire appeared, coming from the roads of Echigo and heading for Etchū. Being a Boronji, or a *Komusō* as they are also called, he carried a shakuhachi flute to play for alms and wore a tengai basket hat to obscure his face. By the side of the road, he noticed a large group of farmers, equipped with spades and hoes in their hands, mending the coastal road.

Approaching them, the Boronji inquired, "I have something I must ask you. There aren't rough waves on the path ahead today, are there?"

The farmers exchanged glances at the question and answered kindly, "Yesterday, the road was battered by high seas. It was so bad that even a guide would have found the traversal difficult. But today is quite the opposite, a true lull in this small spring. Just look at us. We were ordered by our lord to go and mend the road along the shore, but our warm clothes ended up just being in the way. The seas are so unusually calm that it seems they mimic our pleasant state. There is absolutely no danger ahead, so you may proceed at your leisure."

Happy with the news, the Boronji said, "Indeed, what glorious weather we are having. Then I shall continue and cross over this dangerous pass with ease," and headed westward.

On the roadside, the Boronji came across a *Rokubu*, a pilgrim carrying sixty-six copies of the Lotus Sutra to sixty-six temples across the country. The Rokubu had set aside his case of sutras and sat on a boulder, smoking a pipe and having a rest. The Boronji approached, and like the Rokubu, he took a rest while gazing out over the sea.

A spirited and beautiful female pilgrim passed by the coast as well, coming from the direction of Etchū. She too decided to rest, perhaps feeling a pang of jealousy at the two travelers.

The Rokubu, who had been first to take a rest, eyed the Boronji and the pilgrim and asked, "Where are the two of you from, and where are you headed?"

(14.6)

The Boronji replied, "I am on an ascetic practice, following the clouds and the waters, with no specific destination in mind. So, it is difficult to say where I am from or where I am going. But enough about me. What about you, lady pilgrim? What has caused a woman, so young in years, to be here? For you to go on such a solitary journey, your heart is truly admirable."

The female pilgrim smiled and said, "Well, since you ask, I was bereaved of my parents at an early age, and I had no other relatives. Since I have no one in this world, I embarked on a pilgrimage to the sacred places throughout the lands, seeking the blessings of the Bodhisattvas to fulfill a cherished wish I've held in my heart for a long time and for the sake of my parents' future lives."

As she narrated her tale, the Rokubu found himself captivated by her elegance, and without hesitation, he stepped closer and said, "You have endured the loss of both parents and home, yet you travel as a pilgrim to fulfill your wish. Such a story you've shared with us. It must be sad to be a woman traveling all alone. Fortunately, as you can see, I, too, am on a pilgrimage, wandering through these lands. I would make a fitting travel companion for you. With me as your fellow traveler, we can take care of each other and explore the country, side by side. That doesn't sound too bad, now does it?"

14.6

He reached out to grab the pilgrim's hands, but she brushed him off, saying, "I have no wish to become the companion of a Buddhist practitioner, who seems to not even grasp the metaphorical description of hell, despite relying on Buddha and hearing about it. What you are saying is absurd."

The Rokubu's face turned red with anger at being rebuffed so sternly, so the Boronji tried to divert the situation, saying, "I may not have heard your voice back then, but I caught a glimpse of your face, and it has stayed with me ever since. You must be that courageous woman who confronted the rogue near the torii gate of that shrine I visited." The Boronji cast away his tengai.

The pilgrim remembered and said, "You are that person I briefly met at the great shrine on that rainy evening? Your features and stature match the rumors that have spread throughout this floating world. Could you truly be my destined husband, Jiraiya-dono, whom I have been seeking?"

He interrupted her, saying, "To claim such now would be unkind. Nevertheless, I cannot forget the memory of that parting moment," and drew close to the pilgrim.

Bashful, the pilgrim replied, "If you really are him, then there are surely things that even the premonition of the immortal maiden could not tell me in my dream."

Seeing the pilgrim softening up to the Boronji, the Rokubu said, "It is vexing to listen to you uttering those affectionate words, even though

14.7

you are a monk who has learned the teachings of the Zen masters of the Fuke School. I am leaving immediately."

Feeling envious of the emotions between the other two, he wedged himself between them, but a scroll slipped out from inside his breast pocket. The Boronji caught sight of it and went to pick it up, but the Rokubu snatched it and put it away.

The Boronji said to the Rokubu in a demanding tone, "The thing you just dropped was undoubtedly the family tree of my house, which I lost in the foothills of Mount Nunobiki in Musashi!"

(14.7)

Hearing this, the pilgrim said, "I was also there, resting from my travels. As a woman, it's a bit embarrassing, but I was there as well, fishing for sweetfish with cormorants on strings. Consumed by guilt for taking life, I climbed up the rapids until the darkest night, where all light had vanished, and I could no longer see the shape of the fish."

The Boronji interjected, "With great difficulty I had sailed on a raft over the rapids and was waiting for the moon to rise, because I wanted to search for the fortress on Mount Kurokoma in Kai. I had put the raft up next to the shore, and just as I was dozing off, I heard a sound from the shore that shook me out of my dream."

The Rokubu responded, "I, too, was there when it got dark, and was forced to spend the night at the Nunibiki Shrine, using only my arm as a pillow. But that very evening, there was going to be a festival, so farmers had left a chest there for the ritual. They had placed it beyond the door curtain in the main shrine, thinking no one would come there. Inside the chest were clothes for a kagura dance ritual, and I put on whatever I could get my hands on to shield me from the winds of the cold autumn night. Just then, there was a commotion outside and in the light cast by a campfire, I saw two talkative comrades, arguing and fighting over two treasures. Acting swiftly, I swooped down like an eagle, killed them, and stepped out of the shrine."

The Boronji continued, "With the same intention of claiming the treasures, I leapt from the raft. But as I did, the fire went out, and nothing could be seen in the total darkness. I fumbled around and felt a woman's head."

"I also wished to take the treasures," said the pilgrim, "so I stepped off my cormorant boat. But the moment I did, I felt a hand approach my head and swatted it away. When I searched around, I felt the presence of a suspicious man."

The Boronji spoke again, "And a great serpent appeared, both to protect him and to be my opponent. For some mysterious reason, no matter how hard I struggled, my body was paralyzed."

Rokubu: "No, the most eerie thing that happened was a slug that protected the woman bandit. It obstructed me, and as I struggled to regain my freedom of movement—"

Pilgrim: "A great frog appeared in the shadow of the man from the raft. Its eyes were wild with rage, and it would not let me get near him. The battle became like three swirling pools of water at a dam. When one advanced, so did another. When one retreated, so did another. It seemed like it would have no end."

Boronji: "But I made a mistake and was shocked when I dropped the secret family tree. My hands searched for it, but instead what I picked up was the tea container..."

Pilgrim: "And I searched around, eventually finding the tanto..."

Rokubu: "And I had the two treasures that I desired in my heart taken from me, but to my surprise, the Ogata family tree fell into my hands. At that moment there was a firelight from the mountain. It looked like many people were coming our way, and without a word, the three of us dispersed and vanished without a trace, like the wake of a boat. How uncanny that we should meet again in this place."

Thus, their words rekindled the memories of that night among them.

Nonchalantly, the pilgrim then looked to the skies and said, "Despite knowing how winter days come to a close so easily, while we were talking time passed without me noticing. I must be off now." Yet, despite having said this, she left her heart with the Boronji before departing.

Looking like he might be thinking about following after the pilgrim, the Rokubu said, "Indeed, the day is short. I shall take my leave as well," and started walking away.

After he had taken two or three steps, the Boronji stood tall and called out, "Wait a moment, Orochimaru, pirate of Mano!" stopping him in his tracks.

14.8

The Rokubu turned around with a jerk and went back to the Boronji. “Clearly, you have discovered my name. Seeing as a tremendous frog came to your rescue back when I met you at Tama River, you match the rumors of Jiraiya that I have heard. Now, reveal your name!”

(14.8)

“Indeed, your deductions are correct. I am none other than the one they know as Jiraiya, whose real name is Ogata Shūma Hiroyuki. Now, return the scroll with my family tree which I lost back then!” Jiraiya demanded.

Orochimaru raised his guard and replied, “Indeed, the scroll did fall into my possession, and I will return it to you. However, you also have something I want. Mount Kurohime, your stronghold, is an excellent and impregnable fortress, and I have coveted it for some time. Hand the mountain over to me, and I shall give you the scroll in an even trade.”

Jiraiya’s fury ignited, and he retorted, “Your words are cunning and insolent. I will kill you for them and simply take the scroll back afterwards! Now, have at you!”

Jiraiya pulled out a sword, hidden inside his flute, and lunged at Orochimaru to cut him down. However, Orochimaru also pulled out a sword hidden in his staff. Using their mystic fighting arts, they clashed blades. However, the wound that Orochimaru had previously received from Gisuke flared up in pain. His arm grew increasingly tired from the fighting. Sensing an imminent loss, Orochimaru withdrew his blade and

14.9

fled, seeking shelter behind his carrying box which was sitting close by. Jiraiya pursued him and swung his sword, but the blows were deflected by the sturdy box. Jiraiya struck again, this time cutting the box clean in half.

(14.9)

This, however, set off the smoke signal, which Orochimaru had worked into the box. As the smoke rose up, charring the sky, the men who had previously looked like farmers mending the road came armed to the teeth. They were in fact Orochimaru's henchmen surrounding Jiraiya. However, this only made his spirit grow stronger and he cut them down in slews. When one of the henchmen eventually faltered, the whole group crumbled, and like birds scurrying about on the beach, they ran, confused and lost, trying to escape. Jiraiya gave chase, following them for four or five chō.

The area the henchmen ran into was the place Orochimaru had ordered them to rig with landmines earlier. If Jiraiya entered, no matter what jutsu he might possess, how could he possibly escape this underhanded trick? He would be no different from a candlelight before the wind. However, just then, something mysterious happened. Even though it was the start of winter, from far off Koshiji, in between the sprawling mountains covered in a white cloth of snow, black clouds gathered overhead.[4] A single bolt of lightning, flashing bright enough to pierce the eyes and thundering loud enough to burst the eardrums, struck the ground where the landmines were buried. The bolt ignited the

4 Koshiji is present day Nagaoka City.

gunpowder, which exploded, tearing open the ground. Orochimaru's henchmen were launched into the sky and blown to pieces by the very landmines they themselves had buried. You reap what you sow, and they got their just harvest.

Jiraiya returned to where he started, saying, "Now, that just leaves you, Orochimaru!" and went after him with a fierce energy.

Seeing no other options, Orochimaru took out the scroll from within his breast pocket, warning, "Listen to me closely now, Jiraiya. If you oppose me any further, I will take this family tree and tear it to shreds!"

It became a pressing situation, so Jiraiya decided to use his jutsu to seize the scroll from Orochimaru. Jiraiya made the signs with his hands, but because Orochimaru had the protection of his serpent mother, Jiraiya could not perform his toad conjuring. The usually sharp Jiraiya wavered for a brief moment, and the tranquil sea erupted into violent waves. From the ocean depths, an enormous serpent appeared, jumping out of the water with its sights on Jiraiya. Simultaneously, one of Orochimaru's henchmen, hidden among the cliffs, aimed an arquebus at Jiraiya, getting ready to fire. This was a more dire peril in Jiraiya's life. Any more would either be too late or too early.

When she had returned was unknown, but in that moment, the female pilgrim came running, as if emerging from the shadows of the rocks. Sending his head flying through the air, she swiftly decapitated the bandit with the arquebus and wiped the blood spatter from her tanto. With a booming and admonishing voice, she called out, "Evil bandit of Mano, Orochimaru. Heed my words! I am Tsunade of Konoha Village in Etchū. I too am a descendant of the Ogata, and I have come to save Jiraiya-dono, whom I have been destined to be with since a previous life. I heard from the ghosts of Gisuke and his wife that they suffered an unnatural and untimely death at your hands. Now you will come to know their grudge!"

Brandishing the Katsuyumaru tanto, Tsunade slashed at the serpent in the water. The sheer holy power of the tanto made the serpent recoil, and it could not get near Jiraiya.

Seeing this, Orochimaru cried, "You insolent little..." and swung his sword at Tsunade. For a while, they fought, but the light emitting from Tsunade's blade was blinding to Orochimaru's eyes. Realizing that he would not be able to win, Orochimaru turned to flee, but Jiraiya blocked his path and Tsunade chased after him from behind. With no place to either advance or retreat, it looked as if Orochimaru was about to meet his end.

(14.10)

However, a great wave rose up, and from within, the poisonous serpent wrapped itself around Orochimaru, diving into the depths of the sea. Tsunade gnashed her teeth in frustration and was about to give chase, using her training in the ways of the water to chase them however far they might go, but Jiraiya stopped her.

"Even if he escapes now, soon we will have another chance to kill him and take back the scroll. Your bravado is making you impatient," said Jiraiya, his words reining in Tsunade.

14.10

She wiped Katsuyumaru clean of blood and put it back in its sheath. "In order to counter Orochimaru's dirty tricks, there is nothing better than this tanto. Take it," Tsunade said, handing the blade over to Jiraiya. With hurried words, she then shared with him all about the dream message from the immortal maiden, her meeting the spirits of Gisuke and his wife in Hell Valley on Mount Tate, and her decision to take on their vendetta.

Jiraiya accepted Katsuyumaru and said, "For complicated reasons, I have been searching for this tanto in order to save someone for quite some time now." Then he told her about stopping Hamaogi Rokusaburō's death.

As he was about to tell her about the circumstances of Rokusaburō's father, Orochimaru, fueled by a jealous hatred, burst out of the raging waves and onto the shore. Jiraiya and Tsunade split to the left and the right, Jiraiya astride the toad that protected him and Tsunade riding her slug. They went to close in on Orochimaru. However, it was as if fate itself said it was not yet time. A gale blew, and a tsunami approached. With their magical abilities, they simply floated on the water, seemingly undisturbed, like sleeping mandarin ducks. The sudden wave split them up, sending them away from each other. Their destinies were not yet aligned.

(14.11)
We now return to Takasago Yuminosuke, the brave and loyal retainer of the Sarashina clan in Shinano. Previously commanded by his lord to subdue Orochimaru, who resided on Mount Mano, Yuminosuke had sailed to Sado Island and placed his boat near the coast. There, he kept an eye on the comings and goings of the bandits, and one night, while at the shore, he saw two ghostly lights emanating from a hill at the base of the mountains. Subsequently, they would appear in the same place over and over again.

One night, Yuminosuke received a message in his dream from someone unknown, telling him, "You are trying to subdue Orochimaru, but his fate has not yet run its course. Nonetheless, if you destroy his home, it should weaken his spirit. When you spot the ghost lights again, climb Mount Mano. Then you will find that you can easily enter the fortress."

The brave retainer woke up from his dream overjoyed. When the next night fell, he prepared a formidable force and pressed up the mountain. Guided by the ghost lights, they easily broke into the bandit hideout, set it ablaze and captured the people there. However, on that very night, Orochimaru had gone to shore of Ichifuri to try and kill Jiraiya, and thus eluded capture. Nevertheless, Yuminosuke succeeded in apprehending all of Orochimaru's henchmen left to guard the fortress, and the women who had been abducted by Orochimaru were safely returned to their homes.

14.11

Editor's note: The story will continue with Book 14, Part II in Volume II.

The end of Volume 1 of
The Tale of Jiraiya the Gallant

Translator Bio

Andreas Kronborg Danielsen is a Danish translator with a deep passion for Japanese culture and folklore. Holding a Bachelor's and Master's degree in Japanology from the University of Aarhus, Andreas has also studied extensively in Japan at Sophia University in Tokyo, Kobe University, and Tokai University in Kanagawa. Specializing in Edo period culture, he brings a nuanced understanding of Japan's rich literary traditions to his work.

Andreas has previously published *Japanese Fairytales*, a collection of over 45 stories that marks the first-ever translation of Japanese fairytales into Danish, as well as the first full Danish translation of *The Tale of the Bamboo Hewer*. His work has been well-received, with *Japanese Fairytales* earning praise from Danish library reviewing services.

The Tale of Jiraiya the Gallant is Andreas' first book in English, where he combines his academic expertise with a love for storytelling, offering readers a fresh and engaging interpretation of this classic Edo-period adventure.

www.ingramcontent.com/pod-product-compliance
Ingram Content Group UK Ltd.
Pitfield, Milton Keynes, MK11 3LW, UK
UKHW020912070525
5796UKWH00014B/185/J

9 781965 492062